Praise for the National Bestselling
Seaside Knitters Mysteries

Murder in Merino

"This genuinely entertaining and deeply perceptive mystery will transport you to a charmingly tight-knit community."
　　　　　　—Agatha, Anthony, Macavity, and Mary Higgins Clark
　　　　　　award–winning author Hank Phillippi Ryan

"An intriguing mystery, *Murder in Merino* is also a story of a community in which people invest their lives and care for their friends and neighbors. Born of Goldenbaum's fertile mind and generous heart, it's as much a love story as a whodunit, and it satisfies discerning readers on all levels." 　　　　　　　　　　　　—*Richmond Times-Dispatch*

"Satisfying. . . . Fans of previous entries will enjoy spending a few more hours with the Seaside Knitters." 　　　　　—*Publishers Weekly*

"Readers will be entertained from page one to the end." 　—*Gumshoe*

"Goldenbaum has written another perfect cozy . . . delightfully complex." 　　　　　　　　　　　　　　　　　—*RT Book Reviews*

"A compelling story. . . . I recommend it!" 　　　—*Suspense Magazine*

"Characters that every reader wants to know." 　　　—*Fresh Fiction*

Angora Alibi

"Ms. Goldenbaum writes such interesting and likable characters, the reading of one of these [novels] is like a reunion with old friends."
　　　　　　　　　　　　　　　　　　　　　—*Fresh Fiction*

"The sights and sounds of the latest Seaside Knitters story will enchant readers. The mystery unfolds nicely with some surprising and clever turns." 　　　　　　　　　　　　　　　　—*RT Book Reviews*

"Goldenbaum, as always, gives readers an intriguing whodunit with characters they have come to know and love. As if that weren't enough, she again blesses her fans with an eloquent testament to family and friends." 　　　　　　　　　　　　—*Richmond Times-Dispatch*

continued . . .

A Fatal Fleece

"Goldenbaum offers credible characters, a mystery that's uncomplicated without being too obvious, and the knitting content her fans demand in a very readable package." —*Publishers Weekly*

The Wedding Shawl

"Like the best marriages—mystery, romance, and lots of charm."
—*New York Times* bestselling author Nancy Pickard

"This might be Goldenbaum's best so far." —*Booklist*

"A very pleasant read that evokes summers by the sea."
—*Kirkus Reviews*

A Holiday Yarn

"Goldenbaum's plotting is superb, her characters richly drawn . . . and her prose is seamless." —*Richmond-Times Dispatch*

"Goldenbaum's cozy mystery features appealing characters whose relationships will matter to the reader." —*Booklist*

"Death puts a damper on the Christmas festivities in Goldenbaum's engrossing fourth cozy." —*Publishers Weekly*

"Invites you once more to imagine yourself in a charming, if homicidal, town." —*Kirkus Reviews*

Moon Spinners

"Goldenbaum's amateur sleuths are appealing, her plots are intricate and plausible, and the local color of Sea Harbor is interesting without being overwhelming. And you don't have to know a thing about knitting to enjoy this pleasing yarn." —*Richmond Times-Dispatch*

"Delightful . . . well-drawn characters and an intriguing plot."
—*Publishers Weekly*

"The knitters . . . make for an appealing and comfortably cozy coterie of sleuths." —*Booklist*

"[A] diverse yet likable lead protagonist . . . a delightful entry in a fun regional mystery series." —The Best Reviews

"Goldenbaum's writing is clear and evocative. Not only are you reading a well-crafted mystery but you are also, from the first page to the last, visiting a seaside New England village filled with interesting characters, charming shops—scenes so well defined you can almost smell the ocean and taste the food. The mystery itself is multilayered, with plenty of red herrings to keep . . . reader[s] on their toes."

—Gumshoe

Patterns in the Sand

"Engaging. . . . Goldenbaum weaves a tight plot as Izzy and her knitting friends attempt to untangle another puzzler without dropping a stitch."   —*Publishers Weekly*

"A powerful story."   —*Midwest Book Review*

"A good series is like taking a break and going to spend some quality time with friends you've never met. Goldenbaum has constructed a town and its people with care and attention to detail."   —Gumshoe

Death by Cashmere

"Murder in a truly close-knit community—a knitting circle in a New England seaside town. Peopled with characters we come to care about. Add a cup of tea, a roaring fire, and you've got the perfect cozy evening."

—Rhys Bowen, author of *Queen of Hearts* and the Agatha and Anthony award–winning Molly Murphy mysteries

"With all the dexterity and warmth the women of Sea Harbor knit into their sweaters and shawls, Sally Goldenbaum weaves us a tale that combines friendship, community—and crime—without dropping a stitch."   —Gillian Roberts, author of the Amanda Pepper series

"Sally Goldenbaum's appealing world will draw readers to return time and again to Sea Harbor. In this wonderful launch of a vibrant new mystery series, the characters ring true and clear."

—Carolyn Hart, author of *Death at the Door*

"[A] vibrant and earnest portrait of friendship. This is a whodunit with a big heart."   —*Richmond Times-Dispatch*

"[A] charming debut . . . a cozy many will find an ideal beach read."

—*Publishers Weekly*

Murder in Merino

A SEASIDE KNITTERS MYSTERY

Sally Goldenbaum

AN OBSIDIAN MYSTERY

OBSIDIAN
Published by the Penguin Group
Penguin Group (USA) LLC, 375 Hudson Street,
New York, New York 10014

USA | Canada | UK | Ireland | Australia | New Zealand | India | South Africa | China
penguin.com
A Penguin Random House Company

Published by Obsidian, an imprint of New American Library, a division of Penguin Group (USA)
LLC. Previously published in an Obsidian hardcover edition.

First Obsidian Trade Paperback Printing, May 2015

New American Library Trade Paperback ISBN: 978-0-451-41537-0

The Library of Congress has cataloged the hardcover edition of this title as follows:

Goldenbaum, Sally.
Murder in merino: a seaside knitters mystery/Sally Goldenbaum.
pages cm
ISBN 978-0-451-41536-3
1. Knitters (Persons)—Fiction. 2. Murder—Investigation—Fiction. I. Title.
PS3557.O35937M84 2014
813'.54—dc23   2013049946

Printed in the United States of America
1 3 5 7 9 10 8 6 4 2

Set in Palatino • Designed by Elke Sigal

In memory of my parents,
Frances and Armin Pitz

Acknowledgments

$\mathcal{M}$y heartfelt thanks to Cindy Craig, the talented and generous teacher, designer, and manager of the Studio Knitting and Needlepoint shop in Kansas City, Missouri. Cindy not only designed the amazing pattern for Nell and Ben's anniversary throw, but she filled her design with meaning and symbolism reflective of the Endicotts' forty years of marriage. How lucky Nell and the Seaside Knitters are to be beneficiaries of Cindy's talent. A special thanks, also, to Trendsetter Yarns for their generous donation of the merino yarn used to make a replica of Nell and Ben's anniversary afghan.

Many of the "imaginings" for *Murder in Merino* were nurtured by my loyal muses: Sr. Rosemary Flanigan, who years ago mentored me through logic, metaphysics, and Greek philosophy. Her creative suggestions for this book brought alive Socrates' warning about the unexamined life as she urged me to probe more deeply into the psyches and lives of Nell, Izzy, Birdie, Cass, their neighbors, and their friends. And my Minnesota muse, Mary Bednarowski, who reads my often-scattered proposal ideas and runs with them in a dozen directions, imagining all the what-ifs as she helps me follow them to surprising conclusions.

My thanks to Nancy Pickard, who not only provides me with a place to write, brainstorming sessions, occasional egg scrambles, and a glass of pinot grigio at the end of our mutually intense writing days, but who, in word and deed, inspires me to be a better writer.

Acknowledgments · x

Forever thanks to my terrific agents—Christina Hogrebe and Andrea Cirillo—and to my wise and wonderful editor, Sandy Harding.

Warm thanks to my Kansas City friends who show up at book signings, pass the Seaside Knitters along to their unsuspecting relatives and friends, and, most important, are friends—of the very best kind.

And to my sisters, Jane Pitz and Mary Sue Sheridan, always encouraging, always loving, always proud, and always there when a listening ear is needed.

My husband's, children's, their spouses', and my grandchildren's involvement is absolutely essential in getting these mysteries from thought to print. Their loving support—both emotional and practical—makes writing novels possible. Without them, the seaside knitters would be adrift in one of Cass's lobster boats, without a strip of land in sight. They are my life jacket.

Cast of Characters

Annabelle Palazola: Owner of the Sweet Petunia Restaurant; Liz and Stella Palazola's mother

Archie and Harriet Brandley: Owners of the Sea Harbor Bookstore

August (Gus) McClucken: Owner of McClucken's Hardware and Dive Shop

Beatrice Scaglia: Councilwoman running for mayor

Don Wooten: Co-owner of the Ocean's Edge restaurant; married to Rachel Wooten

Ella and Harold Sampson: Birdie's longtime housekeeper and groundsman

Esther Gibson: Police dispatcher (and Mrs. Santa Claus in season)

Father Lawrence Northcutt: Pastor of Our Lady of Safe Seas Church

Garrett Barros: Works at Ocean's Edge

Grace Danvers: Hostess at Ocean's Edge; cousin of Laura Danvers

Gracie Santos: Owner of Gracie's Lazy Lobster Café

Harry and Margaret Garozzo: Owners of Garozzo's Deli

Jane and Ham Brewster: Artists and cofounders of the Canary Cove Art Colony

Janie Levin: Nurse practitioner in the Virgilio Clinic; Tommy Porter's girlfriend

Jeffrey Meara: Longtime Ocean's Edge bartender and co-owner

Jules Ainsley: Visitor to Sea Harbor

Jerry Thompson: Police chief

Karen Hanson: Mayor Stan Hanson's wife

Laura Danvers: Young socialite and philanthropist, mother of three, married to banker Elliot Danvers

Lily Virgilio, MD: Izzy's obstetrician

Mae Anderson: Izzy's shop manager; has twin teenage nieces, Jillian and Rose

Maeve Meara: Jeffrey Meara's wife

Mary Pisano: Middle-aged newspaper columnist; owner of Ravenswood B&B

Mary Halloran: Pete and Cass's mother; secretary of Our Lady of Safe Seas Church

Merry Jackson: Owner of the Artist's Palate Bar and Grill

Penelope Ainsley: Jules Ainsley's mother

Pete Halloran: Cass's younger brother and lead guitarist in the Fractured Fish band

Rachel Wooten: City attorney; married to Don Wooten

Rebecca Early: Lampworks Gallery artist in Canary Cove

Stan Hanson: Mayor of Sea Harbor

Stella Palazola: Realtor in Sea Harbor; Annabelle's daughter

Tommy Porter: Policeman

Tyler Gibson: Esther Gibson's grandson; bartender at Ocean's Edge

Willow Adams: Fiber artist and owner of the Fishtail Gallery

Murder in Merino

$$Chapter\ 1$$

Late September
Sea Harbor, Massachusetts

The wind was coming out of the northeast, blustery and heavy with salt. It stung the woman's cheeks, turning them the color of her bright red Windbreaker. Thick strands of hair flew about her face, wild and free—like the sea she was beginning to call home.

After days of warm sun and soft breezes, the weather had suddenly turned. But she loved it in all its guises—foamy surf crashing against the rocks or water smooth as silk, a chilly wind or sun-warmed sand. Each day was new and amazing and comfortable, as if she'd been born to this place. It had been fortuitous to travel halfway across the country to this strange little town where she knew no one, yet she felt as if she'd finally come home.

She'd awakened that morning to leafy branches banging against the bed-and-breakfast's roof, rattling windows and pulling her attention away from the coffee and blueberry scones the inn's owner had brought to her room. It was a wild sound, unnerving and exciting at once.

Mary Pisano had explained that September was a weatherman's delight. A time of change. A month filled with surprises. An exciting time, she'd said, and then brought Jules another scone.

That was true enough. Already the week had been filled with unexpected happenings—though none a weatherman could predict.

The green-shuttered house on Ridge Road was just the beginning. More would come. She felt it deep inside her with a ferocious certainty that would have made her mother uncomfortable. Penelope Ainsley didn't believe in thinking about the past or in secrets or in peeling away layers of anything, other than expensive wallpaper, maybe, during one of her remodeling efforts. Sad things, after all, disappeared if you didn't hold them in your memory.

She told her daughter often that there was only one reality: the one they were living in at that precise moment. Not what was to be . . . or what had been. The past could bring only pain, she'd say, the warning in her voice sharp.

And in those latter days, when Penelope had lain motionless on the white sheets, the bedside table littered with medicine bottles, she'd repeat her mantra with unexpected urgency to her nearly forty-year-old daughter. Live in the day, my darling. Write your own script. The past is gone; let it be. Let it be . . .

During those last days Jules wasn't sure who was talking—the pills or the mother who had loved her so passionately.

But no matter. She would hold her tongue when her mother talked. And then she would follow her own path, a practice honed at an early age and one that served her well.

Thoughts of her mother squeezed her heart. Her lovely, refined, rigid mother, controlled by her parents. Jules had loved her deeply, but they rarely saw things with the same eye or sensibility. Penelope never wavered in what was correct—the way to act, to talk, to be— never allowing for those shady areas in life where happiness might be found. They were look-alikes, some said, but that was where the similarities ended. One woman sought security at all costs. The other simply wanted to be free and whole. And she couldn't be. Not yet.

Chin tucked to chest, she headed into the wind, climbing the gentle hill to Ridge Road, then turning onto the shady street. *Her* street, as she thought of it. She had intentionally come early, in time to explore before the caller would show up—and before the open house. She quickened her step as she passed the Barroses' place. The small frame house reeked of bad karma. A cranky woman. A weak husband, she suspected. And the grown son. Clarence? Garrett? She'd seen him one day from the road below, standing as still as a rock, looking through binoculars. But the Barroses didn't worry her, not really. She'd turn them into decent neighbors.

Or not.

Some yards ahead, a gray Toyota, the engine quiet, sat at the curb directly in front of the house at 27 Ridge Road. She stopped, startled, and checked her watch again. He was too early.

At first the thought frightened Jules. Maybe the man had ulterior motives for meeting her, maybe ones not as innocent as he'd led her to believe.

No, she scolded herself. Early was fine. The mysterious conversation wouldn't take long, and then she'd spend the extra time exploring the property on her own before the Realtor arrived.

He needed only a few minutes, he'd said when he called. At first, she had tried to put him off, suggesting she stop by the Ocean's Edge the next day—it would be an excuse to have a bowl of the restaurant's mussels, she'd told him, sending her smile across the phone line. Today was bad for her. She had a list of things to do, including this important open house.

Things more important than talking to a man—sweet as he was—whom she barely knew.

But he had been persistent, offering to meet her at the open house so he wouldn't mess up her day. He knew the house well. He'd said the latter words in a way that made her wonder whether he, too, wanted to buy it. Perhaps that was the urgency of meeting her. A worrisome thought. But if that was the case, she'd persuade him otherwise. She was good at convincing men to see things her way.

She walked over to the car window and leaned in, a wide smile in place, a greeting on her lips.

The car was empty.

She stood back and looked around the neighborhood. There were no signs of life along the winding street, and only the relentless wind added movement and sound. She glanced over at the Barroses' house. A curtain in the front window fluttered, then went still.

The watery wind picked up with renewed vigor and slapped a piece of newspaper against her jeans. Jules jumped, a nervous laugh escaping her lips. She pressed a hand against her chest, uncomfortable with the stab of fear that had strained her breathing. Few things frightened her. Certainly not wind . . . a newspaper . . . an empty car.

She looked at the house, trying to dislodge the tightness in her chest. It was beautiful. But so much more than that. It was an unexpected treasure, hidden behind the trees, waiting for her to find it. A key to the life she was looking for.

She was startled the first time she saw it, not believing it was real. The shingles were weathered, the shutters in need of paint. The back swing moving slightly in the breeze. It was a miracle—if you believed in such things. A miracle that she had found it, a miracle that it was to be hers.

Her mother had been wrong in her warnings. There was joy in this house.

Jules glanced at her watch again. Daylight was fading and a flash of lightning lit up the sky in the distance. But she had enough time to explore the back, the view of the sea, the potting shed. She had imagined the porch as wide enough to dance on or to curl up in the old porch swing, a pile of yarn as high as the sky beside her.

She wouldn't allow an irrational fear or a cold wind to color this day. The day was hers, hers to color in rainbows.

And then another thought occurred to her. Perhaps he was here after all, the man she was to meet. Perhaps he, too, was walking about the property, surveying it, imagining it as his own. She looked at the house, listened, then pushed her hands into the pockets of her Windbreaker and walked quickly up the front walk, the ends of a silky knit scarf flapping around her shoulders. If that was the case, she would convince him otherwise. There was no doubt in her mind about that.

The flagstone path led around to the north and Jules followed it past the shuttered windows, the empty flower boxes, the wild rosebushes. She breathed deeply, pushing against the feeling that still clung to her, prickling and niggling inside her chest.

As she rounded the corner of the house and passed the garage, a gust of wind sliced through the trees and met Jules head-on, sending her scarf flapping to the ground. It snagged on a granite boulder beside the path and she leaned over to pick it up, then stayed there for a minute, one hand on the cold, damp surface of the rock. She steadied herself, breathing in and out, slowly and purposefully, pushing away the sudden fear that threatened to disturb this day.

Her eyes were closed, lashes dark on her wet cheeks. She was aware only of the oxygen filling her lungs, and oblivious to the world beyond it. Deaf to the sounds of the sea crashing against the rocks below, to the roar of the wind. Deaf to what lay ahead.

In her head, all was silent.

Chapter 2

The week before

One week before their September would turn foul and troublesome, a shiver had passed through Nell Endicott. It began in her chest and spiraled out, traveling down her arms to the tips of her fingers and defying the warm, sunny Friday. She pulled her sweater tight, then wrapped her arms around herself.

"Chilly?" Birdie quickened her step, trying to match Nell's long-legged stride.

Before Nell could answer, Birdie shivered, too. "It must be catching," she said.

"A storm, maybe?" Nell looked east, beyond the old pier and parade of pleasure boats heading out to sea. Past Gracie's Lazy Lobster Café and a fleet of lobster boats being repaired in their slips.

The sky was flawless—pristine, perfect. No storm was predicted, and the windless day and glassy sea spoke of a lovely Indian summer day.

But sometimes Nell felt things before they actually happened—like unexpected weather or a phone call bringing sudden news—a trait for which her mother took full credit.

"It's genetic, my darlings," Abigail Hunter would tell Nell and her younger sister, Caroline. "A sixth sense. Treat it lovingly and wisely."

Nell's father's reaction was deep laughter and a bear hug for his girls, pulling them close and tousling their hair. Then he'd open his arms and pull their mother into the circle, and tell all of them what a lucky man he was to have such magical ladies in his life.

Nell shifted the bag of knitting hanging from her shoulder, her eyes still looking at the sky.

Birdie looked up, too. "No, it's not a storm," she said. She moved to the edge of the sidewalk to avoid being felled by a redheaded skate-boarder racing down Sea Harbor's main street. Large black earphones covered the boy's head, his lips moving to the music pumping into his ears.

"Freddie Wooten, be careful you don't kill yourself," Birdie called out to the skinny young boy's back.

Nell paused at the curb to let the traffic pass. "Are you as curious as I am about why Mary Pisano wants to have coffee with us at this ungodly hour?"

"Not exactly *wants*. She pretty much demanded it. I suspect she's working on some intriguing story for her column and is hoping to pump juicy gossip out of us to flavor it. Perhaps that's what's making us shiver."

Nell laughed and turned her head to wave to Harry Garozzo. The deli owner was standing in front of his store, his white apron already smudged with an orange-colored sauce.

"Pork and porcini mushrooms with Bolognese sauce," Birdie said. "I can smell it. No doubt Harry has been simmering it since dawn."

At that moment a woman in shorts and a T-shirt, a baseball cap barely controlling a mass of flying hair, approached Harry from the opposite direction.

Nell and Birdie watched the deli owner's face open wide as he wrapped Julia Ainsley in a greeting.

Her arms were slender and firm, her legs long and strong like a runner's, her eyes wide and expressive. With a single smile she fastened Harry to the spot as if she'd poured cement beneath his sneakers.

Harry was in heaven.

"A breath of fresh air, that's what he calls her," Birdie said. The octogenarian took Nell's arm and stepped off the curb.

Nell glanced back and laughed. "Harry's always been susceptible to a beautiful woman's charms."

"That woman is odd in that way," Birdie said. "There's a definite magnetism about her. But she doesn't throw it out there to impress anyone. It's simply there."

Before Nell could respond, she heard their names being called and she looked over at the waving arms of Mary Pisano. She was standing just inside Coffee's patio gate, lifting herself on tiptoe in an attempt to increase her less-than-five-foot stature an inch or two.

Patrick O'Malley's café, Coffee's, was nearly always crowded and today was no exception, which was why Mary Pisano was guarding the wrought-iron table ferociously. She pushed open the gate and ushered them in, pointing to the coffee mugs and plate of chocolate éclairs she had used to mark the table as her own.

"I saw you watching Jules come down the street," Mary said, sitting back down and passing napkins to each of them. "She's hard to miss, isn't she? Such a bundle of energy. She's been here just a short time and she already knows that Harry makes the best Bolognese sauce on Cape Ann. She'll probably be the first in history to wrangle his grandmother's recipe out of him."

"She's interesting," Birdie said in her declarative way. "I like her."

"Of course you do. She's talented and smart." Mary passed around the plate of éclairs. "She's the ideal bed-and-breakfast guest—full of life, friendly to the other guests."

Nell looked back across the street. Harry's group had grown. Julia was still there, listening intently to whatever Harry was saying, her hands on her hips, her cap off now and the morning sunlight painting streaks in her dark hair. Karen Hanson, the mayor's wife, and Izzy's friend Laura Danvers had joined in the conversation.

"Attracts people like bees to honey," Mary said around a bite of éclair.

"She's friendly," Nell said.

"Yes. And beautiful. And did I mention how talented she is?"

"You did," Nell said. "Izzy has said as much. She's doing a beautiful job on a cable sweater."

"She's quite a runner. I see her everywhere—the harbor, the backshore. When does the woman have time to knit?" Birdie asked.

Mary wiped the crumbs from the corners of her mouth, her head nodding agreement.

"You're enjoying having her around, I gather." Nell's words were spoken in a tentative way, wondering where Mary was going with the conversation. The text she'd sent the night before had been brief. *Please meet with me on Coffee's patio in the morning. There's something I want to talk to you about.*

Birdie had received the same invitation.

A meeting at Coffee's to talk about Julia Ainsley's fine attributes?

"How long is she vacationing here?" Birdie asked, picking up on Nell's thought, a trick she and Nell had mastered years before.

"Well, now, I don't know exactly. She's a bit mysterious when it comes to planning for the future. And about her past, too, for that matter. I've asked all my usual questions, but I've learned little. I know she'll be here at least a few more weeks." Mary looked at each of them in turn, her eyebrows lifting.

An odd way of wording it, Nell thought.

Mary went on. "But there is something important I've learned about her: Julia Ainsley knows food." Her words were firm, as if her companions might disagree.

"Well, that's good," Birdie said. "So do we. And we've plenty of good restaurants to suggest. I wonder if she's tried Gracie's Lazy Lobster Café yet? It sometimes gets overlooked once the tourists leave."

"No, that's not what I mean." Mary looked at Nell. "She has a knack for presenting things. So I may urge her to stay on long enough, just to get her ideas."

"Long enough for what?" Birdie asked. Perhaps they were finally getting to the reason for the meeting.

"For the anniversary party." She smiled at Nell. "Yours."

Nell put down her coffee cup. "Mary, what are you talking about? Ben and I are planning a casual early-evening event at our house. Appetizers and drinks. No muss, no fuss."

"Nonsense, Nell. No couple plans their own fortieth anniversary celebration. It will be at Ravenswood by the Sea. I've already asked Jules for ideas. And Karen is helping, too."

"Karen?"

"Karen Hanson. Our first lady, that Karen. She's redesigning some rooms in the bed-and-breakfast. She's an excellent designer, you know—her family owned all those high-end stores. And she's good at knowing what people want, which is partly why her husband has been mayor for the last two decades."

Nell looked relieved at the change in conversation, so Birdie picked it up. "But maybe not for long. I hear Beatrice Scaglia is planning to give him a run for his money," she said.

Mary laughed. "Beatrice will keep moving up the political ladder until she's pope, if you ask me, though I'm not sure anyone can beat Stan. He's a good man. But no matter—you're changing the subject on me. We're here to talk about your anniversary party, not politics."

"Mary, I don't think—" Nell began.

"Shush. We've already talked about it."

Mary continued, her voice tamping down Nell's attempt to intervene. She clearly wanted to get her thoughts out on the table without interruption. "Jeffrey Meara from the Ocean's Edge can manage bar duties; maybe Liz Santos from the yacht club will provide staff—"

"Staff?" Nell's summer tan began to disappear.

Mary's small hands waved her into silence. "It will be lovely. A fortieth wedding anniversary should be a time of joy and celebration without any concerns on the honorees' part. That's just the way it is."

The look Birdie passed over Mary's lowered head said it all. *Let it go, my friend. You have absolutely no choice here.*

How true. Once Mary Pisano settled on an idea, she was a dog with a bone, and there wasn't any way they would be able to wrest the anniversary planning away from her, at least not without being bitten.

Nell sighed, then covered her resignation with a smile, wondering how she'd explain to Ben that their laid-back anniversary plans were now in Mary Pisano's hands. "Laid-back" wasn't a word with which Mary easily identified. The talky columnist and owner of Sea Harbor's elegant bed-and-breakfast was not only involved in every inch of Sea Harbor life, she was as resolute and stubborn as a fisherman's wife, which she also was.

"So it's decided, then? Good." Mary took a last drink of coffee, wiped the corners of her satisfied mouth, and pushed out her chair.

"What's decided?" Cass Halloran walked over to the table, balancing a mug of dark roast in one hand and a blueberry scone in the other. She looked tired, even before she pushed her sunglasses to the top of her head, revealing red-rimmed eyes.

Birdie frowned. "Are you all right, Catherine?"

"Fit as a fiddle." Cass set her things on the table, then leaned down and gave Birdie and Nell quick hugs. "I need coffee."

"And I need to write my column," Mary said, standing up and hoisting her backpack between narrow shoulders. She looked over at Cass. "I could use some juicy tidbits. Any gossip heard on the *Lady Lobster*?"

Cass shot Mary a frown. "Why do you ask that?"

"Because my husband is a fisherman just like you and your brother, and I know what goes on out there on the water. Lots of cussing. Some feuding. Nasty tricks now and then. But always plenty of talk."

Cass swallowed a drink of coffee. "Now that we've added more boats and a ton more traps, I'm in the office managing things more often than out on the water. But there's no new gossip that I know of. If I hear anything, you'll be the first to know."

Mary patted her hand. "As it should be, Cass." She wiggled her fingers in a makeshift wave to Birdie and Nell and headed across the patio to the small round table beneath the maple tree, a table for one, reserved for the "About Town" columnist. In minutes, Mary had opened her laptop and settled in, beginning to compose the day's chatty newspaper column. A dearth of gossip was not much of a challenge for Mary—she'd dig something up or applaud someone's good deeds or expound on a favorite cause or pet peeve. The column would be written no matter how little news was circulating around the seaside town—and it would be read by nearly everyone in town.

"So," Birdie said, the soft word drawn out slowly to relax the lines on Cass's face.

Cass managed a smile. "It's been a long day, that's all." She held her cell phone in her hand and glanced down at a message that pinged into view.

"Cass, it's morning. Early morning." Nell looked down to see Danny Brandley's name being dismissed. She was fond of Cass's significant other and had to tamp down the urge to suggest Cass answer it.

"Morning. Night. Just busy. What was Mary in such a heat about?"

Birdie filled her in on Mary's plans for Ben and Nell's anniversary celebration. "And apparently she's recruiting others to help as well."

Cass glanced over at Nell and spoke around a bite of scone. "Oh, jeez, Nell. I'm sorry—"

"It'll be fine. You know Mary."

"She claims it will be simple," Birdie said. "She's already recruiting help, even trying to get a guest to give her ideas."

"Guest?"

"Julia Ainsley."

Cass's head shot up, sending crumbs and blueberries floating through the holes in the wrought-iron table. "What about her?"

"Mary is looking for excuses to keep her around longer. She's asking her for ideas for Nell and Ben's anniversary party."

Cass stopped chewing and stared at Birdie. "Why would she do that?"

Nell answered. "Mary probably thought she was doing us a favor by taking over planning duties." She paused, confused at the look of disapproval on Cass's face. "Cass, it'll be okay."

"No, I mean Jules Ainsley. Izzy says that's what she wants to be called—Jules. She's just here on vacation, passing through, right? Why is she getting involved in our . . . our lives?"

"She and Mary have become friends. And we all know it's hard to say no to Mary."

Cass washed down her scone with coffee, her silence heavy and uncomfortable.

Cass guarded her feelings closely, but she was as unable as a child to hide emotion in her face. Deep lines formed just above her dark eyebrows, creasing her forehead. And her eyes—a color matching the deepest part of the sea—lacked the clarity and curiosity usually found there. Instead they were filled with emotion, her attractive face a study in frustration. "You're upset," Nell said.

Cass turned her head away from the two older friends who were usually like warm blankets to her, always there, always comforting. Always able to lighten her load when the family lobster business became too heavy a weight on her shoulders.

Cass sat still as a granite rock, staring across the street at Harry Garozzo's deli.

Nell and Birdie turned their heads and followed her look. Harry had gone inside, and Laura and Rachel Wooten were nowhere to be seen. Standing just beyond Harry's wide front window were two familiar figures: Danny Brandley and Julia Ainsley, their heads bowed until they almost touched, their conversation shielded in the cave of their nearly joined bodies.

Chapter 3

$\mathcal{N}$ell carried the image of Danny and Julia Ainsley with her to the market. She picked through the beans, wondering about the conversation. The two figures, standing there, their bodies leaning in toward each other. They had looked like old friends—the sandy-haired mystery writer and the long-legged runner—sharing something important. Something *intimate*.

Cass had been upset, that was clear. She and Danny were close—closer than Cass had allowed herself to be with any man. Her independent streak had been remarkably softened by the mystery writer, causing Cass's Irish mother to light even more vigil lights at Our Lady of Safe Seas in her relentless pursuit of grandchildren.

Nell pushed her cart down the produce aisle in the busy store, trying to imagine Ben in an intimate conversation with a beautiful woman, someone she didn't know well, maybe not at all. She dropped several tomatoes and peppers into the cart and moved slowly down toward the lettuce, the odd scenario playing out in her mind like a movie.

And then she stopped short, her hands tight on the handle rung. What was she thinking? She and Ben were about to celebrate forty years of marriage, but for that split second Nell had felt an uncomfortable pang. An emotion that made her want to confront the imaginary woman, made her want to look her squarely in the eyes and tell her that Ben—*her* Ben—was her best friend, her lover, her husband of decades. She wanted to tell her to go away.

So silly! she thought, and held back an embarrassed half smile at the crazy sensation that had taken hold of her, then left just as quickly. Yes, silly for her, but maybe not so silly for Cass, who had only recently been open about her feelings for Danny and was suddenly faced with Julia Ainsley—bright and beautiful and with that confident glow that many women around forty exhibited. No matter how innocent the encounter on Harbor Road had been, it was not something Cass would take lightly.

"The asparagus is great today. The manager is buying from a local farm over near Rockport."

Nell pulled herself from her thoughts and smiled into the face of Karen Hanson. She was holding up a bundle of slender green asparagus.

"You caught me daydreaming, Karen—sorry." She pushed away the curious sensation that her thoughts might have spilled directly out of her head and were hanging there, right in front of the lettuce and tomatoes, for everyone to see. Including the mayor's wife.

"Don't apologize for daydreaming. I do it frequently."

"You probably have it down to a fine art. I would if I had to attend all the dinners and events you and Stan get invited to."

"Yes, there's that—lots of fried-chicken dinners in campaigning, at least in this campaign." She glanced over Nell's shoulder, then took a step closer and lowered her voice. "I believe in the democratic process, but campaigns were easier when Stan was only running against himself. Madame Scaglia is a challenge."

The edge to her voice caused Nell to turn and look across the aisle. Beatrice Scaglia, dressed in heels and a fitted orange-and-pink dress and jacket, stood nearby. Her eyes were focused on bins of lettuce and fennel and ripe tomatoes, but her body language seemed more tuned in to picking up conversations around her, particularly Karen and Nell's.

"She's putting her heart and soul into beating Stan," Karen said. "Although 'heart' may be a misnomer in this case." Her jaw was set, her fingers wrapped tightly around a set of car keys.

At that moment Beatrice lifted her head and, as if surprised to see her, greeted Nell with a broad smile and a friendly hello. She ignored Karen Hanson.

Karen disregarded the snub and dropped a bag of lemons into her cart. Her understated slacks, silk blouse, and diamond stud earrings were the direct opposite of Beatrice's attire, piece for piece. Karen's appearance spoke of old money; Beatrice's glittery earrings, expensive heels, and bright-colored attire called out for attention.

"It goes with the territory, I suppose," Nell said to Karen, slightly surprised at Beatrice's behavior.

But the look on Karen's face showed little concern with Beatrice's manners. Instead, the usually mild-mannered woman's expression surprised Nell. The public smile was gone and in its place Nell saw a confident woman up for a fight—one she was sure she'd win.

They watched Beatrice move down the grocery aisle, smiling at other shoppers along the way as she campaigned her way to the bakery department.

"Beatrice can ignore me all she wants," Karen muttered. "But a single word against Stan and she will be gone. I won't stand for that."

"I don't think she would do that," Nell said. But her words were hollow, spoken more to soften Beatrice's rudeness to Karen. Beatrice was ambitious—a fact everyone in Sea Harbor was aware of. She'd been on the city council forever and desperately wanted to put Stan Hanson out of office.

What Beatrice would do to win an election was anyone's guess.

"On to more pleasant things," Karen said. "I've been helping Mary Pisano liven up some rooms in her bed-and-breakfast—I noticed when we had guests stay there how shabby it was looking. I'm ordering some things that will help."

Karen Siegel Hanson's grandfather had invested a fortune in high-end furniture stores that catered to the very wealthy—and had doubled the family fortune. As the only remaining heir, Karen dabbled in the business herself when the spirit moved her. "We'll have it looking better in time for the party," she said carefully.

Nell laughed. "The anniversary party, I guess you mean. You know, she's using you, Karen. Who would have more connections than the mayor's wife to help her with the event? But you need to know it's not exactly what Ben and I had planned."

"I know, I know." Karen stopped Nell's words with a shake of her head. "Mary sometimes inserts herself into things. But actually, she's right, Nell. You shouldn't have to plan your own anniversary party."

"It doesn't seem I have a choice. But since you've been recruited to help, I have a favor to ask."

"Of course."

"Mary listens to you. Please restrain her and keep this thing simple. Ben and I refuse to have a fancy, elegant party—it's not who we are. It didn't really need planning to start with."

"You have my word. I will keep her in check. It's something I'm very good at. I practice on my husband daily."

They had neared the front of the store and looked up to see Beatrice handing a balloon to a little boy.

Karen watched her husband's competition in silence, her chin set and her eyes steely. Then she looked at Nell, lifted one brow, and whispered, "I don't suppose I have control over the guest list for your party, do I? There are definitely some people I'd happily eliminate."

The weatherman predicted an evening that would be almost sinfully beautiful, and Ben had gone all out with his fish for the Endicotts' weekly dinner on the deck. The salmon he'd brought home was truly majestic. *King* salmon, Ben announced.

"It might be our last fresh salmon before winter," he said, pulling it out of the refrigerator.

"It's gorgeous, Ben—and there's enough to feed at least half of Sea Harbor." Nell absently whisked wine into the ginger and brown sugar marinade, mentally planning the salad she'd make with the leftovers the next day.

"Any idea who's coming?" Ben asked.

"Oh, who knows? Izzy and Sam will be here—they know I need my daily Abigail fix. Cass said she would be here. She wasn't sure about Danny. Birdie, of course. And I don't think Jane and Ham have ever missed a Friday night since Ham talked you into doing it. Pete's Fractured Fish band has a gig tonight, so he and Willow won't be here." Nell poured a thin stream of olive oil into the pan, mentally going through a list of friends and neighbors. "I don't know about the Wootens."

Friday-night dinner at the Endicotts' was an open invitation, with the regulars nearly always there and sometimes neighbors or friends Ben or Nell happened to run into that day. *Come one, come all* was the standing mantra.

Ben took a drink of iced tea, then pulled his grilling tools from a lower cabinet. "Sam and I were washing down the boat this afternoon and Jules Ainsley jogged by. She's a friendly gal, even offered to help us out. Before we knew it, she was checking the hull and engine cases and discovered some rust we'd missed. Impressive. She used to sail on Lake Michigan, she said. Anyway, we invited her to drop by tonight if she didn't have plans. I told her Birdie lived right across from the B and B and she could hitch a ride with her if she wanted to. She was gracious but didn't commit."

Julia Ainsley again. Nell's mind went back to the scene at Coffee's and the look on Cass Halloran's face. She lifted the pot off the stove and set it on a hot pad. *She knits, she's smart, she's beautiful . . . and she sails.* Nell held her silence.

"I think she'll fit right in with our friends," Ben said, talking over his shoulder as he moved to the liquor cabinet in the family room. The Endicotts' kitchen and family room flowed together, making a comfortable, bright, and airy space. They'd done the remodeling when Ben inherited the house from his parents, and this area—the whole back section of the house—was a dream come true for Nell. Her ideal kitchen and family room, with space for friends to help cut and stir, gather in groups, play music, and sit around the stone fireplace on cold winter nights.

Ben took the martini glasses from the cabinet and lined them up on a tray.

"I don't know her well," Nell said. "But she seems to be everything you said—and attractive, for sure."

"*A looker*, as one of the kids down at the dock put it. He guessed her age at thirty—a decade off, she said."

The infectious sound of a baby's laugh preceded Abigail Kathleen Perry into the room, stopping all talk.

Sam swung Abby's infant seat with one hand, and with each swing the baby's high squeals filled the air.

Nell wiped her hands on a dishcloth and hurried toward her grandniece, leaving all thoughts of Jules Ainsley behind.

Izzy followed, carrying a basket with loaves of French bread peeking out from beneath a checkered cloth. Bringing up the rear was Red, Abigail's constant companion and bodyguard. The golden retriever seemed to have recaptured his youth with the baby's arrival. He left her side long enough to bound around the room, accepting everyone's pats, then dutifully returned to Abby, now cuddled in Nell's arms.

Cass and Danny, carrying a covered pan, arrived next, with Jane and Ham Brewster following in Danny's sweet-smelling trail.

"What do I smell?" Jane asked, depositing a fresh salad on the island and sidling up to Danny. "My nose tells me it's magnificent and will add an inch to my waistline."

"Apple crisp. I picked the apples over at Russell Orchards. You'll love it, Janie."

He leaned over and gave the artist a hug, something people seemed to do automatically to Jane Brewster. She and Ham were onetime hippies who had come upon Sea Harbor by accident in the early seventies and never left. The Endicotts' closest friends, the two artists had single-handedly founded Canary Cove, the art colony that hugged the shores of Sea Harbor, and their largesse had given many young artists their start.

"Of course I'll love it." She looked around and spotted Nell. "And now it's my turn with that baby, Nell." Jane hugged Abby close to her pleasantly ample breasts, then danced the blue-eyed baby to the opposite end of the family room and the Bose dock, where in minutes she'd be twirling Abby to a Beatles or Billy Joel or Joni Mitchell tune.

Nell looked around for Cass. She was out on the deck with Ben, sticking toothpicks into olives as Ben prepared a batch of his martinis. Nell watched them for a minute, the image pleasing her, as it always did. Cass found comfort in Ben's presence, even when she wasn't seeking advice for her lobster company or about an inheritance, or needing help towing a truck. Nell suspected Ben somehow filled a void in Cass, one created when her own fisherman father was killed at sea. She wondered absently whether Cass was seeking comfort now—or simply helping Ben make drinks for the group and poke coals to life.

Danny walked up behind her. "Seen Cass?"

Nell nodded toward the open doors to the deck.

Danny looked outside. "She seems to disappear from my presence quickly these days. I think something's on her mind." The sandy-haired writer had finally resorted to wearing glasses, and he fiddled with the stem now, his eyes on Cass.

The glasses only added to his looks, a fact not lost on a whole parade of Sea Harbor single women. Perhaps Jules Ainsley had also joined that club. But the good news was that it was clear to Nell that Danny had no idea why Cass was acting strange. And surely that signified a man without guilt. They sometimes joked about Danny's being oblivious, his thoughts elsewhere—solving a murder or planting red herrings in his head, all fodder for a future book. Even though he had certainly seen the seamy side of life when he was a prize-winning reporter, he approached people openly and kindly and with great interest. He had probably bumped into Jules Ainsley the same way Sam and Ben had at the yacht club. Or Harry Garozzo had in front of his deli. Or any of them, for that matter. Jules was friendly. They were making mountains out of molehills.

At that moment the front screen door blew open and shut and Birdie breezed into the room, a gigantic bowl of a sweet-smelling quinoa salad in her arms. "From Ella, of course—not me. My dear housekeeper is going all healthy on me, insisting on things like kale and quinoa and what have you. You'll love it, Nell. You, too, Isabel. And I will learn to like it." She allowed Sam to take it from her. "Even our sweet angel Abby will love it, once it reaches her via her mom."

Nell half expected Jules to be following Birdie into the room. She released a sigh of relief that her friend was alone.

Sam noticed, too, and asked whether Birdie had heard from her neighbor across the road. "Ben and I thought Jules Ainsley might be coming with you."

"Jules? Mary's guest? Oh, dear. Was I supposed to invite her? I swear, this head of mine must be shrinking. It doesn't hold as much—though you ask me what my Sonny and I did fifty years ago and I'll be able to tell you down to the wine we drank." Her tiny frame moved with laughter.

While the others conjured up romantic images of a youthful Birdie and the love of her life, Sam explained, "You're fine, Birdie. You didn't forget anything. We figured Harold was driving you over, so we suggested she call you if she wanted a ride."

"No, she didn't call. I saw her out running a little bit ago and she waved in that friendly way she has that makes me think we know each other better than we really do. She was heading toward the beach. It's quite amazing the way she's embraced this town—all of Cape Ann, in fact. She told me yesterday she'd discovered Gloucester's backshore. 'A runner's dream,' she called it. So I'm quite sure she could find Sandswept Lane if she had a mind to do it."

"How long is she going to be here?" Jane Brewster asked, coming in from the deck, where she had regretfully relinquished Abby to Ham's waiting arms. "She came into the gallery last week. She's not your ordinary tourist, is she? She seems more like someone checking us all out."

"Checking us out?" Nell asked.

"Well, the town, I guess I mean. She asked a lot of questions about the area, its history, why people live here. She was interested in Canary Cove, too—how long it's been here, that kind of thing. She likes art and asked if I'd look at a painting she brought with her."

"She paints? I can't stand it. She knits like a pro, she runs like an Olympic athlete, she's smart—and now she paints? Geesh." Izzy took a piece of Brie from a wooden cheese plate and stared it down before putting it into her mouth. "And from the looks of her she doesn't eat much—clearly not the kind of food that keeps me alive and Abby thriving."

Jane laughed. "I don't know if she paints. She just thought I'd be able to tell her something about a painting she owns."

"That's odd," Birdie said.

"What?"

"That she'd bring a painting with her on vacation. Assuming she's on vacation, that is."

They mulled over that fact for a minute before Cass interrupted, stepping through the French doors with a tray of Ben's martinis, a Friday-night staple. "Drinks are ready," she announced.

She seemed more relaxed, Nell thought, and even responded with a smile to Danny's large hand claiming the small of her back. *Good.* And as much as Nell loved welcoming people to their Friday dinners, she was relieved that Jules hadn't shown up.

In the distance, the sizzle of salmon on a hot grill filled the air with the smell of garlic, wine, and lemon.

"Out, everyone," Izzy urged. She handed Cass a basket of pita and followed her to the deck, carrying a round tray of small bowls filled with dips.

Nell followed Birdie into the kitchen and in minutes they'd crisped the bread, checked the quinoa, and then joined the group on the deck. Ben stood at the grill, basting his masterpiece while the others relaxed in the comfortable porch chairs, sipping martinis.

"I was in a meeting with Stan Hanson today," Ben said, stepping away from the cloud of smoke. "I told him he and Karen should stop by if they were free."

"Let me guess," Ham said. "They had yet another PTA or Rotary Club appearance to make."

Ben nodded. "You guessed it. It's all because of Beatrice Scaglia, Karen says. She's campaigning like a human dynamo—although Karen's words were more pointed. She's everywhere, and the Hansons have no choice but to do the same."

"And Beatrice has the energy edge—she's ten years younger." Birdie sat on the glider, gently rocking Abby in her arms.

Sam moved opposite her and snapped a photo of the pure innocence of his baby girl, looking up into the lined face and wise eyes of the woman with whom she seemed to share the most basic secrets of life.

"Such messy business, politics," Jane said. She smothered a cracker with a fig and goat cheese spread and handed it to Ham. "It makes me wonder why Stan would even want another term. He's, what—sixtyish? Why not relax and enjoy life. He's certainly paid his dues."

"But Stan does good things. He's probably done more for social services than anyone in the state," Nell said. "He's a fine mayor."

"He hasn't done much about raising revenues for roads and playgrounds," said Ben. "And Beatrice is beating him over the head with that."

"Well, we know he doesn't do it for the money," Ham said. Although the city council had recently raised the mayor's salary—in spite of Stan's own opposition to the proposal—everyone knew it wasn't what he could have made working in his wife's family's businesses.

"He and Karen live rather modestly, considering the wealth they've inherited," Birdie said. "Their house is impeccably decorated, of course." She handed the baby over to Izzy, who tucked her feet up beneath her and nursed Abby until her chubby body went slack and her curly blond head nodded in sleep.

"Stan's a modest guy," Ben said. "Before Karen coerced him into running for mayor, he was perfectly content working at Father North-cutt's shelter or running the Boy's Club program. He still volunteers with the sailing classes Sam and I run for those kids."

"Good folks," Jane said.

"And now we have the happy excuse to abandon politics for food," Ben said. "The salmon is ready, folks. Let's move this party to the table."

The wooden dining table was Nell's pride and joy. It sat beneath the shade of a maple tree, where it hosted gatherings from April to October and sometimes—with the help of a heater, jackets, and coop-erating winds—into early winter. Nell had set it tonight with the earth-tone pottery Jane Brewster had made for them years before, each piece slightly different from the next. Flickering light from a line of hurricane lamps echoed the warmth of the day and in minutes they'd all gathered around, pulling back chairs with colorful cushions and settling down for a feast. Birdie lifted her glass in a toast to a beautiful night, to Ben's special salmon, to family, and to friends.

"Hear, hear," they echoed as the gentle clinking of glasses filled the darkening sky.

Bowls and platters were passed; wine was poured and a bowl of dog food set out for Red.

"Those no-shows are going to rue the day they missed this meal. You've outdone yourself, Ben Endicott." Ham breathed in the garlicky aroma of the salmon, patted his ample belly, and sighed.

They all laughed. Ham was everyone's most appreciative dinner guest.

Izzy eyed the quinoa and took a generous helping, scooping up capers, snow peas, slices of red pepper, and chunks of feta cheese. "Birdie, let Ella know she can move into our spare room anytime she wants. This is fantastic."

"Speaking of spare room," Sam said, "we're almost ready to put Izzy's old house on the market."

"At last," Birdie said. "That's one distraction you don't need in your lives right now. All attention should go to sweet Abby." She glanced back at the baby, sound asleep in a small cradle with Red at her side.

Izzy raised an eyebrow. "You've heard the complaints, haven't you? Fess up, Birdie."

The small cottage Izzy had lived in before marrying Sam had been rented on and off, but since Abigail's birth it had stood vacant, something to which the neighbors on Ridge Road didn't take kindly.

Birdie held her wineglass up for Ben to refill. "Perhaps a word here and there." Birdie's connection to Sea Harbor news and gossip came to her unbidden, a product of having lived in the town forever and knowing nearly all its residents. And having a large capacity to hold secrets close.

"The next-door neighbors have been a bit cranky," Izzy said. "But probably with good reason."

"The Barroses? They were grouches when I lived in your house, Iz," Cass said. "I didn't mow the lawn in the right direction or something equally ridiculous. They're nosy as all get-out—and not only that, their son Garrett is a pill. He dropped out of junior college and I see him all over town looking as if he's on some awful stuff. Always with those binoculars around his neck."

Izzy laughed. "It was your truck the Barroses didn't like, Cass, not you. For some reason a rusty pickup piled high with lobster traps didn't fit the neighborhood décor."

Sam took a drink of wine and declared that, whether they were nosy or not, he agreed with Izzy—the neighbors probably had grounds for complaint. "I haven't done a great job of keeping the lawn mowed— and one kindly neighbor pointed out a couple beer cans under the bushes. Teenagers using the porch or shed out back, probably. They climb up that small hill from the beach, through that overgrown mess of weeds and trees. It's time for someone to make it a home again."

"So when does it go on the market?" Danny asked. "Need any help getting it ready?"

"Thanks. But I think we're okay. We'll use the weekend to get things out of there, and turn it over to Stella next week."

"Stella Palazola? That's wonderful," Birdie said.

"Her Realtor's license is hot off the press—she's joining her uncle Mario's company. I think we'll be her first listing. She's pretty psyched."

"And I bet her mother is happy, too. The last of Annabelle's children to graduate college and settle into a career. She has a right to be proud," Nell said.

"Selling this house will be a challenge for Stella," Sam said. "It's small and needs some serious work. It will take a special buyer and someone who can see beyond the surface."

"It will sell," Birdie said. "It's a sweet little place, and has a long history here in Gloucester. Someone will fall absolutely in love with it. I may tell Jeffrey Meara about it. He and Maeve have been talking about downsizing."

"Jeffrey from the Ocean's Edge?" Danny asked. "'The Bartender,' as Pete calls him, as if he's the only one in town."

Birdie nodded. "In fact, I probably know a number of people who might want to scale down their lives." Birdie sweetly ignored the laughter that followed her comment. Her own eight-bedroom home was magnificent and could easily house a family of twelve. But it had been Sonny Favazza's home—*their* home—and it would be her final resting place. And all who knew Birdie—including a couple of husbands and myriad developers who had tried to convince her otherwise—knew there was absolutely no way to change her mind.

"Big or small," Ben said, "Stella's enthusiasm will serve her well. I agree with Birdie—she'll find a buyer." He walked the salmon around the table and slid pieces onto Sam's and Ham's raised plates, then headed inside for more wine.

Conversation swirled around the table and it wasn't until Nell noticed a few empty glasses that she realized Ben hadn't returned with the wine. She looked across the deck toward the French doors and started to call out to him. But just then Ben pushed open the door and stepped outside.

"We have another friend joining us," he said.

They all looked up. Just a foot or two behind Ben, framed like a painting in the door opening, stood Jules Ainsley.

Chapter 4

Her smile was open, if slightly embarrassed. She followed Ben, her sneakers silent on the deck floor.

"Excuse my looks," she said, pulling off a baseball cap. She wore running shorts and a tee. Simple and jewelry free, except for large hoop earrings and a thin gold chain with a small locket attached that moved as she walked. Her forehead was damp and the stains on her shirt showed the exertion of her run.

Nell walked quickly across the deck. "No need to apologize, Jules. You found us after all. Come, sit. Let me fill you a plate. We always have extra."

Ben handed her a glass of wine and Danny pulled a chair over to the table.

Jules's ponytail moved with the shake of her head. "No, please. No matter what this looks like, I didn't plan to barge in." Her smile and large brown eyes took in everyone at the table. She fiddled with a chain around her neck, twisting it around a finger, a brief nod to nervousness. "I actually had an early dinner at the Ocean's Edge with Mary Pisano and her husband. I swear I single-handedly ate an entire platter of calamari—the best I've ever had. Honest—I really didn't mean to interrupt your dinner."

Izzy and Nell looked over at Cass at the same time. She was studying Jules, as if trying to figure out what was going on inside her head. Cass's own thoughts were clear: *If not for food, why are you here?*

Jules went on, speaking more to Nell than to the others. "I was running and remembered the directions Ben and Sam had given me to your home, so I thought I'd just try to find it. I'm always looking for new destinations, figuring out where things are. And then, well, I did. I found it. It's so welcoming, and the front door was open. So I walked up, really just intending to peek inside." She looked over at Ben and gave a slightly embarrassed laugh. "But Ben caught me in the act."

"Not true. We invited you, though invitations aren't really needed around here."

"This is an amazing home . . ." She looked across the sloping backyard, the meandering flagstone walkway, the woods and the worn path that wound through the trees to the sea. "If there is a heaven, surely this is a piece of it."

"It's pretty close," Ben agreed. "Come have a seat. Do you know everyone?"

Jules looked around the table again. Nodding. Smiling. "But please, everyone—eat. Don't let me interrupt."

"We're almost finished. We'll be ready for dessert soon," Ben said. "And no one can say no to Danny Brandley's apple crisp. It's not allowed. No matter how many helpings of calamari you had."

"Danny cooks?" Jules's laugh was full and infectious. She walked over and sat down beside the author. "A mystery writer, an investigative journalist . . . and he cooks, too?"

Danny brushed the comments off with a wave of his hand.

Jane picked it up, a hint of teasing in her words. "Our Danny's talents are boundless. He also knits—though he's not very good at that."

"That's all you know, Jane Brewster," Danny said. "Iz taught me how to purl the other day."

"Yes, I did," Izzy acknowledged. "I won't vouch for how good he is, but he can indeed purl. His relatives and friends will be very happy this Christmas that he's moved beyond garter stitch ties and scarves."

"Enough," Danny said, pushing out his chair and holding up his hands. "I'm going to dish up my dessert and he who speaks ill of the cook gets coal."

Jules pushed out her chair. "I'll help you." Her words trailed off behind her as she followed him into the house.

Nell watched Izzy distracting Cass by placing a waking Abby in her lap. The others went on talking, moving from one topic to another, and finally settling on Ben and Nell's anniversary and Mary Pisano's insertion of herself into the planning.

"It will be a lovely gathering, no matter what," Birdie declared, piling empty plates on the tray.

Izzy and Nell got up to help, filling trays and heading toward the kitchen.

Danny and Jules were at the kitchen island, the pan of apple crisp cooling on hot pads in front of them. They were so engrossed in conversation that they didn't realize they weren't alone in the kitchen.

"What about tomorrow?" Jules was saying.

"Tomorrow . . ." Danny scratched his head and pulled out his phone. He checked the calendar.

"Tomorrow. Okay. Maybe the Artist's Palate deck?" He lifted his head and noticed Nell and Izzy. "Sorry. We got talking and I forgot what I was doing in here."

"No problem," Izzy said brightly. "We'll keep you focused." The smile she sent his way was on her lips but not in her eyes, and it came with a warning attached. *Don't hurt my friend Cass*, it said . . . *Or else.*

Danny Brandley was oblivious to the warning. Nor did there seem to be any guilt in his being caught planning a get-together with a beautiful woman—one who wasn't Cass. Instead, he grinned back at Izzy and motioned toward a stack of plates. "Okay, Iz. Here're the plates. Could someone grab the cinnamon ice cream in the freezer and a scoop? We're minutes away from indulging in Granny Brandley's fantastic apple crisp."

"I'll scoop," Jules said, and went rummaging through a drawer in search of a utensil.

She was loving Sea Harbor, she told them as she dug into the cinnamon ice cream. She loved the sea. The boats. The food. It was a perfect getaway spot.

"Getaway?" Izzy asked.

"Oh, you know. Just an expression. My mother died recently after a long illness. I had quit my job in Chicago to take care of her, and after it was all over, I needed to get away. She'd left me a little money to travel or whatever."

"How did you pick Sea Harbor?" Nell asked.

"That's what a friend back home asked me. *See what?* she asked. But it seemed as good a place as any to get away. So here I am."

Though not a town you'd find on any list of top places to visit, Nell thought. Jules was adept at not answering questions she clearly wanted to avoid.

Before the question was repeated, Jules changed the subject, telling them about running in Dog Town the day before. She'd met a group of runners who shared their favorite trails with her.

"Imagine, a place called Dog Town—and strangers who become your friends in the blink of an eye. Friends who'd invite me to a dinner like this. I could get used to this town."

Nell looked at Izzy.

But please, don't. The words weren't spoken aloud, but they were written all across Izzy's face.

And the disconcerting part of it all was that Izzy liked Jules Ainsley. Nell did, too.

But they loved Cass.

Chapter 5

It was a weekend that began and ended with Jules Ainsley. Friday night, then Sunday. Like bookends. Or at least that was what stayed in Izzy's and Nell's memory when they tried to make sense of everything later.

Ben and Sam had arranged the evening—a treat for their wives, they'd said. Reservations for four at the Ocean's Edge.

A double date, Sam called it, and he refused to let Izzy say no.

Cass had been begging for a night with Abigail. She wanted the baby all to herself, and she agreed with Sam that he and Izzy needed a night away.

Izzy didn't think she needed any such thing, but she was overruled.

And they were probably right, she confessed to Nell as they walked up the steps to the restaurant. As much as she hated leaving Abby, it was nice to put on a new silky dress, to brush her hair, to feel sexy. Yes, to be on a date with Sam.

As always, the seaside restaurant was packed inside and out. A large covered deck and outdoor bar wrapped around three sides and hung out over the water, inviting waves and horn blasts from passing boats. A narrow flight of stairs led down to a dock for the water taxi that brought people over from Rockport, Annisquam, and other parts of Gloucester. The driver, amiable and flexible, was willing to go anywhere his boat could get to.

The restaurant's interior was slightly more formal, the large, angular space filled with comfortable leather booths and white-clothed tables, with a wall-to-ceiling stone fireplace in the center, maritime sculptures, and tall, leafy plants that made the spacious room seem private and intimate.

Jeffrey Meara was at his customary post at the end of the bar, directing waiters, greeting newcomers, and shaking a blunt finger at one of the busboys. Jeffrey always dressed for the job, a bow tie and crisp white shirt. But his signature pieces were the knit vests he wore nearly every day, all knit by the woman in his life, his wife, Maeve. Today it was a soft merino vest the color of butter.

Nell waved but the bartender didn't see her. His brows were pulled together, his eyes glaring at a busboy texting on his cell phone.

"Whasmattayou?" he mouthed at the young man, then pointed to a table near the bar, empty of people but crowded with dirty plates, scrunched-up napkins, and a tablecloth stained with wine and coffee. Jeffrey jabbed the air with his index finger, as if the busboy were right in front of him and he was poking him severely in the chest. Then he pointed to the table again.

Nell could read his lips, hear the words inside her head, ones that sent the man backing up against the wall. She imagined the busboy now shaking as he sought release from Jeffrey's stare, wondering how long he'd be employed.

When people talked about "the Bartender" at the Edge, everyone knew they meant Jeffrey Meara, even though Jeffrey had become one of the restaurant's owners and there were plenty of other bartenders on staff. According to those in the know, he was the one who kept the restaurant on the Best North Shore Restaurants list. Co-owner. Bartender. Manager. But his favorite spot would always be behind the well-polished walnut bar, greeting his regulars. Seeing him in this other, more recent role of owner always surprised Nell, and didn't fit in comfortably with the Jeffrey she knew.

He turned away from the offending busboy and noticed Nell and Izzy watching him. The glower disappeared immediately, the wide smile returned, and he walked over, greeting each of them effusively.

Izzy touched the vest gently with the tips of her fingers. "The finest merino your money can buy, Jeffrey. Maeve knit this in my shop's back room and we all lusted after it."

Jeffrey's smile grew soft. "That's my Maeve." Then he looked around and motioned with a wave of his hand. "Can you believe this place tonight? Too many things going on. I need four of me." He laughed, then grew serious. "Here's the thing—here's what I need to say to you. There's a small glitch in your reservations." His perfect Cape Ann accent gave the words an interesting twist as the *r*'s disappeared. "But because you both are so beautiful—and because your table isn't ready yet—I have a special deal for you. My unique, irresistible Cape Ann autumn cocktail is being prepared for you as we speak—and for the gentlemen, too—compliments of Jeffrey." He patted his chest and lifted his bushy brows in his best Danny DeVito style as he looked from one woman to the other.

"There's no need for that, Jeffrey."

"Of course there is, Nell," he said, stopping her words with his raised hands. "And you will love it. It will bring the blush of summer back to those amazing cheekbones. I call it the Forbidden Apple. Hand-pressed apple cider from Russell Orchards, fresh lemon juice, the finest Macallan oak whiskey, and a couple other things I'll take with me to my grave." A blunt finger went to his lips.

Sam walked up at the mention of Macallan's. "Count me in, whatever it is you're talking about. And no need to hurry with the table." He grinned, shaking Jeffrey's hand and straddling a barstool. He looked closer at the bartender. "Hey, what gives? You look tired, Jeffrey. Not an attractive look for you. Summer's gone; fall is the easy time. Lighten up, buddy."

Jeffrey guffawed. "That's all you know, Perry. Spend a day walking in these shoes." But the photographer had drawn a smile from the older man and his shoulders lost their rigid stance.

Ben walked in, the mayor and his wife right behind him. "What's this I hear? A special Meara drink? I'm in."

The mayor glanced over at Jeffrey. He nodded a greeting. "Jeffo," he said.

Jeffrey answered with the same slight nod. "Sage," he said.

Nell looked from the mayor to the bartender. "Sage? Jeffo? It sounds a little vaudevillian."

Karen offered the explanation. "Those are nicknames from a long, long time ago—in a galaxy far away." She looked at Stan, then back to the others. "I think they started in high school."

"High school? Where?" Sam asked.

"Our own Sea Harbor High, home of the Cool Cods," Karen said.

"Cool Cods, that's great," Sam said.

"I sometimes forget that people were actually born here," Izzy said.

"Still are," Ben said. "Abigail Kathleen Perry being one of those very special folks."

Izzy laughed. "You got me there."

"There are lots of us," Karen said.

"Yeah," Jeffrey said. "Some of us stayed. Some—like old Sage here—went away to Yale, got himself a law degree."

"But then he came back," Karen reminded him.

Nell looked up at the hint of criticism in Karen's voice, but it was quickly replaced with a smile. Karen was always diplomatic. The perfect political wife.

Stan stood back as he often did in social settings, watching from the sidelines as Karen took over. He was alone with his thoughts, his face showing little emotion. Ben said he had perfected a politician's best weapon: hiding thoughts and emotions from crowds that were ready to pounce on them, the media eager to interpret and analyze them. Stan Hanson was difficult to read and it served him well.

Karen served him well, too. She was a plain woman, a contrast to her handsome, silver-haired husband, but always perfectly attired.

Tonight the simple black dress, pendant, and diamond stud earrings she always wore blended perfectly with Stan's more relaxed slacks and jacket. She had emerged, some said, from a quiet, mousy woman to one who used the power her money brought to propel her husband into the political arena.

"Jeffrey almost went to Yale, too," she said. "They were all very intelligent. The brainy Three Musketeers, we called them."

The bartender frowned in displeasure at the talk of his teenage past and concentrated on wiping an imaginary water spot from the bar.

"So tell us about this drink," Ben said, easing into a topic Jeffrey might be more comfortable with.

Appreciative, the bartender launched into the origin of the Forbidden Apple, expounding on the health benefits of apples.

"So you're saying it's a health-food drink?" Sam laughed.

Jeffrey leaned in and lowered his voice. "It convinces some of the older crowd. No matter that the whiskey will curl the hair on their chests."

Nell half listened as the drinks were passed around. She watched the homebred bartender. The lines on his forehead relaxed as he talked about the special drinks he concocted for his customers, clearly more comfortable in his present than in his past.

But it was his past that intrigued her. He turned down Yale?

She was as guilty as Izzy of sometimes forgetting that—because she and Ben, Izzy and Sam, the Brewsters, and other friends weren't Cape Ann natives—there were those who had lived their entire lives on the rocky cape that jutted out into the Atlantic. Some went away for school or training, and then returned to live out their lives on the shore, just as their parents and grandparents and sometimes great-grandparents had done before them.

Cass and her family, the Garozzos and Wootens, the Brandleys and Palazolas, Stan and Karen Hanson, and so many others.

People were born here. People lived their whole lives here. And people died here.

She looked over at Stan, polished and handsome, his silvery hair thick and smooth. And across the bar from him, Jeffrey Meara, short and slightly overweight, with tufts of what little hair he had left sticking out at odd angles. One man with a Yale law degree, an accomplished civic leader. The other, a bartender his entire life. The smartest student in the high school class, if Karen was correct.

She looked back and forth between the two men. She knew Stan from social and civic events. Ben considered him a friend. And everyone knew Jeffrey. But she knew little about either man's past. Had they been high school friends? Nell couldn't tell. Stan's face revealed little, and Jeffrey had clearly skirted the conversation. Nor had their nickname greeting to each other seemed overly friendly.

Finally Jeffrey eased away from his guests, sliding a bowl of peanuts and a basket of mozzarella sticks their way. With stubby fingers he straightened his bow tie and moved into the entry, greeting incoming diners, all the while keeping his eye on the kitchen door, the waiters, the busboys, the bartenders.

He did everything at the same time, like the conductor of a well-rehearsed symphony orchestra.

But from the look on his face, the expected harmony and the seamless service weren't pleasing him tonight. Worry lines—angry ones?—once again marred the forehead of the usually mild-mannered man.

The hostess moved over to the group, interrupting Nell's thoughts. The young woman apologized for the wait, then led them across the room and around a corner to a table for four, elegantly set near the wide glass doors that opened to the outdoor dining area. A slight breeze ruffled the edges of the white tablecloth and the salty tang of the sea mixed with the enticing aromas of seafood and garlicky vegetables.

Stan and Karen waved as they walked by, following the hostess to an intimate table on the other side of the fireplace.

"It's nice those two manage to find alone time," Ben said. "A political campaign can't be easy on a marriage."

"If a baby makes spending time with your woman so difficult, imagine what a political campaign would do," Sam said. He wrapped an arm around Izzy's shoulder, edged her closer, and kissed her lightly.

"Your *woman*?" Izzy wrinkled her nose and pulled away. Then she moved in and kissed him back. "Okay, Perry. You were right. We needed a night out." She sighed and looked down the front of her dress. "This is nice—and so far no leaky milk stains."

"And so is this," Ben said, nodding with pleasure at the platter of calamari, shrimp, and chunks of sweet lobster that the waitress was setting down in front of them. Crocks of spicy red sauce and lemon butter were next.

Somewhere in the distance, a band began to play. Not Pete Halloran's band, but a nice jazz combo, filling the ocean air with horns and percussion, the mellow sounds of a piano keeping the rhythm of old familiar pieces. The drinks, the music, and the taste of perfectly prepared seafood quieted the conversation into a comfortable lull, with the pleasure of each other's company, the breeze from the sea, and friendship wrapping around them like a soft merino blanket.

They were nearly finished with the chef's special—crispy sautéed cod with a bright green chimichurri sauce—when Izzy declared her legs in need of stretching. She pushed back her chair.

Sam looked at his wife, one brow lifted. "Izzy, Cass will handle things just fine."

"Shush, Sam," Nell said, slipping off her chair. "I'll go with you, Izzy. I'm a bit stiff, too."

Izzy had her phone out before they reached the restaurant lobby. "Cass is wonderful with Abby. I know she is, Aunt Nell. It's just—"

"Izzy, just call. Cass will wonder about your mothering skills if you don't. I'm off to the ladies' room. I'll meet you here in a few minutes." Nell walked down a narrow hallway opposite the bar, passed the partially opened door to the restaurant offices, and retreated to the restrooms beyond.

A few minutes later she emerged to the sound of angry voices.

Suddenly the hallway seemed smaller, narrower, but there was no one in sight.

"You're a crazy man, Meara!" The voice, coming from the office suites, was low and threatening. "I warned you about this one. It's going to have consequences. Fogarty was a decent supplier and he's furious—he'd like to kill you, given a chance, not to mention the two guys you fired this week. You're going to regret this—mark my words. You'll run us into the ground, you damn fool, and I won't stand for it."

The voice was familiar, but one that at that moment Nell had no desire to connect to a person. She hurried down the hallway, eager to pass the office suites before anyone came out.

But she was three steps too late. A tall shadow backed into the hallway, blocking her way.

Nell stopped short. She took a step backward.

The man was tall, with broad shoulders and a sprinkling of gray hair mixed into the brown. The stance and head of hair were both familiar.

Don Wooten turned and stared at her, as if she had somehow dropped from the sky. Quickly he regained his composure. "Hi, Nell. Good to see you."

Nell smiled and gave her friend a quick hug. "I sometimes forget you're an owner here, Don." Looking around his shoulder, she spotted Jeffrey Meara, stepping back into one of the offices and quietly closing the door.

"A not-so-silent partner," he said, glancing back into the office suites. "Sorry you overheard that. It's nothing, just a minor business disagreement. Par for the course."

"Don't give it a thought. But whatever you're doing to the Ocean's Edge, it's all good. Things just keep getting better and better here."

"Good to hear." Don began walking down the hallway beside her, ushering her out into the lighted entry. "Rachel thought I was crazy when I bought into this a few years ago. But she's so dagnabbit busy managing all Sea Harbor's legal maneuverings at City Hall that I needed something to keep me out of trouble. And I figured I had the necessary credentials—" He patted his midsection. "I love to eat."

Nell laughed. Don often sailed with Ben—he and Rachel Wooten were old friends. And she was well aware of Don's credentials, which were far more noteworthy than his healthy appetite. Having bought and sold several successful businesses on Cape Ann, he knew what he was doing when he bought into the Ocean's Edge enterprise and contributed his expertise to making it one of the most popular restaurants on the North Shore.

Nell looked up and spotted Izzy waiting near the bar. She nodded in her direction, then smiled back at Don and excused herself. "Izzy and I need to get back to the most delicious cod I've had in ages—or at least since I was last here. Ben Endicott can't be trusted around my plate."

Don smiled, looking relieved to end the conversation, and Nell walked over to Izzy's side.

Izzy's smile told Nell that all was well with baby Abigail.

"Of course it is," Nell said aloud, taking her niece's arm. They wove their way between the tables, knowing that if Ben and Sam had their say, there would be a bountiful tray of desserts waiting for them.

She tucked away the curious encounter with Jeffrey and Don. They often kidded Don about the ease with which he approached life, a perfect complement, everyone agreed, to his wife Rachel's lawyerly demeanor. But business partnerships were something Nell had some experience with—Ben's family had owned a successful company for decades. And she knew well that such dealings could bring out personality traits never visible during dinner with friends or afternoons spent sailing at sea.

A short while later, after watching Sam scrape the sides of his empty bowl of crème brûlée with his spoon, they all agreed it was time to go. A perfect evening. Time for bed.

Ben and Sam went on ahead to bring the car around while the women gathered up their things and headed to the front entrance.

Izzy spotted Danny Brandley first. He was leaning on the polished surface of the bar, talking to Jeffrey Meara and nursing a beer.

Danny spotted her at the same time and waved them over. "Hey, you two. I just talked to Cass. She's in her glory. Having Abby all to herself is pretty great, Iz. She refused my offer to help. Next time it's my turn."

Izzy hugged him. "I am crazy about the fact that our baby has so many aunts and uncles loving her. But I'm sorry you're here all alone. You should have joined us for dinner."

"And be the fifth wheel? Just saw Sam and Ben and they made it clear that it was double date night." He laughed. "I'm fine. I'm just here to meet someone for a drink."

He looked toward the front door, then lifted one hand in the air.

Izzy and Nell turned. The entrance door was open tonight to bring in the evening breeze. Esther Gibson, Sea Harbor's longtime police dispatcher, her cane in hand, was tapping her way into the restaurant with her husband, Richard, close behind, her white head nodding to everyone she passed.

But it wasn't the Gibsons who were drawing Danny's attention.

Nell and Izzy stared.

It was Jules Ainsley, walking directly behind Esther and Richard and looking slightly caged in by Esther's slow pace.

She was looking around. It was a moment before she spotted them at the bar, just long enough for them to admire her silky red blouse, the locket that rested between the rise of her breasts. Her hair was loose tonight—a tangle of waves that Nell suspected was the result of a quick brushing—yet looked like some stylist had spent hours making it appear casually glamorous. Her skirt was breezy and her manner the same.

Spotting Danny's raised hand, she hurried over.

"Sorry I'm late, Dan." She smiled at all of them. A generous smile, unaffected, seemingly oblivious to the emotions that her meeting with Danny Brandley might generate.

"Wine?" Danny asked, but Jules shook her head and pointed to his dark beer. She focused her smile on the bartender.

Jeffrey smiled back, but it was a curious smile that quickly turned to a puzzled one. "Have we met?" he asked her.

She extended her hand across the bar. "You're the second person who has asked me that this week. But no, I don't think so. I've seen you around, but we've not actually met. I'm Jules Ainsley. And you are the Bartender, or so the locals tell me."

Jeffrey didn't seem to notice the outstretched hand or anything she was saying. Instead, he leaned a little closer, continuing to scrutinize her face. His brows pulled together in concentration. Finally he said, "I guess you're right." But his eyes remained fixed on her face.

Jules wrapped her necklace around one finger, the small charm sliding through her fingers. Her words were quick, as if wanting to appease his stare. "Well, I don't think we've met, though I might be wrong. I've eaten here before. I love this place. The calamari alone has added five pounds to my hips. Maybe you've noticed me because of that. The gal in the corner chowing down all those squid." Throaty laughter followed her words.

"Tell her she's not alone, Jeffrey. The Edge's calamari is famous," Nell said. "She has good taste."

Jeffrey finally released his stare. He filled a mug with beer from the tap and slid it across the bar.

Jules thanked him and took a sip.

"You been here before?" he asked.

"In Sea Harbor?"

He nodded.

"Not exactly. Well, no."

"You like our town?"

"I love it here. It's an amazing place."

He nodded. "Why do you think that?"

"Why do I think it's amazing? I don't know. The people. The sea. I feel at home here in an odd way. Like I *have* been here before. Even though I haven't."

Jeffrey's eyes narrowed, his look intense.

Nell felt the awkwardness of the conversation, with Jeffrey's scrutiny unnerving all of them. "Jules is from Chicago," she said. "She's a runner, and is enjoying exploring Cape Ann on foot."

Again, Jeffrey wasn't listening. Instead, his eyes were moving from Jules's face to her blouse, to the finger twisting around a gold chain.

"Okay, then," he said finally. His eyes focused on the necklace, shiny against a tan chest. "That's nice. Your locket. It's a clamshell, right?"

She nodded. "It's old. You can hardly see the shell anymore. I should probably stop fiddling with it. Nervous habit."

It looked for a minute as if Jeffrey was going to reach out and lift the jewelry up to the light. But instead, he forced himself to look away. He smiled at the rest of the group, the expression familiar and one they were all more accustomed to seeing on Jeffrey's face. He shook his head as if ridding it of cobwebs. "'Scuse my questions. I like to find out about people visiting our town. Two more beers, Danny? On the house." He looked over as Ben and Sam walked in. "Ben? Sam? Any takers?"

Ben dangled his keys. "We've got to get Izzy home. A hungry baby awaits."

"Sure. I get that," Jeffrey said as Ben moved his group away from the bar and toward the door.

But the bartender's words were distracted, muted.

Nell followed Ben through the door. She paused and glanced back before heading down the steps.

Danny's elbows were on the bar, his head lowered, his attention on whatever Jules was saying. She was talking quietly, leaning toward Danny to be heard. One finger twisted her necklace chain around and around, as if tugging on it brought some clarity to her thoughts. The conversation seemed serious, intent.

And off to the side, his blunt fingers drying the same wineglass over and over and over, Jeffrey Meara watched the conversation as if it was about to change the course of his life.

Chapter 6

"Oh, you know Cass. Cass is Cass," Izzy said. The fat wheel of Abigail's beach stroller moved smoothly along the sand.

It was the early morning, a clear Tuesday with a slight breeze and only an occasional whitecap rolling up on the shore. Abby loved movement, and her tiny pink hands clapped as she lay back in her padded cocoon. Beside her, Nell and Birdie worked to keep pace with the stroller.

"She can't be happy about Danny spending time with Jules," Nell said.

"When we got home Sunday night, she already knew about Danny being at the Edge. He called her earlier and told her Jules had asked to meet with him there."

"Of course he did," Nell said, her voice filled with the need to keep Danny's integrity firm, to protect this quiet man they all loved.

"But why?" Birdie asked. "What could Jules possibly want from Danny?"

Nell looked at Izzy. She had wondered the same thing, and had asked Danny as much when she'd run into him at his parents' bookstore the day before. His answer then had been a nonanswer. He'd shrugged and said Jules was a mystery fan. And she needed some help with something. She'd heard he was a reporter, and didn't reporters know everything? It wasn't a typical Danny answer. Danny didn't claim to have fans and rarely talked about the fact that he had been a recognized and respected reporter. That he had won awards and was sought after as a special guest at conferences. He had "made it" in a world that didn't make that easy.

"I guess that's the mystery in all this," Izzy said. "Cass was trying really hard to handle it without showing anger or jealousy. She asked him that exact question: Why was he spending time with a gorgeous woman, at a bar, at night—without her? I'll tell you right now that if she invites Sam Perry for a drink, I'm going along. Or better yet, Abby will go along, nicely parked on Sam's back, preferably right before a feeding."

Nell and Birdie laughed, imagining the scene.

"So what did Danny say?" Nell asked.

"Nothing, really. Just that she was interested in mysteries and the fact that he'd been an investigative reporter."

"Fiddlesticks," Birdie said. "That's a conversation you have at a party or when meeting Danny in the bookstore. You don't invite a handsome young man to have drinks with you to discuss it. Especially one who is involved with another woman."

Izzy picked up her pace and Nell and Birdie huffed to catch up. "I was upset when she told me, but the more I think about it, I think Jules is oblivious to the fact that Cass might not like her hanging out with Danny. And I don't think she's really flirting, either. Jules doesn't strike me that way. She was in the shop yesterday, talking to everyone, asking a million questions about Sea Harbor, why people lived there, who lived where, who was who. How great the food was. How friendly the people. You'd think she was writing a history of the town or an article for a travel magazine instead of just visiting. She sat with Esther Gibson for a long time in the shop, knitting away, and Esther was in heaven—she loved having someone interested in all her old stories.

"Customers liked her, too. Even Mae likes her, and she's a pretty good judge of character. She likes that Jules seems unaware of her looks, as if it's totally irrelevant to anything important. She's almost careless about herself."

Nell had noticed that, too. Unlike many beautiful women, Jules didn't try to bring attention to herself. She was who she was—that was the message she gave out, and whether people liked her or not didn't seem to be anything she worried much about.

But there was something else about Jules Ainsley. Something just beneath the surface. A kind of determination that Nell couldn't quite put her finger on. She was friendly, but directed, and Nell suspected she wouldn't take kindly to people getting in her way.

"Do you know if she's been married?" Birdie asked.

"No husband, now or ever. Mae came right out and asked her."

Nell laughed. "Mae Anderson is the perfect shop manager for you, Iz. She probably knows the complete history of every deliveryman who steps into the shop. No unsavory characters allowed."

"Was Jules offended?"

"Not at all. She laughed, in fact, and told Mae that she'd had a couple of relationships but none that ended in permanency. She said she probably wasn't cut out for that kind of commitment."

A familiar voice traveled across the sand beach and stilled the conversation. They all turned toward the sound.

"Hi, guys," Jules Ainsley called out from the water's edge. She waved a baseball cap in the air.

A bright red tank top was plastered to her damp tan skin. Green sneakers kicked up sand as she jogged along the beach, her shoes just touching the tide. A headband was only partially successful in holding her hair in place.

They waved back, but Jules had already passed them and soon was just a moving dot in the distance.

Jules's appearance caused an end to the conversation. The feeling that somehow they'd been gossiping hovered uncomfortably as they kept up with the fat wheels of the stroller moving along the sand. For a while they walked in silence, the breeze off the water blowing away remnants of the uncomfortable conversation and energizing them with the smells of the sea. When the beach narrowed to a sliver, they turned their backs on the beach and headed toward the road.

"Is your house on the market yet?" Birdie asked, looking down the road to the hilly neighborhood that Izzy had lived in before her marriage to Sam. The cottage was at the top of a gentle rise in the land on the quiet Ridge Road cul-de-sac. Trees, brambles, and bushes crowded the low hill that led up to the homes.

Izzy laughed. "Supposed to be. But no. We thought it'd be ready to show sooner, but Abby put her chubby little foot down. It's amazing how a person as sweet and tiny and wonderful as Abigail Kathleen can determine our days with such indomitable force. With a tweak of her finger she pushes everything else in our lives to the backseat."

"As it should be. And you love it, Isabel," Birdie said.

Izzy nodded happily. She looked back at the hill. The potting shed and back porch were just visible above the trees. "As for the house, Sam did some minor fix-ups last night. We didn't get around to the potting shed as we'd planned—it's still a mess from the last tenant. Gloves and tools all over the place. But Stella thinks that's okay since, as she so sweetly put it, we're selling a house, not a place to pot plants. She's having an open house Friday. She even bought a new dress for it. Can you believe it? She's so excited."

Watching Stella Palazola, a young Sea Harbor resident they'd known nearly her whole life, setting out on a new career was nice to see.

Izzy turned Abby's stroller down the beach road and toward a shortcut that would take them back to Nell's house, where scones and iced tea were waiting.

Birdie paused for a minute, looking back toward the hill leading up to the Ridge Road neighborhood. She pushed her sunglasses into her short white hair and squinted. "Isn't that Jules down there?"

Izzy and Nell stopped and looked back down the road toward the hill.

Jules Ainsley stood at the edge of the road, her profile visible as she stared up the hill. For a moment she appeared to be frozen, her body unnaturally immobile. Then one hand lifted to her mouth, as if suppressing a cry.

Birdie started to move in that direction, to call out, but she stopped before the words were formed, instinctively knowing it was a moment that defied interruption.

An eerie moment.

Jules's head was held back as if tethered in place. Her eyes were focused on something in the trees and bushes that covered the hill like a briar patch, as if seeing something visible only to her. It was a look of awe, they agreed later. A look of disbelief.

A look that was seeing a mirage, or a miracle in motion, or something else entirely.

A look that was aimed directly at the hill leading up to the Perrys' cottage.

Chapter 7

*B*en said they were all overreacting. "You're forgetting that she's a tourist. That's what tourists do—look at things." He put the morning paper aside and took off his glasses.

"Stare," Izzy corrected around a mouthful of scone. "Definitely a stare." She checked her watch.

"It was a bit unusual," Birdie agreed. "And not to disparage Izzy's old house, but that hill behind it isn't very pretty. Jules could have found many more beautiful spots to admire if she was out seeing the sights."

"You're absolutely right," Izzy agreed. "That back area is a mess. Sam kept thinking he'd do something about it—a person could die in that tangle of weeds and bushes and never be found. But in the end we decided to lower the price and leave the yard work for the next guy. That land is actually owned by the city, so it's always iffy who should take care of it."

She knelt down beside the stroller, her long legs bending like a ballet dancer's. She touched Abby's cheek, then looked up. "I need to get home, shower, and get to the shop. You're sure you don't mind keeping Abby today, Aunt Nell? The class I'm teaching should be over around four."

Nell simply smiled. *Mind?* What a silly question. Mind watching this beautiful baby who had brought such joy into their lives? Her day with Abby, written on the calendar with a bright red marker, was the highlight of her week.

The day was planned. She'd take Birdie home, run errands, and then lunch with Ben at the yacht club, where they would show off Abby's smile to the hostess, Liz, to the bartenders, the diners. Later she and Abby would head to the Sea Harbor Historical Museum for a short meeting in which Abby would be welcomed by the board members as warmly as an unexpected donation to fix the roof. Amazing the power babies had.

Izzy planted one last kiss on Abby's plump cheek and was out the door, followed in minutes by Ben, off to a meeting at City Hall.

"It doesn't happen often, but he's wrong, you know." Birdie looked at Ben's departing back. She gathered up her sweater and backpack and headed toward the door.

Nell picked up the infant seat with its precious cargo and followed her to the car without answering. Birdie was absolutely right, of course.

Tourist or not, Julia Ainsley couldn't possibly have been in awe of the tangled jungle that had once been the hill in Izzy's backyard. Something else had stilled the lovely runner into that silent stare. In whatever form it had come—a sudden memory, a dream, a thought—Julia Ainsley had seen a ghost.

A ghost on Ridge Road.

It was nearly two in the afternoon when Nell and baby Abby finished their errands and parked near the museum. With both Beatrice Scaglia and Karen Hanson on the museum board, it was certain the premeeting chatter wouldn't be about politics. Laura Danvers, chairwoman, ran a tight ship and avoided confrontations. A relief to Nell. Beatrice was everywhere these days, and the tension caused by a heated campaign was difficult to avoid in such a small town.

She carried the car seat with a sleepy Abby into the redbrick building that housed Sea Harbor's past in glass cases and exhibits. Its viewing rooms were filled with models of fishing boats, photos of early settlers, maps, and exhibits of the once thriving granite industry. It never failed to make her proud of the place she and Ben had chosen to live after leaving busy corporate lives in Boston.

Laura Danvers was waiting at the door of the meeting room for a peek at baby Abby. "I just came from the yarn shop and Izzy mentioned Abby was joining us. I need my baby fix," she said, bending down to meet Abby at eye level.

"The meeting will be short, I promise you, sweet Abby," she whispered, then rose and, with a smile, promised Nell the same.

Nell slipped inside and took a chair close to the door, settling the car seat on the floor at her feet and nodding a greeting to other board members. Rachel Wooten sat down next to her. She leaned toward Nell. "Don mentioned you ended up in the wrong place at the wrong time the other day and were forced to hear an argument. He was so sorry. Those things can be messy."

"It was nothing, really. Not even messy. Business dealings can be tense—it's the nature of the beast."

"'Beast' is a good word for it."

"My bet is that whatever it was, it's settled by now."

Rachel smiled. "You're probably right. Don says business arguments are easy to handle. It's the personal ones he has trouble with."

"Personal problems? Are you talking about Jeffrey?"

Rachel nodded. "He didn't show up for work yesterday. I've known Jeffrey since I was a kid—it's not the way he is. Don was worried enough about it that he stopped by his house."

"Was Jeffrey okay?"

"He wasn't there. Then today he missed a meeting with the accountants, but at least he called and made some excuse. So I presume he's fine, though it's odd. He loves the Ocean's Edge. He's never delinquent, never misses a meeting."

"Maybe he was sick. There's a stomach bug going around."

Rachel agreed. "Or maybe he just needed a day off. Who doesn't want to miss work now and then? That's one of the reasons I'm on this board. It's a fine board, but also a good reason to get out of the courthouse legal offices every few weeks."

"Definitely true," Nell agreed. Everyone needed a break. Even Jeffrey Meara, who never took one.

. . .

But later that afternoon, while pushing Abby's stroller down Harbor Road, Nell wondered whether both she and Rachel had been too quick to fabricate excuses for Jeffrey Meara.

She had stopped on the harbor bridge to watch several stately sailboats making their way to inland waters. Leaning over the railing, she spotted Jeffrey sitting on a stone bench, hunched over, his elbows on his knees. The bench was below the bridge near the concrete pilings, not easily visible to people walking by.

Next to him, also leaning forward, was Stan Hanson. The two men were huddled together as if planning the next play in a tie Patriots game. Stan's face was in profile, his chin set, his brows pulled together tightly.

Nell stood there a minute watching the muted conversation. The two men's body language spoke of a somber conversation, with Jeffrey Meara doing most of the talking. Stan Hanson's expression seemed to shift with Jeffrey's words: surprise, dismay, a touch of anger. Sadness. Every now and then he'd take a deep breath, sit back on the bench in silence, and look out over the water. Then, when Jeffrey began to talk again, he'd resume his listening posture.

Nell pulled herself away. Even though she couldn't hear a word they were saying, she felt like an eavesdropper. Abby's soft gurgles were a welcome relief. Quickly she turned and pushed the stroller away from the bridge and down Harbor Road, toward friendly faces and conversations she was meant to be a part of.

"Nell, you're just the person I want to see." Mae Anderson rushed from behind the checkout counter as Nell pushed the stroller into Izzy's yarn shop.

"You don't fool me for a minute. It's Abigail Kathleen you want. I am simply the means to your end."

Mae laughed and leaned her needle-thin body down to peer into the stroller. Abby was fast asleep, but that didn't stop Mae from carrying on a sweet and intimate conversation with the baby.

"Well, you truly *are* the person *I* want to see." Beatrice Scaglia appeared from behind a display of merino yarn. The soft skeins were piled high in all the colors of autumn—burnished gold, honey maple, sage green, rich reds and oranges, several of which Beatrice held in her hand. Although Beatrice was rarely seen knitting, she was a devoted customer and often attended Izzy's classes, disguising her true intent with a pile of yarn, bamboo knitting needles, and a stack of pattern books at her side while she listened to every conversation spinning around her.

"It helps her to know what people are saying and thinking about the town," Izzy explained with a shrug.

Nell looked at the skeins of yarn in Beatrice's hands. "Those are beautiful, Beatrice. You have good taste."

"No, it's Izzy with the taste," Beatrice said. She motioned for Nell to follow her to the side of the room, out of traffic. "I tried to talk with you at the museum earlier today, but sometimes it's hard to talk privately with Karen Hanson around."

When she noticed Nell's frown, her words came more quickly. "I'm sorry if I sound disrespectful, but for all her smiles, she has somehow managed to push me off the speaking platforms of nearly every social group in town by pulling her first-lady card and suggesting that she do it herself. I suppose growing up in the lap of luxury gives one that feeling of power. And somehow—though it seems inappropriate—being the mayor's wife holds more weight than being a hardworking councilwoman." Her voice trailed off.

"Beatrice, campaigns are difficult for sure. But Karen has done a lot of good in Sea Harbor during Stan's tenure as mayor."

"All calculated," was Beatrice's retort.

Nell looked around for an escape.

"I know I shouldn't be venting to you, Nell," Beatrice said, her voice softer, and one hand resting on Nell's arm. "It's not what I really wanted to talk to you about anyway. I want to help with your anniversary party."

Nell sighed. Before long, the planning committee would include the whole town.

"I will give a toast, of course, but I could also serve as an unofficial emcee? Welcome people, make everyone feel comfortable. And my nephew has a band I will contact—he's playing at all my political gatherings."

Nell could imagine the scene—an American flag hanging in the background, Beatrice in a colorful suit at the microphone commanding attention, a band playing somewhere in the distance. A political rally in disguise. "Beatrice, you're generous," she said. "But we don't need a thing. It's going to be a casual gathering of friends and family. Hopefully something like lobster rolls and beer."

Beatrice frowned and took a step back. "I heard that Mary Pisano is helping organize things."

Of course, Nell thought. And she probably knew that Karen was helping Mary. Nothing escaped Beatrice.

But this time Beatrice focused on a new target. "Mary told me the woman staying in her inn is offering suggestions. Surely you don't want a stranger involved."

This time Nell laughed. "Jules used to cater parties. Mary is simply asking her for ideas."

But Beatrice wasn't listening. "The woman is pleasant enough—but she seems a bit inappropriate, don't you think? I've seen her jogging through town in those skimpy shorts. Asking questions, nosing around. I even saw her over at City Hall this afternoon."

"Oh?"

"In the records library. How many tourists do you see in the records office?"

Beatrice let her words hang in the air between them, casting them in an ominous light.

"I think she makes the most of places she visits, absorbing the town's spirit and history, getting to know people. It's a good idea, don't you think?"

It was a thought that developed as she said it aloud, and hearing her own words, Nell decided there was probably truth in what she was saying—even though her intent was to keep Beatrice from imagining nefarious scenarios.

Beatrice didn't answer, but her lack of a reply, brief good-bye, and quick exit told Nell what she thought of her opinion. And of Jules Ainsley. And definitely of Karen Hanson.

Nell watched her walk away. The councilwoman was unique, and in spite of her idiosyncrasies and sometimes irritating manner, Nell admired her. She'd undergone a tragedy in her own life when her then husband was found guilty of a murder in an attempt to cover up an affair. Somehow she had come out on top of it all, holding her head high and resuming her place in Sea Harbor's political scene. Beatrice Scaglia was a survivor and Nell liked that about her.

Through the shop window she watched her climb into her white Mercedes, as immaculate as the first snow. She slipped on her sunglasses, then sat still for a few minutes, staring across the street. Finally she started the engine and pulled quickly away from the curb.

Curious, Nell looked across the street.

Gus was in his usual spot, standing on the sidewalk in front of his store.

Today he had company.

Late-afternoon sunlight fell across the sidewalk, stretching the two shadows onto the street. Julia Ainsley, sunglasses pushed to the top of her head, stood next to the friendly hardware store owner.

Gus was listening intently to whatever Julia was saying. Finally he nodded, then took her by the arm and walked with her to a doorway between his store and Scooper's Ice Cream Parlor. The door, nearly hidden in the shadows, opened to an inside staircase and a second floor of small offices, including that of Nell and Ben's dentist. Did Jules need a dentist? Being in an unfamiliar town and needing medical care could be difficult.

When Nell looked out a few minutes later, Jules was still standing there, listening to Gus while she scribbled something on a piece of paper. Then she slipped the paper into her pocket, flashed Gus a brilliant smile, and sprinted down Harbor Road.

Whatever she was up to didn't involve having a cavity filled after all.

Jules Ainsley looked more like a woman on a mission.

Chapter 8

It was two days later when Nell discovered what Jules Ainsley had written on that sheet of paper. And it came to light only after a head-on collision with Karen Hanson.

She and Birdie were walking through Archie's bookstore toward the exit, their arms filled with books and their heads bowed in conversation, catching up. Birdie had agreed that Jules Ainsley was an odd sort of tourist and her interest in the town did seem a bit peculiar, but there had been no recent sightings of her with Danny, and that pleased them both.

Outside the bookstore, Karen Hanson, herself distracted, pulled on the heavy glass door just as Birdie was about to do the same. The unexpected movement as the door opened wide caused the small, white-haired woman to lose her balance, sending several of Danny Brandley's mysteries to the sidewalk. She tottered, regained her balance, and stepped quickly to the side with Nell close behind, closing the heavy door behind her.

Karen, muttering apologies, crouched down and scooped up the books. "So terribly clumsy of me," she scolded herself. She looked up. "Are you all right, Birdie?"

"Fit as a fiddle." Birdie held up Danny's newest release, diverting attention from Karen's embarrassment. But the absent look on Karen's face stopped her short from expounding on the dramatic cover. "Karen? Are you all right?"

Her face was the color of Archie's gray, sea-washed door.

"I should have been paying attention to where I was going. My mind was elsewhere." She stood up and handed Birdie her books.

"Campaigns can be killers," Birdie said. "We understand."

"Yes." The single word carried unusual force and brought some color to her face. "But Stan and I will get through this." She paused, then said, with clear determination, light coming back into her eyes, "Stan will handle it. He will. He promised me —"

Nell wondered briefly whether Beatrice Scaglia had anything to do with Karen's distress. It was out of proportion to a few dropped books. But before she could ask, a familiar voice shouted at them from across the street.

"Miz Favazza!"

It had come from Gus McClucken's hardware store and was followed by a truck screeching to a stop as Stella Palazola, her hair flying behind her, raced in front of Shelby Picard's tow truck. She sent an apologetic wave to the frustrated mechanic.

"Stella, you're going to get yourself killed," Birdie said as the Realtor leapt up on the curb and rushed across the sidewalk.

But Stella heard none of it. She wrapped her arms around Birdie and spun her in a circle, lifting her small feet clear off the sidewalk.

"Stella?" Birdie mumbled from the folds of the young woman's sweater.

Finally Stella released her and took a step back. Her green eyes sparkled. "You're like my guardian angel." She turned toward Nell and gave her a quick hug. "You, too, Miz Endicott. Two guardian angels. Aren't they the best, Miz Hanson? And that's why I'm so lucky. Can you believe it?"

"Believe what?" Birdie asked. She had known Stella since she was born, and she also knew her enthusiasm could signal a range of things—from a lottery win to an invitation to a party, or the fact that she'd finally found her favorite shoes on sale. Patience would eventually be rewarded by clarification.

"It's the house," Stella said breathlessly. Her cheeks were bright pink. "Izzy's house. *My* house. My first listing."

"Izzy has a fine Realtor, that's for sure. You're going to do a great job," Nell said.

"Izzy and Sam are selling their house?" Karen asked.

Stella turned toward the mayor's wife and put on her more professional face for the city's first lady. "Her old house, Mrs. Hanson. Not the one she and Sam and Abby live in. I'm selling it for her. You're welcome to come to my open house tomorrow."

When she turned back to Nell and Birdie, unbridled enthusiasm once again filled her voice.

"I'm almost ready for the open house. It'll be so cool. It's going to be at the cocktail hour—fancy, right? Sam said he'd go over there with me tonight to check last-minute things. Make sure all the lightbulbs work, toilets flush, that kind of thing."

"That is smart, Stella," Birdie said. "I knew you'd be good at this. Izzy mentioned the open house."

"But wait—I haven't told you the most amazing news. The *real* news. I already have someone who wants to buy it! Can you believe it?"

Nell took off her sunglasses and stared at Stella. "But it hasn't even been advertised. There's no 'For Sale' sign up, is there?"

"Nope. Not yet. I'll put it up today. But people hear about things like that. You know how news travels in this town. Izzy has been talking about it and my mom tells people who come into the Sweet Petunia. And of course I've told anyone who looks at me."

"So how did it happen?" Birdie asked.

"Well . . . when I got to the office today . . ." She grinned as she said the word "office," and pointed across the street to the windows above Gus's store, where a new sign read: PALAZOLA REAL ESTATE. "Uncle Mario said that getting a partner—that's me—required a new sign. Anyway, when I got to work, there was someone in the hall right outside my office, just sitting there, waiting for *me*. Someone who wants to buy my very first listing. And here's the kicker. They want the house without ever even stepping inside it!"

"That's great, Stella," Nell said. "But odd, don't you think? I can't imagine anyone making an offer on a house they haven't seen."

"Yeah, it's weird. But here's the thing—it's really none of my business, as long as there's legitimate financing, so if that's how it goes, I'll take the offer to Izzy. But here's what I'm thinking—and this *is* my business," Stella said, her brows shooting up into her bangs and her eyes growing larger behind her green-framed glasses. "If one person is that enthusiastic about the house without even seeing it, then maybe there are even more people who might want it. I've put an ad in the paper for the open house, so I can't just pass this offer along—not until the open house. I can't just cancel it, no matter what the offer is. But the real reason is that maybe we'll have lots of people bidding on it."

"I suppose that's true," Nell said slowly, trying not to put a damper on Stella's enthusiasm. Izzy's house was cute and cottagelike, but in need of repair, and the neighborhood wasn't as kept up as it once was. A bidding war was probably wishful thinking on Stella's part. On the other hand, the fact that someone had actually made an offer on the house without even seeing it was equally preposterous.

Karen Hanson listened, but with little interest, her mind elsewhere. Finally she checked her watch, and once again headed for the bookstore entrance.

"Who wants to buy it?" Birdie asked.

"You'll never guess. That's the weirdest thing of all," Stella said.

The mystery in Stella's voice stopped Karen at the door. She paused and looked back.

"Who?" Nell asked. It had to be a contractor—Davey Delaney would be her guess—someone planning on doing something to that small neighborhood, like buying up the small homes and turning them into condos. Davey had a keen eye for turning a profit.

"It's that lady who runs every day, even when it's raining."

Nell's brows lifted.

"Who?" Karen turned around. Her voice was tight.

Stella's head bobbed with excitement.

"You know her. The runner—that's what Pete Halloran and his buddies call her when she jogs by Coffee's every morning. All the guys—the early-morning coffee drinkers—they all stand up and watch her fly by. It's Jules Ainsley, that's who. She's fallen in love with Izzy's old house, sight unseen."

Chapter 9

"It doesn't make sense." Cass refused the news, pushing it away with a sweep of her hand. She walked over to the large wooden table in the yarn shop's back room. Food would calm her down.

She spooned a small mountain of shrimp scampi onto her plate, scooped up a helping of rice pilaf, and returned to her overstuffed chair near the fireplace corner.

Thursday-night knitting with Nell, Izzy, and Birdie was the mainstay of Cass's week. Great friends, Nell's cooking, and the sensuous pleasure of soft, vibrantly colored yarn. It calmed her down, revitalized her, and refreshed her spirit. Lobster traps, ever-changing fishing regulations, and pressing business matters facing the Halloran Lobster Company were put aside for three hours of bliss.

How dare Jules Ainsley interfere with her Thursday night?

"Stella said she was insistent," Nell said.

Izzy concurred. "She came rushing into the shop late this afternoon, right in the middle of a class on intarsia knitting. She was concerned about Stella's open house tomorrow. In her mind, there was no reason for it, because she knew she wanted the house. Couldn't I simply accept her offer and that would be that?"

"That's crazy," Cass said. "Doesn't she know she doesn't live here? What does she need a house for?" Purl flew up next to Cass. Absently, she scratched the calico cat's neck, her sweet purring bringing Cass's blood pressure back down to manageable levels.

Birdie filled wineglasses all around, then settled back in her chair. She speared a buttery piece of shrimp and chewed it thoughtfully. "Perhaps she's looking for a vacation house. She seems to like Sea Harbor. It might be a wise investment for her."

Nell disagreed. "I saw Mary Pisano earlier today. She said Jules mentioned the house to her last night and then asked her a million questions about the neighborhood—she even brought up the names of other people who live on Ridge Road, wanting to know how long they'd lived there, if there was much turnover, that kind of thing. And she asked about Sea Harbor winters. That doesn't sound like a house she wanted to spend two beach weeks in."

"What does Mary think about it?" Birdie asked.

"She is dumbfounded. Jules hadn't mentioned anything to her about looking at property. As far as Mary knew she was here for a relaxing vacation and then would be leaving. The only unknown was how long she was staying."

Birdie sipped her wine. "Stella said Jules was looking into financing, talking to the bank. It might simply be a lovely dream on her part. Perhaps we're all overreacting a bit."

"Birdie is probably right." Nell passed around a basket of warm rolls and Irish butter. "I can't imagine a stranger doing something so impulsive. Buying a house is an important decision, not something you jump into. A finance person may help her see that."

Cass held her glass out for more wine. "There's something about her—and it's not just that she seems to be putting the moves on Danny. It's something else. I mean, who comes through town, 'just visiting,' then suddenly is trying to make friends right and left? Something about her really gets to me."

"Maybe it's because she's interesting, and she has this big personality—so we want to like her, or at least get to know her better," Izzy said. "But she makes us uncomfortable because we don't really know what she's all about, we're not sure why she's even here, and we certainly don't like her hanging on Danny." Izzy picked up her glass and swirled the wine around. She was quiet for a moment, as if wondering how far to take this discussion without seeming disloyal to Cass.

She went on. "I remember vividly the first time I met her. It was shortly after hearing Pete and Andy Risso discussing her jogging prowess. She had 'admirable form,' they said. Ha. But anyway, I had Abby in the shop with me that day. We had a ton of customers, and in came Jules in running shorts and an old T-shirt—'parting the sea,' as Mae later put it. You know how people are. A stranger in town—and an attractive one at that. Everyone looked her way, though she seemed not to notice.

"Abby was still in her car seat near Mae's checkout counter. Jules looked around for a few minutes, getting the lay of the store. But then she spotted Abby in the corner. She stopped for a minute, and then walked directly past that exquisite new display of alpaca yarn as if it weren't even there. And she crouched down beside Abby, looking at her with a look that said she was the most exquisite child she'd ever seen."

Izzy grinned, then added, "I thought she was the wisest, most perceptive customer I'd had in my yarn shop all year."

Even Cass smiled, and then the group fell silent, spooning up the last bites of shrimp and rice and relishing the rich, garlicky wine sauce Nell had snuck into the recipe. In the background, Adele sang about rain and relationships, her husky voice a comforting blanket as the night breeze grew more robust.

Nell got up and rinsed her plate in the sink, then closed the casement windows above the window seat. The sea was black and active, with harbor lights catching waves as they crashed against the shore. She had met Jules for the first time at the yacht club buffet, not a usual destination for tourists, but Mary and her husband had brought Jules as their guest that night. It was a gracious gesture, Nell said, and the more practical Ben had laughed, wondering how quickly the B and B would go broke if the Pisanos treated every guest to a lavish spread at the Sea Harbor Yacht Club.

It was Jules's look that Nell remembered from that night. The even stare that seemed to see clear down to your soul. And yes, she'd liked her, too.

It would be easier, maybe, if Jules Ainsley were obnoxious and they couldn't bear to be in her presence.

But she wasn't.

Finally Izzy spoke again. "She's not likable in a warm and fuzzy way. But yeah—I admit it. I'd like to know her better, maybe even as a friend. But I also know what you mean, Cass—there's something about her, some kind of mystery. As if what she lets us see might be sincere, but there's a lot going on there that we don't see, something hidden beneath the covers."

"That could be said of most people," Birdie said. She put her empty plate on the table and walked back to the group. "We all have secrets, don't we? It makes us interesting." Her infectious laughter softened the seriousness weighing down on the room. "I think one solution to these mixed feelings would be to get to know her better. Invite her to Friday-night dinner, but not as an afterthought. Even if she leaves town soon—which I suspect she will—it's a nice thing to do." She looked at Nell.

"That's a good idea, but only if you're comfortable with it, Cass."

They all looked at Cass. She turned toward the window and the darkening sky. "I think it's going to rain tomorrow," she said.

"Well, whether we get to know her better or not, it will probably never happen—her moving here, I mean," Izzy said. "I can't imagine anyone buying a house without looking inside it. I told Stella she was absolutely right to hold the open house as planned. For starters, we can't let that new dress she bought for the occasion go unused."

She cleared the last of the dishes and wiped off the table, readying it for yarn and needles and the pieces of the afghan they were knitting for Ben and Nell's anniversary gift.

"Yes, an evening together might be just the ticket," Birdie said, pulling out a ball of ruby red yarn. She fingered it lightly, then spread a piece of her knitting out on the table—a long stretch of stockinette, outlined in lacy hearts and knit in the softest of merinos. "Maybe we'd find out why she wants a house on Ridge Road so badly, don't you think?"

Cass leaned over Birdie's shoulder and looked down at the work taking shape right there in front of them, blocking out Birdie's question. The afghan's ruby red color symbolized the fortieth anniversary. Izzy had designed the blanket in sections that could be worked on individually, then sewn together to make a whole. A gorgeous tapestry, knit by those who loved her aunt and uncle.

Nell moved closer to the table. When she looked down at Birdie's panel, the threads of their previous conversation faded away, replaced with the simple stitches on the table, now being worked into art. "This is . . . it's truly the most . . ." She sat down beside Birdie, the rest of her words swallowed up in emotion.

They hadn't shown Nell Izzy's pattern. It was the one secret they'd kept from her. But to bar Nell from their knitting sessions was an awful thought, so they had decided instead she could watch the afghan as it evolved on knitting nights. At first the sections were simply a series of rows, mostly in stockinette, a lacy band here and there, that graced Cass's and Izzy's and Birdie's laps each Thursday. But now, as if by magic, the shape was becoming more than that. It was becoming a whole, a true tapestry, with hearts and cables defining the work.

When Nell looked up, her eyes were moist, but Birdie was disallowing emotion. "You may be teary when we present it to you and Ben, if you like. But not before." She hugged her friend lightly, picked up her needles, and in the next breath moved everyone's attention back to a topic that was less emotional: Jules Ainsley.

"One thing that puzzles me is why and how Julia even knew to ask about Izzy's house," Birdie said. "No one—including Mary Pisano, who knows everything—mentioned before yesterday that Jules was looking for a house. Yet suddenly here she is, wanting to buy a house."

"And it's not just any house she wants," Nell said. "It's Izzy's house on Ridge Road."

"You're right," Izzy said. "Stella hasn't advertised it, not really, so she wouldn't have seen a 'For Sale' sign. And it's not a neighborhood she'd run in anyway. So how?"

In the next second it dawned on Nell, Birdie, and Izzy, all at the same time.

"She saw it from the beach that day!"

"We thought she was looking up at the woods behind the Ridge Road houses," Nell said.

"But it wasn't that at all. She was looking at the house."

Birdie explained to a confused Cass how they'd seen Jules running on the beach that morning. And then spotted her again, a short while later, staring up at the house.

"It was as if she'd seen a vision. Like a ghost or something," Izzy said. "It was weird."

They remembered the look on her face. She'd been mesmerized.

"That was Tuesday morning. Beatrice saw her in City Hall after that—maybe she was finding out more information about the house," Izzy said, putting her deductive skills to work.

That would make sense. A map would help her find the neighborhood and information on the house as well. And if Jules had asked, lots of people who worked there would have told her it was empty and going on the market sometime soon.

"But then there's the bigger mystery. She could barely see the house from where she was standing—the edge of the potting shed with that little overhang that I painted yellow, the porch, maybe the old swing, but not much else. Not much of the house, really," Izzy said.

The room fell silent, with only the click of knitting needles filling the night air.

Finally Cass broke the silence.

She looked around at her circle of friends. "That's the point exactly. Why would anyone in her right mind make an offer on a house she'd never seen? *She wouldn't.*" Her last words attacked the air as if it were a punching bag. "Julia Ainsley is a certifiable nutcase. It's what

I've been saying all along. Now let's get back to things that matter, like Ben and Nell's incredible, amazing, and soon-to-be-finished anniversary throw."

She lowered her head and vigorously ripped out the last row of her knitting, blaming every single missed stitch on a crazy Julia Ainsley.

Chapter 10

Dinner on the deck was not promising to be wrapped up in a warm Indian summer evening, maybe for reasons other than the weather.

The day itself had begun with a vengeance—a north wind carrying wet air that chilled all the way to the soul.

But it took more than weather to deter Ben and Nell's friends from planning their Friday evening around Ben's grilled trout or cod or salmon and Nell's special sauces. Not to mention the friendships that seemed to be the perfect antidote to a long week. No matter what the week had wrought, people would come, and it was helpful to have food when they did.

Birdie and Cass had insisted on helping Nell with the shopping. Birdie had nothing on her calendar for the day except for the delicious meal at Ben and Nell's that night, and Cass was giving herself a day off. "To clear my head of fuzzy things," she told Nell. Spending the afternoon tagging along with her and Birdie was a good enough way to do it.

They headed over to the fish market in Gloucester and found several pieces of fresh haddock, the skin translucent and perfect. Ben would be pleased. After a quick stop at Savour Wine and Cheese for hunks of Gouda and Stilton, they headed home, stopping at a vegetable stand along the road for spinach and kale.

"I read that you're supposed to massage the kale," Birdie said, climbing back into the car. "Imagine, massaging your vegetables."

"I'd like someone to massage me," Cass said.

Birdie laughed. "I know a nice mystery writer that might be perfect for the job."

"Speaking of mystery writers, Jules called the one I know this morning while he and I were sitting out on the back deck having coffee and actually enjoying each other. After our talk at knitting last night I decided to simply let things be. Danny said there was nothing going on, so who was I to say there was? She simply wanted his help doing some research. 'Research?' I asked. He just shrugged. So that was that. But it was okay. I was going to be cool with it. But when she called, my stomach knotted into a ball. I hated that feeling. Hated it. I don't like myself at all when I'm like this, worrying about who he sees or doesn't see, worrying about my feelings. Crap. That's not who I want to be. Maybe I'm not cut out for a relationship."

Birdie and Nell were silent. Cass was fiercely independent, and having her emotions dependent on another person was bound to be difficult for her. But it certainly didn't mean she wasn't cut out for a relationship. It meant she was human.

They had all rejoiced when she had finally let the low-key Danny Brandley into her life. And if they had anything to say about it, they'd make sure he stayed there.

But the truth was, they didn't have anything to say about it.

Cass looked up into the driver's mirror. "She told Danny that you invited her to dinner."

Nell nodded. "I was about to mention it." She turned onto Harbor Road and headed toward Birdie's house.

"Is she coming?" Cass asked.

"Yes. Stella's open house is late afternoon, so she'll come over after that, she said."

"It will be fine, Cass," Birdie said.

But Cass had rolled down the window, and Birdie's words were pulled out to sea, carried on a rush of wild, wet wind.

. . .

"Inside or out?" Ben picked up the grill lighter and opened the French doors to the deck.

Nell walked out behind him and looked up at the threatening sky. The air was damp, but it was the wind, whipping in from the ocean, that was menacing. Branches of the old maple tree that shaded the deck danced wildly. "Let's not set the table out here. We'll keep things on the kitchen island and we can do potluck."

"I hope the weather doesn't mess up Stella's open house." Ben began igniting the burners on his oversized grill. He'd start with a batch of fresh vegetables, then free it up for the haddock later, once the appetizers, martinis, and being in the company of old friends had done their magic, softening the week's tensions.

Noise from the kitchen drew Nell back inside, where Red, Izzy and Sam's adopted golden retriever, was sitting calmly beside a smiling Abby. Nearby Izzy was tossing lettuce in a giant wooden bowl.

"I didn't hear you come in," Nell said.

"Probably because of the commotion outside," Sam answered from the family room. He was pulling a diaper out of a polka dot bag. He walked over and gave Nell a hug.

"Commotion?" Nell asked, but before Sam could answer, the intrusive honking of emergency vehicles pummeled the air. Sirens followed, swooping high and low like diving birds, then settling into a shrill refrain.

Ben walked in. "What's going on?"

Izzy walked over and hugged him hello. "We don't know. We were halfway here, coming down the old beach road, when all hell seemed to break loose. Chief Thompson was leading a string of police cars, headed north. I didn't know we had that many police cars."

"An accident?" Nell asked, memories of a horrible wreck a few years before filling her head. Sophia Santos, the construction magnate's wife, had driven off the side of a hill, directly into the ocean. And the sound that had followed was the same: soul-shattering sirens and cars moving too quickly along quiet streets.

The sounds of danger, of lives being altered in minutes, seconds.

She rubbed her arms briskly, fighting away the goose bumps that rose instinctively to the surface.

Ben noticed her discomfort and walked over. He wrapped an arm around her shoulders, his voice low. "It's probably nothing, Nellie. A cat in a tree. A boat pulled away from its moorings. Remember when the Seroogys' boat dock pulled loose last year and crashed into the neighbors'? It was a domino effect. This wind is wicked strong."

Nell forced a smile, knowing her worry was often a false alarm. It came too fast, unwarranted. Irrational. And Ben was always there to tamp it down and put it in its place.

Jane and Ham walked in carrying several ceramic pots. "My Janie made these," Ham said, handing Nell the pots. They were molded and fired into the shape of wrinkled paper bags and each held a fat candle.

"They're for your deck or whatever. Just in case we lose electricity," Jane said. "It's a crazy night out there."

"These are beautiful," Izzy said, fingering the delicate folds. "You're brilliant, Jane Brewster. Oh, and you, too, Ham."

"Yeah, I suppose so, Iz." His blue eyes laughed above a bushy white beard. "But what's even more brilliant is the sky. Not only is there some lightning over Canary Cove, spinning red lights are headed toward the north beach."

"So we hear. Do you know where they're going?"

"Dunno, but maybe Cass and Danny followed them. They picked up Birdie and were behind us on Harbor Road for a bit, before Tommy Porter nearly cut us off in his police cruiser. And the next time I looked in the mirror, they had disappeared."

Nell placed hunks of cheese on a platter and filled a basket with pita chips. "If it's near the water, it probably has something to do with a fire or fallen tree or some such thing. It wasn't a good day to be on the beach or the water." Fallen trees, empty boats, cats in trees—those were all things Nell could deal with.

The sound of the front door scattered her thoughts and she welcomed Cass, Danny, and Birdie into the mix, each one carrying something—wine, a bag of fresh rolls, a tin of buttermilk brownies. Birdie's cropped hair was windblown and glistened with raindrops.

"We look like something the cat dragged in, don't we?" she said, handing Ben the brownies and suggesting a martini wouldn't be ignored.

Danny relieved Cass of the wine and took everything into the kitchen. He grabbed several dish towels and handed one to Cass. She took it, then moved across the room to where Ben was mixing drinks.

"Ham thought you might have gone ambulance chasing so you could bring us the scoop." He poured the liquid into several glasses.

She shook her head and took the glass Ben offered her. "Someone probably skidded off the road. It's getting nasty out there."

"There was a lot of noise for a simple car mishap," Izzy said. She scooped up Abby and danced her way across the room, plugging her iPhone into the amplifier and turning on a music track. Soon Norah Jones's husky voice traveled across the room.

"Tommy told me things are pretty dull at the station," Cass said. "Once the tourists leave town there's no one left but law-abiding citizens. Boring, he said. Maybe that's why so many cars responded to whatever the call was—they needed something to do."

Soon the smell of grilled haddock filled the air and Nell checked her watch. She looked around the room and asked no one in particular, "Is there anyone we should wait for? Pete had another gig tonight. Anyone else?"

Cass looked over at Danny. "Danny?"

Danny looked back at her. He seemed about to say something, then changed his mind and simply shook his head. He looked worn-out, Nell thought, and strongly suspected Cass had done the wearing out.

"Well, then," Nell said, walking over to the counter, where her chimichurri sauce was awaiting a final stir.

Cass was at her elbow in a minute. She took the fork from Nell and began stirring sauce, muttering an apology. "I will brighten up, I promise. Is it possible for a nearly forty-year-old woman to not know herself? To not know why she feels the way she does? What she wants to be when she grows up?"

Nell gave her a quick hug. "It's possible for a sixty-year-old to question life's mysteries, sweetie. Just be sure you don't confuse what you're questioning."

Cass looked over at Danny. He was holding Abby now, standing at the windows that looked out over the deck. He rocked her gently back and forth, humming softly.

Nell followed her look. Her heart swelled at the image of the gentle, sandy-haired man cradling the baby girl. Sometimes things seem so simple. But for Cass, that time wasn't today.

Sam held open the door for Ben and he came inside, along with a mighty gust of wind, carrying a platter of fresh grilled haddock. The mild fish rested on a bed of thick grilled tomatoes, topped with an herb and fresh bread-crumb mixture. The fragrance of lemon and garlic, rosemary and thyme floated up in the air and stopped conversations around the room as Ben invited the crowd to satisfy their growling appetites. In minutes white plates were piled high with grilled fish and vegetables that Nell topped with her own version of chimichurri sauce. Izzy's toasted pecan and pear salad was on the narrow table against the wall, along with carafes of wine, water, and iced tea and a basket of crusty Italian rolls.

Ben left the doors open a crack to bring in night sounds and the smell of rain on freshly mowed grass. Soon the sounds of forks and conversation mingled with cool jazz as they put the week to rest. "All's well," Birdie said, holding up her wineglass.

It wasn't until Danny and Nell began spooning up the bread pudding an hour later that Birdie's comment was shattered.

The call came to Sam's phone. It was from Stella Palazola.

"Please come over to your house," she begged. "Bring Ben."

Stella didn't say much more, but the choking plea in her voice was enough for Sam to promise that he and Ben would be there in minutes.

"Maybe a pipe burst in the middle of her open house," Sam said as he grabbed his keys. "Stella and I didn't check the ones in the basement." But his words were hollow. A broken pipe would be a blessing.

"A possibility," Izzy said. She got up and hugged Sam tighter than usual, then pushed him toward the door.

"We'll let you know what's going on," Ben said over his shoulder, grabbing his rain gear and following Sam to the car.

The Ridge Road house was filled with lights when Ben and Sam arrived. There were several police cars double-parked in front of Izzy's old house, just behind a Toyota Camry. Up and down the row of houses, residents stood out on their front steps holding umbrellas, watching the commotion, and texting to friends whatever they supposed was happening. In front of Izzy's old house, two policemen kept people at bay.

But the activity wasn't inside the well-lit house. Flashlights, voices, and a young policeman directed Sam and Ben around the side of the house to the small backyard.

Chief Jerry Thompson met the men at the corner of the house. In the distance, just at the edge of the potting shed, a figure lay still on the sodden ground. Several police officers and the county coroner hovered over the form.

"It's Jeffrey Meara," Jerry said quietly. "He's dead."

Chapter 11

It was midnight when Sam and Ben returned to Sandswept Lane. The bread pudding was gone, but the Friday-night group was still there, and except for Abby, who was sleeping soundly in the guest bedroom, they were all wide-awake. Nell had put on a pot of coffee; Ham had found Ben's cognac and had glasses waiting.

The story they brought back to the group was simple—and horrifying.

Ben had found Jules and Stella on the back porch, sitting on the swing. They were talking to Tommy Porter, the young policeman who'd been a part of the Endicotts' life since he mowed Ben's parents' lawn years before. In his usual efficient way, Tommy carefully recorded everything the women said.

Stella's face was streaked with tears, her hands knotted in her lap, Ben said. Jules sat expressionless, her face impassive except to offer brief answers to questions. She'd heard nothing. Seen nothing. Until the moment she walked over to the potting shed and stumbled upon a pool of blood—and Jeffrey Meara lying in it. His hand-knit sweater was matted, the soft merino wool soaking up the blood like a sponge.

When Stella arrived shortly after, she had found Jules leaning over the body, futilely pressing a scarf to the wound. A serrated garden knife lay on the dirt beside the body.

Stella leapt from the swing when she saw Ben. She melted into his arms, tears flowing freely, along with choked and needless apologies to Sam that she had screwed up the open house.

Jules had been strangely calm, the two men said. Her only visible emotion—and that wasn't much—had come later when she thanked them for driving her back to the Ravenswood B&B, where Mary Pisano was waiting for her. Esther Gibson had been on duty at the police station and alerted Mary, thinking Jules might need someone to be with her.

The group sat in silence for a while, each nursing private thoughts of a friendly bartender who made the Ocean's Edge a little bit like Boston's Cheers, a place where Jeffrey, at least, knew everybody's name.

"Dear Jeffrey," Nell whispered softly. "Everyone loved Jeffrey."

It was a refrain that would be echoed from Coffee's patio to the Ocean's Edge, from Gloucester to Rockport, one that would roll down the streets of Sea Harbor, gathering momentum and passion in the days and weeks to come.

Even when it was challenged.

Chapter 12

By Saturday morning the rain had stopped, the wind had relaxed, and white clouds scuttled across a blue sky. It was as if the storm itself had provided a background for the horrible happenings at Izzy's cottage. And then it was over.

Today was a new day, a beautiful day.

Except it wasn't.

Ben was already up and the coffee was brewing when Nell came down the back stairs. She had slept little, her dreams tangled up in a jumble of images—Jules Ainsley, a tearful Stella Palazola, Jeffrey Meara. So many lives shaken by a horrible act that had happened while the rest of them were going about their ordinary lives, making dinner, checking the weather, cleaning up the family room.

Ben wasn't alone in the kitchen, as often happened on Saturday mornings. Usually it was because he made blueberry or Scottish scones on weekends. Today it was simply for a cup of coffee, maybe a hug. Today it was for friendship.

Birdie looked up as Nell walked into the room. Izzy sat across from her, poring over the *Sea Harbor Gazette*.

The headline was big:

STABBING DEATH ON RIDGE ROAD

The article was short.

"There isn't much to say," Ben said. "Not yet."

Nell nodded and leaned over Izzy's shoulder, reading the article, which talked more about what a Sea Harbor legend Jeffrey Meara was than about the cruel way his life had ended.

"Sam is meeting Jerry Thompson over at the Ridge Road house this morning," Izzy said. "There's yellow tape all over it right now and they're pulling up Stella's 'For Sale' sign."

"Poor Stella," Nell said. "This must be absolutely awful for her."

"It's awful for everyone. I saw Mary Pisano out walking this morning. She was clearly upset," Birdie said. "Jeffrey was a longtime friend."

Izzy looked up from the paper. "Was Jules with her?"

"No. She was out running. Mary said she left at the crack of dawn."

It was probably a panacea for Jules. Nell pictured her running into the breeze, hair flying, escaping from the haunting images. She was happy Jules had an outlet. She would surely need one to get through all this.

"I wouldn't blame her if she was running as far away from Sea Harbor as she can get," Izzy said. "It must have been terrible for her, finding Jeffrey like that."

Ben poured Nell a cup of coffee. "No, she won't be heading away from here—not soon anyway."

"I don't mean literally," Izzy said. "But imagine, being here on vacation and finding the dead body of someone you barely know at an open house?"

"Not a pleasant thing, for sure, but Jules may have known Jeffrey better than we think. Apparently he had called her and insisted on meeting her at the Ridge Road house yesterday. That's why he was there, she said. They were supposed to meet before the open house."

"Good grief. Why?" Nell asked.

"That's the question. Jules told the police she hadn't the faintest idea. She had met Jeffrey, but only casually."

"That's how it looked to me when I saw them talking at the

Ocean's Edge a couple times." Nell thought about the previous Sunday night—which now seemed like a lifetime ago—when Danny had introduced Jules to Jeffrey. Or was it the Hansons he had introduced Jules to? It was all hazy, even though it had been only a few days before. Death seemed to squeeze time into a meaningless blur.

"That's what Jules said, too. That she'd met him at the Edge bar. He had seemed a little odd, she said."

"That isn't a word any of us would use to describe Jeffrey," Birdie said. "*Odd?* Why would anyone think sweet Jeffrey Meara was odd?"

"She had the feeling he was staring at her, as if he'd met her before," Ben said. "But in any case, Jerry Thompson has asked her not to leave town for a few days, not until they get their arms around all this."

"No wonder the poor girl was out running," Nell said. "That's awful, Ben. Surely they don't think she had anything to do with it." But even as she said the words, she knew the police would most certainly look at Jules.

Ben spelled it out. "At this point they have to suspect everyone," he said. "But Jules was right there at the scene. She was meeting him, according to phone records. Her fingerprints were all over the knife. And the fact that she's a relative stranger here certainly won't help."

"Geesh," Izzy said. She walked over and impulsively wrapped her arms around her uncle.

Ben hugged her back, smiling down into her hair. "I love you, too, Izzy. And the chief is on this. Don't worry."

But she was worried. They all were. Nell watched her niece and her heart ached. Izzy was a mother now, and the thought of evil lurking in their town was doubly awful with baby Abby to protect.

Izzy finished her coffee and was off to the yarn shop to teach a beginning knitters' class—a futile effort to make it an ordinary Saturday.

Ben left to meet Sam at the Ridge Road house. "Moral support, if nothing else," he told Nell, and kissed her, a little longer than usual.

"Father Northcutt is over at Maeve's," Birdie said. "She's in good hands."

Nell nodded. "Jeffrey told me about his love affair with Maeve the very first time I met him. 'I fell in love with an *older* woman,' he said. 'And me just a bumbling kid.' And by some miracle, he said, she had noticed him. Then, years later, after she went to college and lived for a while in the big city, she came back to Sea Harbor and she remembered him—still a bachelor, much to his mother's dismay. And a few years after that . . . she married him. It was a long time in coming, Jeffrey said, but well worth the wait."

They seemed to be the perfect pair, balancing out each other's personalities. The social bartender and his quiet wife. He had his restaurant; Maeve had her garden and her crossword puzzles. It worked for them.

"I don't think Jeffrey showed his face around Our Lady of Safe Seas much, but Maeve more than made up for his absence and knows Father Larry well," Birdie said, getting up and slipping on her sweater. She looked out the kitchen window at the sun-splashed yard. A light breeze moved through pine trees. "He'll take good care of her."

She turned back to Nell. "And you and I, Nell, we need to take care of us. Before the day gets away from us, let's get in that walk you promised me. I'm in need of stretching these legs and cleaning out my head."

They went out the back way, across the deck and backyard and down the wooded path to the beach road. Several runners passed them, and an old man with his dog walked slowly along the narrow stretch of beach. Teenagers sat on the rocks, tapping messages into cell phones. But even on the beach, a feeling of sadness weighed down the air.

It was the weight of *death*—for that's how people would talk about it for a while. "Murder" was too harsh a word, too awful to comfortably weave into September days.

"It doesn't seem real," Nell said. She watched the waves lap up against the smooth sand, then suck it back into the sea. Retreat. Return. Retreat. Nature's simple rhythm usually brought quiet to her spirit, but today the waves seemed somehow menacing.

Birdie nodded and quickened her pace, as if speed might put some time and distance between them and Jeffrey's death.

They walked up the winding road at the end of the cove and through a neighborhood of fine, elegant homes, then around a bend to another stretch of beach, where Izzy liked to push Abby in her stroller. Pete Halloran jogged by, arms pumping. When he noticed Birdie and Nell, he slowed to a walk, moving in step with the women.

His face was somber. "Old man Meara gave me my first busboy job," he said, wiping away the beads of perspiration dotting his forehead. "I sucked at it and he fired me. He said I needed to make better use of my time and suggested practicing the guitar. He was right."

"There'll be lots of Jeffrey Meara stories being told this week," Birdie said, patting Pete's arm. Cass's lanky brother dwarfed the older woman by nearly two feet and he lowered his head to hear her, a band of sandy hair falling across his forehead.

"Losing the Bartender is a sad thing. But having it happen the way it did . . . that's . . . it's . . ."

Trying to grasp the horror of murder defied words. They'd try and try, but it was a reality that shunned adequate emotional descriptions. It happened. It was awful. And that was that. There was nothing they could do about it.

Except find the person who did this, who ended a life so purposefully and cruelly. And then begin to piece their lives back together again.

As the beach narrowed further, Pete waved them off and picked up his pace, running down to the water's edge and around a mound of granite boulders.

Birdie and Nell walked back toward the road, suddenly aware of how far they'd come. Birdie sighed. "Was it just a heartbeat ago we were standing in this same spot with Isabel and Abby, enjoying the breeze and the magic of a September day?"

"A simple day," Nell murmured. She looked down the road, toward the bushy hill that climbed up to the house on Ridge Road.

"Birdie," she said suddenly. "Look."

Birdie stopped and followed the point of Nell's finger. "Good grief. Déjà vu."

Jules Ainsley stood at the foot of the incline, staring beyond the yellow tape that marked the property, up through the trees to the top of the hill. To the top of the house. The porch with the hanging swing. To the potting shed.

"Come." Birdie touched Nell on the arm and they walked briskly down the road. Jules seemed not to notice when they stopped beside her. Instead, she remained focused on the hill, as if waiting for something to happen. Maybe for time to turn back. For yesterday to be gone.

Nell tried to imagine what she was seeing when she looked up at Izzy's old house, tried to read what was going through her mind. But beyond the trees and bushes, all she could see was the scene Ben had described to them the night before. The awful scene of a man dead outside a potting shed, lying in a pool of blood. The same scene, she supposed, that was even more vivid in the memory of the woman standing beside her.

Finally Jules turned toward them and managed a sad smile. "Who was he?" she asked. "Why was he wanting to be in my life? Why did . . . ?" Her words dropped off. She shook her head as if dismissing them, and then she looked back up at the house, her hands on her hips, as if somehow the answers she sought would be up there, hanging from a bush or the yellow tape that was visible through the trees.

"He was a good and decent man," Birdie said. "That's who Jeffrey Meara was."

Jules was so quiet Nell wasn't sure Birdie's words had registered.

Finally she asked, "When will the police take the tape down?" Her voice was neutral now. Almost businesslike, as if she were asking what time the bank opened or when the train left for Boston.

"The police tape?" Nell asked. Her brows lifted in surprise. Somehow, the day after a terrible death, police tape seemed supremely unimportant.

Jules turned away from the woods, the house, and Nell's words. She climbed onto a bike that was leaning against an old post and said, more to herself than the others, "Maybe the Realtor will know."

"Why is it important?" Nell asked.

Jules looked puzzled and taken aback, as if she had asked a most logical question, perhaps *the* question that needed to be asked at that precise moment, and Nell was somehow remiss in not having the answer.

Then she said slowly and patiently, as if speaking to someone who might have difficulty understanding: "So I know when I can move in."

Chapter 13

*L*ater that morning, Nell and Birdie ordered an antipasto plate and a selection of Garozzo's choice cold cuts and Italian bread to be sent over to Maeve Meara's house. As an afterthought, they had Harry pack up a bag of sandwiches for themselves and headed down the road to the Seaside Knitting Studio.

The encounter with Jules lingered with both women, her odd comments troubling. They had wanted to comfort her, to ease the awfulness of what she'd so recently seen.

And Jules wanted to take down police tape and move into a house where a man's blood still stained the potting shed floor and walkway.

Perhaps Izzy would know more.

Mae sent them immediately to the back room. "Stella Palazola just flew by me on her way to see Izzy. The poor girl looked awful," Mae said. "White as a sheet. No young girl should be witness to such a horrible thing." She turned back to the computer and a customer wanting to place a special order.

Stella was sitting at the old wooden table, looking like she hadn't slept in days.

Izzy looked relieved when Birdie and Nell walked down the steps. She eyed the familiar white bag Birdie carried. "Harry's sandwiches? You're an angel, Birdie. Stella needs food."

Birdie set the bag down and gave Stella a hug. She noticed several sheets of paper on the table in front of her. "These look official," she said.

Stella fidgeted with one, curling back the corner. She nodded. Her light brown hair was pulled back into a makeshift ponytail, the scattering of freckles across her nose looking more prominent than usual. She had contacts in today, swimming in watery eyes.

"Has Jules Ainsley contacted you?" Nell asked. She sat down on the other side of the table.

"We're closed today," Stella began, as if the answer to Nell's questions required some background information. "Uncle Mario was a friend of Jeffrey's and he didn't want us opening the office. Mostly, I think he wanted me to get some sleep if I could. Wishful thinking, I guess."

Birdie patted her hand. "It wasn't a good night for sleep. Tonight will be better."

Stella managed a half smile and then went on. "I was in the shower when she knocked on my door. Jules, I mean."

"She came to your apartment?" Izzy asked.

"Yes. She went to the office first, and when it was closed she somehow found out where I lived."

Izzy picked up one of the papers and looked at the PALAZOLA REAL ESTATE heading at the top. She scanned the text, her eyebrows pulled together. "This is an offer on my house."

"She wants it, Izzy. Real bad."

"She wants that house. Now? Today? Even after—?"

"That doesn't seem to matter to her," Stella said. "She doesn't want to wait. She even offered more money than you and Sam are asking, just so you wouldn't have to wait for other offers and would feel okay about it. She wants it now—like right now."

"Other offers?" Izzy said. She looked up at Stella, then stared again at the formal offer. "She wanted you to bring this to me today? What was she thinking?"

Nell told Izzy about their morning walk. "It was just like the other day, when we saw her staring up at the house from the street below. But this time, we thought she was there because of the murder, that maybe she was in shock, or trying to make some sense out of what she'd seen, or maybe she'd gone back to see if it was real or simply a bad dream."

"But we were wrong. It wasn't any of those things," Birdie said. "She was wondering when she'd be able to move in."

Stella shook her head, her ponytail swinging back and forth. "It's nuts. Uncle Mario says houses where someone has died in such an awful way are hard to sell. Sometimes they never sell, and the house is taken down and something else built in its place. Or maybe they put in a park on the land. Like with a memorial. You know—like Cass did with old Finnegan's house over near the water. Jules told me that was her fear, that someone would tear the house down. Maybe even you, Izzy. She said that we can't let that happen."

Izzy ran her fingers through her hair, trying to make sense of what she was hearing. "Sam and I haven't even talked about what we want to do with the house. It seems so unimportant in the light of what's happened, especially while everyone in town is trying to come to grips with the awfulness of Jeffrey's death and to help Maeve deal with the tragedy. The man isn't even buried yet."

Her words matched Birdie's and Nell's thoughts perfectly.

Nell pulled out the sandwiches and passed the wrapped parcels around. Stella opened hers immediately and bit into a juicy Reuben on Harry's homemade rye bread. Thousand Island dressing oozed out the sides. Izzy was right—Stella hadn't eaten in a while.

"I'm mystified about something, Stella," Birdie said. "Maybe you know the answer. What does Jules find so unique and special—not to mention urgent—about that particular house? What does she love so much about it?"

Stella shifted in the chair and looked at Birdie sadly, as if regretting her whole decision to become a Realtor. Her buoyant enthusiasm of a week earlier was buried somewhere deep beneath the tragedy that should have been her first open house.

"She hasn't even seen the inside the house, Miz Favazza. All she's seen of the property is a dead body on a stone floor. What is there to love?"

. . .

Izzy tucked the papers into her purse and brought them with her to dinner that night. Cass and Jane Brewster had gone early and saved a large table in the corner of Gracie's Lazy Lobster Café. The unpretentious restaurant was out on the pier and Pete's band often performed on the deck, a wide structure that hung directly over the water. No one was in the mood for a night of fun, but Gracie needed the business, and Pete, Andy, and Merry—the Fractured Fish threesome—needed the moral support. Playing in the shadow of the Bartender's death would be difficult.

Merry Jackson, singer and keyboard player in the band, came over to the table and hugged everyone. "The loss of someone we all knew and liked is awful enough," she said, repeating aloud what all of them were thinking, "but beneath all that, beneath the sadness of Jeffrey's passing, is the scary and horrifying fact that someone murdered him."

Jeffery was a man who had never left his hometown for longer than a honeymoon trip to Nantucket, a fishing trip in the White Mountains, and infrequent errands in the city—certainly not places or events where one went out of his way to make enemies—so his murderer was likely a resident of Sea Harbor, Massachusetts. Someone they knew. Perhaps someone seated in Gracie's lobster shack that very night, listening to the Fractured Fish play a medley of old Beatles tunes.

Ben looked over the papers Izzy handed him while Sam flagged down a waitress and ordered Gracie's lobster special for the table.

"Did you see this, Sam?" Ben asked. He pointed to a line in the offer.

Sam's eyes widened. "I missed that."

"It's a cash offer," Ben explained to the others. "Not unheard of, but a little surprising." He moved aside several water glasses so the waitress could fit a plate of crab-stuffed mushrooms and a pitcher of beer on the table.

"Especially for someone who has never seen the house," Izzy said. "The offer is more than generous. In fact, it seems wrong to sell it for that price. I can't imagine how Jules can afford it. Mary Pisano got the impression money might be tight for her."

"The offer looks legitimate. Earnest money and all, and it doesn't sound like Jules cares much what an inspection might turn up," Sam said.

Ham Brewster stroked his beard. "I dunno. It somehow seems disrespectful. Not that it makes a lot of logical sense, I suppose. But the property is a crime scene right now. A man died there. Can't she wait until we've gotten through these next few days?"

Izzy nodded. "I'm with you, Ham."

"I am, too," Ben said. "Let's get through the next few days, do what we can for Maeve. Try to deal with the rumors that will surely begin to fly with Monday's paper and the workweek beginning." He looked at Sam and Izzy. "It's something you don't need to deal with this weekend."

"Wednesday," Sam said. "Jules had Stella write in that the offer was good until Wednesday."

"Geesh," Cass said, then hid her own thoughts behind a frosty mug of beer.

Two waitresses appeared with the lobster special served family style—bright red lobsters, baked potatoes with sour cream, coleslaw, and Gracie's famous garlic bread. A pile of lobster utensils sitting on top of plastic bibs filled a basket at the end of the table.

Nell sat at the one end, her back to the wall, listening to the hum of conversation around her but only tuning in to bits and pieces. Concentration didn't come easily and she finally gave up, letting the Fractured Fish music take over.

She was surprised at the number of people filing into Gracie's tonight. Perhaps it was the same need she and Ben had felt. Not a desire to go out for fun or food, really. But to be in the gentle embrace of friends.

She looked around and spotted the mayor at a table near the deck, sitting with his wife and the Pisanos—Mary and her husband, Ed. A mayor, his wealthy wife, a bed-and-breakfast owner, a fisherman. It was one of the things Nell loved about Sea Harbor: the blurred lines of social standing.

Stan looked tired, Nell thought. The campaign was getting to him. Karen rested a hand on his sleeve, a sweet gesture, even from where Nell sat. Stan was exceedingly handsome, she thought, realizing she rarely had the opportunity to observe him like this—quietly, discreetly. Next to him, Karen's pleasant appearance was almost diminished, but her presence always carried a certain control. A helpmate, a perfect first lady—roles she seemed to cherish.

Izzy followed her aunt's look. "Do you suppose Beatrice is here?" And then they both spotted the councilwoman at the same time. Her bright green dress was difficult to miss. She was sitting with Rachel and Don Wooten and another councilman Nell knew only slightly. Their conversation looked to be engaging, though somber, to all except for Don, who sat slightly removed from the others, nursing a beer.

Thinking of his partner, Nell thought. This would be a difficult time for Don. The angry exchange she had overheard came back to her as she watched a range of emotion wash across his face—sadness, frustration, weariness. The unpleasant encounter he'd had with Jeffrey would make this all even more difficult for him, to have had such unpleasant words with Jeffrey and then have him gone so tragically.

She didn't see Jules Ainsley in the small café and felt a momentary twinge at forgetting about her. No matter what she and Birdie had seen that morning, one didn't easily erase the image of finding a murdered body. Nell knew firsthand what that was like, about the haunting images that appeared at the least-expected moment. Jules couldn't be immune to that, however it might have seemed. And unlike those sitting around Nell's table, unlike Stella Palazola and others so intimately connected to this crime, Jules had no one to comfort her.

Nell pivoted toward Cass, sitting next to her, her chair slightly turned. She, too, had removed herself from the conversation and seemed to be wrapping herself up in the music, her meal untouched. Not a usual scenario for Cass.

Nell leaned over and asked softly, "Where's Danny tonight?"

"He said he'd stop in later. He had something to do first." Cass's eyes remained on the band, her fingers strumming on the table along with her brother's guitar. Finally she scooted her chair closer to Nell's and looked at her, her palms flat on the table. "He went over to Mary's B and B. He said it was the right thing to do—Jules doesn't know a lot of people in town."

"Maybe it was the right thing to do."

Cass's fingers began their light tapping again. "Maybe."

"It had to be awful for her, finding the body like that."

"If that's what happened," Cass said.

"What do you mean?" Nell picked a piece of lobster meat from the shell and dipped it in a pot of lemon butter.

"I don't know what I mean. But why would Jeffrey call her and insist she meet with him like that? It doesn't make sense. It sounds . . . it sounds made up."

Nell had played with the same thought, but excused it by admitting that Jeffrey was looking strangely at Jules that night at the Ocean's Edge. Izzy said she'd noticed the same thing. It could have been for the same reason a lot of people looked at Jules—she was striking looking, attractive in an unusual way. She turned heads. But when she replayed the scene, she realized it was a different kind of look the bartender had sent Jules's way. It's why Jules thought the bartender was odd. It was as if he had seen her before and was trying to figure out where. "There are certainly missing pieces," Nell admitted. "And it's true we don't know Jules very well, but she certainly seems like a straight shooter, even when it might not be to her advantage. I can't imagine why she'd lie about this. Besides, all the police have to do is check Jeffrey's cell phone."

Danny Brandley's long shadow fell over the table. "Mind if I sit?" He squeezed a chair in next to Cass, greeted the others at the table, and then turned toward Nell and Cass. His face was somber. "I caught the end of your conversation. You're talking about Jules."

"Cass said you went to see her. How is she?" Nell asked.

"She's a survivor, that's for sure. And it's a good thing, I guess. She sure didn't plan on all this when she came to Sea Harbor."

"What did she plan on?" Cass asked. Her layered message was carried in the hard tone of her voice.

Danny took off his glasses and rubbed the bridge of his nose. He ignored the tone in Cass's voice. "That's the question, isn't it? I don't know for sure. Originally she just wanted my help finding out how to access old records, that sort of thing. She wanted to know more about the town, she said, and she figured since I was an investigative reporter I should know how to do those things."

"What was she looking for?"

"Just things about the town, its history, maybe some genealogy stuff, she said." He took a pair of tongs and transferred a lobster from the platter to his plate. "And she asked me not to talk about it, so I didn't."

"But why?" Nell asked.

"At first I thought it was because she was on a wild goose chase and didn't see any reason for the whole town to know it."

"And now?"

"I don't pretend to understand Jules. But . . ."

"But?" Nell said.

Danny took a long swig of beer before he answered. "But now I think she's afraid of what she might find."

Chapter 14

onday. That was the day that Ben predicted the rumor rock would start to roll down the mountain, gathering moss. The weekend was for absorbing the sad news that Jeffrey Meara was dead. The beginning of a new week would bring out other things.

And so it did—the harsh, relentless dissection of a crime that rocked a town, by folks desperate for it to be solved.

The first thing Monday's *Sea Harbor Gazette* did was give the murderer a name:

POTTING SHED MURDERER
LEAVES FEW CLUES

Nell folded the paper to the article and smoothed it out on the yacht club dining table.

"Potting shed murderer?" Nell said, looking up from the paper. She stared again at the headline. "That's ridiculous."

A couple sitting at the next table looked over, then quickly went back to their tuna salad.

"Read on," Ben said. His voice was controlled, but the set to his jaw told Nell exactly how he felt about the press coverage so far.

It was the tagline that would give legs to a rash of rumors and that caused Ben to swear, something he rarely did in public.

UNREST AT THE OCEAN'S EDGE: FACT OR FICTION?

The article itself contained little that related to the tagline, except for innuendos, things culled from an ambitious young reporter's interviews with a few friends who worked at the restaurant. Seeds that would soon grow wings.

"What does Jerry Thompson think about this?" Nell asked Ben. "He was at your meeting this morning, right?"

At first, Ben didn't answer. He finished off his glass of iced tea and pushed away his plate, empty now except for a few remnants of lettuce. He looked out over the ocean, peaceful and calm, the waves lapping up on the club's carefully tended beach. All around them, yacht club diners lunched on lobster rolls and salads, fish and chips, while waiters scurried about the flagstone patio refreshing drinks and pushing the dessert cart from table to table.

It was an idyllic setting, masking a cloud of fear.

"No," Ben finally said. "He was invited, but brainstorming programs for Sea Harbor at-risk youth—as important as it is—was probably not high on his to-do list today. But Don Wooten was there. He asked if I'd have coffee with him afterward. He was upset."

"Because of the article?"

Ben nodded. "But it was more than that. Even though the reporter did a mediocre reporting job, there's some truth to it."

"Unrest at Jeffrey and Don's restaurant? What does that mean?" Birdie asked. She nibbled on a sliver of pretzel bread.

Nell's thoughts turned to that recent Sunday night when an argument had trapped her in the restaurant's back hallway.

"Partnerships can be tricky," Ben said. "Even when you know your partner well."

"But as you yourself said, tricky partnerships are a part of business. They don't merit a tagline in an article about a murder investigation." Birdie motioned to the waitress that they were ready for dessert. "I feel a need for sweetness," she said.

Ben allowed a half smile and pointed to the fruit cup for himself. Birdie and Nell would split an enormous slice of lemon cake.

"They were friends," Nell said.

Ben agreed. "But the previous owner of the Edge was an absent landlord for the most part. He lived in Boston and rarely came up here. He let Jeffrey pretty much run the show, making big decisions, signing supplier contracts, hiring people, the whole shebang. When he and Don bought the old man out, it changed things. They're cut from different molds. Don, with his Harvard MBA and business successes, and Jeffrey, the longtime bartender who knows everyone and everything, and who pretty much considered the restaurant as his own. Don said they've had some heated exchanges about major things, like vendors and accounting practices."

"But what difference does any of that make? It certainly doesn't fit in an article about a murder," Nell said.

"You're right. It shouldn't be there—at least not until there's something concrete to say about it. But when there's been a murder, everyone who has ever had anything to do with Jeffrey will be in the limelight. His partner would be among the first, I'd guess."

"I suppose that makes sense, awful as it is," Birdie said.

"The police are already exploring it. They told Don to come down to headquarters for questioning today. I tried to convince him that it's routine, but it's still damn unnerving. I think he just needed someone to talk to, to hear himself think it through."

Nell knew that was an understatement. Ben Endicott had many friends, and the chief of police just happened to be one of them. It also didn't hurt that he had both a law degree and a business degree and was fair and honest to the core. His strength was in his kindness, and he had helped many friends in matters from negotiating contracts and deeds and wills to listening to personal issues and offering wise moral support.

"Poor Rachel. How upsetting for her," Birdie said. She moved her glass as the waitress brought dessert plates to the table.

"I don't think he's told her yet. He'll get the questioning over with first. I told him I'd go over with him this afternoon."

"Not much escapes her, working in City Hall," Nell said. "She'll know soon." She cut into the rich lemon cake.

"Well, she's a smart attorney. She'll see it for what it is." Ben speared a strawberry out of the parfait dish. "She's known Jeffrey since childhood. His death will be hard for her."

"It makes me wonder how many of our friends will be touched by this. Mourning Jeffrey or being suspects. It's insidious," Birdie said. "And entirely too close to home. A good friend, murdered. Our dear Izzy and Sam's house sullied in such a terrible way. Don Wooten being called into the police station and questioned. And imagine what Jules and Stella are going through. Who is next?"

It was a rhetorical question, of course. Who would be affected next by this senseless crime? It was a question Birdie really didn't want an answer to—unless that answer was no one.

It would all go away, and they'd wake up and have their ordinary lives back in place again.

Chapter 15

The church service was set for Wednesday.

Maeve Meara wanted it to be held as soon as possible. There were no out-of-town relatives to wait for, and she wanted her Jeffrey's spirit at peace, wanted the blessings Father Northcutt's service would bring to his soul.

It would have to be a memorial service, the priest explained, because it would take a while to get the body released, and that was fine with Maeve.

So Mary Halloran, the parish secretary, managed to move schedules, contact florists, undertakers, and cemetery folks, and made sure the Altar Society ladies would have plenty of food at the church hall reception afterward. It would be something Jeffrey would have been proud was held in his memory. "You know my helper won't settle for anything but the best," Father Larry told Maeve, then added in a whisper, "Sometimes I think Mary Halloran only keeps me around for comic relief." And then he kissed her gently on the top of her head.

They all knew it to be true. Cass's ma was truly the power behind keeping Our Lady of Safe Seas functional and efficient, and she left no detail to chance for her friends Maeve and Jeffrey Meara.

Don Wooten had offered to have a reception after the memorial at the Ocean's Edge, but Maeve thought that was an inappropriate venue, no matter how much her Jeffrey loved his bar, his beer, and his signature drinks. The church meant prayers and comfort. That was where it should be. That was where *he* should be, she'd added with some emphasis.

"This is Maeve's big chance to get him into the church," Father Northcutt said with a hint of a smile.

Wednesday dawned bright and glorious, a day that brought out nearly the whole town to listen to the priest's kind words and humorous anecdotes. Close friends mixed with the curious, the well intentioned, and some who didn't want to miss out on the bountiful reception in the basement of the church.

Father Larry closed his eulogy with words that Maeve herself had handed him that morning, handwritten on a piece of linen stationery. They were words that would serve the devout woman well in the days to come:

My dear Jeffrey loved life, loved all of you here today, and loved me with his whole heart. He lived a wonderful, full life, filled with good friends. He wanted for nothing. He did what he loved doing: watching the sun come up out of the ocean, making me popcorn and watching every single Star Trek movie six times, reading his favorite philosophers in front of a roaring fire. He enjoyed beating our police chief at poker and working at his bar, where he knew every single customer's name. He did what he loved—all those things that filled his life with happiness.

How many people live much longer than my darling Jeffrey did and yet never experience that kind of love and joy? Jeffrey's life was glorious—and for that we cannot be sad. We can only be grateful.

Thanks be to the good Lord.

With that Father Northcutt completed his prayers and walked with Jeffrey's widow down the long aisle to the hall below.

As they inched their way down the crowded steps, Nell mentioned to Ben that she had spotted half the police force in attendance. He'd noticed the same thing, some in uniform but many in suits milling around at the back of the church and now headed downstairs.

They caught up with Jerry Thompson at the bottom of the steps to the parish hall. "Looks like your whole force is here," Ben said.

"Almost." Jerry nodded and moved over to the wall to let people pass. "The crowd had me worried," he said. "The harsh fact is that there's a murderer on the loose. Although nothing so far leads us to believe that this was a random killing, you can't take anything for granted."

Ben listened carefully, his brow creased. "I can't imagine it was random—but I can't imagine anyone intentionally killing Jeffrey Meara, either." He looked around at the crowd, the faces, some chatting as if at a wedding reception, others with tears in their eyes. "I understand murderers often have a compulsion to show up at press conferences or funerals of victims."

Jerry managed a laugh. "So you watch *CSI*, Ben? Who would have guessed? But yeah, it's true. The guy could be in there eating Harriet Brandley's potato salad or Gracie's lobster rolls or Harry's cold cuts. So all my crew are spies today. Maybe someone will hear or see something, catch a look or some movement, something that doesn't quite fit in at a wake." He shrugged. "We're looking under every stone. We'll solve this. Tommy Porter is my right-hand guy on it, and he's definitely motivated. Jeffrey was a friend of his grandmother."

Nell saw the fatigue and sadness on the police chief's face. She and Ben had talked about it for a long time the night before, the difficulties built into his position. Senseless loss of life was an awful thing. And when it was a friend, a man who was a fixture in a small town, it was awful—and personal. Having Tommy, a young man they'd known almost since his birth, on the case was a good thing, too. Tommy and his girlfriend, Janie Levin, were special to all of them.

They left the chief and walked by some of the Ocean's Edge staff making their way out of the church. Some were kids just out of college, looking to move on to better jobs but content to have one at the Edge in the meantime. Most had probably been hired by Jeffrey himself. And if rumor had it right, fired by him as well.

Inside the large hall, Maeve sat in a semicircle of chairs not far from the food buffet. The long folding tables nearly groaned beneath the weight of hams and seafood salads, platters of lobster and chips and dips, pies and cakes. The widow was composed and gracious, a small, peaceful woman who believed with all her heart that her Jeffrey hadn't left her. Not really.

People circled around her, murmuring kind words, then moved on to let others take their place.

Ben and Nell stood in line with Izzy and Birdie, just in front of Stan and Karen Hanson. They exchanged a few words, but Stan was clearly not in the mood for small talk, and Karen, one hand on her husband's arm, watched him closely, her face composed.

Nell thought about the conversation they'd had just days before. Stan and Jeffrey had been friends. And however long ago it was, it appeared fresh today in Stan's face. Fresh and very sad.

The Three Musketeers, Karen had called them. The third in the trio hadn't been mentioned by name. He was likely one of the Sea Harbor High graduates who didn't come back after college and now lived in Boston or New York or someplace more exotic.

Maeve looked up as Nell and Ben approached. She smiled, her eyes focusing first on Nell. "Jeffrey loved you, you know," she said to her. "You and that big Ben of yours. And sweet Izzy." When she saw Birdie, her eyes filled, but she wiped away the gathering tears immediately. "And my dear Birdie." She held out both hands.

Birdie leaned over and hugged her, a gentle embrace to a fragile form.

"Birdie was at our wedding. All those many years ago," Maeve said.

"And you were at mine, Maeve."

"All three of them, I believe," Maeve said, chuckling.

Looking at the weaving line of people waiting behind them, Ben and Nell began to move on. Maeve stood briefly and moved close to Birdie, her hands on her friend's shoulders, their eyes at the same level, one looking into the other's. Two women small in stature and big in all the things that matter. "Come visit me," she said. "We will talk."

Birdie promised as much and moved away. They walked single file through the crowd, over to a small table where Cass, Sam, and the Brewsters sat together, drinking glasses of iced tea.

"She's quite a lady, isn't she?" Sam said.

"I wonder how much she's really grasped of what's happened," Birdie said. "I got the feeling that maybe the way Jeffrey died has escaped her completely."

"Which might be a good thing for now," Nell said.

They looked back at Maeve. She greeted the mayor and his wife graciously, smiling. Karen sat down next to Maeve, taking her blue-veined hands in her own. She smiled, that sad way people did at funerals. Next to her, Stan stood silently, awkwardly, looking down at the two women. He appeared slightly rumpled today, a look out of place for the distinguished mayor.

Next in line was Beatrice Scaglia, her eyes scrutinizing the group in front of her. She watched each movement, each gesture, her own face still and in mourning mode.

"Beatrice wants to be sure she gets equal time," Cass whispered. "There are lots of voters here."

Birdie tsked at her, but with a half smile.

Cass feigned regret. "I shouldn't be snarky at a funeral, should I?"

"But you're right," Izzy said. "Our Beatrice is a good politician. Funerals are fair game, I guess."

Minutes later, their attention shifted back to Maeve. She moved forward on her chair, her hands grasping the edge, then slowly got up and stood in front of Stan Hanson. She tilted her head back, looking up into his face. She lifted one hand to his cheek and touched it gently, then spoke quiet words, as one might to comfort a child.

In the next minute, Stan Hanson, mayor of Sea Harbor and a man known for keeping his emotions in check, seemed to shrink in size. Maeve stood still, not moving away, her hands now resting on his arms.

Mayor Hanson lowered his head as unchecked tears rolled down his cheeks.

Karen rose from the chair immediately and gathered up her things. She offered her husband a tissue, and then she gently ushered him through the crowds of people and out of the crowded hall.

Ben suggested they leave shortly after the mayor and his wife. Birdie declined, saying she was going to stay on a while longer and make sure Maeve got home safely. "She'll be here a couple more hours at least. I'll stay with her."

Ben gave her the look that questioned her mode of transportation and she assured him her driver, Harold, would be in charge of getting them both home. Ben's personal mission to keep Birdie's Lincoln Town Car in the capable hands of Harold Sampson, especially after she'd ruined several parking meters near the police station, would be honored. Birdie took Ben's reminders in stride. Besides, the thought of marring her deceased Sonny's cherished Town Car was nightmarish, and though she'd never tell Ben, that fact went much further than Ben's concern in convincing her to let Harold take the reins.

Nell looked back at Maeve once more before following the group out of the hall. Beatrice had now claimed the widow and was sitting next to her in her tailored black suit, offering water and condolences.

"Stan Hanson was having a hard time. What was that about?" Cass took two steps at a time, up the basement steps and into the sunshine.

"I was surprised, too," Ben said. "I've never seen him show much emotion, not even during the fiercest city council fight. That was the private side, I guess."

Nell squinted in the brightness of day, then slipped on her sunglasses. "I think it was about a sweet man showing us that even real men cry," she said.

Cass scoffed. "Real men do lots of things, some not so nice."

Nell put an arm around her shoulder and they began walking together down the wide granite steps that fronted Our Lady of Safe Seas. "Speaking of real men, I didn't see Danny."

"He's watching the bookstore," Cass said. "His parents were good friends of the Mearas."

"Of course," Nell said. "See? Good men do nice things."

Ham interrupted before Cass could manage a retort.

"We're off to the gallery. No rest for the wicked," he said, taking Jane's arm and guiding her through a crowd gathered on the steps.

"And I need to get back to work, too," Izzy echoed. "Mae's nieces are minding the shop." She looked over at Sam and Cass. "Anyone want to grab a coffee on the way?"

Sam was checking his messages but dutifully followed behind the two women.

Nell watched them walk off. It was the middle of the week, a Wednesday, but the weekday seemed out of place. It was a different kind of day, not one with a name like Wednesday. Nell felt unsettled. She looked up and down the street, as if something should be happening, a second act. As if something she couldn't quite see would add some closure to the day. She looked at Ben and saw in his eyes that he sensed what she was feeling.

"It's an uncomfortable feeling, isn't it, Nellie? Funerals are so final. But nothing about this is final. We're in a time warp, and we're stuck here until the murderer is found."

Nell let out the breath that had been trapped inside her chest and nodded, somehow knowing that Ben would manage to crawl inside her thoughts and make sense of them. She smiled and took his arm, her heart holding him there, next to her, forever.

They walked out of the long shadows of the church toward their car. Ben had parked just past the small corner park near the Sea Harbor Historical Museum.

Nell noticed Tyler Gibson, a bartender at the Ocean's Edge, standing in the middle of a group near a small fountain that centered the park. Nell recognized several members of the restaurant's waitstaff.

"Nice funeral," Tyler said as they drew near. His cheeks reddened as he heard his own words. "Geesh, Nell, Ben. Sorry. That doesn't sound right. What should you say?"

"It's fine," Nell said. "It *was* nice. Very personal, and that meant something to Maeve."

"It's nice that all of you came," Ben said. "Jeffrey would have liked his staff being there."

Ty smiled and shifted from one foot to the other, his blond hair flopping over his forehead. "Truth is, Ben, Wooten closed the restaurant until four today so we would all come, kind of like we should, you know?" Then he added quickly, "But we'd've come anyway—sure."

Zack Levin, Janie's younger brother, stood next to Tyler. He cleared his throat, then looked at his older friend and shrugged. "Speak for yourself, Gibson."

Nell looked at Zack. Poor kid. She remembered seeing him the other night, trying to hold it together under Jeffrey's anger when he caught him texting someone and neglecting a table littered with dirty dishes. Janie had told her later that Jeffrey had fired Zack that night.

"It's nice of you to show up, Zack, considering everything. And if you need suggestions in your job search, Ben and I might be able to help." Zack Levin was a nice kid—not completely responsible, but well intentioned. And they all adored his sister, Janie, the wonderful nurse who lived in the apartment above the yarn shop. Ben would surely be able to find someone to hire him.

Zack brightened. "Hey, thanks, but I'm good. Surprise, surprise. Don Wooten hired me back a couple days ago—that's why I'm here all duded up like this." He flipped his tie.

Nell held back her surprise. Without looking, she could feel Ben's similar reaction. Their friend Don Wooten hadn't wasted any time in overturning his dead partner's decisions.

Behind Zack, Ryan Arcado, the fire chief's son, stood with his hands in his pockets. He had been fired, too, according to M.J., Nell's hairdresser and Ryan's mother. A month or so earlier, M.J. had said. Nell had been in the salon for a trim the day before Jeffrey's murder, and M.J. had not minced words. "Jeffrey Meara wields a mighty stick with his employees. He's tough," she had said. "I know Ryan can be a hothead, but the man could have been more forgiving and given him a second chance. It's impossible for these kids to find jobs and Jeffrey knows that. He's so smooth and gracious to diners, but let me tell you,

Nell, he can be a beast to work for. He was much nicer when all he did at the Edge was tend bar."

The portrait that M.J. had painted of Jeffrey had surprised Nell at the time. Ben had been more circumspect when she repeated the conversation. "Ryan can be bullheaded. Maybe he deserved it. Who knows? He has some growing up to do." He had paused and chuckled as he went on to share an old memory. "I got fired from busing tables at the Harvard Club because I tossed out a bunch of silverware with the trash. As my manager politely explained, 'It wasn't a good thing to do.'"

Nell had laughed. A decades-old mistake was humorous in the retelling. But one that happened a day or week before had not had the chance to be softened by time.

Zack looked over at Ryan and pointed. "Arcado is back, too. Jeffrey took his phone from him the day he caught him texting and threw it in the trash bin outside. Not a happy sight. There's a bunch of us who got canned. We're the Ocean's Edge's returning alums."

Ryan tugged off his tie and sat down on a bench. "Yep. It's good to be back. Wooten called me Monday. He's cool. Old man Meara could be wicked hell to work for. I'da liked to have killed the guy a couple times," he said.

"Zip it, Arcado." It was a hostess Jeffrey had introduced Ben and Nell to early in the summer, Laura Danvers's cousin Grace. Jeffrey had liked her, and today she looked both sad and disgusted.

"Sometimes you're as appropriate as my kid brother. Just let it be. The man is dead." She looked over at Nell. "It's sad. As soon as Mr. Wooten was out of sight today they peeled out of that church as if it were on fire. I don't think they even stayed long enough to hear the nice eulogy Father Larry gave." She glared back at her coworkers. "In fact, I didn't see some of you in the church at all. I think you just got dressed up, made sure Mr. Wooten saw you, and then probably went over to the Gull and drank beer. How juvenile. You guys are supposed to be grown-ups."

"Grace's right," Tyler said, holding up his hands as if to stop a fight. "Let's be fair about old Jeffrey. He helped put that restaurant on the map." He looked around for nods, then added, "Best on the North Shore, bar none."

Nell watched Tyler change the course of the conversation with a charming smile. He was a good guy—not to mention a good grandson to Esther. He'd brought real joy back into that house when Esther offered him a place to stay. And maybe because of his grandmother, he seemed to be learning from his rather numerous youthful indiscretions. Hopefully Ryan Arcado would learn a thing or two from the handsome bartender. And Zack Levin could use a role model, too, although she suspected his sister stayed on top of his missteps.

As Nell started to turn away, she noticed another familiar face just behind the stone benches. At first she couldn't place the tall, dark-haired man with the square chin. But then she realized who it was. Garrett Barros had been Izzy's neighbor when she lived in the house on Ridge Road. Nell had talked to him a few times while visiting Izzy. And more recently she'd seen him at the Ocean's Edge.

Was he on Jeffrey's good side? she wondered. Or had he suffered the fate of Zack and Ryan? He had always been pleasant, which she remembered specifically because his parents had been curmudgeonly, criticizing everything from Izzy's placement of her trash to the length of her grass. She looked again at Garrett. Yes, he was pleasant enough, but there'd been something about him, something . . . What was it? She pulled her brows together as she tried to tug up the memory. But it was gone, so she smiled instead, waved to the group, and followed Ben down the pathway toward their car.

Sam was standing at the curb checking his watch, his Jeep parked next to the Endicott's car. He looked up.

"I have a favor to ask."

"Go for it," Ben said.

"The police chief has taken down the yellow tape from the Ridge Road house. They're through with whatever they needed to do and it's been tossed back into our lap. Stella wants to meet over there to go over some papers, look at the inspection report. Izzy won't go. She says it gives her nightmares. I thought maybe one of you would want to come along."

They both agreed to join him.

"Funerals have a way of discombobulating me," Nell said. "I won't get anything done at home anyway."

They drove over in Sam's Jeep, Ben in the back, straddling his long legs across the floor mat. Sam rested one arm on the window edge and headed the car north. "Izzy gave a fleeting thought to tearing the house down and selling the property. There's always a market for land close to the water. But that would be a mess, finding groups who'll reuse the bricks and wood. Somehow, I don't know, some crazy voice in my head rejected that idea."

"And it would certainly crush Jules Ainsley."

"That it would. She's been calling Stella every day, even though we haven't signed anything and told her we needed some space to say good-bye to our friend Jeffrey. I went ahead and had the house inspected, even though Jules offered to buy it as is. It didn't seem right to take her money and have the house fall apart the next day."

"Was she at the funeral? I didn't see her."

"She told Izzy she wasn't going," Sam said. "She didn't know Jeffrey, and she thought her connection to him might make it awkward for everyone. She was right. I saw her headed into the bookstore when I picked Izzy up at the shop."

The Brandleys' bookstore. Nell looked up, about to say something, then thought better of it, and instead turned and watched the neighborhoods roll by until Sam finally turned onto Ridge Road. They drove past the Barroses' house and pulled up behind Stella Palazola's small Toyota. She was standing on the front step.

Beside her, her hair pulled back into a ponytail, was Jules Ainsley.

Chapter 16

H er smile was more subdued today, but she was just as striking, even in jeans and a faded T-shirt. She stood still, watching them walk toward her, her brown eyes large and expectant and welcoming.

Almost as if welcoming them into her own house.

Nell returned her smile.

"Jules has been waiting patiently to see the inside of the house and this seemed as good a time as any, since Sam and I were coming over," Stella said. "I hope you don't mind, Sam." She looked at Nell and Ben and her smile grew, relieved to have the extra support.

"Of course not." He looked at Jules. "I guess that means the week hasn't changed your mind about things."

"No," she said.

"If the week's events haven't, the house may," he said, then suggested to Stella that they all go inside.

The house had a stale smell, the smell of perspiring police officers tromping through it looking for whatever they thought might lead to a murderer. Mud covered the hardwood floors and a small accent rug was rolled up, as if someone thought there might be a valuable clue beneath it, perhaps a trapdoor in the floor.

"Chief Thompson called and apologized for the mess," Sam said, looking down at the muddy boot prints. "It was raining that night. It couldn't be helped."

Jules stood in the center of the small living room. Izzy had left behind some furniture for renters—a couch and chairs, a kitchen table, beds. The furniture made it easier to imagine the house as it might have been.

But Jules wasn't interested in the furniture. She was looking through to the back of the house and the yard beyond.

"It's a great view, once that weedy mess on the hill is cleaned up," Stella said, then sent a silent apology to Sam, her brown brows lifting up into her bangs.

They all walked through a dining alcove to the kitchen, where large windows framed the backyard, the porch, and a wooden swing that Nell knew well. It had been the main selling point for Izzy when she had purchased the house. The swing was old—even back then—with rusty chains and squeaky brackets, but Izzy had fallen in love with it. And she'd spent more money than she probably should have restoring it, replacing parts, repairing the wood, and refinishing it to what it must have looked like years and years before. Today it was as polished and smooth as Sam and Ben's sailboat.

Jules stood still, taking in the swing, the yard. When she spoke, her voice was tight and filled with emotion. "It's . . . it's perfect."

Sam stared at her, at the yard, at the muddy footprints on the hardwood floors. And most of all, at the potting shed at the edge of the yard, where a man had recently been killed. *Murdered.* It was as far from perfect as could be imagined.

Nell looked at the emotions flitting across Sam's face, then pushed the images of the past week out of her mind and walked over to the windows. She looked out, lost in her own emotions, seeing the same beauty Jules Ainsley somehow was seeing. "Izzy and I spent many nights on that porch, dreaming of her future here in Sea Harbor," she murmured.

"Was I in those dreams?" Sam asked softly, standing close behind her.

"Someone exactly like you, Sam Perry," Nell said. "I think we dreamed you into being."

Sam chuckled. "I didn't have a chance, huh?"

"Not in the slightest."

"Sam, why don't we sit over here and go over things," Stella called to them, motioning to the dining table, where she had laid out papers. Ben was already seated and had taken out his reading glasses.

"Nell," Stella asked, "would you mind showing Jules through the rest of the house?"

"Stella is being all business," Sam whispered to Nell. "We best comply."

Nell chuckled and motioned to Jules. "It's not really big enough to get lost in—except for what we used to call the hidden bathroom—but follow me. The bedrooms are back this way." She headed through the living area to the small bedroom hallway. She reached the first bedroom before she realized Jules wasn't with her. "Jules?" She retraced her steps and found Jules still standing in the kitchen, looking outside. "Jules?"

She spun around. "Oh. Sorry, Nell. I'm coming." She hurried after her, taking in everything Nell pointed out: two small bedrooms, a walk-through closet, with the single bathroom on the other side.

"We used to tease Izzy about this bathroom. Her closet always had to be neat and tidy so guests could walk through it on their way to the restroom. One of the house's idiosyncrasies."

"It's charming," she said. "The whole house is."

"It needs some sprucing up. Years of renters can take a toll on a house, but when Izzy lived here it was a lovely, cozy cottage."

Jules didn't answer. When Nell looked over at her face, all she saw was happiness.

They stayed another hour, waiting until just before leaving to venture out into the backyard. But it was out there, with the wind blowing up from the ocean and the tangle of weeds waving wildly, that Jules seemed to be most at peace. She sat on the swing, her flip-flops falling to the floor, and swung slowly back and forth, as if she were alone in her own private universe.

Sam and Ben walked back to the potting shed. It was a small structure, with a semicircle of flat granite stones outside the door. The stones had been scrubbed clean. They pushed open the door to the shed and walked into a small space with gardening implements, potting equipment, and lawn tools scattered about. The potting work-bench was littered with trowels, gloves, and miscellaneous items.

"Jerry thinks Jeffrey and his killer moved in here to talk privately, out of view of neighbors," Ben said. "It must have been someone Jeffrey knew, because there were no signs of a fight. The serrated knife that killed Jerry came from that bench. From the bloodstains, they know he was stabbed, then staggered outside and collapsed on the stone path outside the shed."

"Izzy's last renter loved gardening," Sam said. "She left this stuff behind when she skipped out on two months' rent and disappeared. The tools must have been hers."

Ben nodded. "The police took the knife, of course."

"Which sounds like whoever did this didn't plan ahead?" It was Nell, standing in the doorway, grimacing at an image of the grisly scene that had played itself out where she was now standing.

"It sounds like that, doesn't it?" Ben said.

Somehow it lessened the horror of it a small bit, the idea that no one had plotted out the murder. Yet someone did kill Jeffrey Meara. Why?

She looked out the door at Jules Ainsley sitting on the swing, her mind a million miles away. Was she seeing it all over, finding the bar-tender in a pool of blood? If she bought this house, would she wake up in the middle of the night thinking about it, replaying it?

Somehow Nell didn't think so. Jules looked more peaceful at this moment than she had when Nell first met her—or on any of the inter-vening days. Even her necklace was at rest, the charm hanging quietly from her neck, not from a chain twisted around nervous fingers.

Sam checked his watch. It was getting late. "Stella, let's go over Jules's offer again and get out of here before it gets dark."

They headed inside, Ben leading the way.

Sam held Stella back and apologized to her. "I know this isn't the way you've been taught to sell houses and negotiate contracts, Stella. It's . . . well, not the norm, I guess."

"Sam, do you have any idea how relieved I am that this whole thing is happening with you and Iz and the Endicotts? A few days ago I was ready to burn my license, but Uncle Mario talked me out of it. He told me to calm down, that the nicest people in Sea Harbor had my back on this whole awful thing. That would be you guys. And he's right." She took a deep breath and let it out slowly, her eyes filling. She took off her glasses and blinked away the tears. "The miracle of it all is that it looks like I'm actually going to sell this house."

"We're an inch away," Sam said.

"And that's because of all of you. I love you guys."

Sam gave her a hug, then led her through the door and to the table, where the others were already seated.

Sam sat and looked at the official offer one more time, then the bank statement, the earnest money already deposited. The inspection report was better than he'd anticipated, with no major repairs needed. "Your offer is more than fair," he said, looking up at Jules.

"It's all relative. It's fair to me." Jules sat beside Stella, her face still.

"We'll cover your closing costs—it'll make Izzy feel better. And we will have the whole place cleaned. I had Stella write that in." He glanced down at the papers again.

Stella laughed. "How am I ever going to handle another sale, one where sellers actually try to get buyers to fork out more money and buyers try to whittle down the price? You guys are ruining me."

They laughed and Sam pushed out his chair. "I think we've removed everything from the house that needs to go—mostly junk left by old tenants. The furniture is yours to use or give away. Izzy had it cleaned, but who knows what's happened to it this week."

They looked around the table.

"That's it?" Jules asked.

"Almost," Stella said, trying with great difficulty to hold back her excitement and present a professional face. "I need to run this by

Uncle Mario. If you could come by the office tomorrow, we'll seal the deal and give you the keys."

And in the next breath she let out a squeal that everyone present was sure was heard in Rockport, Gloucester, and perhaps the northern edge of Boston.

"Sorry we don't have champagne," Sam said, laughing. "Maybe at a later date."

"Later is fine," Jules said. Her smile was wide, filling her whole face. She looked at Stella. "You're great, Stella. I will be sending everyone I know to you."

"But . . . but you're on vacation, right? This will be your vacation house? I guess in all the commotion I never asked."

Jules smiled again, a smile none of them could begin to read. And Stella's question lay unanswered on the kitchen table.

They walked out into the fading light of day. Nell felt a weariness clear through to her bones, deep and suddenly overwhelming.

They all paused at the end of the walkway and, as if by plan, turned and looked back at the small house that had been Izzy's first home in Sea Harbor. Cass Halloran had lived there for a while after Izzy had moved to the home she and Sam shared, and after that a succession of not always ideal renters moved in and out.

And now the torch was passing to Jules Ainsley. A stranger in their lives who had somehow become—in a very short time—a very intimate stranger.

It was then, when they turned back to the house, that they saw him.

He was standing near his parents' rosebushes, still dressed in the suit he'd worn to Jeffrey Meara's funeral. In one hand was a pair of binoculars attached to a black cord around his neck. On his face was a crooked smile.

Garrett Barros released his grip on the binoculars, letting them fall to his well-muscled chest, and waved.

Chapter 17

It wasn't the kind of news anyone wanted to wake up to, especially after the emotions of the day before.

It came in a phone call just as Nell was making her way down the back stairs to the kitchen, barefoot, with her hair still damp from a quick shower.

Ben picked it up. When he hung up a few minutes later, he hadn't spoken more than a dozen words.

"That was Birdie. Someone broke into Maeve's house during the funeral yesterday."

"No. Oh, Ben, that's terrible. Is she okay?"

"She's fine. There's something hauntingly serene about Maeve Meara. And Birdie's fine, too—she and Harold were with her when she went into the house. She noticed right away something wasn't right. Her mail had fallen to the floor from a small table in the front hallway, and Maeve is fastidious about things like that."

Nell poured herself a cup of coffee. "Birdie said Maeve resisted having anyone stay in the house during the funeral. She said she didn't have anything worth stealing."

"Apparently the thieves thought so, too, because, as Maeve told the police, nothing was missing, at least as far as she could tell— Jeffrey was a bit of a pack rat. They made a mess, that was all, she said."

"Not even a television or computer? Jeffrey had plenty of electronics."

"He did. And that's why the police don't think it was an ordinary thief. Tommy Porter was on duty last night, and he sat and talked with Maeve for a while, walking her through things."

"Are there any hypotheses?"

"Probably the one running through your head right now. That somehow . . . somehow this is connected to Jeffrey's murder."

Nell shuddered. "Where was the mess?"

"In Jeffrey's den. Drawers pulled out, that sort of thing. Birdie said it was 'interesting' and that she'd fill you in on everything tonight."

"That sounds cryptic."

"It's probably because Birdie, wise as she is, knows that the details you might want to hear would be of less interest to me."

Nell nodded, her mind's eye still seeing a fragile widow walking into a ransacked house. It was unnerving and unpleasant.

But the most unnerving thing of all was that, had the timing been different, Maeve Meara and Nell's cherished friend Birdie might have come face-to-face with a murderer.

Thursday dinner for the knitters would be simple, and Nell knew no one would mind. She was watching Abby for the afternoon—Red had come along, too—but she also needed some time to clear her head, to try to deal with the fact that a murderer was inching his way into their lives in a most frightening way. She needed time to calm the fear that closed her throat and tightened her chest when Ben told her about the danger that Birdie had narrowly escaped.

Ben had tried a distraction before leaving the house earlier. He brought up their wedding anniversary, something they hadn't talked about in days. "Nell, let's just pack a bag and escape to Costa Rica for a couple weeks. Forget about everything else. Just you and me and the deep blue sea."

He lifted one brow in what he hoped was a sexy way.

Beneath it, his eyes were tired, too.

In one movement, Nell was close enough to feel his breath on her cheek. She wrapped her arms around him tightly. *Costa Rica. Beaches, rain forests. Alone with Ben for days and days.*

She sighed, her head rubbing against his chest. "If only . . ."

"If only," he whispered into her hair. "But this, too, shall pass, Nellie. Soon."

They finished the Israeli couscous salad in record time, down to the last piece of feta cheese and lone chickpea on the bottom of the bowl. Soft, flaky rolls were washed down with Birdie's pinot gris, and the meal was applauded.

"It looked way too healthy to be good, but that salad was great," Cass said. She slathered the last roll with butter and began to collect empty plates.

"You outdid yourself, Aunt Nell. When did you have time to make it? My daughter isn't usually so unselfish with people's time," Izzy said. "She definitely doesn't like people cooking when she's there to be cuddled."

"I didn't."

"You didn't what?" Izzy's eyes grew large. Never—not once in all their Thursday nights in the back room—did Nell not cook.

"I didn't make the salad. Abby, Red, and I went over to Gloucester and bought it at that sweet little tea shop on Pleasant Street. We sat there for a while, just the two of us, with Abby captivating everyone who came in. It simply wasn't a day for cooking. It was a day for playing with Abby, for marveling at the magnificent schooners in the Gloucester harbor, for feeling the breeze in our hair as I pushed her stroller, and visiting that little park near the water where Abby shrieked with delight when I bundled her into a baby swing and pushed her back and forth. It was a day for clearing my head and being thankful for all sorts of wonderful things. That's what today was for. Not for cooking."

For a few minutes the room was quiet. Then Birdie reached over and touched Nell's hand. She said softly, "Yes, Nell. It was a day for all of those things. A small babe puts everything in its place."

Nell hadn't realized the enormity of the emotion that had been trapped inside her until Birdie's gentle touch released it. She cleared her throat and brushed the moisture in her eyes away. "It's been a long week, hasn't it?" She managed a smile.

"Long weeks need chocolate," Cass said, moving quickly to the side table. She picked up a box of Masala chocolates and passed the pear-shaped candies around.

Nell nodded a silent thanks to Cass. She could always be counted on to lighten an awkward moment. She had almost forgotten Cass's own emotional baggage—it had all been lost in the shuffle of the past week. She looked at her face, trying to read there how she and Danny were getting along. And how they were both greeting the news that the house on Ridge Road was being passed along to Julia Ainsley, a Sea Harbor visitor who seemed to be overstaying her welcome.

Izzy plopped down on the chair next to her aunt's. She nibbled on a chocolate and took a sip of wine. "Okay, first, let's get the elephant out of the room." She looked at Birdie.

"You want to talk about Maeve's house, about the break-in," Birdie said. "Tommy Porter called it a 'minor' break-in, and maybe you can't even call it a break-in because Maeve never locks her doors."

"*Sergeant* Tommy Porter," Cass said. "He just got promoted. And it sounds like Sergeant Tommy Porter handled things well," Cass said. "We actually heard the whole story from the horse's mouth. Tommy came by here last night."

Izzy picked it up. "Cass and I were here late, just sort of, well, solving life's personal problems without men around. Tommy was picking Janie up and saw our light on the way up to the apartment. He probably also spotted the beer and pizza on the table. He and Janie came in for a while."

"It was a careless break-in," Birdie said. "That's what Tommy said, done by someone who probably didn't even know what they were looking for. Amateurish."

"Did he have any ideas?" Nell asked.

"First he did a masterful job of calming Maeve," Birdie said. "That young man is number one in my book. He will go far."

"But who does he think did it? And what were they after?" Nell asked.

Izzy pulled out the section of the anniversary afghan she had almost completed. The soft red yarn coated her finger. "He wouldn't commit to anything. He wouldn't even say it was connected to the murder. But it must have been."

"Except," Birdie said, "Maeve never locks her door. It could have been someone walking by, looking for cash. For food."

"In the den?" Nell said. Birdie was trying to calm everyone's fears, and especially Nell's worry over Birdie and Maeve's close call. But the very thought of it caused the fear to worm its way back inside her. "Birdie, it could have been awful—you and Maeve, you could have—"

Izzy spoke up. "Aunt Nell—you can't live your life on what could have been. How many times have you said that to me? Birdie is fine. Maeve is fine."

"But there's some creep out there who isn't fine," Cass said. "That's what we need to be thinking about. And we still have some dribbles of pinot gris left to help us think it through."

She walked around and refilled glasses. Cass couldn't sit still for long. Perhaps hours spent on lobster boats did that to her. But tonight she seemed especially on edge.

Nell watched her circle the room, her Irish features—"black Irish" features, according to Mary Halloran—stunning. High cheekbones and a defined chin were the only traits that linked her to her mother, but those who had known Patrick Halloran said she was the image of her father in looks and temperament—thick dark hair, dark eyes, pale olive skin, and a stubbornness mixed with good humor that served her well as co-owner of the lobster business her grandfather and father had built all those years before.

Nell took a drink of wine and pulled out a sweater she was knitting to add to Abby's growing collection. Navy blue was difficult to knit on, but it would look wonderful with the baby's blond curls and would be perfect in the coming months—a warm, cozy cardigan for stroller rides down to Paley's Cove when the winds blew in from the northeast.

"Tommy said they've run into a brick wall with their investigation," Izzy said. She pulled out a loose stitch and redid it, smoothing it in place with a finger until the tension was perfect. "Actually, it was Janie who said it—Tommy tries to be mum about police business—but it wasn't exactly news. I think everyone in town knows that there are no good leads."

"The police have talked to Don Wooten," Nell said. "He and Jeffrey were having some difficulties with their partnership." She told them about the night she'd been caught in the middle of one.

"Don got angry? Geesh," Izzy said. "I don't ever want to go into business with a friend if that's what it does."

"Pete and I argue all the time. It's part of the game. But I'd never murder him so I could make all the decisions." Cass paused, then joked, "Well, at least I'd give him a chance to behave first. Seriously, though, I can't imagine Don doing that. He's been such a success in the businesses he's run, and you don't get to be on top by being a temperamental schmuck. It doesn't make sense."

"Of course, that's how all of us see it," Birdie said. "Don is our friend—we like him and we're crazy about his wife, Rachel—so it's easy to decide that he couldn't have done it. But what if you didn't know him? What if all you knew about him was that he was Jeffrey's partner and he didn't like the way Jeffrey ran the restaurant—and he threatened him to back down or else. That's what the police will look at. The facts."

"Another thing that's not in Don's favor—he wasted no time at all in negating many of Jeffrey's decisions, hiring back people Jeffrey had fired just days before he died. And he did it all before the body was even cold."

"What did he do?" Cass pulled her hair back from her face and fastened it with a rubber band. Dark strands escaped and curled around her flushed cheeks.

Nell told them in detail about the conversation she and Ben had had the day before with some of the Ocean's Edge staff.

"Wow. That's pretty sudden, don't you think?" Cass asked. "I wonder if he's making other changes that quickly, before Jeffrey is in the ground. It almost sounds like he'd thought them through and as soon as he had a chance, he went into action."

None of it sat well, of course—none of them truly believed Don Wooten could be on the wrong side of such a tragic situation. Yet Nell had been wondering the same thing as Cass, and so had Ben. Usually those kinds of business decisions took time and thought, both examined from an HR standpoint and looking at the legal ramifications. Don was a businessman. He would know this. Had he known for a while what he was going to do?

Ben had been especially interested in the vendor accounts the two men had argued about that night. Vendor accounts in a restaurant business were very important, relationships to be nurtured and fostered. What happened there? Nell wondered. She made a mental note to check whether Ben had gotten more information. She knew Ben thought she should talk to Jerry Thompson about the conversation she had overheard. Yet it made her feel like a traitor, and she cringed at the thought of providing any information to the police or anyone else that would draw more suspicion to Don Wooten.

"Who else are the police talking to? And who would have known that Jeffrey was going to be at the house that day?" Birdie asked.

"Jules, of course," Izzy said. "And maybe Don or others working at the Edge that day. He would have taken time from work."

"The police have probably covered that," Birdie said. "But it certainly wouldn't hurt to have lunch over there tomorrow." She looked up, her eyes bright at the prospect of clam chowder, but brighter still at the thought that sometimes, as she often said, the devil was in the details. And often those details escaped the notice of professionals who weren't encouraged to bend the rules.

Nell held up the back of the soft sweater as she watched Birdie's mind work. All the pieces of her sweater for Abby could be knit perfectly, but the trick was in piecing them together smoothly. And that's what Birdie was thinking. The pieces of a murder. Gathering them, laying them out, and removing fear and danger from the town they loved.

"If the person who killed Jeffrey ransacked his house, he was looking for something. Something that was worth killing for," Izzy said. Her logical, orderly thinking had served her well as a lawyer in Boston—and in other ways, too.

"So it was someone who skipped the funeral when he knew the house would be empty?" Nell thought of the waitstaff. They'd all been at the church, or so it seemed.

"Not necessarily," Birdie said. "Maeve stayed until the last person had left the church hall, as everyone knew she would. It was dark by the time Harold and I took her home."

"Then pair up the two things. It had to be someone who knew Maeve was at the church—someone who wasn't at the funeral, or maybe left early—and someone who knew Jeffrey was going to Izzy's old house that day, who knew where it was, who knew about the back way up the hill." Cass listed the items, her knitting needles tapping out each one. She stopped and looked around.

Izzy continued with Cass's thought, with a fact none of them wanted to say out loud. "Someone who knows Maeve doesn't lock her door. And someone who knows what a mess the back of the Ridge Road house was and that they could easily go up through the bushes without anyone seeing them. Someone who . . ."

"Lives in Sea Harbor," Cass finished.

"Or . . ." Birdie said slowly, bringing a reality check to the discussion, "the break-in and Jeffrey's murder behind the Ridge Road house might not be related it all. We need to be very careful that what we are knitting together is tight and even and doesn't fall apart with a slight tug."

The room fell silent, save for the sweet sound of a saxophone cushioning their thoughts.

Minutes later the silence was disrupted by tires on the gravel alleyway between Izzy's shop and the bookstore, followed by the banging of a tailgate and the sound of voices. Izzy and Cass stood up and looked out the window; then Cass walked over and fiddled with the sound system while Izzy stepped outside.

"It's just Danny and Sam," Cass said to the others.

Nell and Birdie looked at each other. Then back to Cass, who was forcing a smile to her sad face. "Did Danny come to pick you up? I could have taken you home," Nell said. The spacious house Cass had inherited recently wasn't on anyone's direct route home, but it was a drive they all loved. It sat beyond Canary Cove, up a winding road in a quiet neighborhood overlooking the water. The house was airy and bright, and Cass had put in new windows in a second-story den so that on a clear day, she said, Danny could see to the end of the ocean while penning his popular mysteries.

"Ride?" Cass shook her head. "No, I'm fine. I . . . ah, I'll drive my truck back when they're through emptying it. I had talked all this over with Izzy earlier and should have said something to both of you. I meant to. But . . . well, it didn't seem to fit into a conversation about murder very easily." She forced a laugh and absently pulled the band from her hair, shaking it loose. She looked from Nell to Birdie. She smiled again. Then frowned. And finally finished her thought.

"Okay, here's what's happening. Danny's moving out. He's going to stay in that little efficiency above his parents' store, at least for a while. It's not such a bad place. He can write there, too, and come over here to drink Izzy's awful coffee. That's it. That's my news."

Chapter 18

*C*ass's words thudded to the floor, ponderous and unpleasant.

Birdie and Nell got up and looked out the side window. Izzy was standing in the alley, talking to Sam. Danny was lifting cardboard boxes out of the truck bed.

"Hey," Cass said, pulling their attention back to her. "Danny didn't die. I didn't, either. It'll all be fine. He'll be fine. I'll be fine."

Fine was Danny and Cass together. That's what fine was.

Birdie managed a smile that said it was Danny's and Cass's lives, not theirs, and that of course they were always here for her, no matter what decisions she made about her life.

Nell said nothing, although questions were forming in her head, along with warnings to herself to give Cass some room. She was a private person in many ways, and even dear friends might need to keep some distance.

Cass frowned. "I've never known you two to be at a loss for words. Come on, what are those faces?"

"It's a surprise, that's all," Nell said. "I suppose Jules Ainsley—not to mention her very recent purchase of Izzy's old house—has something to do with all this. And her friendship with Danny."

Cass chewed on her bottom lip and seemed to be giving Nell's words more attention than they deserved. Finally she said, "I don't know. Jules and Danny are friends, and that's about all I know. He doesn't talk about her, except to say that's all it is, and that he doesn't even know her all that well. She asked him for some help, he gave it, he thinks she's a nice person, he thinks I'm overreacting. That's it. And I get it. Sam and I are friends, Andy Risso and I are friends, Ben and I are friends, I have lots of male friends. So why shouldn't she and Danny be friends?"

"That's a thoughtful question," Birdie said.

Izzy walked in, bringing with her a fresh breeze and strains of music from some distant place. It eased the uncomfortable moment slightly. She tossed Cass the keys to her truck. "All done. He said he'll see you later."

"See?" Cass said. She twisted the key chain around her finger. "This isn't Armageddon. Danny and I are friends. He's maybe the best friend I've ever had—well, except for you guys. And of course there was that goofy kid I hung out with in third grade." She looked around for smiles. Nell managed a weak one and Birdie chuckled.

It was clear Cass and Izzy had talked this through—Izzy was showing no surprise at anything that was being said. Nell was relieved that Cass hadn't kept her feelings all bottled up inside her until her Irish temper finally got the best of her and she made a rash move or decision. Like bolting out of a relationship.

Birdie leaned forward. "There must be a 'but' on the end of that sentence, dear. It's just hanging there, without much meaning."

Cass smiled sadly. "You're right, Birdie. Sure, there's more going on. But it's hard to talk about it. I promise I will, but not tonight, not with all this funeral and suspicion and awful murder stuff going on. But please know this: it has to do with me, not Danny, not really Jules, even—though I could have lived a long, long time without her barging into our lives. Enough said. More than enough, in fact. Birdie, do you have any more pinot?"

There wasn't any more wine. And there didn't seem to be enough air in the back room, either. It had become still and stifling in the last hour.

Nell folded up Abby's sweater and put her knitting back in the basket. It was still early by Thursday-night knitting standards, but no one made a move to return to their balls of yarn and patterns. Although knitting had taken the four friends through deaths and births, sorrow and pure joy, weddings and anniversaries, tonight they needed something else. Their bodies needed to move; minds needed to be refreshed.

Sam walked in through the side door. "The night is young. There's lots of life out there on Harbor Road. And great music, too. Pete and the Fractured Fish have set up shop in the park across from the museum. Ben said he'd walk down and meet us there if anyone wants to mosey over that way."

Of course they did. Music, a big golden moon. And being together.

Izzy went up and kissed him full on the lips.

It took minutes to put things away and turn out the lights. Grabbing sweaters and bags, they moved out the side door, up the short alley, and onto the sidewalk.

It seemed it was what the whole town needed. Laughter. Talk.

And everyone in groups of at least two or three. Safety in numbers.

Across the street, the line outside Scooper's Ice Cream Parlor stretched down Harbor Road toward the Gull and the Ocean's Edge. In the other direction, Gus McClucken stood outside his store, greeting and gossiping. And a half a block farther up, in the tiny patch of green across from the historical museum, Pete Halloran's voice belted out sing-along songs that pleased the gathering crowd.

"And he's not even getting paid for this," Cass said. "Let's make sure that's really Pete."

Willow Adams, Pete's girlfriend, stood on the fringe of the growing crowd and assured them it really was Pete. And Merry on the keyboard, and Andy Risso on the drums. And no one was paying anyone. "Goodwill," she said. "And it's working. Look at the smiles."

The patches of green between the crisscrossing pathways were filled with people sitting on benches or grass, or standing together, mouthing the words and leaning into each other as the music took hold and somehow made things seem better.

"The universal language," Birdie said, her small body swaying as the whole crowd joined Pete and Merry in a robust rendition of "Sweet Caroline," as loud and raucous as if they were standing in Fenway Park during an eighth inning.

Nell looked around for Ben, and spotted him just as he stopped to talk to someone hidden from her view by a lamppost. Ben looked over and saw her. He waved for her to join him.

She circled the back of the crowd to where Ben was standing, talking with Jerry Thompson.

Nell gave Jerry a hug. "You need some sleep," she said. In her opinion, he also needed someone special in his life. Someone with whom to share the burdens of his job—and the good things in life, too. Tonight he seemed especially alone.

"Sleep?" Jerry said with a laugh. "What's that?"

Ben wrapped an arm around Nell's shoulders. The night air was chilly and his arms brought immediate warmth. She leaned into his side. "This is tough, isn't it, Jerry? Do you have any leads?"

"Oh, sure. Lots of them. But they're about as thin as Harry's angel-hair pasta. But we'll find the person who did this. There's not a doubt in my mind."

"It must be difficult probing into Jeffrey's life—someone we all liked."

"Well, not everybody liked him. And that's coming out in spades. Lots of disgruntled employees at the Edge."

And owners, too, Nell thought. But she kept the thought where it belonged. In her head. She knew nothing more than what she had overheard—a conversation that probably had layers to it that she didn't understand.

"But mad enough to kill him?" Ben asked.

"I guess that remains to be seen."

"And the break-in at Maeve's house?" Nell asked, knowing full well that Jerry wouldn't offer up any information. But the break-in had already been the subject of Mary Pisano's morning "About Town" column, in which she took full liberty in chastising anyone who would dare trespass in a grieving widow's home—her *private, personal* space, as Mary put it. It was a despicable act.

Mary hadn't connected the break-in to the murder of the man who had once lived in the house. The police hadn't done that, and Mary showed great restraint in not coming to her own conclusions, as she so often did. Nell thought that Mary probably had another reason for not connecting the dots. She suspected that she—along with all the rest of the town—couldn't bear the thought that a murderer was freely walking down their streets and could have gone into Maeve Meara's home in broad daylight. Or could be here, tonight, on Harbor Road, listening to Pete and Merry singing.

Nell shivered.

"Cold?" Ben asked, tightening his hug.

"I need to move along," Jerry was saying beside her. "I was taking a break and heard the music. It's a good thing Pete's band is doing here. People are smiling, even me." He checked his watch. "Now, back to things that aren't quite so pleasant."

As if summoning him, his cell phone rang. He shrugged. "No rest for the wicked." He took a step away to answer it. The lines in his forehead deepened as he listened. Although the words were muffled, Nell could hear the strain in his voice, the terse words, the listening with all his senses.

He silenced his phone and stood still for a moment, staring down into the shadows of the lamplight, his jaw set. Then he turned abruptly, and with an unreadable wave to Ben and Nell, he hurried across the park.

In the next minute, he was swallowed up by the night.

Chapter 19

"Jerry Thompson didn't show up today," Sam announced the next morning, walking into the Endicotts' kitchen with Abby in his arms. "We were going to go for an early sail. Maybe he slept in."

"He could use sleep," Ben said. "But I don't think that's what kept him away. He got a call last night that sounded important and clearly upset him."

"A break in the case?" Sam asked.

Nell brightened at the sight of the baby, and immediately took her from Sam. "That would be our hope," she said. "But his expression didn't exactly say that."

"Whatever it was, it was important and worth paying attention to. He took off in a hurry, hardly said good-bye, and that's not like Jerry. I checked the morning paper and there wasn't anything about the case, almost as if it were being swept under a rug."

"Or was simply a terrible nightmare," Nell said.

The ringing of a cell phone caused all three people in the room to rummage for phones.

Nell handed Abby back to her father and answered. Mary Pisano was upset. She was looking for Jules. "I don't think she slept here last night," Mary said.

Nell cringed. It was Danny's first night alone in his new place. She hoped it had been exactly that. *Alone.*

Aloud she told Mary that she hadn't seen Jules, but she'd ask Sam and Ben if they had.

"She has the keys to the house," Sam said. "Stella handed them over yesterday. It's all final. 'Cash to keys,' the Realtors call it. She's probably checking things out over there. As anxious as she was to get into the place before she bought it, I can't imagine she'd be holding back now. I told her we'd help her move anything that needed moving, but she doesn't have much."

Nell repeated the message to Mary, who seemed slightly relieved. But her voice still held concern.

"I'm sure she's fine, Mary," Nell said. "She's a grown woman." But as soon as she spoke, Nell realized how empty her words were. She was a grown woman, true, a grown woman wandering around a town with a murderer on the loose.

Mary didn't buy Nell's assurance, anyway. But her concern went in a different direction. "Nell . . ." she began, pausing. And then she proceeded to share the reason for her concern.

Nell listened carefully, then dropped her phone into her bag and turned to Sam and Ben. "It seems Mary isn't the only one looking for Jules. Tommy Porter came by the bed-and-breakfast looking for her, too."

"Oh." Ben poured Sam a cup of coffee, then refreshed his own. "Did he say why?"

"No . . ."

"No, but . . . ?"

"Mary said he was in full uniform, shiny shoes, pressed pants . . . and he refused one of Mary's cinnamon rolls. He meant business."

It was another hour before Sam left. They took Abby out on the deck and drank coffee while they explored possible reasons for Tommy's visit to Ravenswood by the Sea. And in the end, they convinced themselves that it was probably routine—Tommy had become a top-notch member of the police force who didn't let details slide away from him.

He probably had a few more questions for Jules about what she'd seen that awful day.

"My guess is that Jules is at the house," Sam said. "She probably slept there, just to make sure no one snuck in somehow and bought it away from her. I've never seen anyone so determined to own something. I need to run anyway—I'll drive by on my way home and have her call you. Or Mary. Or someone. Probably not Tommy Porter. I'm sure she's had her fill of questions."

Sam put down his coffee mug and packed up baby Abby. "My Abby and I are doing a photo shoot, aren't we, darlin' daughter?" His face lit up as he kissed her on the top of her head and then on the tip of her nose. Izzy's nose. Then he held her at arm's length and soaked in every inch of her with his eyes. "She's really something, isn't she?" he said, his words catching in his throat. Then he brought her to his chest and, with her tiny hand in his, waved to them good-bye.

Jules's disappearance didn't take long to solve.

First, Sam texted that her car was at the Ridge Road house, parked in the drive, but she wasn't around. Garrett Barros was standing out front and said she'd gone for a run. All's well. Mary Pisano needn't worry that she was lost at sea.

Jane Brewster called next to ask whether she could bring coleslaw to Friday-night dinner. And then, in passing, she mentioned that she'd just had a nice talk with Jules Ainsley, who was enormously interested in the gallery and some of the artists she and Ham represented. "She's an interesting person," Jane said. "And knows a lot about art."

"So she came to the gallery?" Nell asked.

"Actually she was meeting Rebecca Early for coffee on the deck at the Artist's Palate. I ran over for a quick bite and they invited me to join them. She came back to the gallery with me afterward to see a new exhibit I had told her about. She mentioned you had invited her to dinner tonight and she was looking forward to it. Then she left to jog back home."

"Home?"

"Izzy's house—well, *her* house, I guess. She's moving what little she has into the new place. I think she wants to stop paying for that expensive room at the B and B as soon as possible."

"I see," Nell said, processing the information as Jane talked.

"So, about the coleslaw? It's a new recipe I want to try."

"Absolutely. That's great, Jane. As far as I know right now, your coleslaw and Ben's martinis may be all we have. By the way, how does Jules know Rebecca?"

"Hmm. I think it was when she first got to town and she was exploring Canary Cove. She fell in love with Rebecca's lampwork beads and they've become good friends. But then"—Jane laughed—"is there anyone in Sea Harbor Jules Ainsley hasn't met?"

A point well taken. Maybe they weren't all friends exactly, but Jules certainly knew a good portion of Sea Harbor residents.

Nell hung up and grabbed her bag. A late start to a busy day. She called Mary Pisano on her way out the door to the market. "Jules is safe," was the message she left on her phone. "She's at her new house. Safe and sound." Or as safe as any of them were these days.

Cass came over early for Friday night on the deck. She had called an hour before, offering to pick up cheese and crackers on the way, and anything else Nell needed.

Nell was in the kitchen slicing zucchini and orange peppers for the grill when Cass walked in. Ben was still at the boat slip doing some minor repairs on the *Dream Weaver*, but Sam and Izzy were on their way, she told Cass.

"People seem a bit at loose ends these days, don't they." Nell took the paper bag from Cass. "Did you take the day off?"

"No, I fiddled around in the office, paying bills, ordering new buoys, hired a new guy. But my head wasn't really there, so I left and went home. But that was a mistake. The house seemed way too big. Too empty. So here I am." She opened the refrigerator and pulled out a diet soda.

"It was probably an empty night for Danny, too," Nell said. "Change is hard."

Cass focused on her soda, taking a long drink. She found a tray in the cupboard and began arranging rounds of Brie and Camembert.

"It wasn't working, Nell," she finally said.

The sound of footsteps put a halt to the conversation and Cass looked visibly relieved.

Birdie's words preceded her into the family room, as they often did. "Maybe it's just me," she said, "but the awful pallor over this town is slowing down thinking, walking, talking, living. Pretty soon we'll be at a dead standstill. Just a bunch of people looking sideways at their neighbors, wondering if the sacker at the Market Basket is a bad person, or the waiter at the Ocean's Edge, or the baker or grocer."

She walked across the family room and put a freshly baked apple pie on the island. "Stan Hanson was in the bakery when Harold and I stopped in for the pie. He was picking up five dozen cookies that Karen had ordered for yet another campaign event. He looked very preoccupied but managed a weak hello. It can't be easy being mayor of a town where a murderer lurks."

Nell agreed. "It's a double burden for him—trying to keep the town safe, help people with their fears, while grieving for someone he's known for a long time."

"His emotion at the funeral was a surprise, now, wasn't it?" Birdie said. "He's a dear man but usually holds his feelings in check."

"I think his wife was embarrassed," Cass said. "She holds everything together—including Stan."

Ben came through the back door, struggling with a case of beer. He set it down beside the refrigerator. "I heard Stan's name. I ran by the library on my way home and Karen was there, standing in the foyer, fuming. Stan was supposed to speak to a group of seniors but apparently didn't show up. It's been a miserable week for him. Jerry Thompson mentioned to me that Beatrice Scaglia is spreading the word that Stan should drop out of the race and take a long vacation. He's been a great mayor, she said, but his time is over."

Nell shook her head, putting the beer in the refrigerator. "Beatrice better watch what she says. Her words could turn on her. People like Stan."

"On the other hand, he does deserve a vacation," Birdie said. "Maybe Beatrice has a point—a mayor needs to handle business even if it is personal. I can't imagine wanting to keep that job a second longer than he has to."

"I'm not sure Karen would let him quit," Ben said. "And he is a damn good mayor, in my opinion. Karen wouldn't take his resignation sitting down." He pulled out his phone to check his messages. "I forgot to turn it on when I got out of the library."

Jane and Ham Brewster walked in with a bouquet of gerber daisies, and a hand-painted bowl, filled to the brim with Jane's new recipe for coleslaw.

"The secret is in the peanut butter," she said. "Who would have thought?" She busied herself in the kitchen while Ham went through cupboards looking for a vase.

Nell suggested Cass put some music on since Izzy, their usual DJ, hadn't arrived yet. She and Birdie got out iced tea glasses and Ham took over uncorking wine until Ben could replace him.

Nell looked over at her husband. He had moved to the den doorway and was scrolling through the messages slowly.

"Ben?" Nell saw the lines in his forehead deepen, his face still. He scrolled back through the messages, then began all over again. "Ben, what is it? Is it from Jules? She said she'd be here tonight—"

Just as he lifted his head to answer, the doorbell rang, a sudden, invasive sound. Nell started toward the door, but Ben held up his hand, stopping her, as if he knew who it would be, and that it would be for him.

He strode through the family room to the front door.

Tommy Porter stood on the steps, his face somber.

"I just got your message, Tommy. Jerry's, too. So sorry I didn't respond—my phone was off." He clenched his jaw, anger at himself tightening his face.

"No, no, it's okay. I hope it's okay that I just came over."

"Of course it is."

Nell came up behind him. "Tommy? What is it? Is Janie all right?"

"It's Jules Ainsley, ma'am," he said, his manner professional but his eyes filled with apology. "I thought she might need company. And you folks are friends she mentioned."

Nell's confusion was softened by Ben's assurance that Tommy had done the right thing. He seemed to somehow understand what that was and why he was standing on their doorstep. It must have been the barrage of texts he'd just looked at.

"Is she in the car?" Ben asked.

Tommy nodded and Nell looked out to the curb, where the policeman's patrol car was parked. A woman sat in the backseat, her eyes straight ahead.

"She's a tough lady," Tommy said. "But she's scared. And she didn't have any way to get back home or here or anywhere."

"Where is her car?"

Tommy sighed. "She'll explain. Chief Thompson said she needs to talk to a lawyer. He gave her your phone number, said you'd know someone."

"I got that text," he said, and headed out to the car. "She needs to come inside."

"Tommy, what's going on?" Nell asked. She could feel bodies behind her, keeping a distance but straining to hear what was going on.

"I'm really sorry, Nell. We're pulling you right into the middle of this. Izzy and Sam, too, it being their house and all. I shouldn't get involved like this, I suppose, but Janie would shoot me if I just dropped Jules off at an empty house, her not being from here and all. And Janie likes her. 'Innocent until proven guilty,' she keeps saying to me, and it's the truth. But it doesn't look good. That's why the chief gave her Ben's cell number. He says even though Ben's not practicing law, he gives the best advice on Cape Ann—and he thinks about the people getting the advice while he's doing it."

Ben walked up with Jules beside him, pale as a ghost, but holding herself in check. She wore slim jeans and a sweater, her hair loose and curling around her shoulders. She looked at Tommy and forced a smile, holding out her hand. "Thanks, Tom. It's your job—I know that."

Tommy shook her hand, then walked as quickly as appropriate back to his car without appearing to run from the scene. His shoulders were slightly slumped and his tires screeched as he made a U-turn and headed back to the station.

It was the first time Nell had ever seen Sergeant Tommy Porter look anything but proud of his profession.

Sam and Izzy drove into the driveway just as Ben was ushering people inside. Danny Brandley sat in the back next to Abby in her car seat. They got out and walked up to the door, puzzled expressions on their faces, but one look at Ben held their questions in check.

He held the door open for everyone to come inside.

Ben eased the initial awkwardness by suggesting Sam open a couple of bottles of the wine. The martinis could wait. "And you and I can talk in here if you'd like," he said to Jules, motioning toward the den. His voice was kind.

Jules forked her fingers through her hair, pushing it back over her ear. She nodded. "But could we . . . could I talk to everyone first?" She looked around at the people standing in the family room, trying to be welcoming and nonchalant, while all the while wondering what their Friday night was turning into.

"Of course," Ben said.

"You are . . . all of you . . . kind, good people," Jules began. "And I can't just descend on you like this again, not without an explanation."

"We invited you," Nell said. "Maybe not this way, but you know you are welcome here, Jules."

"Thank you. Your kindness is kind of overwhelming. But you deserve an explanation, whether you think you do or not. Other people, well, they will think what they want to think no matter what, and there isn't anything I can do about it.

"But you—" She looked around again, directly into each person's face, begging them with her eyes to listen. "I care what you think. And I need you to know the truth. I need you to believe me. No matter what the police think, no matter what they found, no matter what they say or anyone else says, I need you to know.

"I came here to Sea Harbor to find myself, my life. Not to take someone's away. Please believe me. I did not kill Jeffrey Meara."

Chapter 20

The room was silent, save for Cass's iPod music soothing the mood with the throaty sounds of Norah Jones singing about needing a friend. "A fortuitous choice, my dear," Birdie whispered to Cass.

"All right, then," Nell said, breaking the silence. "First things first. Please let's all sit down and be comfortable." She touched Jules lightly on the shoulder and pointed to one of the sofas near the fireplace. It was a cozy area, with a wooden coffee table anchoring it and light sisal rugs covering the polished cherry floor. Slipcovered chairs and sofas in greens and blues and golden tones reflected the colors of nature outside the wall of windows. It was a spot that had harbored more than a few traumas—and many triumphs as well.

Ben had opened the French doors to bring in a breeze, and Sam was already setting out wineglasses, filling each one with cabernet. Birdie placed the cheese board on the coffee table and the group gathered around, with a snoozing Abby adding a comforting note to the tense scene.

Jules took a sip of the wine, then plunged in.

"The police searched my car today."

"Why would they do that?" Danny sat opposite Cass and adjacent to Jules. He leaned forward, his elbows on his knees, listening intently.

Jules looked at him and smiled slightly, as if grateful to have a question asked, helping her story to come out. Or perhaps grateful for Danny's presence?

"At first they wouldn't tell me, only that they had a warrant. Then Tommy Porter showed up and he explained that someone called the police station and said they might find something in my car that would be important to Jeffrey Meara's murder. They're following all the leads they get, so of course they would follow this one. They looked for me, equipped with a warrant. They had trouble finding me at first, which probably made them even more suspicious, thinking maybe I was hiding or had left town." She looked down at her up-turned palm, tracing her lifelines with the tip of one finger, crossing and turning and twisting across her hand.

"You were hiding in plain sight, then, for heaven's sake," Jane Brewster said, a motherly tone coating her words. "You were having lunch with me—which I thoroughly enjoyed."

Jules looked at Jane's kind face. "Thank you. You don't know me very well, none of you. And yet you say things like that. Such very nice things." For the first time her voice broke, a slight crack that she quickly tried to hide by clearing her throat. She took another drink of wine.

"What did they find in the car?" Ben asked. In all the messages he'd received that afternoon, none of them went any further than to say "incriminating evidence" had been found.

"A garden glove."

Ben nodded. One of the few pieces of evidence uncovered so far were some threads, presumably from a garden glove, that had stuck to the murder weapon, fibers glued to the knife with blood. The garden glove itself hadn't been found. "It matched the threads on the knife?"

"I don't know. They're testing it to be sure."

"Where did they find it?"

"They wouldn't tell me. Just somewhere in my car."

"Who called it in?" Danny asked.

Ben answered the question. Jerry Thompson had told him how they knew to look in the car. And he also made it clear to Ben that, although he didn't like this kind of lead, he had to follow it. "It was an anonymous caller," he said.

For a moment there was relieved silence. Anonymous callers were cowards, after all. Why hide your identity if you're doing something good, like helping the police solve a murder case?

And then the realization that there were plenty of reasons someone might not want to identify himself intruded on their short-lived relief. Especially in a small town, especially with a killer on the loose. Fear of retaliation, fear of a mistake. Ugly, ubiquitous fear.

"When?" Ham broke the silence.

"Last night. In fact, Jerry must have found out about the call when talking to Nell and me at the concert."

Jules agreed. "I had moved my things from the bed-and-breakfast last night—my car was full. I emptied some of it before I went for an evening run. So someone could have put the glove there anytime last night—while I was running or sleeping."

She said the words definitively—*put the glove there.* As mysterious as Jules had been about why she had come to Sea Harbor, about *who* she was, there was no mystery about how she thought this all happened. Someone, for whatever reason, had planted incriminating evidence in her car. Someone wanted Jules Ainsley to be arrested for murder.

If Jules's story was the truth.

She was forthright in answering the questions that followed, relieved that there were people who cared enough to get to the truth. She had absolutely no idea why anyone would think she killed Jeffrey Meara, she said. She had met him at the Ocean's Edge a couple of times and that was the sum total of their relationship.

Until she got his phone call.

"You have no idea why he wanted to talk to you?" Izzy asked. "The police are going to need to come up with some kind of a motive, and they may zero in on that."

Jules shook her head. "It was strange. A part of me thought maybe he was interested in buying the house and wanted to talk me out of it. An even crazier thought was that he knew something about the house that he wanted to warn me about. But, Izzy, you lived there—and I heard you lived there, too, Cass. Clearly one of you would have known if there was some kind of ghost in residence?" She pushed a weak smile into place.

Cass hesitated, then managed a smile back—or half of one, at least. "The only ghost I remember was definitely not the see-through kind. It was that creepy Garrett Barros, who spent an inordinate amount of time outside with binoculars around his neck. Bird-watching, he claimed. He was spooky."

"Garrett. I'd forgotten all about him," Nell said. "He works at the Ocean's Edge. I wonder if the police have talked to him. Maybe he saw something—"

"Or *did* something. He knew Jeffrey, he lived next door to where the man was killed. I wonder what his relationship with him was," Cass said. "Some of the staff liked Jeffrey, but he was pretty rough on some others."

Without a word to Nell, Ben had slipped away and ordered several of Garozzo's biggest pizzas, one with five different cheeses, alive with green and red roasted vegetables, and another with Italian sausage, cheese, and Harry's special sauce. Food for thinking.

Then he stood at the side bar, listening carefully to the conversation while he mixed a batch of his famous martinis.

"Did the police take your car?" Sam asked.

Jules nodded. "They were at the house when I got home this afternoon. Fortunately, I'd unloaded most of my things in the morning before jogging over to Canary Cove for lunch. So my paintings and photos and clothes are at least safe—I think all that was left in the car were some sheets and pillows. Tommy Porter showed me the warrant, asked me to wait inside, and they did a search right there. Apparently the caller hadn't told them where the glove would be, so it took a while. I didn't see anything when I was packing or unpacking. But then, I wasn't looking for a garden glove."

And the anonymous person probably knew that, Nell thought. Then she realized with a start that she was believing everything Jules was telling them. She looked around at the others. The questions they were asking indicated they believed her, too, but whether it was out of politeness or something else, she couldn't tell.

"Was your car locked, dear?" Birdie asked.

Jules looked up at the question. Then she looked surprised, but more at herself than at the question. "I used to lock my car. I even had one of those awful-looking steering wheel locks for a while. My mother insisted. But somehow, Sea Harbor doesn't seem to be the kind of place where people do that. I don't think I've seen anyone lock a car since I've been here. Besides, my car is old. I can't imagine anyone wanting it. And if they do, maybe they need it more than I do."

"How long was your car parked at the house?" Sam asked.

"Since yesterday. I packed my stuff up at the bed-and-breakfast, then drove over to the house and unpacked some of the things until it got dark. I spent the night over there in a sleeping bag. The car was pulled up in the driveway the whole time, close to the back."

"So someone could have done it anytime during the night," Ham said.

"Or during the evening, I guess. I ran along the beach for about an hour before I went to bed. The moon was full and that always relaxes me."

Nell looked over at Cass. She was listening carefully, but Nell wasn't sure whether she was making the same connection she was: Danny *had* been alone last night. Nell guessed right.

"Chief Thompson is a decent guy." Jules looked over at Ben. "He certainly thinks a lot of you, enough to share your phone number with a person that some of the guys over there probably think is a murderer."

"Yes, he is a decent, fair man." He looked down at his phone, seeing a message ping into view. He frowned, read the note, then looked up.

"The chief isn't going to release this new information, Jules. He'd like it if we would be discreet as well."

Relief washed over her face. "He is a good man," she whispered.

"And he didn't arrest you," Izzy said. "So the evidence is circumstantial right now."

"No, he didn't. Not yet . . ." Jules's voice dropped off.

The determined look, the smiles that usually flashed so quickly and took over her whole face were gone. She looked smaller. Vulnerable.

Cass was watching Jules closely, listening to everything she said. Her face registered little, but Nell knew that Cass Halloran was fair and smart and flexible. And she wondered how those traits were faring in her friend right now.

Danny was listening, too, with glances at Cass now and then when he didn't think she would notice. He was taking in Jules's story with his author's sensitivity and curiosity. His face reflected empathy as one would show for a friend—but not necessarily for a lover. At least that was the way Nell interpreted it.

Danny knew Jules a little better than the rest of them did. Nell could see in his eyes that he believed her. And he seemed upset with the injustice being heaped on her. He'd do what he could to right it, because that's who Danny was. But what she didn't see was a man attracted to a woman, at least not in a sexual way.

Ben and Sam began passing out martinis to any takers, and Ben announced to everyone that the best pizza on the North Shore would be delivered soon.

"Perfect," Jane said. "Pizza and my peanut coleslaw—I can't imagine a better combination." Throaty laughter followed her words. "I think this will be a Friday-night dinner to remember."

Everyone agreed it would be perfect, and would be topped off memorably with Birdie's apple pie. Nell urged them all to take advantage of the late September breeze and move outside—it was Friday night on the deck, after all—and though the grill was idle, the martinis and music were not.

Ben and Jules went into the den and Izzy switched the iPod to more body-moving music. She waltzed out onto the deck, urged along by Justin Timberlake beating out the rhythm to "Take Back the Night."

"Yes," she answered the singer. "We will do exactly that."

Sam gave his wife a hug, gyrating around her, with Abby squealing from the baby pack he'd strapped to his back.

Music, friends. They'd do it, even if not in the way the singer meant. They would take back the night, the day, and the whole town, too.

Nell watched from the sidelines as Danny took over for Ben, filling drink orders, then giving in to Birdie's charms as she showed him what a longtime tap dancer could do with a good partner and some jazzy music.

Nell laughed and then noticed Pete and Willow rocking their bodies up the back deck stairs. A nice surprise on an evening that was slowly filling up with the unexpected. Willow scurried across the porch to wrap Nell in a hug. Nell loved the waiflike artist who had wormed her way into their hearts the summer she lived in Ben and Nell's backyard guesthouse—she'd been a part of the family ever since.

Nell looked down at the guesthouse now. The high bed that Izzy used to love as a child was still there, made up with fresh linens. The little step stool in place beside it. The place was aired out and ready to be used. The bathroom was always stocked for unexpected guests—toiletries, thick towels, and nightclothes. Of course—it was a perfect place for Jules to spend the night, she thought suddenly. It had been a harrowing day, and being alone in a house with the knowledge that there were people in this town, perhaps even neighbors on Ridge Road, who thought of Jules as a murderer might not be conducive to—or safe for—sleeping.

She'd invite her to stay the night, or until she could get her own house in order. Get her *life* in order. Something, Nell realized, that would take more than a night to accomplish.

Ben and Jules emerged a short time later, just in time to take the pizzas from the arms of Harry Garozzo's son, Harry Junior.

The enticing aroma of warm homemade crust, fresh tomatoes, garlic and basil, and grilled vegetables wound all the way out to the deck and pulled Nell inside, where she met Ben, Jules, and the pizzas in the kitchen. Nell repeated her thought out loud, that Jules spend the night in the most comfortable bed on Cape Ann. Ben seconded it.

Jules paused for a moment, her face registering first surprise, then gratitude. "It would beat that old sleeping bag—at least until I can get my car and my sheets back. You're very kind—both of you. Thank you."

Jules Ainsley didn't accept help easily, Nell suspected. She was beginning to trust them. The next piece that hadn't yet fallen into place completely was a huge one: could they trust her?

She looked over at Ben, who was explaining to Jules the secret recipes for Italian cooking that Harry Garozzo had extracted from his grandmother on her deathbed. "For pizza dough, you must always, always, *always* use doppio-zero flour," Ben quoted in his best Italian accent.

Nell began pulling plates and napkins from the cupboard. Jules looked better after talking with Ben, calmer. There were traces of tears on her cheeks, but that was a good thing. Too much bottled-up emotion wouldn't help anything, especially the hurdles that lay in her path in the days ahead. And Ben was very good at handling a tear or two. Patiently. Kindly. And with enormous respect.

Jane appeared beside her, her long skirt creating a breeze. "Coleslaw time," she announced, and took the heavy bowl from the refrigerator. Nell turned the oven on to low.

Time to warm up the apple pie.

In minutes the outdoor table was lined with pizza and plates and bowls for Jane's juicy slaw. Nell lit a row of hurricane lamps while Birdie uncorked more wine. It was going to be buffet, Nell declared. Although most Friday nights were spent sitting around the old deck table, shoulders touching, voices overlapping and tangling and layered on top of one another, tonight called for moving around. There were too many emotions hovering in the night air and she didn't want anyone to feel trapped. A comfortable chaise or overstuffed wicker chair with room to spread out would be fine.

The pizza was as good as Harry claimed, and Jane's coleslaw a perfect match, much to nearly everyone's surprise. The jalapeno and fresh ginger added the perfect tang to the dressing; the radishes, carrots, and scallions gave a nice crunch to the slivered cabbage. "A success," Birdie declared, and Jane said, "Of course."

Nell was in and out, slicing additional pizzas, refilling wineglasses.

She paused at the doorway, taking in the activity around the deck.

Willow and Pete seemed to have adopted Jules, pulling her into a conversation with Ham Brewster about his and Jane's early years as Berkeley hippies.

Jules was quieter than Nell had seen her be in the preceding days, the days before her life had changed. The days when she happily met strangers on Harbor Road, charmed shopkeepers with her smile, jogged through town in the early morning, unaware of the male admirers watching her from behind the windows of the deli or coffee shop. When she seemed to have her life under control.

Nell wondered what she was thinking now that she'd lost at least some of that control. Sometimes even people proclaiming their innocence were sent to prison.

How would Jules weather this storm?

On another side of the deck, close to where Nell stood, Ben and Izzy were doing the unthinkable: asking Danny how his next book was coming along. Danny's good nature took the question all writers dread hearing in stride, and then he told Ben he owed him another martini. "Immediately would be good," he added.

There was laughter and serious talk. And the quiet swaying of shoulders on the deck when Aretha Franklin's unstoppable voice took over their senses with her "Soul Serenade."

From everything Nell could see, Jules had been accepted into their gathering. Even Cass's chill had warmed a degree, although she kept her distance from the newcomer, and from Danny, too.

By the time Birdie brought out the warm pie, the night sky was studded with stars and the mood was as mellow as the breeze.

Nell looked around at the candlelit faces of the people she trusted and loved and walked over to Ben's side. He stood at the portable bar, handing out brandies or coffee, water or small glasses of juice.

"A nice evening," she murmured.

"An unexpected one," he said, watching her watch the others.

"The lull before the storm?" Nell's eyes went from group to group, reading their faces, their eyes, trying to see into their souls. "Do they believe Jules?"

His arm went up around her shoulders and she could feel Ben's heart, the gentle beat, the deep breathing.

Jules was slightly removed from the others, sitting off to the side, her face unreadable.

"Do you?" Ben asked.

Around the deck a few people got up from their chairs and began collecting pie plates and coffee mugs.

"Yes."

"Yes," Ben agreed, reading her face. "Yes, but . . ."

"That's the question, isn't it? Yes, but if she didn't do it, who did?"

Chapter 21

*N*ell carried a carafe of coffee and a plate of cinnamon toast across the backyard to the guesthouse. The cottage faced what the locals called the Endicott Woods—a thick acre of pine, birch, and maple trees that separated the back of the property from the beach road. A path, worn smooth by generations of children and neighbors taking a shortcut to the beach, wound through the woods.

Although Jules had mentioned that she was usually up with the birds, it was only the sound of birds that greeted Nell as she walked around to the front of the cottage. The front window was open a crack with the curtains pulled back, and she looked in. On the small table beneath the window, a white card was propped up against a vase of flowers on the dining table.

Nell knocked, then opened the door. Inside, all was bright and airy, skylights painting rectangles of light on the old pine floor. A white slipcovered chair near the corner windows held an open book, and the light beside the high four-poster bed was still on, signs of life. The guesthouse was a cozy, welcoming haven, a quiet spot away from the noisy Endicott clan, who had gathered there for decades each summer. And it continued to be exactly that. Nell suspected it had been the perfect place for Jules to be last night.

Jules's note was gracious, written on the thick stationery Nell left in the desk for guests to use. Tiny embossed shells decorated the corner. She'd gone for a very early run with a friend—her therapy, she wrote in parentheses. But she would be back to properly thank them for their generous hospitality and the best night's sleep she had had in many days.

It was signed *Affectionately, Jules.*

It wasn't until she met up with Izzy, Birdie, and Cass on Merry Jackson's deck later that morning that Nell wondered who Jules was meeting. She was happy that friends had already become a part of Jules's days in Sea Harbor. It was what the town was all about and something Jules could certainly use right now.

"How is she?" Izzy asked as she made room for Nell on the bench beside her. Birdie echoed concern and even Cass threw out a caring comment. She understood probably better than any of them what Jules was going through.

Nell repeated Jules's message and said they'd talked little after everyone left the night before. Jules was exhausted. They were in a wait-and-see mode, according to Ben, but he would be getting in touch with attorney friends who might be able to represent Jules if she was formally charged.

"Murder, geesh," Cass said. "This is a mess. It's gone on too long."

Nell agreed. She looked around the deck to see who might be sitting nearby. They often met at Merry's place on Saturday mornings when the weather was nice. Usually the deck was nearly empty at this time of day, one thing they liked about it. At noon it would be filled with people craving Merry's burgers and at night it rocked, with area bands performing and Merry's wall of beer bottles meeting everyone's taste.

But in the morning hours, the owner didn't mind if people just came and sat, watching the fog burn off the harbor. Sit, gossip, work on laptops, knit. Merry was fine with any agenda, even those that didn't include coffee and her homemade granola. Today Izzy and Cass had claimed a table beneath one of the trees that grew up through carved-out holes in the old wooden deck.

But it was always good practice to check out the other tables, a practice that often dictated the flow of the conversation—what to say or not to say, when to keep some things to a whisper. Nell spotted Danny Brandley, and realized with a start that she was happy he was there, and not the friend who was running with Jules. He was sitting at his usual table, tucked away in a corner on the ocean side, right beside the back stairs that led down to an uneven dock that the artists claimed as their own. The coffee break dock, Ham Brewster called it.

Danny was staring at his laptop screen, a large mug of coffee next to it. His writer's expression was intense behind his glasses. She waved at him, but suspected he wasn't aware of other living people as he hammered out another chapter or played with a plot.

Several artists waved at them as they gulped down coffee and picked up Merry's granola-to-go, then hurried back to their galleries to prepare for serious Saturday business. Merry appeared, one blond braid swinging between her narrow shoulder blades. Four coffee mugs hung from the fingers of one hand, and in the other the spirited owner carried a carafe of hot coffee. "Here you go, friends. I'll be back for gossip later. Have to take a new batch of granola from the oven." She waved and was off across the deck before they had a chance to say hello.

Izzy took the carafe and filled their mugs with coffee, then pulled out a skein of orange yarn and the beginnings of a pumpkin hat she was making for Abby. She looked at Birdie. "What do you think of Jules?" she asked. The sudden question startled them all to attention.

"That's a layered question," Birdie said carefully. "Are you asking me if I believe her when she says she didn't kill Jeffrey Meara and that someone planted that garden glove in her car?" She reached down and took a half-finished pair of socks from her bag. Her purse project, she called it—soft and completely portable. These were for her grand-daughter Gabby, stripes of orange and green and pink in soft sock yarn.

"I guess that's one of the layers." Izzy looked around at the others. "It's the one question that floated around in the air last night. I think each of us was trying to read one another's mind. Did we buy her story? And if so, why? That glove was probably worn by the murderer. That's serious stuff."

"I believe her," Birdie said. She looked at Izzy. "I believe that's layer number two."

Izzy nodded. "I believe her, too. I'm not sure why. But I do."

Cass thrummed her fingers on the table. She looked across the deck at Danny, then back again.

Nell watched her thoughtful face. Cass was honest through and through, a trait that sometimes caused her great grief in a business where poachers were plentiful and lobster traps pilfered, where lines might be cut one day and the truth clouded over easily.

"Yeah," Cass said finally. "I don't think she did it. She might be guilty of other things, but not murdering Jeffrey Meara. I'm not sure why I believe her, either, but there it is, for what it's worth."

"If we knew more about her, we might not only believe her but be more sympathetic," Nell said. "And if we're going to help her out of this mess, maybe that's the first thing we need to do."

Cass cleared her throat to get attention and Nell looked up.

Jules Ainsley and Rebecca Early were walking up the steps to the deck, both in running gear and hair held back with wide headbands. Together, they were striking—the flyaway, dark-haired Jules, oblivious to her looks, and Rebecca Early, her platinum hair smooth as glass and nearly blinding in the morning sunlight. She looked around and spotted the table littered with yarn, nudged Jules and pointed, and together they headed toward the table.

The blown-glass artist had come to Sea Harbor several years before and had barely set up Lampworks Gallery when she began winning awards for her amazing pieces. It was Nell's favorite place to shop for birthday and holiday gifts, and over the years she had become fond of the platinum-haired woman, too, even though her temperament sometimes put her at odds with others working in Canary Cove. She was simply opinionated, Ben said. And certainly nice to look at.

Today, in running shorts and a bright pink Lululemon Bitty Bracer, Rebecca was turning heads. And, unlike the woman beside her wiping away the perspiration from her forehead, she was enjoying the attention.

"It's time for Jules to try Merry's homemade granola," Rebecca announced. "She needs to eat better." Her words came out in starts and stops as she caught her breath. She looked at Jules. "Okay, I'm off to shower and open the gallery. The granola is on its way—you need the protein right now." She paused, then said softly, "You'll call me if you need anything?"

Nell heard the concern in her voice and watched Jules nod as Rebecca headed across the deck. Though younger than Jules by a few years, Rebecca had clearly taken charge, and her concern for Jules's plight was nice to see.

"How did you sleep?" Nell scooted over on the bench so Jules could sit down.

Before she could answer, Merry appeared with granola, a spoon, and another cup of coffee. "You'll love it, Jules," she said, and hurried off.

"I didn't think I would sleep much. But that breeze off the water and the most amazing bed I've ever slept in were pure tonic. Images of police warrants and garden gloves flew out the window the instant I hit those down pillows."

"That's good—and not a surprise," Birdie said. "Nell's little cottage has magical powers."

Jules's smile was weak, and the sleep she claimed to have gotten didn't erase the exhaustion in her eyes. "I need some magic," she said, fiddling with her necklace chain. The tiny embossed seashell on the charm would be rubbed smooth soon if things didn't settle down. The confident woman who had jogged the streets of Sea Harbor and put strangers under the spell of her smile had been swallowed whole in less than a day. Even finding Jeffrey's dead body hadn't done to her what a garden glove had accomplished.

They heard Danny's voice before they saw him. "Any coffee left in that carafe?" An empty mug appeared next to Birdie's shoulder.

She patted the bench beside her. "Sit with us, Danny." She filled his mug while he swung one long leg over the bench, straddling it. He dropped his backpack on the floor and looked across the table at Jules. "How are you feeling today?"

"Unraveled," she said quietly, her dark brows lifting with her words.

"Sure," Danny said. "Stands to reason."

"I came here with such good intentions, and now here I am, a mess. So that's how I feel, as if my life has become a messy ball of yarn."

"What were those good intentions?" Nell asked. Her voice was soft, unthreatening, but holding a question they'd all been reluctant to ask. "Most people come to Sea Harbor to relax, to enjoy the beaches, the ocean, the sea air. Why did you come?"

Danny's eyes remained on Jules's, holding her to Nell's question. She returned his gaze, almost as if asking his opinion. Then she nodded, as if it were time she took charge of her own intentions—especially with people who had offered her support.

"I came here to find out who I really am. I came here to find my father," she said.

Chapter 22

A brief silence met Jules's reply. It wasn't what any of them had expected, but it wasn't a completely startling story. People wanted to know who brought them into the world, from whom they'd come. Even Sam Perry had once journeyed back to Colorado and Kansas to find his roots. But nevertheless, it wasn't what they were expecting. Not today.

Birdie broke the silence. "That's interesting. Have you found him? Does he live here?"

Jules looked over at Danny again, as if the answer would come from him. He straddled the bench, listening, but offered no comment.

"No," Jules said. "I haven't found him yet. I don't know if he's dead or alive. I told Danny why I came here, but I asked him not to tell anyone."

"Why?" Izzy asked. "Wouldn't telling people make it easier to find whomever you're looking for?"

"I thought the same thing," Danny said. "Especially since the time I was spending with Jules was raising eyebrows."

Jules looked genuinely puzzled. "What do you mean, raising eyebrows? Why?"

Nell swallowed her surprise. Jules clearly didn't know how her behavior was interpreted. "Because you are a very nice-looking woman and Danny is a handsome guy," she said. "And suddenly you were asking him to meet you for drinks or talks or walks. Danny's right. It raised eyebrows."

"But that's ridiculous," Jules said. The words came out forcefully. She stared at Danny. "Why didn't you say something?"

He shrugged. "I am a well-trained secret keeper. Years of investigative reporting will do that to a person. And frankly, I thought I did explain it as well as it needed to be explained. You asked me for help, and I was trying to give it to you. That was what I told people."

Nell listened to the exchange, and then watched the others listening to it. Cass's eyes were on her coffee, her face unreadable. His comment was pointed at all of them, of course. That was the explanation Danny had given each of them in one way or another. And none of them had believed him. At least not entirely or with great assurance.

"Izzy has a good point," Birdie said, shifting the conversation. "Why were you keeping it a secret? People on Cape Ann know each other. Some have lived here all their lives. If your father was from around here, someone probably knows him or at the least could lead you to someone else who might be able to help you find him."

Jules was quiet for a minute, as if wondering how much of her life she wanted to pour out on the table. Finally she said, "I think my father might have done something bad. He might have been a criminal. That's not something you readily tell people, especially people you don't know. And I don't even know his name. So asking for help when the information I have to start with is so scanty would definitely make people wonder about me."

"But you told Danny," Izzy said.

"Because I didn't have a clue where to start. I was messing around in the bookstore, looking for something that might help me, and his dad told me that Danny had done investigative reporting and that he was an expert at tracking things down. Danny agreed to meet with me, and he's been giving me a list of places to start—court records, mapping dates, checking old newspapers. My hope is something will pop out at me. I was beginning to do that when this . . . when the murder happened. And then the glove."

Nell watched Cass's face as Jules talked. She was listening carefully.

"What did your mother tell you about your father?" Cass asked.

"Not much at all. She had a terrible time talking about it, as if she was the one who had done something wrong. I think whatever happened crushed her. My mother was always a religious person, a good person with very high standards. Her church was very important to her, and she saw the world in black and white. When I'd try to bring up my father, she would insist that my life began when Gordon Ainsley adopted me and gave both of us his name. My father was dead to her."

"Why do you think your father did something wrong?"

"It was always there, lurking beneath her words—what few there were—that this man she had conceived a child with had done something shameful, and she didn't want me touched by it. Sometimes I had the feeling she didn't really believe it herself, but was repeating what she had to repeat to live with herself. And maybe to protect me.

"Because she was so reluctant to talk about it over the years, I settled for reading emotions, expressions, innuendos, storing them all away. I am fairly sure he isn't alive, but even that wasn't made clear to me."

"What name is on your birth certificate?" Izzy asked.

"My mother's name. Johnson. Father unknown."

"The second most common name in the United States," Danny said. "A needle in a haystack, especially if he wasn't a resident of Sea Harbor. It was summer. He could have been vacationing here."

"So they met here one summer, do you think? Where was your mother from?" Izzy asked.

"She was raised in the Chicago area. I don't even know if my father was from here—like Danny said, he could have come up for a job, like she did. I found some old papers in a box after she died, things from her college years—she went to Bryn Mawr. And apparently one summer she got a job on Cape Ann. She worked at a resort that burned down a few years later."

"Lots of us did that," Izzy said. "We got jobs at ocean resorts during summer breaks, waitressing or lifeguarding or whatever." She laughed. "Especially those of us who didn't want to go back to the sizzling Midwest, where there was no ocean in sight."

"But my mother didn't just wait tables or whatever it was she was paid to do that summer. She got pregnant."

They all listened, thinking back to their own summer college breaks. Summer meant freedom. Fun. Parties. Crazy times when falling in love was as easy as skinny-dipping on a hot summer night. They wondered where Jules's story was going and exactly how it had brought her here to Sea Harbor, all these years later.

"So you know your father was here that summer, at least," Birdie said.

She nodded. "Yes. I have been living with my imaginings of what happened that summer for a long time, wondering, wanting answers, piecing things together. And then, when my mother was dying, I realized that any answers would be up to me to find. So much of it didn't make sense, knowing my mother as well as I did. Like I said, she was a good person; she always did the right thing. Not like her daughter—" Jules managed a short laugh. "And I know that she wouldn't have hopped in bed with just anyone. So whatever happened that summer, I feel sure that my mother loved the man who fathered me."

Izzy leaned forward. "Would she have fallen in love with a criminal or someone who had done something bad?" She spoke gently, the voice she might have used as a lawyer preparing a client for trial, guiding her through any inconsistencies in her testimony. Helping her understand clearly what she was saying.

Jules toyed with the flaw in her own reasoning. "No. And that's a contradiction, I know. It's one of the things that has baffled me. Her parents were very powerful, strict people. They took over her life. And whenever I would ask about the past, my mother left me with few answers, but always with the impression that trying to revisit the past would only leave me with heartache." She stirred her coffee, then looked up, her brown eyes thoughtful. "But somehow I don't think that's what I'll find."

"What do you think you will find?" Birdie asked.

"I think I will find a love story."

She spoke softly, but in her words they sensed the hope that had brought Jules Ainsley to Sea Harbor. Birdie leaned forward, reaching across the table and placing her blue-veined hand on top of Jules's. "I'm all for love stories. If it's there, we will help you find it, my dear," she said.

Danny sat quietly, tracing a line in the weathered picnic table with the end of his finger.

"Danny, what do you think?" Nell asked.

He looked up. "I think Jules will find some answers, maybe not all. She knows which summer it was. Her age plus nine months. That's a starting point. But right now what I think is that it's a good thing that all of you are hearing Jules's story." He looked over at her. "If you could pick any support team on the Eastern Seaboard, you couldn't do better than the four women sitting at this table." He took a drink of coffee, then met Jules's eyes again. "And Rebecca Early is a pretty good friend to have as well."

Nell poured some cream in her coffee and stirred it around with a spoon. "Have you told the police about this?"

Jules looked surprised and slightly agitated. "The police? Why would I do that?"

Why indeed? A random idea had scuttled across Nell's mind that there might be a connection between Jules's father and Jeffrey Meara's murder. But when she let her mind touch on the possibility, it instantly fell apart, into loose, frayed pieces of yarn. She looked over at Danny and saw that he was considering it, too—and getting nowhere.

Jeffrey Meara would have had no way of knowing why Jules was in Sea Harbor. Danny had been her only confidant. But yet . . . he had insisted on talking to her. And it was important to him.

Important enough to get him killed?

Danny left the table soon after, back to his corner table to rework a stubborn character, he said, and figure out a tricky motive.

Nell watched him walk across the deck. Would that it were so easy in real life. Now there were two mysteries, not one. A murder, and uncovering a past. One was drowning a town in fear, the other filling a woman with hope.

As the deck began filling up with the early lunch crowd, they realized the morning was rushing by. Coffee cups were drained, bills pulled out, and tips slipped under the creamer as they waved a good-bye to Merry.

Birdie told Jules they would talk soon. She was an old-timer, and though she sometimes had trouble remembering what she had for dinner the day before, remembering what happened thirty or forty years earlier would be a breeze. She would certainly give it some thought.

Jules was grateful to Birdie, to all of them, she said. She had no doubt Danny Brandley was right: they were formidable allies. Just as he was. She looked across the deck at the writer. "You know better than I do what a good and decent man he is," she said. Her words were spoken to all of them, but her eyes were on Cass.

As soon as Jules had left, Nell took out her phone and sent a quick text to Ben to check on Jules's car. Surely the police were finished with it by now. Jules was headed back to her house—she would need a car. Maybe Ben could speed it up. As she punched the Send command, she looked over the deck railing and noticed that Jules had stopped in front of Lampworks Gallery, looking in the window at the colorful handcrafted beads.

Izzy stood and followed her look. "I like Danny and I like Rebecca," she said. "But Rebecca is much better for Jules right now than Danny Brandley."

Nell laughed. "That's only because you have other plans for Danny."

At the table, Cass gathered up her bag and ignored her friends. She wasn't laughing.

Chapter 23

Birdie and Nell left the Artist's Palate together, stopping briefly at Birdie's home in the Ravenswood neighborhood to pick up a chicken salad Ella had prepared that morning. "Enough for three," Birdie had requested.

They drove north along Ravenswood Road, past the bed-and-breakfast and the elegant homes hidden on wooded acres. A mile later, they turned west onto a side road that wound around to the smaller, more modest neighborhood where Jeffrey and Maeve Meara had settled.

Birdie had suggested to Maeve that she and Nell stop by. She wanted Maeve to try her housekeeper Ella's incredible chicken salad.

But mostly they both wanted to check on Maeve, to see for themselves how she was doing and to make sure she wasn't spending too much time alone. And as Birdie said, one learns a lot from sitting in another's home. Things you never noticed before sometimes became significant, the minutiae of living a life. When she and Harold had taken Maeve home the night of the funeral, all they saw was the results of someone's invasion of a grieving widow's privacy. Perhaps a friendly visit would give them a much better picture of what might have been going on in Jeffrey Meara's life in the days before he died.

They pulled up in front of the neat, two-story frame house. The grass was trimmed, and Mexican urns filled with orange and crimson chrysanthemums sat on either side of the front steps—as welcoming as Maeve herself was when she appeared in the doorway and ushered Birdie and Nell inside.

It took them less time than it did to settle around the pine dining table to see that Maeve was going to be fine. Although her eyes were lined with grief, there was something else in this small woman who had just buried the love of her life: Maeve Meara held an extraordinary ability to understand life—and death—and whatever lay beyond.

The table was bright, cheery, with a vase of gerber daisies in the center and three of Jane Brewster's signature pottery plates on bright green place mats.

Maeve immediately scooped up a forkful of Ella's chicken salad. "This is quite amazing," she said. "Now tell me what these little buds are?" She pointed to one of them with a tine of her fork.

"Capers," Birdie said. "As my granddaughter says, 'Capers and olives and avocados in a chicken salad. How cool is that?'"

"It's very cool," Maeve said, going for another forkful.

The dining area was an extension of the living room, the short end of the L. Above the credenza on the wall facing Nell was a wall filled with framed photographs. Her eyes moved to a wedding photograph of Jeffrey and Maeve. The age difference was evident but not pronounced, and the look of happiness on Jeffrey's face lit up the photo.

"I remember that day," Birdie said, following Nell's look. "I was older and wiser, of course, and from my vantage point it was a marriage made in heaven."

Maeve laughed. She welcomed the chance to bring Jeffrey Meara back into the room with them. "In those years before we married—when I was off at college and then experimenting with living in a big city— Jeffrey was kind of a lost soul. He had put off college for a year to care for his father, who was dying of cancer. But then, after his father died—I don't know. My family and friends said that something happened to him, changed him, and he seemed to lose his way. Jeffrey was very smart—Yale was holding a scholarship for him, but he didn't honor it."

"Did you ever ask him why he didn't go?"

She sighed, as if she'd like to go back right then and talk to him about many things. "Sometimes we would touch upon our pasts, but not too often—and that particular time seemed to be a touchy subject. Jeffrey would clam up when I asked too many questions and I would back off. I didn't want him to think I was disappointed that he didn't have a college degree."

"But he planned on going to college?"

"Yes. He kept in touch with several good friends, and they all went off to college. I'm sure they encouraged him that way. But then— well, somewhere along the way he changed his mind. Something happened—something traumatic—and his life turned around and followed a different path. But the good thing is that it was a path that crossed over mine.

"I knew Jeffrey because our families had lived here forever, but when I came back to Sea Harbor, I wasn't looking for a man. Then one day I walked into the Ocean's Edge with some friends and there he was—the man I wasn't looking for. This short little man with a bow tie who was already going bald, even way back then.

"Jeffrey used to say that I gave him a second life, and that it began the day we were married." Maeve turned and looked up at the wedding photo. "He was a romantic, my Jeffrey. My Renaissance man, I called him."

Her gaze lingered on the photo. The couple stood side by side, dressed in simple clothes, a short white dress for Maeve, a dark suit for Jeffrey. They were nearly the same height. They weren't touching, except for a brush of their hands, but the look on their faces told a deep and intimate story.

Maeve turned back to the table. "Memories," she said softly, then picked up her fork and scooped up the remaining traces of Ella's chicken salad, smiling with pleasure.

"Do you suppose his father's death changed him?" Birdie asked. "Perhaps that's why he didn't continue his schooling."

Maeve thought about the question, but rejected it. "No, I don't think so. His father died that next winter after Jeffrey got out of high school. My sister worked with him at a resort near Long Beach and she said Jeffrey contacted the school after his father's funeral and told them he'd be coming the next fall and they should activate his acceptance papers. He was going to sell this house—who needed four bedrooms? But then at the end of that next summer, when he should have done all those things, he didn't. He didn't sell the house, and he didn't go to Yale." Maeve thought about the question some more, as if in the retelling it made even less sense to her.

"Jeffrey told me he wasn't close to his father. He cared for him when he was ill, but I suspect it was out of duty, not affection. Jeffrey was the kind of man who would do that. He was as loyal as the day is long. And his father appreciated it. He thanked him by leaving him this house." She looked around the room. "This is where he was living when I moved back to town."

They looked around at the cozy and well-kept home. Nell's guess was that Maeve had lovingly torn the entire place apart and transformed it into the cheerful and inviting home that they now sat in.

"It was a bit of a wreck," Maeve mused, as if reading their thoughts. "Too many bachelor parties, I suspect. The only decent room was the garage."

Nell laughed. "Now that's a switch. Our garage is a mess."

"Ours was—is—spotless," Maeve said. "Jeffrey kept a car out there, a Sprite—one of those tiny British cars that looks like it's smiling. And he kept it in perfect condition—always."

"Jeffrey had a Sprite?" Birdie's silver brows lifted in surprise. "My Sonny had a Sprite and he loved it dearly. The two of us would drive up the coast—all the way to Maine and back—my hair flying in the wind, young and carefree and alive." Her voice grew soft with memory. "May I see it, just for a moment?"

"Of course." Maeve got up immediately and led the way through the kitchen to a back door that opened onto the driveway. She pressed a button just inside the door and they heard the garage door lift.

"I can understand Jeffrey's pride," Birdie said, walking down two steps to the gravel drive. "Sonny's Sprite was his true joy—well, after me, of course."

They stood on the driveway looking into the immaculate garage.

Looking back at them were the bright bug eyes of a pristine British racing green Sprite. The small open-topped car, facing out, commanded center stage in the spotless garage. With the headlights staring straight ahead and the wide oval grille below, it did look like it was smiling at them.

The three women smiled back.

"What a gorgeous car," Nell said.

"It's beautiful," Birdie said. "A beautiful beast. But I never once saw Jeffrey drive it. I could barely pry Sonny out of his. There was only one way"—she lifted her eyebrows—"and this isn't the time or place to talk about it."

Maeve laughed. "Jeffrey never did drive it. Never once that I know of, though he certainly might have before I came into the picture."

Birdie was in disbelief. "This amazing car sat here alone?"

"Oh, no. Not alone. Jeffrey spent a lot of time with it, just not behind the wheel. He got the car from a great friend, someone he was tight with when he was young. He had promised his friend he'd take good care of it. Jeffrey was a man of his word—take care of it, he definitely did. He polished it every single week." Maeve spoke in the indulgent tone reserved for talking about husbands who did irrational things.

They started to walk back inside, when Maeve stopped and turned back to the car as if remembering something.

"One curious thing. Jeffrey spent more time out here than usual the last week before he died. I remember because it wasn't the usual time to polish it, but he gave it a complete once-over. I heard him rummaging around with some things he kept out here one day. After a couple of hours I came out to check on him, and there he sat, relaxing on the black leather seats, his head back and his eyes closed. He must have been revisiting old times. He had a box on his lap and he was smiling. A kind of sad smile, I remember. I snuck back inside, not wanting to disturb his reverie." She smiled at the memory, then shook it off and motioned Birdie and Nell back inside.

"Well, your whole house—not just the garage—is lovely," Nell said as they walked back inside.

Maeve glanced back one more time, then shut the door behind her. "It's interesting how memories come to me now, some from long ago, some from last week. In no order. No reason, except maybe triggered by a comment made here or there. And the need to keep Jeffrey close."

"Are you remembering something about the car?"

She nodded. "Something he said in passing recently, something that was a surprise. He said he had found someone to give the car to. And that thought seemed to make him inordinately happy. It surprised me."

"Who?" Nell asked.

"He didn't say—and I didn't ask. I assumed it was one of the collectors who occasionally called about the car. Someone who would want an old Sprite in pristine condition. It was just the day before . . ." She didn't finish the sentence, but the drop in her voice made it clear. *It was the day before he died. The day before he was murdered.*

"We had recently talked about moving, maybe finding a smaller, one-story place. And it might have been related to that. Perhaps the person he talked to will call about it."

She walked into the dining room and began carrying the empty dishes from the table back into the kitchen. She called over her shoulder, "You tell Ella for me that your granddaughter is absolutely right. This salad was amazing. Cool, indeed."

Jeffrey's British racing green Sprite had slipped back into her memory, tucked carefully away with decades of others.

Nell walked through the living room to a back window that looked out over Maeve's garden. A vine of small pumpkins wound around the spinach and kale and the border of bright dahlias and nasturtiums. She could imagine it all summer long, carefully tended, bearing tomatoes and zucchini and peppers.

Maeve came out of the kitchen and pointed to glass-paned doors that opened into the den. "That's the room where someone thought Jeffrey had hidden money or gold or something worth dumping out drawers for. Birdie knows—"

Birdie looked through the doors, a slight shiver bringing back the image of the chaos they'd found there just a few days before. "I'm sure the police have been over all this with you again, but do you have any idea what the person was after?"

"I try not to dwell on it," Maeve said. "But of course I've thought about it. I've gone through the room myself and there's not much there anyone other than I would want. I know every inch of what's on the bookshelves. Nothing was missing. I think it was a random happening."

A random happening that had nothing to do with her husband's murder. That, of course, was the hope. It was simply a curious person who knew Maeve wouldn't be home that day and that she rarely locked her doors—and took advantage of it. It was a scenario that was far easier to deal with than the thought of a murderer's presence in this lovely home, and Nell wondered whether she might have felt the same way had it happened to her. Imagining a murderer in your personal space was a nightmarish, nearly unbearable thought.

Maeve walked into the den and Birdie and Nell followed. It was neat and clean now, the pine floor polished and small rugs vacuumed. A vase of colorful dahlias sat on a small table near a leather love seat. "Jeffrey loved this room—it's where he worked on his restaurant business but also where he spent hours and hours reading. Originally, it was his mother's sewing room, but together we turned it into a den for him. He called it his haven."

One wall was floor-to-ceiling bookshelves. Nell read the titles and held back her surprise at the collection: a shelf of Proust; Aristotle and Plato, Sartre and Heidegger sharing space with postmodern philosophers; French poetry and British mysteries. The classics and volumes of history books. Jeffrey Meara may not have made it to Yale, but he was well educated. Maeve was right. He was a Renaissance man.

Maeve followed her look. "He read them all, Nell. Sometimes he'd read poetry to me. He loved every inch of those books, from his bartending volumes to literature to philosophy. That was my Jeffrey."

Interspersed with the books were mementos, photos, and framed certificates. "I found boxes in the rafters of the garage with all this old stuff of his. I pulled out some of it and surprised him with it. He protested at first—he said he stashed all those old things so no one would find them. But then he looked at it all carefully, walking around the room, and it must have brought back some good memories because he got a bit teary—and he let it all be, exactly as I arranged it. I think it taught him that the past wasn't always a bad place to go. Recently I found him rummaging around out there in the garage, looking at some other things he'd stashed. Memories."

There were plenty of framed photos of Jeffrey holding giant fish down on the pier, of his bartender licenses right alongside an old National Honor Society membership certificate, and a photo of him on his first day on the job at the Ocean's Edge. Maeve had even put his high school graduation diploma in the mix. It was on a top shelf so he couldn't get it down easily and pitch it, she explained smugly.

Next to it was his senior photo in cap and gown with "Class Valedictorian" written below it in gold script. A collage of black-and-white photos was also on the top shelf, one with the words "Cool Cods" written in block letters in the center of the picture with an array of black-and-white photos displayed around it—the kind of page kids put together for a yearbook ad.

"Cool Cods," Nell murmured. "I've heard that recently."

"It used to be the high school motto—even back when I was a student at Sea Harbor High a millennium ago."

Birdie smiled. "No, dear. Millennium history is mine."

Maeve chuckled.

"I remember now where I heard it," Nell said. "We were talking with Jeffrey at the Edge one night and Stan Hanson came in."

"Our mayor. A very nice man," Maeve said.

"He and Jeffrey greeted each other with nicknames that night,"

Nell said, trying to remember what they were. "Yes, I remember now. Jeffo and Sage. Apparently they were old high school friends?"

Maeve mulled over the nicknames. "Now that's interesting, isn't it? I never heard Jeffrey called that. As for the mayor, I suppose it fits—he appears to be a wise man. Those names must have been left behind when they all grew up. But then, I was far enough ahead of Jeffrey in school that I wouldn't have paid much attention to his friends or nicknames. You know how those things go. Underclassmen were so *irrelevant*." She laughed.

"So you think Jeffrey and the mayor's friendship wasn't one that lasted into adulthood?"

"That happens. But sometimes the affection lasts even when the friendship doesn't survive maturity. They were good friends a long time ago, Jeffrey told me once. And Mayor Hanson was clearly moved at Jeffrey's funeral." Maeve frowned as she explored the relationship between the two men. "Yes, good friends, I think. Yes. But in later years, not so much. But then, Jeffrey and I were a bit odd in our social life. Together, in this little house, we were somewhat cloistered. When we stepped outside these doors, we entered into our almost separate worlds; when we came back together we brought with us the best of where we had been and simply enjoyed each other. It worked for us. Jeffrey did so much socializing at the Ocean's Edge that I think he was happy to put it all behind him when he got home and settle in with me and with his books. It worked for me, too. I had my Altar Society and the women's guild. Helping at the soup kitchen downtown. My bridge group. And at home I had Jeffrey. A long answer for a rather easy question, isn't it? Sometimes I ramble." Maeve's smile was apologetic, but she was clearly enjoying herself and her chance to share.

Nell thought back to the day she'd walked Abby over the bridge and spotted Stan and Jeffrey down below, sitting on a bench in an out-of-the-way place, deep in conversation, the way friends would do. It was a serious conversation, not a casual catch-up—that much she had been sure of. And Stan's emotional reaction at the funeral. Perhaps old memories, old friendships ran deep. Or perhaps Nell had misread the encounter entirely. So much had happened since that day.

Birdie and Maeve were looking up at a framed article about the Ocean's Edge that had been printed in a travel magazine.

"The Ocean's Edge has become a destination for people. Jeffrey must have been proud of it, and deservedly so," Birdie said. "There have been a lot of changes over there since he signed on all those years ago. And I've eaten my way through every one of them."

"Not all the changes have been good ones, I'm afraid. Jeffrey was an excellent bartender and did a fine job keeping track of things for the precious owner, who lived in Boston and wasn't around often. Jeffrey enjoyed that—not having the responsibility of an owner but being able to make decisions. When he bought into the restaurant, the responsibility grew more onerous and I think it ceased to be fun for him. He worried about it all the time. And the worry was making him cranky, even with the staff. Another problem was with his partner. He and Don Wooten have known each other a long time—Jeffrey and Don's wife, Rachel, were friends since high school. But Jeffrey and Don were cut from different cloths. They didn't agree on much when it came to business, and Jeffrey spent long hours in this very den, poring over numbers and trying to figure out how he could buy Don out. He'd had it, he told me, but I wasn't sure what he meant by that.

"Then late one night Don called here. It was on a Sunday night, shortly before Jeffrey passed away," she said. "He turned the tables on him and suggested that *he* buy *Jeffrey* out. He said he'd give him a fair offer and it made good sense. It was the only way it would work, Don said."

"And what did Jeffrey say?"

"He said . . ." Maeve looked at each of them, a slow blush creeping into her cheeks. "I don't choose to repeat all the words he used—I'm not even sure I'd pronounce them right. But the last one, the important one, was 'no.' And he made it very final by hanging up on Don. I remember it clearly because I was irritated with Jeffrey for his rudeness. It wasn't necessary."

"But the restaurant was like a child to him," Birdie murmured.

Maeve nodded. "The truth is, I would have been all for him selling out to Don—I didn't like seeing him come home weary and frustrated. When he became an owner, he refused to give up his old job: the world's finest bartender. And he wouldn't admit he was no longer twenty-nine. It was taking a toll on him. But I wouldn't have wanted him to sell unless he found another passion he could wrap himself up in. He would have failed completely at sitting in a recliner and watching football. And he couldn't quite abide my bridge club. But he had his books . . . and, of course, polishing his Sprite." She laughed softly and sat down on the love seat.

It was near Jeffrey's old desk, and Nell could imagine the two of them in this room, Jeffrey in the swivel chair behind the desk working on his numbers or reading Proust or some obscure philosopher, and Maeve cuddled up on the couch reading or doing crossword puzzles. Together.

"That last week, especially, made me think Jeffrey should sell. Or I should say, 'we.' He always insisted we both owned the restaurant, though I would have preferred a new stove or maybe an Alaskan cruise."

"What happened that last week?"

"He was anxious, concerned about something. But he didn't want to talk about it. Jeffrey was like that, keeping anything he thought would upset me locked up somewhere inside him. Usually I was able to get to the heart of the problem by simply being patient and waiting for the right moment, the right words. Sometimes making his favorite lobster macaroni and cheese would loosen him up. But it wasn't so easy to find the key to what was bothering him this time."

She tucked her short legs up beneath her with an agility that defied her age, and urged Nell and Birdie to sit in the two chairs facing the small couch. She was feeling the need to talk, she said, and they complied.

"This time it was different somehow. I could feel the tension in his body. He wouldn't talk about it. But Jeffrey had developed a habit as he got older of talking to himself when he'd shower or shave. Or when he thought he was alone outside or in the garage polishing his car. Sometimes it was simply cussing, using words I wouldn't let him use in the house. And sometimes he'd just mumble on about this or that. I heard him one day talking about righting wrongs, and I thought at first that maybe it was a religious thing. Maybe he was going to start going to church with me. But it wasn't that, and I knew it immediately when I saw his face. It was a sad face, weary and worn. I knew it was one of those things he had to work out by himself. But his eyes held a resolve. He was going to do something."

"For someone? To someone?" Nell asked.

"For himself, I think."

Chapter 24

*N*ell and Ben drove the long way around to get to the Sweet Petunia Restaurant Sunday morning.

"I'm sure she's fine," Ben assured her, but Nell suspected it was his stomach speaking. And the desire for Annabelle's special omelet. And his quest to curb her tendency to worry.

"I'm sure she is, too, but imagining her in that house alone, not knowing the neighbors. With a murderer on the loose. It's unsettling. Driving by the house certainly can't hurt."

Ben slowed and turned onto Ridge Road.

The green-shuttered house had new life today. Windows were open wide and somewhere in the background music filled the air.

Sitting in the driveway was Jules's car.

Nell looked at it, then leaned over and kissed him on the cheek. "You got Jules's car back for her. Thank you," she said.

Ben smiled. "Not a biggie. The police had finished going through the car and had neglected to return it."

On the side of the house, beyond the car, a clothesline held several small rugs and curtains. The gauzy fabric waved in the breeze.

"It's beginning to look loved again, just like when Izzy lived here," Nell said.

"Maybe Jules would like to go to Annabelle's with us," Ben said, turning the car around at the end of the cul-de-sac and driving slowly back down the street.

As they approached the house, Rebecca Early appeared from around the back with a mop in her hand and began beating one of the rugs with great vigor. The music grew louder and her body rocked to the lyrics of "Safe and Sound" as she pounded a thick flurry of dust motes into the air.

Nell laughed, straining to see through the gray cloud.

Ben laughed at the scene. "On second thought, I don't think even Annabelle's amazing omelets would entice a cease-fire."

Nell agreed. "Jules wants nothing more right now than a clean and well-lighted place, as Hemingway would say. And I'm so happy she has friends to help her get it. Brunch is probably the last thing on her mind."

Ben drove on, stopping at the corner to allow a stream of traffic to pass by.

Nell turned and looked back at the house again. She frowned. "Ben, look—"

A figure was emerging from behind the house next door to Jules's—a tall man with a muscular build and dark hair. Nell stared at Garrett Barros as he edged his way close to a copse of pine trees that separated the two properties.

She looked at Ben. He'd shifted in the seat, his hands on the steering wheel but his eyes on the pine trees.

Garrett moved into the dense shadow of the trees, then stood as still as the trunk in front of him—a dark statue.

"He's spying on them," Nell said. "We should go back. Or call Jerry."

Ben shook his head. "Your nerves are getting the better of you. He lives in that house, Nell. It's rude, but he's not doing anything wrong—at least not legally. It wouldn't hurt to let Jules know she has a nosy neighbor. Maybe send her a text later?" Ben looked back again.

He was still there, still not moving. One large hand was gripping a pair of binoculars that he raised to his eyes, and with his free hand he pushed aside a branch, finding just the right spot to see clearly through the trees. *And into the house*, Nell thought, *if he so pleased.*

. . .

The Endicotts' usual table at Annabelle's had grown. Stella Palazola, helping her mother out by filling in for an ill waitress, had pushed two tables together. "Somehow it seemed like a two-table Sunday," she explained as she led Nell and Ben through the restaurant and out to the deck.

Annabelle's Sweet Petunia Restaurant was built into the side of a hill, and the deck off the back of the restaurant hung right over the trees. At the bottom of the hill was Canary Cove, with its bustling galleries, the Artist's Palate Bar and Grill, boutiques, and a tea shop. But up in the trees Annabelle's was removed from it all—and filled with the amazing aromas of eggs and butter, cinnamon and freshly baked dough, bacon and sausages, and strong Colombian coffee. It was Ben's favorite place to spend a Sunday morning.

"Voilà," Stella said, waving her arm toward the end table on the narrow porch.

Stella was right: it was a two-table Sunday. Birdie, Sam, Izzy, and Cass were already there, mugs of hot coffee and a basket of bite-size cinnamon rolls in front of them. Abby was happy in her carrier, seated next to Sam.

"Where's Danny?" Nell asked Cass.

"I haven't talked to him," she said, and took a cinnamon roll from the basket.

Although they'd all been diplomatic and not asked, Izzy, Nell, and Birdie had assumed yesterday's conversation with Jules should have gone a long way in mending fences between Danny and Cass. Now Nell wasn't so sure.

"Here he comes," Sam said.

Danny walked over with his usual grin and slightly disheveled look, his hair curling slightly around his collar. He pulled out a chair next to Sam and sat down, his long legs finding room beneath the table. He nodded toward Cass, sending a smile along with it. Cass looked slightly uncomfortable but smiled back.

"We couldn't wait for the slowpokes," Izzy said, biting into a buttery roll and looking over at her aunt and uncle. "What kept you two?"

Nell and Ben sat back while Stella filled their mugs, and then told them about their patrolling duties that morning. "I just wanted to be sure she was okay before we came over," Nell said. "It was a long day yesterday. And I think pouring her heart out to us the way she did took a lot out of her."

"Izzy told me about your conversation," said Sam.

And Nell had told Ben.

But the two men hadn't heard the story from Jules herself the way Danny had. They hadn't been privy to the expressions that had flitted across her face as she had talked or to the emotion that coated her words, which made it easier for them now to concentrate on the practical—and poke holes in her story.

"So . . . she thought her biological father lived in Sea Harbor because her mother worked at a resort around here? Why not Gloucester or Rockport or Manchester-by-the-Sea?" Ben asked.

"And how does she think she can find anyone with such sketchy information?" Sam wondered.

"O ye of little faith," Danny chided. "There are ways and there are ways. And when you're as determined as Jules is, those ways will bear fruit. She'll find some answers. I'd bet my life on it."

"Danny's right," Izzy said. "She knows there's more to the story than her mother told her, and she has good reasons for thinking so." Her voice held a note of defensiveness and she held back from launching into Jules's description of her mother, of what she would and wouldn't have done, of how she'd never have gotten involved in a relationship just for the fun of it. Of the emotions and intuition driving her journey. The women understood that immediately, but it might not carry much weight to the more practical men sitting around the table. Except for Danny.

And then Sam surprised them. "I understand the need to find your roots. And I think it becomes more important as you get older. I felt that way before marrying Izzy." He smiled at her, then looked down at Abby, her fingers clutching a tiny wooden rattle and her eyes closed. "I didn't want to bring any surprises to our marriage. "But I had a little more to go on. I think Jules is going to have a harder time."

"Maybe," Nell said. "But Danny gave her some direction, and Birdie knows a lot about Sea Harbor history. We'll all pitch in. We'll find her father—or at least we'll find out who he was. Jules is assuming he's not alive."

"I'm assuming from what you've said that all of you are convinced Jules Ainsley did not murder Jeffrey Meara," Ben said.

"Of course she didn't," Nell said without a pause. "And I think in his heart Jerry Thompson believes in her innocence, too. He's simply doing his job."

Stella came back to the table carrying an enormous tray. She settled it on a folding stand and began filling the table with plates of creamy omelets. Flecks of chervil, tarragon, and spinach poked out of the cheesy eggs. Chunks of fruit, strips of crisp country bacon, and tiny roasted potatoes circled the plates.

"Stella, tell your mother she is amazing," Ben said, tilting his chair back and looking up.

Stella grinned. "I do. Often."

"And I bet she tells you the same," Nell said. "Here you are with your first house sold within a month after getting your license."

"Twenty-three days," she said, and laughed. Then she sobered up quickly and looked over at Izzy. "So do you think she's okay, Iz? Jules, I mean. Do you think she'll be okay in the house?"

"She's going to be okay," Izzy said. "What about you, Stella? This was awful for you, too. It's not easy to erase those images."

Stella nodded and they could see in her expression that the images still visited her. Probably in the middle of the night. "But at least I have all of you and my family. I get hugs at every turn." She looked down at the tray, then back at the faces around the table. "And you know, I have another edge. No one looks at me and wonders if I had anything to do with Jeffrey Meara's murder."

"You're absolutely right. It's not easy being Jules Ainsley right

175 • *Murder in Merino*

now," Nell said. "But I know for a fact having a new house to make her own is going to help her a lot."

"So you think she's really, like, going to live here?"

Nell looked at Danny. He shrugged.

"Well, whatever she does, she's a nice lady. She can be pushy, but I don't think she murdered Mr. Meara. When I got there that day, she was kneeling down next to him, trying to pull—well, to pull the knife out of him. He must have staggered out of the little shed and fallen. He was just lying there. And I think she was trying to help him, not kill him."

A waving hand from a few tables down pulled Stella back to her job and coffee mugs that needed refilling. "Oops, gotta go."

Nell watched her walk down the row of tables lining the railing. She stopped at the Wootens' table, where Rachel and Don were eating alone, talking in serious tones. They stopped talking briefly while Stella filled their cups, then went back to their conversation, their heads nearly touching over the small table.

"I wonder what they'll do about the restaurant now," Ben said, following her gaze.

"They're doing plenty already, from all reports," Cass said. "I hear via the docks' grapevine that Don is painting, hiring, changing menus. And he's reversed some of the decisions Jeffrey Meara made in the past couple weeks, some of the firings. Jeffrey would be turning over in his grave."

"I wonder if he checks with Maeve first," Birdie said, more to herself than to the others.

Ben caught her words and nodded. "That's a good point, Birdie. Maeve owns half the restaurant now."

"Don is nothing if not a businessman," Nell said. "I'm sure he's covered all his bases." But deep down she wondered the same. Maeve hadn't talked about the restaurant's future—only its past.

Birdie looked at Ben. "Has Jerry said anything about the investigation?" She kept her voice low, and Ben answered in like manner.

Although they were seated at the end of the porch, sometimes the breeze picked up and carried voices down the row.

"I talked to him yesterday when I went in to check on Jules's car. He said they had asked Jules to come in for some more questioning—it must have been after all of you met over in Canary Cove. This time Jules told them why she had come to Sea Harbor in the first place, making it clear she had never met Jeffrey before coming to town and he had nothing to do with her coming here. It cleared up one mystery for the police, anyway, and I think that was a good thing. Her presence around here was a real curiosity, and in the light of what's going on, it made her appear suspicious from the very beginning, even before Jeffrey was killed. Tourists don't ordinarily act the way she did. And that made it even more difficult to believe her when she was found kneeling over the body, and now there's this whole glove thing. I don't know how much her explanation for being here will help in the long haul, but at least it cleared up some of the mystery over why she's in Sea Harbor."

"Except . . ." Nell said.

Ben looked over at her.

"Except, what if there is a connection? Looking for her father—and then meeting Jeffrey at the house that day."

"I asked Jerry about that."

"And?"

"He wondered, too. But it didn't really go anywhere. If Jules is telling the truth, she didn't know Jeffrey—and that probably is the truth. How would she? She's never been here before, and Jeffrey never left. The police toyed with the idea that Jeffrey was wanting to buy the house. I guess he and Maeve had played with the idea of moving to a smaller place, and Jeffrey sometimes moved ahead with things without telling Maeve."

Birdie and Nell nodded. Maeve had said as much to them.

"But murdering him because he wanted the same house? A little outlandish—and those were Jerry's words, not mine."

"I don't think it's leaked out yet about the glove they found in

Jules's car," Cass said. "I'd have heard—that would be something that would get bounced around and chewed to pieces in the rumor mill. Have the police decided that's not important?"

"No. It's still important. Jerry said he's keeping it from the press. It wouldn't help the investigation any and it could make Jules's life miserable in the short term. He's a believer of the 'innocent until proven guilty' dictum."

"As he should be," Nell said. "Good for Jerry."

"I wonder how closely the police are looking at the people Jeffrey fired," Birdie said. "And the business dealings going on over at the Edge."

Ben looked at her, wondering what she was getting at, but before he could ask, a shadow fell over the table and they looked up into the smiling face of Don Wooten—a longtime friend—and the same person Birdie was about to shed suspicion on.

A second later Rachel walked up beside her husband. "Look at all of you—you aren't having a secret anniversary party here without us, are you?"

"Not on your life," Ben said. "And miss the fireworks Mary Pisano is probably planning?"

Rachel chuckled and looked over at Izzy. "I hear your house sold, Izzy. To Jules Ainsley? What's that about? A vacation home?"

"Maybe," Izzy said.

"I hope all this blows over soon so she can get on with her life. Poor girl," Rachel said. "But at least she has a place to stay while she's here. She certainly doesn't look like a murderer to me."

As city attorney, Rachel Wooten saw all sides of Sea Harbor life—its beauty and its underbelly—and she probably knew as much of what was going on at police headquarters as anyone did. Nell was happy that Rachel wasn't eager to condemn Jules. Her opinion was greatly respected in Sea Harbor.

"So, Don," Ben said, looking at the less outgoing half of the couple, "you have a lot on your plate right now over at the Edge. How's that going?"

Nell listened for his answer, wondering whether he remembered the last time they'd seen each other—in a dark hall, in the middle of a fierce argument between Don and his now deceased partner.

"We're in a bit of an upheaval, as you'd imagine. It's a sad time—Jeffrey had been a presence at the Edge for as long as some people can remember. People loved him. It's difficult."

"Maeve said he was getting a little cranky at work recently," Birdie said. She followed her words with a smile. "That happens to the best of us sometimes."

Don nodded. "He was a little frustrated, that's true. His way of managing became a little stricter when he became owner. I suppose that's true of all of us in one way or another. When responsibilities change, sometimes we do, too."

"So maybe Jeffrey was happier as a bartender than as an owner with problems," Ben said.

Don didn't answer.

"Maeve said you knew Jeffrey in his youth, Rachel," Birdie said.

Rachel smiled into the memory. "It's true. Everyone liked Jeffo. He hung around Stan Hanson, I remember." Her brows pulled together as she traveled back into memory, trying to remember something. "And Karen, too, maybe. We were in different crowds but sometimes met at parties—you know how that goes in high school. It's all kind of a blur, a lifetime ago. Don here was never a Cool Cod. He went away to school. A fancy guy." She nudged him in the side.

"But I came back for you," Don said. "Surely that made me cool." Then he placed one hand on Rachel's back and suggested they leave these nice people to enjoy their breakfast before all those great omelets turned cold.

Nell watched them walk away, Don's reticence to talk about Jeffrey trailing behind him.

"Don and Jeffrey weren't getting along," Nell said. "Don wanted to buy Jeffrey out."

Sam looked over at Nell, then at the other women sitting around the table. "It sounds like you've been doing some sleuthing."

"Just visiting grieving widows," Birdie said. "One hears things, that's all. Jeffrey said no to Don's offer."

An angry no—and he'd hung up on his partner, who very much wanted the Ocean's Edge to be under single management. But neither Nell nor Birdie said that out loud. It wouldn't go down well with Ben's remaining eggs.

Soon Birdie pushed out her chair and rummaged around for her bag. Cass, Izzy, and Nell followed. Cass's mother was sitting in her usual spot across from Father Northcutt. And the Hansons were at the next table down. It was time to say hello—and time to remove themselves from the remaining cinnamon rolls sitting in the basket while the men settled up with Stella.

Ben scraped up the last traces of eggs with his fork and a piece of toast, watching the women walk down the row of tables. They were being sociable, friendly. That was who they were.

But no one knew better than Ben Endicott that being sociable often disguised their very adept manner of collecting information, of looking for innuendos, of exploring how and why people sometimes did evil things.

When he looked up, Stella had brought the check and Sam and Danny were digging in their pockets for bills.

"This isn't a game," he said to no one but himself. He looked over the edge of the deck, over the treetops to water so blue it melted in with the sky, one giant sea. Someone had been killed. Someone they knew, behind a house they also knew. It was too close—and too dangerous—in spite of the cloak of safety Sea Harbor tried so hard to wrap them all in.

Sam and Danny were standing, shoving receipts into their wallets, looking at Ben and reading his worry.

"They need to let this thing go, let the police do their job," Ben said.

But the only people around to hear were Danny and Sam. Ben was preaching to the choir.

Chapter 25

$\mathcal{B}$en came in with the paper and slapped it down on the kitchen island.

"What's wrong?" Nell rummaged around in her bag, looking for her cell phone.

"Jerry said he was keeping this quiet."

Nell walked over and read the headline.

GLOVE MAY GIVE A HAND TO INVESTIGATION

Nell stared at it. "Ben, this is terrible. Everything about it is awful, even the silly pun." She reached for her coffee cup and scanned the first paragraph. The reporter had some information, but not all of it. Enough to insinuate that the missing garden glove that was possibly used in the Bartender's murder had been found. The reporter went on to say that although the police were not commenting, a reliable source said it was found beneath the seat in a car found at the scene of the crime.

Nell's head shot up. "Beneath the seat? Ben, we didn't even know that."

Before he could answer, Izzy came in, a rolled-up paper in her hand. "Rebecca Early called me. She got a call from Jules and went right over."

"Have they seen the paper?"

"Apparently Jules's neighbor brought it over to her this morning. Rebecca wasn't sure which bothered her most, seeing Garrett Barros at her front door, or the horrible headline."

"Garrett Barros?" Ben asked.

Izzy nodded.

Nell looked at Ben.

"I'll call the chief," he said and walked into his den.

Nell explained her concern to Izzy. "We saw Garrett hiding behind a tree yesterday, keeping tabs on Jules. I think the chief needs to know about it."

Ben was back in minutes. "Jerry is as furious as we are about the story. He's calling a meeting this morning to see if there was some kind of leak in the department. He's mystified. He has a select group working on this case—Tommy Porter and some others whom he considers the best, the brightest, and the most trustworthy. He can't imagine that any of them would talk to the press."

"If not the police, then who . . . ?"

Ben shook his head and reviewed the possibilities. Somehow it helped to repeat it out loud. "Who else knew about this? We did. The police, of course. But Jerry hadn't told me where in the car the glove had been found. Purposely. He didn't tell Jules, either."

None of them would say the word. It simply hung out there in the middle of the Endicott kitchen.

The murderer knew.

When Rebecca had called Izzy earlier, she suggested they stop by Jules's house later that day if they had time. She had to leave for the gallery and thought Jules would like the company. "She is as strong as they come, but it might be nice to see someone who didn't look at her and imagine her standing in a potting shed wearing a bloody garden glove. Besides," Rebecca added before hanging up, "the house looks terrific. I know she'd like to show it off to someone else who might care."

The day was packed with work and meetings for all of them. But the evening looked better. Monday night was Ben's chamber meeting night, and Sam was teaching a class in photography at the junior college. Cass offered to pick up a lasagna at Garozzo's—Harry's was the best in town. Birdie would bring wine, Izzy would bring Abby, and Nell would drive. They were set.

A quick call to Jules revealed she'd love the company. She hadn't been up to facing folks at the Market Basket, so the salad and lasagna would be welcomed with eternal gratitude. She was starving.

As Nell drove up the shady street and turned onto Ridge Road, she mentioned to the others something Ben had said earlier that day. "He suggested we put our energy into helping Jules find her roots. A healthy quest. A safe one."

"And of course dear Ben is right," Birdie said. "I agree with him. I think we're exactly the right people to help Jules put the puzzle pieces of her past together."

Nell looked over at her.

"I do, Nell—I agree with your sweet husband. He wants us to be safe. He's concerned that there's a murderer out there on the streets, and he's right. There is. And if the glove was planted in Jules's car, this person is determined not to be found.

"And he's also correct that we're the people to help Jules find her past. I've been around forever; we are good at patterns and stitching things together. Geniuses, maybe." She smiled, that sweet Birdie smile that carried such weight that nearly anyone in Sea Harbor would do her bidding simply because of that look. And, of course, because she was Birdie, always wise and fair and loving.

"But here is what I'm not sure of and neither are you. I'm just not sure one mystery precludes the other," she said. "But we could be dead wrong."

Nell pulled into the driveway and parked behind Jules's car, Birdie's words ringing in her ears.

She looked ahead, seeing only the battered fender on the old Volvo. She turned and looked at sweet Abby in the back, her car seat fastened securely between Izzy and Cass. Safe and sound. *May we all be*, she thought.

They sat in the car for a minute, silently mulling over Birdie's observation.

Finally Nell said, "I agree with both you and Ben. When I think about someone walking around the town—someone who has ruthlessly taken another's life—it pains me. And it frightens me. But the only way to get rid of that feeling is to find the person who did it. And yes, there's a connection, if only in proximity. Jules was trying to find out who her father was. Jules was new in town. She met Jeffrey. And Jeffrey was murdered. Somehow it feels like there should be a connection. But the stitches don't fit together—it's like a 'yarn over' that shouldn't be there. Maybe what's important right now is helping Jules find her father—and hopefully bringing a small iota of comfort to her."

Birdie reached over and touched her friend's hand. Then she turned and smiled at Cass and Izzy and Abby. "All right, then. Shall we go in?"

"What do you think, Abby?" Izzy asked, looking over at the round pink cheeks of her golden-haired child.

"Goo," Abby said.

Jules was waiting inside the front door. Soft jazz played in the background and the open windows welcomed the evening breeze. The house smelled of the sea and daisies and fresh linens.

"It's just beautiful, Jules," Izzy said. She looked around at the amazing transformation of a house that had looked ready for a wrecking ball not a month before.

"You have a knack for the beautiful, my dear," Birdie said.

"What I've done is all pretty cosmetic," Jules said, clearly pleased with the accolades. "Sam gave me some ideas for making the place a little more open, a wall or two that maybe could come down. But for now, I love it. And I love having its former owner and occupants be my first guests." She looked at Cass and Izzy, the wide smile that had been absent in recent days easing its way back. "No matter what's happened on this property, I feel safe here."

Nell thought of the shadowy figure lurking around the pine trees and made a mental note to talk to her about Garrett Barros before leaving. For now she enjoyed Jules's pride in the house and followed her through the cheerful living room to the kitchen, which ran along the back of the house. Izzy had added a wall of windows and a wide door to the backyard when she'd bought the house, and Nell had almost forgotten how they brought light and magic into the kitchen and eating area. Magic and the magnificent light of a darkening sky over the ocean.

"The backyard needs some pruning and fixing up, but come look at the porch. It's my favorite part of the whole house." She pushed open the kitchen door and stepped onto the open porch, which ran the length of the house. The roofline of the house covered it and pillars held it up, but the porch itself was open to the world. Its wooden floor and pillars were scrubbed clean, the wooden swing smelled of Murphy's oil soap, and several Adirondack chairs were softened and made welcoming with bright pillows. A basket of knitting sat beside the swing and a pile of books anchored a small white table. Beyond the trees and hilly tangle of vines and bushes was the sea.

"You did all this in just a few days?" Cass asked. "Amazing. I lived here for two years and never got around to putting up curtains."

"It's how I handle stress—doing this and running are keeping me sane. Friends like the four of you. And Rebecca. She's been a rock. A bonus I never expected when I came here."

Cass went back inside and put the lasagna into the oven. Birdie followed, arranging a basket of rolls and a salad on the small kitchen table.

"This will be ready whenever we are," Birdie called through the door. "But first we need to see every inch of what you've done. We are a very nosy group and make no apologies for it."

"That will take all of three minutes." Jules laughed. "But come. You've seen the living room. We're off to the bedroom, the hidden bath behind the closet, and the den." She led them into her bedroom, transformed now with a bright yellow duvet, gauzy curtains, and a dresser that Rebecca had brought over, its mirror distinctive, with several pieces of inlaid handblown glass.

The den was last on the list, a small corner room with windows on both sides, one that looked out over the patch of backyard and the sea below, and the other framing the side yard.

"I'm using that old desk you left here, Izzy, and Rebecca gave me a sofa she wasn't using." She pointed to the corner where a soft merino afghan was angled over the back of a buttery yellow sofa. "I love this room."

Nell looked around at the finishing touches, a plant in the corner, a small throw rug. And then she looked at the wall. Jules had brightened the white space by placing a small painting above the couch, an impressionistic blend of soft greens and blues, a whitewashed porch, and a basket of hanging flowers that caught the sunlight and reflected the soft canary color of the couch. She walked over to get a closer look. And then she stared hard at the painting, one hand lifting to her mouth.

"How amazing. Jules, where did you find this? Did you paint it?"

She realized the answer before the question was out. It was an old painting. The frame was weathered and the painting inside slightly buckled from humidity. Some areas were darkened, probably brittle beneath the glass. But it wasn't its age that kept Nell staring at it, and that drew the others in the room to her side; it was the subject of the painting.

It was an old painting of the house they were standing in.

"Oh, my," Birdie said. "What a treasure. Wherever did you find this, Jules?"

There was no mistaking the view. It was painted from the side of the backyard and captured a glimpse of the sea and sky in the background. But mostly it featured the porch, the swing, a basket of yarn on the floor. A bright green shrub with soft edges caught the sunlight, much like the overgrown cypress that still hugged the railing of the porch. The artist had layered magenta, cyan, black, and yellow, creating a vibrant bush that reflected the light.

"It's this house, this porch," Izzy exclaimed. "Wow. And look—" She pointed to the background. "It was painted a long time ago, before the hill became dense with undergrowth and trees, so you can see the ocean clearly in the distance. It's beautiful. Was it in that smelly old attic above the bedroom? Or did you find it in Canary Cove? I wonder who painted it."

For a moment Jules just stood there, still looking at the painting as she soaked in their surprise and praise and wonder. Finally she turned around and smiled.

"My mother," Jules said quietly. "My mother painted it."

Chapter 26

A hush fell over the room. And then curiosity took over and the questions began.

"Your mother painted this?"

"How do you know?"

"Where did you find it?"

Their voices collided in the small den, their eyes still glued to the painting.

Jules stood close to the painting now, one knee on the couch, and pointed to the initials painted into the corner—scrolled initials worked right into the shadows of one of the pillars as if part of the painting. *PTJ*. "Penelope Theresa Johnson. I found the paintings in a trunk after she died. I brought them with me—I'm not even sure why. Except it was easy to do—they were small—and somehow I knew they were from a time in her life that I wanted to discover. A time when she was happy. And I didn't want to leave them in a storage unit.

"Then one day I was running along the beach. I stopped to catch my breath, lifted my head back, and there it was—or a glimpse of it at least. My mother's painting, come to life." She turned and looked at them. "I think I saw some of you walking with Abby that day. Remember?"

They nodded. The memory of a mesmerized Jules staring up at nothing was fresh and vivid. They had thought that day that there was something wrong, that she had been running too hard or too long. That she was seeing something that wasn't there. A mirage.

The smell of the lasagna heating in the oven was the only thing that lured them away from the painting, but a string of questions remained. They went back into the kitchen and filled their plates with Harry's cheesy dish, then filed out onto the porch. Birdie brought the cabernet and Izzy passed around rolls for everyone. And although they were starving, the questions lined up like a thick barricade, preventing the food from going down comfortably without at least a few more answers.

Jules confessed that she had come back that day, the day she'd discovered the house, after they were gone. She had worked her way up through the tangle of bushes and scrub trees until she found herself on the edge of the backyard. From there she could see it all, every detail. The swing, the tapered pillars, the slight overhang of the roof. It was just as her mother had seen it. She snapped a string of pictures, then slowly made her way back down the rise, trying not to be caught trespassing.

"I got the painting out of my car and compared it to the photos I had just taken. There was no mistaking that it was the same house—the house my mother had painted forty years before. I knew it was a sign, somehow. A sign that I was on the right path, that this house was important in my search.

"I went to City Hall to learn more about the house, but I was too excited, too caught up in the experience, and I wasn't quite sure what I was looking for." She looked out toward the water, slowly sipping her wine, tracing back over her footsteps that day. "I ended up at the Ocean's Edge. It seemed an easy place to go and think—and I'm hooked on their calamari. I sat at the outdoor bar and asked a few people who were milling around about the house, trying to describe where it was. It was mostly staff because it was still early for dinner. A waitress told me her friend was a new Realtor and was listing a house in that neighborhood. Then she pulled over another waiter whom she thought lived near Ridge Road. Maybe he'd know more, she said. It turned out to be the guy who lives next door."

"Garrett Barros," Birdie said. She looked at Nell, but Jules went on.

Jules nodded. "I know people think he's odd, but he's harmless, I think. It's probably a result of very cranky parents. He told me the house was empty. Haunted, probably. But here's the really odd thing. It's ironic, thinking back over it now, although I never gave it a thought at the time.

"As Garrett and I were talking, Jeffrey Meara walked around the bar, checking on the waiters and bartenders, making sure things were ready for the dinner crowd. He saw Garrett and pulled him away, chewing him out for bothering a customer. I spoke up and said that wasn't the case, that I had been asking him a question and he wasn't bothering me—he was just answering it.

"Then Garrett spoke up, too. He tends to talk more than he has to, but I think he wanted to make sure Jeffrey wouldn't fire him. So he told him I was asking about an empty house that was right next door to his parents' on Ridge Road, so I had picked a good person to ask and he was just trying to be helpful."

She paused, remembering the conversation more vividly as she revisited it now. She took another drink of wine and frowned. "Maybe I'm seeing things that aren't there these days—especially in retrospect—but it seemed to me that Jeffrey Meara's face froze when Garrett mentioned the house on Ridge Road. And then he stared at me, a stare that even that day seemed a little odd and out of place."

"Did Jeffrey say anything more to you?"

"No, but he kept staring at me, just like he had done a few days before when someone introduced us. It was uncomfortable, and then some emergency in the kitchen called him away, and he left, motioning to Garrett Barros to get busy and clean up a wait station. But I didn't have any more questions for Garrett anyway; I was ready to go. The waitress had given me an address and a name: Stella Palazola at Palazola Real Estate on Harbor Road. They'd know more about the house, she said."

Nell remembered what happened next. She had watched Jules talking to Gus McClucken in front of his store, looking up at the window of the real estate firm, closed for the day. She had thought Jules needed a dentist. Now the thought made her smile. How very far off she was.

Izzy put her empty plate on the table and picked up Abby, waking now from a nap. "You decided right then that you wanted to buy the house?" A question they'd all been wondering. "Because of a painting?"

Jules half smiled. "It sounds crazy, doesn't it? I came here thinking I'd spend two weeks tracking down my past, the things my mother refused to talk to me about. I would file the information away, and get on with my life back in Chicago. Before my mother got sick, I was managing a catering company. I liked it—I met great people—and they wanted me back. I had good friends there. And look at me now—I own a house halfway across the country in a place I've never been before."

"It is a bit crazy," Birdie agreed. "What are your plans? Will you stay on here in Sea Harbor?"

There was an awkward silence as they all realized that Jules's decisions right now were limited.

"Even if I wanted to leave, the truth is, I can't. Not until the police are convinced I didn't kill Jeffrey Meara." She twisted her necklace, the small charm glinting in the porch light.

Although she spoke in a matter-of-fact way, her words held an emotion that Nell suspected Jules Ainsley didn't often reveal: fear. A certain amount of trust had come into the small house on Ridge Road, circling around them and emboldening the conversation. It was a shift in relationships, an opening to let out—and in.

"But once I get my life back, I don't know what I'll do. There are still many things I don't know about my mother's life forty years ago. And about the man she was with here in Sea Harbor. Finding this house, though, and looking at the painting again, is telling me one thing, something I'm sure about now, no matter what my mother led me—or herself—to believe."

Nell had pulled out the small sweater she was knitting for Abby. She put it in her lap and looked over at Jules. "What is that, Jules?"

"I know that my mother was happy here, at least when she painted this house. That painting is a happy painting."

It was definitely that, they all agreed. *Happy*. Nell thought back to the summer Izzy lived in the house, the same summer Sam showed up in Sea Harbor to teach a photography class. The summer they fell in love. That summer, the house looked exactly like the painting in Jules Ainsley's den. Filled with love. A happy house.

Jules got up and went inside. Soon strains of "Waiting on the World to Change" drifted over a small speaker. She returned with a plate of chocolate chip cookies that a neighbor across the street had brought over that morning. "It was a welcome to Ridge Road," she said, passing them around.

They savored the cookies in silence, content to let John Mayer's soulful voice fill the porch and roll softly down the hill.

Cass took another cookie from the plate and sat back, looking over the trees at the sky, dark now with a sprinkling of stars. "You mentioned that you brought *paintings* with you," she said. "Do you have more than one?"

Jules nodded. "She did three paintings of the house. Growing up, I never saw them. They were in an old trunk in the corner of her bedroom. The other two paintings were slightly damaged and I haven't had time to get them repaired yet. But I will. They will go right next to the first one, along that wall."

"What else did your mother paint? Did she have a gallery?" Nell asked. "She's very good. I love the light and shadow she's created in the painting of the house. I'd love to see more of her work."

"She didn't ever show in a gallery, although my grandmother told me once that my mother would have been a fine artist, a well-known artist. If only . . ."

The sky was dark now, and somewhere in the safety of the evening shadows Jules spoke more frankly. "'If only,' my grandmother would sometimes say, 'she hadn't gone to the ocean that summer and let her life be ruined by an evil man.'"

The word "evil" was punched out, as they imagined Jules's grandmother might have said it.

"My mother got her rigid code of ethics in the womb, I think. My grandmother didn't allow much give when judging people and actions."

"Your grandmother knew who your father was?"

"I think so. But she took the information to her grave. My mother's parents took her away from Sea Harbor, away from Bryn Mawr, away from the life she had found in the East. They sent her to a home run by the nuns until I was born. And then they hired a nanny for me in their own home and enrolled my mother in Northwestern University. Soon after, they encouraged her relationship with a law professor at the school, a nice, quiet, respectable man who was fifteen years older than my mother. He adopted me and gave me his name."

She looked out into the vastness of the sea, her voice barely audible.

"And my mother never painted again."

Chapter 27

*N*ell hurried toward Archie Brandley's bookstore, checking her watch as she pushed open the door.

Ten minutes to spare before meeting Mary Pisano at the Ocean's Edge. A drink, a simple plan for the anniversary celebration, that would be it, Mary promised. Ben couldn't join them, but Cass and Birdie said they might stop by to provide moral support and keep Mary's plans under control. Nell wanted to tell Cass that she shouldn't come. Any extra time she had in her busy life should be directed toward Danny Brandley.

But she'd never say that, of course. Cass hugged her personal life close to her chest, sometimes even shielding it from the people who were closest to her. Sometimes Nell thought that was to ward off unwanted advice; other times she thought Cass did it to protect those she loved. They were all invested in one another's lives—they celebrated joys and suffered one another's sadness. But they did both gladly, something that maybe Cass hadn't grasped yet.

She walked in to the wonderful dusty smell of books and over to the counter, shielded behind the new-books display.

"Danny," she said, surprised.

Danny Brandley looked up from the computer. "Hey, Nell. Good to see you. I bet you're here for Ben's weekly stash. When are you going to open your own bookstore with the books he finishes?"

Nell laughed. "I recycle a lot of them right back to your father. Or the community center. What puts you behind the checkout desk?"

"Dad took Mom into Boston for a doctor's appointment and the guy who usually helps them out on Tuesday afternoons is sick. That leaves me."

He straightened his glasses and pushed a shock of hair off his forehead. "I'm cheap," he said. "It works well. Free digs, free labor."

Nell's eyes rotated up to the ceiling as if she could see the small apartment off the back of Archie's store. "You're still staying here?"

"Yep. It's not a bad place, though my feet hang over the end of the bed and the hot plate doesn't work. I'm thinking Tommy Porter will soon get up enough courage to propose to Janie Levin and she'll move out of Izzy's apartment above the yarn shop. And then I'll pounce on it, promise to love Purl the cat forever, and I'll once again be able to walk into the bathroom without cracking my head on the slanted ceiling."

"That sounds like long-term planning."

Danny thought about Nell's pointed words, then crouched down and pulled a stack of books from beneath the counter. He set them on the counter and pulled out a bag. "Long term? Who knows?" The look he leveled at Nell was thoughtful and steady—and noncommittal.

And, Nell thought, sad.

Danny slid the books into a bag and handed it to Nell. "Cass needs time. She doesn't want to simply pick up where we were, and I need to respect that. This whole thing shook her in a way I wouldn't have expected, and I'm not sure I can do anything about it. She needs to figure it out."

"What thing?"

"Oh, the Jules situation. Being upset that we were spending time together, imagining false scenarios. It was like a bad movie."

"But she understands now what that was about."

"Yes. But she didn't for a while—she was angry and upset. And she didn't believe me, not completely. Those are big things."

"So this is simply a cooling-off time?" Nell pushed away the sinking feeling inside her.

"I don't know exactly what it is. I'm forty, Nell. For a while I was okay with being a bachelor—I liked it. I was happy doing my thing, being completely independent. But coming back here to Sea Harbor gave me a different perspective on things, changed me, I guess. That and getting older, maybe. I want to have a family, kids. I look at you and Ben, my parents, Sam and Izzy, and I think, Yeah, that's what it's about. That's why we work hard, why we try to be good people. It'd be for all that. For having an Abby, a lifelong partner, a family. A life."

"For a Cass?"

Danny didn't hesitate. "I love Cass, there's no question about that—crazy and ornery as she sometimes is. But whether that's enough right now, I don't know."

The ringing of the bell above the door sliced through the conversation, severing it as Stan Hanson walked over to the counter to ask about a book.

"Hi, Stan," Nell managed to say around the catch in her throat. "It's nice to see you out in the middle of the day. Giving a talk to some civic group, I'd imagine."

Stan smiled, but it wasn't the usual polished meet-and-greet smile Nell was accustomed to seeing from the mayor. Stan Hanson looked diminished somehow.

"No. I've put the kibosh on some of that for a while. I have plenty of things on my desk needing my attention—wind turbines, trying to help the fishermen, things I've started and need to finish."

Nell smiled as if she understood. But her mind was back behind the counter, where Danny Brandley busied himself and hid his feelings behind the computer, looking up the book Stan had asked about.

Nell took the bag from the counter, nodded her good-bye, and walked out into a brisk September day, the breeze a welcome salve for the feelings collecting inside her.

Birdie and Cass were walking up the steps to the Ocean's Edge as Nell approached from the other side.

Nell forced a smile to her face and tried to push aside her conversation with Danny. As Ben reminded her with some regularity, there were some things that weren't within her control.

"Is Mary here yet?" she asked. She glanced automatically over to the bar. It was dotted with customers, some stopping for a drink on their way home, others finishing up a meeting in the comfortable lounge. Tyler Gibson was behind the bar mixing a drink. He looked over and waved.

Tyler was one person to be crossed off the list of those having had a problem with Jeffrey. They liked each other, even if they had a few differences, which Esther Gibson wasn't shy talking about. She said Jeffrey was good for her grandson, a good role model.

Ryan Arcado was there, too, near the bar, dark hair flopping across his forehead. Several customers at round bar tables vied for his attention, but Ryan had his back turned, a grin on his face as he scrolled through texts, neglecting his waiter duties. Nell looked around, half expecting to see Jeffrey coming around the corner to scold the young man. But no one came, and Ryan continued to text.

I coulda killed the guy. The words echoed in Nell's head. It's what Ryan had said right after the funeral when talking about Jeffrey tossing his cell phone in the Dumpster. And Zack Levin hadn't praised Jeffrey, either.

"It's not the same, is it?" Nell looked over at Cass and Birdie.

They looked at the bar and nodded. It wasn't. It wouldn't be. Jeffrey's familiar figure, his warm hugs, would not be back.

But hopefully justice would be, and soon.

"Mary Pisano is waiting for you in the outdoor lounge," a hostess told them, walking across the entry with menus in her hands. "It's chilly today, but we turned on the heaters and lit a fire. It smells like fall." She smiled and led them through the nearly empty restaurant to the deck.

Mary sat at a tall round table, her feet barely touching the rungs of the stool. Beside her sat Karen Hanson, her fingers tapping on a yellow pad.

"I've ordered something for us to taste called a cucumber fizz," Mary said, bypassing hellos. "It might be nice to have a refreshing drink at the party."

Karen looked indulgently at her. They were an odd couple, the mayor's wife and Mary. Both had husbands with demanding jobs that often kept them away from home—one a fisherman and the other a city official. Perhaps that's what made their relationship work.

Nell sat on one of the stools and looked over at Karen. "I just ran into Stan."

"Stan?" Karen looked surprised. "Where? He was speaking at the hospital guild volunteer event today. Were you there?"

"No. He was in the bookstore, on his way to the office, when I saw him. He didn't mention giving a talk." But he mentioned *not* giving talks. Nell wondered whether he had forgotten it, something that never sat well with voters. From the look on Karen's face, she was thinking the same thing.

"Sometimes Stan gets his priorities mixed up. I lined this talk up weeks ago," Karen said. She checked her phone, as if expecting an explanation—an apology?—on the small screen. Then she slipped it into her purse and concentrated on the waitress passing around five tall cucumber fizzes. "Enjoy," she said, then disappeared back inside.

Nell watched Garrett Barros walk out, his shirt straining slightly over his wide chest. Their eyes met briefly and he offered a tentative smile, then followed it with a nod. It was meant to be friendly, she thought, but there was something that added an edge to it, as if he wasn't sure he wanted to be smiling at her.

"Nell, does three weeks from now sound good to you? It will be the actual week of your anniversary, and the back of the inn will be beautiful then, the leaves just starting to turn. The swamp maples will be brilliant—the beeches and oaks, also. And we'll keep it simple; I promise," Mary began.

Nell pushed her doubts away and simply smiled. Ben had told her that business at the bed-and-breakfast was a little slow, and having a party there would remind all their friends that Ravenswood by the Sea was the perfect place to put up visitors and hold events. It was the least they could do for Mary.

Karen slipped Nell a sheet of paper with a menu written in her neat printing style—a distinctive combination of block and script that was utterly legible. Nell found reading Karen's thank-you notes pure pleasure, simply because of the handwriting. She read through the list with Cass and Birdie peering at it from either side of her.

It was all the things Nell and Ben loved—Gracie's lobster rolls, Harry's pasta salads with fresh grilled vegetables. Lots of finger food—calamari and sea salt shrimp and tiny crab sandwiches with sprinkles of the Cheese Closet's feta on top. It read like a menu Nell would plan herself, a gift to her friends.

A river of relief passed through her, followed almost immediately by gratitude and a twinge of guilt at her reticence in letting Mary take over the celebration. Her friend was saving her from details that wouldn't fit easily into her life right now. Not until Jules Ainsley was released from the cloud of suspicion smothering her—and until a murderer was safely behind bars.

She looked at Mary again, this small dynamo of a woman sitting quietly with a smug smile on her face. "Didn't I tell you I'd treat you and Ben right? Especially Ben. I plan on marrying him after you and my Eddie are gone."

They laughed at the image of the not-quite-five-foot Mary Pisano alongside Ben Endicott, his six-four frame belying the fact that the only basketball he ever played was Sunday pickup games at the Y.

"I asked Karen to contact the purveyors of this fine menu, and in her persuasive way she has brought everyone on board."

"But Mary has everything else organized, which is how it needs to be. I have a full plate right now, helping Stan with his campaign. He needs me by his side."

Nell looked up. The words were said with a tone that Karen didn't often use. She thought of the expression on Stan's face in the bookstore. In hindsight, it wasn't a tired look at all. Instead, it was the look of someone distracted, someone grappling with a difficult decision that had no good answer.

"Of course Stan needs you," Birdie was saying. "I told Mary a million times, I'm just across the street and I will be on call for anything you need."

"That's nice, Birdie," Mary said, "but you have a few other things on your mind."

"I suppose we all do," Birdie said. "It's difficult when friends are in pain."

Nell caught the word "friends," and realized that included Jules as well as Don Wooten, Maeve, the chief, and others so affected by Jeffrey's death. Perhaps that's what she had seen on the mayor's face. Grief for an old friend. Worry about a murderer walking freely somewhere. A shared anguish that they needed to bring to an end—soon.

Mary motioned to the waitress for the bill. "How do you think Jules is doing? She stopped by today and mentioned the support you've given her. Thank you for that. I feel a little bit like I took her in when things were happy, then abandoned her."

"Of course you didn't. And she knows that. This house was important to her. It's a good place for her to be right now," Nell said.

"She told me about the painting," Mary said.

"Painting?" Karen looked up.

They had all decided the night before that it had taken great courage for Jules to share her life with them. It wasn't intended for the rumor mill. Nell wondered now how much she had told Mary about her life. As much as they all loved her, holding confidences wasn't Mary's long suit.

Mary went on, explaining to Karen, "She came across a painting that resembled the house on Ridge Road. She loved the painting, and when she saw the house, it seemed like kind of an omen to her. A vacation place here would be a nice investment, I told her, and fixing up that place might help her get through all this mess."

So Jules had been cautious in talking to Mary. They would be cautious, too. "That's a good thought," Nell said. "She certainly has a lot on her mind. But she's a strong woman, and she will somehow survive all this."

Karen leaned in, her voice lowered. "How is she really doing? She used to run through town daily, but not lately. The article in the paper yesterday shocked all of us. It's started a barrage of rumors all over town. People are talking about the garden glove as if it has put the nail in the coffin for her. People can be cruel. I can't believe that what they're saying is true."

"It's *not* true," Mary said. Her words were definitive. "And someone will find something that proves it." She stared at Nell, Birdie, and Cass as if to ask them what they were waiting for.

"Frankly," she went on, "it was a coward who leaked that information to the newspaper. I mean, think about it. It would have had to be someone who actually saw her put the glove in her car, because—according to Esther Gibson—the information didn't come from the police. And if someone had seen Jules put it there, don't you think they'd have run to the police with the information to speed up the investigation? Good grief. We need this solved so everyone can stop looking over shoulders and around corners and double locking their doors at night."

Mary stopped, but only because she needed to breathe. Her cheeks were red and the vehemence of her belief was spread out over the Ocean's Edge lounge. Several people looked their way. Beyond the bar, Nell spotted Don Wooten, his forehead creased as he watched the heated exchange. Normally at this time of day, his lounge was quiet with people drinking Chablis and sherry and not looking for a fight.

"I think you said it very nicely—and you're right," Birdie said. "Finding the glove in Jules's car was to be kept confidential. The information didn't come from the police."

Birdie tapped her pencil on the yellow pad. "We have three weeks."

"To get ready for the party?" Karen said. "That's more than enough time."

Mary stared at her. "Three weeks to find a murderer. I refuse to have the Endicott anniversary party clouded by a murderer on the loose."

They left the lounge a short time later, judging the cucumber fizz a must for the anniversary party—as long as they had plenty of beer, wine, and coffee. They filed back through the restaurant, which was now filling up with early diners.

As they passed the swinging doors to the kitchen, Garrett Barros walked out, a white apron tied around his waist. He walked immediately their way, as if he'd been looking through the small window in the kitchen door, waiting for them. He stood directly in front of them, blocking them from moving forward.

"Hello, Garrett," Nell said.

"Miz Endicott, Miz Favazza," he said. His eyes flitted over Karen, then moved on to Cass. He frowned. "I remember you. You used to live next door to me." He paused, then said, "I'm glad you don't live in that house anymore."

"Me, too, Garrett. Your binoculars got the better of me."

"Binoculars?" Karen asked, trying hard to follow the conversation.

Garrett glared at Cass. "You should be nice like your ma. I watch birds."

"That's wonderful, Garrett." Nell's voice was kind. "That's a noble pastime. But watching people in their houses or yards with binoculars isn't noble."

Garrett jerked his head around and looked at Nell, his face clouded. "I don't do that. Sometimes people get in the way of my birds."

Don Wooten walked over, but Garrett held his ground. "Jules is a nice girl. I don't watch her."

"What's going on, Garrett?" Don asked. His voice was even, but his frown caused Garrett to shift from one foot to the other before answering.

"Nothing, Mr. Wooten. We were talking about my neighbor. Her name is Julia."

Don nodded. "Julia," he said. "Julia Ainsley?"

Garrett nodded.

Don looked at Nell. "Is there a new development? Has she been arrested?"

The wording offended Nell, and then she realized that it was what the town was thinking—that Jules Ainsley was quite possibly a murderer. They wanted more information. They especially wanted her to be in jail. Many people didn't know Jules, at least not beyond her name and face, and what they read in the paper or heard on Coffee's patio, the Gull Tavern, or at the Ocean's Edge bar was what they knew to be true. Jules wasn't "one of them," after all. Nell shouldn't blame Don for being on alert, just like the rest of the town.

Ben called it unintentional viciousness. The longer that the rumors churned and gained weight and substance, the more difficult life was going to be for Jules. And that thought was awful.

Don Wooten took Garrett aside and talked to him briefly, then watched him while he walked back into the kitchen. Then Don turned back to the group of women. "What's going on?"

The kitchen door opened again almost immediately and Garrett came out. "I know Julia didn't murder Jeffrey Meara," he said, his words clear and his expression one of absolute certainty.

He spoke as if he knew Jules didn't murder the Bartender—because he knew who did.

Chapter 28

Before anyone could utter a word, Garrett turned around and walked back into the kitchen.

Don looked at the swinging door, then back to the women. "I'm sorry if there's been a problem out here. I'll talk to Garrett."

"There isn't any problem, Don," Nell said. "You don't need to talk to him."

"Except for the binoculars," Mary Pisano said, standing as tall as her wedge sandals allowed. "What was that about, Nell?"

"He uses binoculars to spy?" Karen said, her voice laced with concern.

Don asked, "What binoculars?"

Mary looked at Cass. "You lived next to him for a while. What do you think?"

Cass shrugged. "Garrett likes to use binoculars. I'd see him outside all the time, night and day. Looking at birds, he'd tell me, though it struck me as odd that he'd be out there at midnight. Don't birds sleep at night?"

"A Peeping Tom," Karen said.

Don stared at the kitchen door. "Binoculars?" he repeated, as if unsure of the word.

Nell spoke up. She wasn't sure what was motivating her—maybe that Don Wooten seemed to think there was something menacing about Garrett Barros having a pair of binoculars. Without his being there to defend himself, it seemed unfair to him. He had struck a surprising chord in her today, especially since just two days before the same man had frightened her as he stood behind the bank of pine trees with binoculars in his hand—and with Rebecca Early and Jules just a few yards away.

Today was different and she had no earthly idea why. But somehow, for some reason, she believed him.

She looked at Don. "I don't think there's anything to worry about. Jules isn't worried about Garrett."

"But he's watching her house with binoculars?" Karen asked. She looked at Cass. "He's been doing this for a long time?"

"We don't know that," Nell answered. "Maybe he simply likes to keep an eye on what's going on in his neighborhood, along with the birds, and in a good way. Not to hurt anyone. Jules is probably safer being next door to him than anywhere else in town right now."

With that, Nell reminded Birdie and Cass that she needed to stop by Izzy's shop before the store closed. A new shipment of wool had come in. Perfect for winter projects.

"I'm not sure what to make of all that," Birdie said, climbing into the front seat. "But I think a talk with Garrett Barros outside his place of employment might be worthwhile. He's an interesting young man, not what I expected. But then, I've never spoken with him before."

Birdie thought about what she had said. "That's a shame, isn't it? To form an opinion of someone without really knowing who they are, except for the way they smile or the way they walk or their mannerisms. Without letting them reveal themselves."

Nell started the car, Birdie's words hanging there in front of the steering wheel. Yes, it was a shame, and she'd done the same thing—how many times?—without even being conscious of it.

"Do you think the police have talked to Garrett?" Cass asked from the backseat. "Could he have been home the day Jeffrey was killed? He seemed pretty sure Jules didn't do it."

"They must have talked to all the neighbors," Nell said. "But I'm not sure he would have mentioned bird-watching in a police interview. Or even his binoculars. We could easily find out if he was working that day."

"And what we're assuming is that he might have seen something, not that he might have done something . . ." Cass's words lingered there, syphoned out of everyone's thoughts.

Nell thought back to the Ocean's Edge staff that had stood outside the church that day. According to one of the hostesses, some of the staff had snuck out of the funeral service as soon as they could. Maybe just stayed inside the church until their boss noticed their presence. Garrett was there. Was he one of those who had fled? More important, probably, was whether he was one of those who had been fired and carried a grudge against Jeffrey Meara.

"Doesn't your Ella bird-watch?" she asked Birdie. Birdie's housekeeper had some interesting hobbies and, if Nell remembered correctly, bird-watching was one of them. "Maybe she knows Garrett."

Don Wooten sounded skeptical about the bird-watching explanation. Karen Hanson didn't buy it, either. Were they being naive?

"I was thinking the same thing, Nell. If he is in any way serious about getting to know our fine feathered friends—which, by the way, is the name of Ella's bird-watching club—Ella will know it."

The image of the tall, narrow housekeeper in bird-watching gear, a safari hat shielding her from the sun, lightened the mood.

Cass leaned forward in her seat.

"Garrett Barros moves to the beat of his own drum, my ma always said. Pete thought I was too hard on him."

"Pete knows Garrett?"

"Oh, you know, everyone around here knows everyone. He and Garrett were in some youth explorers group once upon a time."

"He's Pete's age," Nell mused. "Somehow I thought he was in his early twenties."

"No, closer to thirty," Cass said. "He just looks young."

"Did you get to know him at all when you stayed in Izzy's house?" Birdie asked.

"No, not really—I wasn't around much. That was during the time the lobster business was in turmoil. But I admit he gave me the willies sometimes. I'd see him out in the potting shed, fiddling around, or standing on the rocks out in the back with those binoculars. One time I asked to look through them, but he refused. He said he had to get a specially made pair, and he was the only one who could see through them."

"Why was that?"

"He's left-handed, he said, and had to get a specially modified something or other. Controllers, I think. He was very protective of them."

It sounded like an excuse, Nell thought. "So he knew that backyard well," she said.

"Sure. He had easy access, just like the Seroogys next door to you and anyone else who uses your backyard shortcut," Cass said.

Of course. That's what neighborhoods in small towns fostered: sharing. The winding trail in her backyard was worn smooth by neighbors making their way to the beach. It was what one did.

Cass continued. "If Garrett was home the day Jeffrey was killed and saw him walk around the house—and Garrett doesn't miss much—it would have been simple for him to meet Jeffery back there."

"And he could have left the funeral early and rummaged through Maeve's den, I suppose," Nell said, though her voice lacked conviction.

"So we need to find out how Garrett felt about his boss," Birdie said. "At least for starters."

Cass sat back in the seat, looking out the window, quiet and thinking. Though as Nell caught a glimpse of Cass's expression in the rearview mirror, she wasn't sure she was thinking about Garrett Barros.

When they pulled up in front of the yarn shop, Cass got out, looked over at the bookstore for a long moment, then followed Nell and Birdie past Izzy's colorful window, filled with yarn and matching autumn leaves.

Fall. A time of change.

It was near closing time and the shop was nearly empty. Mae stood behind the checkout counter, talking with Laura Danvers as she scanned several skeins of soft yellow and deep blue merino yarn into the computer. They looked up as the bell chimed over the door.

"You look like a posse," Laura said with a grin. "Red Ranger rides again."

Nell looked at the stack of yarn Mae was loading into Laura's bag. "And you look like you are outfitting the Sea Harbor fishing fleet. I hope you saved some for us."

Laura laughed. "I can't resist. Besides, like everyone else around here, we're spending more time at home these days and knitting is a great escape. Usually in the fall my girls love to hike over in Ravenswood Park—even Elliott—but it's just too forbidding right now. The girls sense it, though we try not to talk about it in front of them."

Birdie nodded. "This, too, shall pass," she said, touching Laura's arm lightly with her hand. "It will."

Nell watched Laura's eyes, the eyes of a mother bear protecting her cubs. And hating the atmosphere wrapping her family in fear.

The bell above the door rang again and attention turned to Beatrice Scaglia, carrying a large Italian leather briefcase, her heels clicking on the hardwood floor.

"I'm not too late. Good," she said.

Mae looked at her over half-moon glasses. "What are you not too late for? We're just about to close—you know that." In spite of her tone, Izzy's store manager liked the brassy councilwoman in the ridiculous—in Mae's opinion—heels. She found it amusing that Beatrice hadn't completed a single knitting project in five years—and was probably less adept than Danny Brandley in mastering the stockinette stitch—but she was a store regular.

As Mae often told Izzy, "She's probably our best customer—she has more yarn stashed in her house than we have in the stockroom. If this place ever burns down we'll set up shop in her basement."

Beatrice bought yarn, but it was the conversations she overheard in the back room of Izzy's shop that she stored away in her razor-sharp mind and memory—and that led to her claim that she was Sea Harbor's most well-informed council member on women's issues.

And no one doubted that she was.

"Oh, Mae. You're so . . . so Mae." Beatrice laughed, a well-controlled and lilting laugh that served her well on the campaign trail. "I'm here to give you some flyers and posters. You'll thank me. You're the first to know." She looked around at the others. "All of you. I couldn't have asked for a better crew to distribute these."

Laura frowned. "Distribute flyers?"

"Flyers? What for?" Izzy walked up from the knitting room carrying a box of yarn.

"Izzy, sweetie, come here," Beatrice said, gesturing to the round oak table centering the room. She pushed aside a basket of yarn and replaced it with her large leather briefcase. Pulling out a stack of colorful flyers, she handed each of them a pile, then pulled out a large poster and handed it to Izzy. "For your window," she said.

Izzy scanned the poster. "A debate?" The headline was bold:

SEA HARBOR'S DEBATE OF THE CENTURY

Mae looked at the matching flyer, then pushed her glasses into her thinning hair. "This sounds formidable, Scaglia. What century are you talking about exactly?"

Beatrice ignored Mae and looked at the others. "It's a wonderful idea, don't you think? I've reserved the community center. Everyone will come and decide for themselves whom they want as their next mayor. But I need to get the word out. It's scheduled for next week."

"Well," Birdie said, the single word seeming to take up an inordinate amount of time. Her eyes scanned the flyer. "I think this will be an interesting evening, Beatrice. How nice that you and Stan have agreed to have a public conversation."

Beatrice looked down at her bright red shoes. Then she lifted her head and smiled at the circle of women looking at her, the same smile she used when trying to convince the council of some unpopular project. "I haven't talked to Stan about it yet. But he is such a broad-minded, intelligent man, how could he say no?"

Chapter 29

Ben laughed when Nell told him about the debate being planned. "There's not much Stan can do about it now, is there?"

"He told me he was cutting back on events like this. I wonder if Karen knows about it?"

Birdie stood nearby, half listening. Her hands were flat on the stone railing of the yacht club veranda. Her look traveled beyond the terraced lawns to the carefully groomed beach. It was nearly empty tonight, even of stalwart twilight swimmers. The water temperature had finally given in to autumn, and it would be months and a new year before towels and blankets and umbrellas dotted the wide expanse of sand. North of the beach, sailboats, anchored in their slips, rocked gently in the breeze. "It's so peaceful," Birdie murmured. "So deceptively peaceful."

"The lull before the storm." Ben excused himself to check on the others, who were watching the last inning of the Sox beating the Yankees on the wide-screen television in the bar.

"Ben looks tired," Birdie said, watching him walk away.

The terrace was nearly empty, the breeze encouraging diners to eat inside. Nell pulled a pale blue shawl around her shoulders. "Some of it doesn't deserve sympathy. He and Sam were sailing today and this wind created quite a challenge. But the other part is concern. He isn't as convinced that Garrett Barros is entirely harmless. I think that's one reason he insisted Jules come with us tonight. He wanted to talk to her about it."

Coming to the club for dessert and drinks wasn't something Ben and Nell usually did. But tonight the management had asked board members to come to encourage attendance at their chocolate dessert night, and Ben found it difficult to explain that he'd planned an evening at home in sweats watching the ball game. Sam, too, had been recruited and was equally at a loss for an excuse. Cass, on the other hand, wouldn't pass up a chocolate dessert buffet if her life depended on it.

They'd found Danny in the bar alone, and he had joined them for dessert. He and Cass were cordial and friendly—and distant.

"What will Ben say to Jules? Beware of the neighbor?"

"I suppose something like that. He plans to ask Jerry about him at a meeting tomorrow."

"Game is boring." It was Izzy, coming up behind them.

Jules and Cass trailed a few steps behind, carrying on an animated conversation. Nell was pleased to see the ease with which Cass greeted her, and the easy conversations that flowed between them during the dessert buffet.

"Try banding lobster," Cass was saying. "I always try to get the left-handed ones."

"You're talking Jules into banding lobsters?" Izzy said. "Don't do it, Jules. I almost lost a finger the first time she and Pete took me out."

Jules laughed. "No. Cass kept knocking into me during dessert. I thought she was still huffy with me, but it turns out she's left-handed. Now she's trying to convince me that some lobsters are left-handed, too, and I should go out on one of her boats and see for myself."

"Honest," Cass said, taking in their looks of disbelief. "Some lobsters are left-handed crushers. Like me." She clenched her jaw and left hand fiercely.

They laughed at the sight of the lobsterwoman, dressed in a silk blouse and skinny jeans, forcing a Rosie the Riveter pose. It was a contradiction that Nell often marveled at. Although Cass did much of the office work now in managing the family lobster business, for years she was out on the boats hauling in traps, checking buoys, banding lobsters—and Nell could never quite reconcile that woman with the attractive one she saw every day. Even back when Birdie had to remind Cass to shower before showing up for knitting night and make her promise not to touch a single strand of yarn until she had. She obeyed Birdie's dictate. But she was always Cass, always the intriguing, dark-haired woman who looked less like she could tend hundreds of lobster traps than the man in the moon.

The laughter traveled across the terrace.

Don Wooten, standing with his wife a few yards away, turned around at the sound. Nell caught his look and waved them over.

"I thought it was an all-woman's enclave," he joked.

"It is," Cass said. "But you're allowed."

"Game's over, Sox win another," Sam announced. He and Ben walked up to the group. Ben carried a tray with glasses and a bottle of port, another of cognac. "Coffee and Baileys are on the way," he said.

"They've hired you, Endicott?" Don said. "About time you got a real job."

"He's in training," Sam said. "Be patient with him."

The mood passed through the group, jovial and welcoming, and for a brief time they felt safe, cushioned by friends, the ocean breeze, and a sky littered with millions of stars.

How could evil exist in this place? Nell wondered, her eyes examining the canopy above her. She looked over at Don Wooten. He looked tired, not entirely himself, but putting up a strong front. The kind that says everything is normal. Everything is good. But maybe it's not.

When the group moved on to replaying Cass's claim of left-handed lobsters, Nell pulled him aside. "About earlier today—"

"I'm sorry about that. Garrett was out of line."

"I think he was trying to be helpful."

"It's not very helpful to spy on people. I talked to the police today. I've never had reason to not trust the guy, but everything needs to be checked out now. Even me."

Nell looked at him, her brows lifting.

"You're not surprised, Nell. You heard firsthand how Jeffrey and I got along. I know he was a tradition at the Edge, and he was loved by lots of people for good reason. But frankly, he wasn't much of a businessman. He wasn't a good owner. And he was a terrible partner."

"Maybe it was just a matter of different methods, Don. Maeve said you wanted to buy him out. Is that true?"

He looked surprised. "Yes. I thought it was the only way to save the restaurant."

"And he said no."

"You know a lot about this, Nell." His tone had changed, his words defensive.

Nell was quiet.

"Yes, you're right. He said no. I think in time he'd have changed his mind." He looked out over the sea, took a drink of the brandy Ben had handed him, and looked back at Nell. "Jeffrey and I did things differently. He changed when he became an owner. He thought he had to make strong decisions or he wasn't carrying his weight. But his decisions were driving off some vendors and creating staff problems—and you can't get away with that in a small town like this."

"And he didn't get away with it," Nell said quietly.

Don clenched his jaw. He took a deep breath and leveled a look at her, his voice more weary now than defensive. "Nell, we've been friends for a long time. Do you think I could have killed Jeffrey Meara?"

Nell was saved from answering by a sudden gust of wind off the ocean, tossing napkins in the air, sending scarfs flying. "Saved by the wind," was how she would later describe the awkward moment to the knitters.

Ben announced it was time to go, past his bedtime. An early morning was staring him in the face.

Don helped Nell untangle the shawl that had whipped around her neck. "Sorry," he said.

Nell watched them walk away, not at all sure what her old friend was sorry for.

Chapter 30

*J*ane Brewster was dying to see Jules Ainsley's painting. "Nell, I love you, but you don't describe paintings well. I need to see it. And you mentioned there were others. I'd like to see those, too."

Jane was with art the way Ben was with a new sailboat, or Cass with a new lobster buoy, or Izzy with a new knitting needle. Tools of their trade—or their passions, as the case may be. And they would drive across heaven or hell to take a peek.

"I don't really know if it's good. I just know I liked it very much. It was alive to me, and expressed something. As Jules said, 'It's a happy painting.' "

"Good. Don't we all need a little bit of that? Wednesdays are slow days and Ham can handle things at the gallery without me for an hour or so just fine. Let me know what time is good."

Nell hung up, checking her own calendar before going upstairs to shower.

Ben had left at the crack of dawn, or so it seemed to her. "This is retirement?" she had murmured that morning as he'd dropped kisses into her tousled hair.

They had both awakened early, reaching out for the other in the tangle of sheets. Nell wasn't sure what woke them, whether it was the rattle of the shutters, the strong ocean breeze, or simply something more basic—a need to be together, their bodies pressed to each other. A need to be touched.

With great reluctance Ben had finally left their bed, promising he would cut back on retirement commitments the first chance he got.

But he wouldn't do that. Of course he wouldn't. Nell stepped into the bracing spray of the shower, smiling as the lovely morning wakeup played itself out again in the steam of the shower. He wouldn't be Ben if he weren't using the keen intellect she'd fallen in love with on a Harvard campus a million years ago. She'd often teased him that falling in love with him was all about the brain, the fact that he helped her through a dreadful symbolic logic course the semester they'd met. The intellect, the brain. And the kind, funny, gentle man who marched beside her in peace rallies and argued with her deep into the night about war and peace, good and evil, poverty and wealth. And the way he kissed her in the rain. Those things, too.

Wednesday was busy, but not too busy to find time for Jane. And she felt sure Jules would like the company. She had been staying close to home, Izzy told her, painting and polishing, planting flowers along the front walk. She'd joined Izzy for a few runs, but mostly in the early morning or in the evening. When beaches were empty. There were plenty of things to do getting the house up to par, but Nell knew there were other reasons, too. Not the least of which was avoiding the stares of people who were frightened of anyone whose name had been connected to a murder. Frightened, cautious, and sometimes mean. It wasn't about fairness. It was about fear.

Birdie said she'd like to check in on Jules, too, as Nell thought she might. She had morning appointments but could be free by noon.

"Perfect." Nell would pick up Birdie first, then a seafood salad at the Ocean's Edge. That and a sack of sourdough rolls and they'd be set.

Besides, Nell had a question. And a stop at the Edge might satisfy more than their hunger.

The restaurant was already busy when Nell and Birdie walked in. Tyler Gibson spotted them from behind the bar. He held up a white sack with a handle.

"Our seafood salad?" Nell smiled.

"The best in the world," Tyler said. "Shrimp, mussels, sea scallops—and not a drop of mayo in sight." He came around the bar and gave each of them a one-armed hug. The blond bartender considered Birdie Favazza his guiding angel for reasons none of them could figure out, though Nell suspected Birdie had kept some of Tyler's earlier indiscretions out of reach of his grandmother's ears. For whatever reason, his loyalty knew no bounds. "I threw in some calamari, too," he whispered to her now. He motioned for another bartender to take his place so he could talk to "two of my favorite women."

"Thank you for not saying 'young ladies,' Ty," Birdie said, her expression one of mock sternness. "I don't despise many things in my very fine life, but that's one of them. I am not young and don't want to be."

Ty laughed. "May I call you ageless? You're definitely that."

"That's fine, dear. Now we need some information from you. Do you have a minute?"

"For you? Is the moon made of butter?"

Tyler's malapropos remark was met with affectionate smiles—such remarks were one of the many things that endeared the lanky bartender to all of them. As his own grandmother often said, he wasn't the brightest puppy in the litter, but definitely the most lovable. And certainly the best looking.

Nell scribbled down the date they were interested in on a piece of paper, and Birdie suggested to Ty where he might find the answer to their question. The young man dutifully went to the computer at the hostess station and began punching keys.

Nell could tell that the date hadn't registered with Tyler. To him, it was a Friday. Any Friday, and that was fine. There was no need for Tyler to make inferences.

Schedule, he typed in. *Garrett Barros.* He looked up at them while the computer was pulling up pages. "Garrett's an okay guy. Don't know him too well. He doesn't hang with us. Mostly keeps to himself. But he's cool."

And he watches birds? Nell wanted to ask, but instead she waited for the computer to answer their question.

"Do the owners put their schedules in the computer?" Birdie asked.

"Nah. No need. Jeffrey was always here, except when he wasn't. And then he'd call out to someone where he was going, when he'd be back. And Don Wooten? I guess he probably put it in his own calendar—he's really organized like that. Wants to be sure we know where he is if we need him. They both were like that in fact—made sure we could get ahold of them."

He looked back to the computer. "Okay," he said, pleased with himself. "I have it right here. It was Friday you wanted, right?"

Nell nodded.

"Yeah, I got it. Garrett was here that Friday morning helping to stock the meat delivery in the freezer—sometimes Jeffrey gave him crappo jobs like that, but Garrett seemed okay with it. Things like emptying garbage, cleaning out the ovens and wait stations. And it looks like he was on garbage detail after he finished with the meat."

"And the afternoon?"

Tyler looked back at the computer. "Hmm. Looks like he left here about two. Odd time. That shift usually goes till four. But maybe Jeffrey let him go early. Sometimes he did that if we weren't busy."

Nell's heart sank, and only then did she realize how much she wanted Garrett to have been safely collecting garbage or cleaning kitchen sinks or lugging beef carcasses into the freezer that whole long afternoon.

The afternoon Jeffrey Meara was killed.

A quick call to Izzy revealed that she was starving and would give away her very special Signature needles for a taste of the Edge's seafood salad. Well, maybe not really. But would they please pick her up in five minutes?

Nell drove down Ridge Road and parked in front of Jules's house. A minute later Jane Brewster pulled up behind her. They piled out of their cars and stood on the sidewalk for a moment, looking at the house.

"It looks different by day," Nell said. "I swear, each time I see this house, it is more a home."

"Where was Jules when I bought it?" Izzy wondered aloud. "I could have used her magic touch."

A giant pot of autumn-colored mums graced the front stoop. The flagstone pathway that wound around the house had been swept clean, and debris around the Knock Out roses cleared away. Newly planted holly bushes replaced the dead evergreen shrubs and the garden was tilled with rich dark mulch.

The small mailbox was now painted a deep verdant green, matching a fresh coat on the front door and shutters. It was simple and clean and had the look an artist might bring to brightening up a home.

"I love what she's done," Izzy said. "Jules was right. It was an omen that she buy this house."

Jules opened the front door. "Come in, come in, come in." She stepped out and hugged them as they walked up the steps.

Nell and Birdie were surprised; spontaneous warmth wasn't what they'd come to expect from Jules Ainsley. Something about this house was bringing out her softer side.

Instead of analyzing it, Jane Brewster and Izzy simply responded in kind, hugging her back. Jane looped one arm around Jules's waist and walked into the house with her, a barrage of questions matching their footsteps.

Jane's first request was a tour. "I'm the latecomer to all that you've done here. We had some great times in this house when Izzy and Cass took turns living in it," she said, "but not since. I love getting to know people through their living spaces. Come, let me get to know you."

Jules was only too happy to comply. She suggested they start outside and work their way in. She'd done some clearing in the back that the others hadn't seen, either, opening the yard.

"Some clearing" proved to be a panorama. They stepped out the back door onto the porch, and looked out in amazement.

"Good grief," Izzy said. "You must have had one powerful weed-whacker."

"His name is Garrett, believe it or not."

"Garrett Barros?" Nell asked. She forced a judgmental tone out of her voice. Right now, at this moment and until they knew more, Garrett Barros was the last person who should be spending time in Jules's backyard.

Jules nodded. "He saw me out here trying to clear a view of the sea and he offered to do it for me. And voilà—isn't it grand?"

It was grand, and then some. How he did it was a mystery, but trash trees had been pulled out, bushes pruned, the winding path that went down the hill defined and tended, roots dug out and discarded. The result was breathtaking. A million-dollar view.

The hill had just enough of a rise to provide a window to the sea. From her spot on the swing, Jules could watch sunrises and the darkening of the evening sky, the incoming tide and the rush of the water moving back out to sea.

"Stella told me the land wasn't really a part of the property, but no one would care if I wanted to tame it."

Izzy laughed. "For me, not owning it was a nice excuse not to spend time on it, unfortunately. I asked the city a couple times to clean it up, but they had more pressing things to spend money on, and so did I, opening up the new shop. But I never imagined how beautiful the view would be."

"Garrett's one strong brute of a guy and he seemed to know the land well. Where the path was, how to avoid the poison ivy."

Nell listened carefully, but without the gratitude Jules was feeling. She looked over at Birdie and saw that she was storing the information away, hoping it meant absolutely nothing.

Jules was moving off the porch and along a stone path to the potting shed. The Knock Out roses and small shrubs hugging the sides of the building had been neatly trimmed but left in place, keeping the shed in the background.

"I haven't done much in here," Jules was saying, opening the door to the dank-smelling shed. "But someone used it a lot, apparently, and even put her own version of a skylight in." They looked up to a crudely opened roof with a piece of scratched Plexiglas covering the hole. "But at least it brings in light."

A workbench spanned one side with a pegboard above it. A smattering of garden tools hung from metal hooks and several more were scattered on the workbench. Stacks of seedling flats were piled against a wall and an old wheelbarrow and several hoses hung next to rakes and spades and shovels. There was a larger door on the other end, one big enough for a lawnmower. It hung slightly open on a broken hinge.

Izzy looked around. "The last renter left all her tools behind. She was in a hurry to get out before the rent came due."

Nell remembered. It had been the last straw for Sam and Izzy. One too many renters skipping out on their rent and leaving a mess behind.

"Well, I'll clean everything up and use the shed while I'm here. I love to plant." She picked a trowel off the workbench and hung it on the pegboard.

Nell looked around. Ben had told her Jeffrey was killed inside the shed, then stumbled outside, where Jules found him. The inside area was small—a place to go for a private talk, she supposed, if that's what Jeffrey was doing inside. It was hard to imagine any other reason, but all Jules had said was that he'd wanted to meet at the house. Why the potting shed? She looked over at the empty flats, at the tools and a garbage bin near the door. It didn't make sense.

She turned around and watched Jules absently straightening things, piling small seed pots together and stacking several dirty gardening gloves.

Izzy looked over at the gloves. "Those orange ones were mine. They probably should be tossed."

Jules held them up. Dried dirt fell out of the holes in the palms. "You're right." She dropped them in the trash bin. "That leaves three.

Looks like one got lost, like socks." She lined them up on the work surface. A pair of denim gloves and one striped one. They were all dirty, with mud and grass stuck to the cloth.

Jules shuddered.

Nell looked over. And then she remembered and knew what caused Jules to wrap her arms around herself and look away. The glove found in Jules's car was a patterned glove, described in the article leaked to the press as a purple-and-orange-striped glove. Its mate now sat alone.

They all stared at the work top, imagining that inclement afternoon when the sky was dark with storm clouds, the makeshift skylight rattling.

The afternoon someone grabbed a glove and a garden knife from the workbench and stabbed Jeffrey Meara to death.

Jules walked quickly out of the shed and the others followed. They gathered on the porch, welcoming the cool breeze and fresh air.

Nell took a deep, cleansing breath and looked out over the sea, erasing the disturbing images. "Jules, I know remembering that day is awful for you, something you don't want to do, but—"

"I think about it all the time, Nell. There's only one way to get it out of my mind."

Of course there was. Jules was right. Find the person who did this. And put them where they couldn't hurt anyone else. It was the one thing the whole town agreed on.

"Here's something that's been bothering me . . ." Nell began. She hesitated for a minute, and then went on. "I know the police have asked you a zillion questions, but are you up for one more?"

"From you, yes. I'm not sure there are any new questions, but maybe you can find something in my answers that the police might have missed. I think . . . I think it's difficult to interpret what I say without the glove in my car somehow creeping into the picture and coloring it shades of 'she's guilty.' Tommy Porter tries to see beyond it, I can tell. Tries to listen. But even for him it's difficult. That glove grows larger than life."

Izzy frowned. "The glove. Wait a minute." She was in and out of the shed in a split second, holding the striped glove in her hand. "This is the right-hand glove."

For a second her comment fell on deaf ears. Then Jules raised her hand and stared at it. "I'm right-handed."

Nell looked at Jules, then the glove in Izzy's hand. "And whoever used the other glove probably wasn't."

Another thought followed immediately and Nell pushed it to the back of her mind, to a dark corner, along with the hope that she wouldn't have to bring it out again.

Garrett Barros used only binoculars with a modified controller for lefties.

"The glove they found was dirty, messy. I suppose they could say a right-handed person could have grabbed it, forced it on."

"But it wouldn't give the person a good grip on a knife. It would have been clumsy," Jane said. "The Kevlar gloves I use when firing in the raku kiln are larger than garden gloves, but even so I have to have them on the correct hand or my fingers would be twisted and I could drop a pot."

Jules looked over at the glove, as if it were somehow her friend. "I don't know if the police have thought about the glove thing—no one asked me if I was right- or left-handed. But it doesn't matter—I know the truth. And I think the glove does, too." She forced a smile. "Was that your question, Nell?"

"No, but I'd like to pass the glove along to the police. Maybe have Ben take it over." She took it from Izzy and dropped it into her bag. "I think all these things will add up to a whole. And the whole will lead us to the right person."

Birdie had been standing at the edge of the incline, listening and looking out over the sea. She turned and walked back to the edge of the porch. "Jules, I'm wondering about the phone call you got from Jeffrey that day. Did you talk about where you'd meet?"

Jules turned the question over in her mind. "I don't think we were specific," she said finally. "He knew I was going to an open house on

Ridge Road, but didn't even ask the address. He said he knew the house."

"He knew this house?" Nell asked.

Jules nodded. "I didn't think much about it at the time, but . . ."

"But . . . ?" Birdie said. "Did he say anything else?"

"Now that I think back over the conversation, he didn't 'know' the house because he'd driven past it or anything like that. He made it sound more intimate. Like he knew the house well. I wonder if he ever lived here?"

Izzy looked around. "It's possible. But I bought it from a rental company, not the Mearas."

"Did Jeffrey say he'd meet you in the backyard?" Nell asked.

Jules frowned. "I think he just said 'at the house.' But the one thing we were very clear on was the time. Twenty minutes before the open house. I was adamant about it because I'd told Stella I'd be here as it started." She looked slightly embarrassed. "I wanted to challenge any competition, I guess. I don't know how, maybe point out the house's failings, pretend I saw rats." She laughed. "I was determined this house would be mine."

"Why was that odd—about the time, I mean?" Izzy asked.

"He didn't need much time, he said, but he wanted to get it off his mind. And it was something I should know. He could sneak away from work for twenty minutes, which was all he needed. So that was how I set the time. Twenty minutes before the open house.

"But then I decided I'd get here earlier and look around the house by myself, the back, the view of the water, the porch. I hadn't had a chance to really get a good look, and I wanted some time alone before the open house. Strange, I know. But you can't always explain emotion . . . and that's what was driving me. So I got here a full half hour before Jeffrey was supposed to show up."

"And he was already here," Nell said.

"And already dead," Birdie finished.

The silence that followed was uncomfortable, and completely devoid of answers.

Finally Jane said, "I think we need something lovely to cleanse our palates."

Jules brightened. "Like my mother's painting."

"Exactly."

They went through the cheery kitchen and into the den, where Jules had done some more decorating. Cheerful geometric-patterned pillows filled the leather couch, and a new piece of furniture had been added. The chair, upholstered in a bright green, yellow, and rose print, filled a corner of the room. Beside it, a reading lamp and small table invited a cup of tea, a book, and a warm body.

Jane immediately went over to the painting. She got as close as she could, then stepped away, to take in the watery nuances, the play of light and shadow. "Your mother was talented," she said softly. "This is lovely. Ham will want to see it, too—he's the watercolor expert. But I know enough." She looked back at the painting. "It was probably midday when she painted it, I think. And late summer, from the way she painted the light. You mentioned that you had others?"

"Two. I got them out when I knew you were coming, but I had forgotten the terrible shape they were in. My mother hadn't framed them." She untied a brown portfolio case leaning against the desk and pulled out two more paintings, the same size as the one on the wall, and placed them on the desk.

They all gathered around and peered at the hazy images that shined through decades of dust and grime.

"I think both paintings are of the house, but it's hard to tell. I was afraid to touch them. I thought water would probably ruin them."

Jane was quick to agree. "Absolutely don't touch them. Ham can clean these. He's magnificent at many things, and restoring old water-color paintings is one of them."

They looked carefully at both paintings. Glimpses of color came through, the same blues and greens.

Light came through.

Jules's mother had been happy.

Chapter 31

I f she hadn't run into Stella Palazola the next day, Nell might have completely forgotten about the odd comment Jeffrey Meara had made to Jules about her new house. And Izzy's house. And Cass's, too, for a while, anyway. A small home that melted into the Sea Harbor terrain as easily as sand castles.

A simple house that might have remained simple, if Jeffrey Meara hadn't been murdered in its backyard.

A house, Jeffrey had said, *that he knew well.*

Seeing Stella brought Jeffrey's comment to mind, and when Nell spotted her walking toward her office, she motioned for her to wait, then hurried across the street, narrowly avoiding Tommy Porter's cruiser.

"I have a favor to ask of you."

Stella's smile was contagious, matched only by her renewed enthusiasm for her job. When she heard what Nell wanted to know, she nearly puffed up with pleasure. "Absolutely. I know exactly what to do. Sometimes the info is available online, but I might have to go to the courthouse—we learned all about it in school. I will find you everything you want to know, and maybe more. I'm on it."

Nell had no doubt that she was.

She walked back across the street feeling somehow like she was the one who was doing the favor. She turned and watched Stella fairly bouncing through the door on her way up to the real estate office.

Stella would soon be Sea Harbor's top Realtor—there was no doubt about it. She was a young woman who knew her own mind. And she knew other people's minds, too. That was her secret.

The class Izzy was teaching on finishing knitting projects had already begun when Nell walked in. She had promised to be there in case Izzy needed help in working with individuals, although help in finishing sweaters was not exactly her strong suit. She approached each finishing project with fear and determination. Sometimes the determination won.

There were about a dozen people in this class, small enough that Izzy didn't really need her, but she liked being there, she enjoyed watching her niece teach, and she had carved out that hour, so she would stay.

She stood on the top step and looked around. It was a new crowd, new college graduates doing jobs they didn't go to college for—people who worked shifts. Hospitals. Restaurants. Yacht clubs. Galleries. Earnest young people who would someday move on to other jobs, maybe even in their college majors. And in the meantime, they were learning in the trenches, as her mother used to say. And that wasn't always a bad thing, in Nell's opinion.

She noticed the pretty Ocean's Edge hostess Jeffrey had hired that summer sitting with a woman who was now working with Rebecca Early at her Lampworks Gallery. And another who waitressed at Merry's bar and grill. They had good role models, Nell thought. Tyler Gibson, Rebecca Early, and Merry Jackson. They would learn and achieve and move on to their chosen professions with tools they might not have gotten otherwise. Sometimes life worked out that way.

When the class came to an end, Izzy invited people to stay if they had questions or needed extra help. She gestured to where her aunt was standing and told people Aunt Nell would be happy to help, too.

As several people gathered around Izzy, the hostess from the Ocean's Edge approached Nell, her almost finished sweater in her hands. "Mrs. Endicott?" she said.

Nell smiled and said, "Call me Nell." She complimented her on the cable sweater, finished except for the side seams and a button panel.

"I'm Grace," the young woman said. "I've seen you at the Edge."

"Of course. Grace Danvers, right? I know your mother and your cousin Laura—and I know that Jeffrey Meara hired you. He introduced us once, and then bragged to me about you, saying that he had hired the best and the brightest."

Grace blushed. "Mr. Meara was a good guy. He liked that I had a degree in philosophy. Sometimes on breaks we'd argue about Plato's dialogues. He was really into the *Euthyphro*—that's what we were pulling apart that week, that week when he died. Trying to figure out if *Euthyphro* should have done what he did, turning his dad in like that. Even though *Euthyphro* thought his father had done something bad, should he have let it slide for the sake of the relationship? he'd ask me. He liked all those ethical dilemmas. I did, too. The philosopher bartender, I teased him. He knew how to make the philosophers—like Plato—real. He would have been a great teacher."

Nell took the sweater and spread it out on the table, showing her how to line up the seams. "I agree. Jeffrey was very smart. And nice. But not all the staff saw that side of him. If I remember correctly, you called some of them out the day of his funeral."

Grace looked down at her sweater and smoothed down a cable. "You're right. Some of the staff didn't like him much. Jeffrey fired some guys, but it was because they were screwing around. Mr. Wooten hired them back—he just didn't want the repercussions from the families around here, but he made them go through extra training. Probably a good thing."

"Grace, were you working the day Jeffrey died?"

She nodded. "I remember it because we were really busy that day."

"Why is that?"

"It was a Friday, and that day is always busy. Plus, the mayor was talking to the women's guild in the private dining room. Also, we had to close the outdoor dining room because of the weather, so we were crowded and had to shove tables together to accommodate a couple large groups. The Ravenswood B and B staff was here, I remember—Mrs. Pisano treats them to lunch once a month. The gardeners, maids, decorators, painters—you name it, everyone. One time she had so many people we had to put them in the private dining room. She didn't have that many the Friday we're talking about, though—it was kind of a small group. Anyway, she's another one of the good guys."

Nell smiled. Young Grace was a fine judge of character. "But Jeffrey left that afternoon, even though you were busy?"

She nodded. "But he said it'd just be thirty minutes, max. When he found out his meeting was moved up, he was mad at first, but then decided it'd be okay—he'd be back in time for the dinner crowd."

"His appointment was moved up?"

"Someone called the front desk and left a message for him. I gave it to him myself."

"Do you know who called?"

"I assumed it was the woman he was meeting, Julia Ainsley—the one—" She stopped, then dropped her thought and said, "But I don't know. Somebody else took the message and gave it to me."

"Did Garrett take the message?"

"Garrett Barros? Oh, no, no." She answered as if to say, *Of course not*, but was avoiding being rude. "It was another hostess, I think. She asked me to give it to Jeffrey. So I did. And then—I don't know why I did it, but I stood there and I watched him leave that day. Watched him rush down the steps and off to his car. He turned back once, saw me watching him, and waved. And then he was gone."

Her eyes fell to the sweater again, and she cleared her throat, then quickly wiped her eyes with the cuff of her sleeve. "I miss him, you know?"

They had already finished their Thursday-night meal at the yarn shop—lobster corn chowder with a generous splash of sherry added to the potatoes, vegetables, bacon, and chunks of fresh lobster.

Comfort food, Nell said.

Knitting needles filled the coffee table, along with carefully cleaned spaces to rest the sections of the anniversary afghan.

It was nearly finished.

"It's beautiful," Nell whispered. "Every inch of it, every single stitch." She touched the zigzag cables on one of the pieces and thought of Ben, of their life. Walking together through all the curves and winding paths. Moving on. Together. Izzy had it all here in knits and purls, cables and lacy hearts. Their life together.

A loud rapping at the side door brought her out of her reverie and Izzy scrambled across the room.

Stella Palazola stood in the doorway. "Hi, guys," she said. "I came out of my office and realized it was Thursday. Perfect, I said. They'll all be over there in the back room knitting up a storm, and here you are." She flapped several pieces of paper in the air.

"What's up, Stella?" Izzy asked, her eyes on the moving pieces of paper.

"It's for Nell." She looked across the room and grinned. "Told you I'd get it all. And more."

"Stella, you're wonderful." Nell walked over and gave her a hug. "Thank you."

"And now I'm out of here. I have a big date. Ty Gibson. Who would have thought he'd ever look at me?" She laughed, completely unaware that over the years she had left the gawky teenager with braces behind and morphed into a lovely young woman. Stella was neither fat nor thin, neither ravishing nor unattractive. But her personality transformed the ordinariness into a presence that no one could overlook. Stella brightened up a room. As Harry Garozzo said recently, "From head to toe, our grown-up Stella is simply *bella*."

"He'd be crazy not to look at Stella," Cass said as the door slammed shut behind her. "She's definitely a keeper. Now what did she bring you?"

They settled back into the chairs around the fireplace and Nell put on her reading glasses. "Jules told us that when Jeffrey called her that day, he didn't need directions to the house. He knew it well, he said."

"But in a personal way, right? Like maybe he had visited someone there?" Izzy said.

"Or even lived there himself maybe. That house is old," Birdie said.

"Exactly. I don't know how it all connects together, but there aren't any real coincidences when you're trying to find a murderer. So here we have these two things lining up beside each other: Jeffrey wanting to talk to Jules. Jules wanting to buy a house that Jeffrey knew well. So I asked Stella to put together a history of the house for me."

She looked down and began reading the information on the top sheet. "And you're right, Birdie. The house is old. Over a hundred years. I suppose we knew that when Izzy bought it, but I'd forgotten."

"Although that's not terribly unusual for this area," Birdie added.

Nell scanned the sheet, her finger moving from line to line. "The little Ridge Road neighborhood was part of a fishing community. Not the fleet captains, but the crew. They couldn't afford widow's walks on their homes, so they built homes up on that hill, where they could look out to sea, waiting for the boats to come in." She paused and skipped over some mundane facts. Stella had been quite complete in her task.

"It looks like houses changed hands every few decades, and then in the fifties Jules's house, along with some others, were bought by families who modernized them and used them as vacation homes. Actually, it looks like a Sea Harbor family owned this house, but they had another house they lived in. The Brogans." She looked up and took off her glasses. "Does that name sound familiar, Birdie?"

Birdie wrinkled her forehead. "Hmm. Yes. There was a Brogan family. I think it was *James* Brogan. He owned some companies in Boston, but he had a huge house over near Elliott Danvers on the Point. Quite enormous. No one knew them well because they spent most of their time in the city, although the mansion here was supposed to be their primary residence. They were an older couple."

"Kids?" Cass asked.

"I think so. Raised here, probably by servants."

Nell looked back at the sheet. "They owned the Ridge Road house from the fifties until . . ." She took off her glasses and looked up. "Until the year that Jules Ainsley was born."

They sat quietly, processing the time frame in their heads.

Izzy spoke up, detailing the facts. "So the house was owned by the Brogans when Jules's mother did the painting of the house. They owned the house when Penelope Ainsley got pregnant with Jules."

"And they sold it the next year," Nell said. "That's interesting."

"I don't see Jeffrey's name on the list of owners, so that rules out him having lived there—at least as an owner. After the Brogans sold it, a couple lived there until they moved into retirement. And then Izzy bought it."

"This could mean something or nothing, but it would be helpful to find out more about the Brogans."

"I can do that easily," Birdie said. "Tomorrow afternoon is teatime with the old gals. Someone will have the scoop."

That brought a chuckle. It was Birdie's affectionate description of a group of mostly wealthy Sea Harbor residents of her own generation who, like Birdie, could buy and sell the town if they so chose. They met semiregularly, though "tea" was a misnomer, that having long ago been replaced by fine sherry.

"So do we think there is something about the house itself that got Jeffrey killed?" Cass asked.

"It's the dead man who has the answers," Birdie said. "We need to get to know Jeffrey even better. Figure out why he wanted to talk to Jules. And if that was the reason he was killed—or was it simply where he happened to be when the murderer acted?"

Nell repeated her conversation with Grace Danvers. "Someone had called and asked Jeffrey to come early that day, before Julia got there. Perhaps someone wanted to talk to him before he talked to Jules."

"That means someone knew he was meeting her that day—and when," Izzy said.

"Which could have been anyone at the Edge. Jeffrey always let people know where he was going," Nell said. "Even customers could have overheard him. Jeffrey wasn't the quietest man in the world."

Customers. Nell repeated Grace's list of groups who ate there that Friday afternoon, including Mary Pisano's group. Looks passed around the room as they silently thought about people who might have seen Jeffrey leave that day.

"There were people at the Edge who would have been thrilled if Jeffrey hadn't returned. Pete hangs with some of the guys he fired," Cass said. "They were furious, especially because jobs are hard to find."

Nell thought about Zack Levin and Ryan Arcado. And about their parents. "We're talking about good families here," she said. "Good people with good habits and sound values that rule their lives."

"People break rules all the time," Cass said.

"Those boys had already lost their jobs when Jeffrey was killed. What would they have gained by killing him?" Birdie asked.

"But Don Wooten hadn't lost his partner. And he wanted to." Nell spoke the words quietly, as if she didn't want anyone to hear.

But of course they did hear her.

Don and Rachel were their friends.

Good people with good, sound values.

It sobered the conversation, stilled them, while Birdie got up and refilled everyone's glass. She sat down again and took out her section of the anniversary afghan, her needles magically knitting a row of lacy hearts. "Taking the personal out of this," she said matter-of-factly, "Don had motive and opportunity. He knew where Jeffrey was going and he would have known when."

"As did the others who worked there. They may have known Don would hire them back—as he, in fact, did—if Jeffrey wasn't around."

And Jules. Opportunity, but what earthly reason would she have had to murder a man she barely knew . . . ?

"And Garrett," Birdie said. "I think our feelings for him have softened. But he may have known the property better than anyone."

"According to Grace Danvers, Jeffrey gave him grungy jobs to do at the Edge. But she said Garrett didn't seem to mind," Nell said. "And there's the spying, if that's what it was—"

Birdie leaned down and dug around in her purse. She pulled out a brochure. "Ella gave me this." She flapped it in the air. "It's the Feathered Friends brochure. Garrett Barros was a bona fide member, and an avid one at that. He especially enjoys their night watches." She looked over the top of her glasses. "Yes, for anyone who doubted it, one can go bird-watching at night." Then she read from the brochure. "'It's the best time to hear a black rail, least bittern, or barred owl.'"

Nell nodded, somehow relieved. The answer would come in the details, and eliminating those small items that pointed to one person or another was a helpful thing.

Izzy leaned forward in her chair, her elbows on her knees. "One of my law professors always warned us against committing what Sherlock Holmes said was a capital offense—theorizing who did it, and then twisting the facts to support it. I think that's what is happening with Jules. People want it to be her because they don't know her. She doesn't live here. Or Garrett, because he's a little off the grid. So we try to twist the facts to seal the deal."

"I agree," Nell said. "We need to find out all the facts first, line them up." She looked down at the beautiful pieces of the afghan in front of them, the gentle zigzag of the cables winding through the design. They were zigzagging, too, this way, then that. But without the beauty of the whole, their zigzags were getting lost.

"I agree with Birdie that the person with the answers is Jeffrey. If we could walk in his shoes that week, figure out what was going on in his head and his life, maybe we could solve this," Izzy said.

They all thought back over the week and tried to pull up the things they'd seen or knew to be true. The steps Jeffrey Meara had taken the last week of his life.

"He had a terrible argument with Don Wooten on Sunday," Nell said. "Don came an inch away from threatening him. And within days of the funeral, Don was reversing plenty of decisions Jeffrey had made, hiring back people and vendors." It didn't at all convince her that Don had done it and she didn't like talking about it. But those were clearly facts.

"We know Don called him at home, the day before he died, trying to buy him out," Birdie added.

"There was something else about that Sunday night that was odd," Izzy said. She looked at Nell. "Remember? Jules came in, and we talked for a few minutes at the bar."

Nell's brows lifted. "Of course. I had forgotten that. Jeffrey acted strangely."

"As if he knew Jules."

"How could he?" Birdie asked.

"Exactly. He couldn't. But he kept asking her questions about why she was there, staring at her the whole time, as if memorizing her face."

"It was uncomfortable," Nell remembered. "And Jules said he did the same thing another time, when she was at the Edge trying to get some information on the house she'd seen."

"Maybe he finally remembered why he thought he knew her, and he was going over that day to explain it. Apologize for making her uncomfortable by staring at her that way," Izzy said.

It was a logical explanation, but one that didn't explain why he ended up dead.

Nell thought back through that week, still trying to follow Jeffrey through it. They knew from Maeve that he had been troubled about something that week. He'd left work a couple of times, missed several meetings, someone had told them. Nell had seen Jeffrey again that week but couldn't remember where. It wasn't where she would expect to see him. Somewhere else, but where? And there was something else, too. Another loose strand they hadn't explored. "Jules mentioned that Jeffrey wasn't the first person who thought she looked familiar. There was someone else."

"Did she say who?"

She hadn't. But intuition told Nell they should find out.

Garrett. Don. Julia Ainsley, someone they had never heard of just a few weeks before, who now had a front-and-center role in their lives.

Harbor Road was quiet when they finally cleaned up the last of the dishes and packed up their knitting, calling it a night.

The room seemed crowded, somehow, with bits and pieces of their conversation strewn everywhere, vying with scissors, needles, and balls of yarn for space. In spite of the food and luscious yarn around them, the air was heavy and they all felt a need to walk outside and breathe in the chilly night air.

"Sometimes things make more sense in the light of morning," Nell said.

"I think it will come together. We have the right ingredients. Now we need to figure out the pattern."

They waved good-bye to Izzy and walked toward Cass's truck.

"You're quiet tonight, Cass," Nell said.

Cass shrugged. "Tired, maybe."

"A long week?"

Cass looked over at a single stream of light on the side of Archie's bookstore. It cast a narrow shadow onto the alley. It was coming from an upstairs window. She looked back at Nell and Birdie.

"It's hard," she said.

Birdie nodded. "Yes. You still love him, don't you?"

Cass didn't have to answer. It was in her eyes, her face, and the sadness that drew her eyes back to the window in the cramped apartment where Danny probably sat, a laptop in front of him, a single bed up against the wall.

"Love isn't always the answer," Cass said.

"The answer to what?" Nell asked gently. The three women stood together, speaking into the space created by the circle of their bodies. Their voices were low and intimate.

"To relationships. Ours hadn't been tested much, but it was this time."

"Danny was true to you."

She nodded. "He was, and I love him even more for that. But what I didn't like was me."

Birdie and Nell were quiet, not wanting to impose on Cass's thoughts. Giving them time to breathe.

She went on, sorting through her words and feelings until she thought she had them right. "Danny's a great guy—and yes, he explained to us why he was with Jules. Even though he didn't owe us an explanation, not really."

"No, dear, he did," Birdie said, looking into the sadness filling Cass's face. "Sometimes one needs to explain things that are out of the ordinary to people they care about. We're human. And Jules aligning herself with Danny the way she did deserved an explanation."

Cass conceded. "But either way, the experience brought out some things in me that I didn't much like. I felt so vulnerable that I wanted to curl up in a ball. I hated that. The whole thing made me feel weak. I hated that, too. And sure, for a while I even felt some jealousy. And that's abominable to me. I didn't like me. I didn't like what loving Danny was doing to me."

"You should look in a mirror more often, Cass. Maybe you would see the many marvelous things loving Danny—and having Danny love you—has done for you," Nell said. "Those of us who love you see them."

"You sound like your niece, Nell. Izzy says the same thing. But she doesn't have to live with me. I do."

She turned toward the truck, then stopped and turned back. "I remember watching my ma after my dad died. I was just a little kid, but my ma seemed to shrink. She was so vulnerable—because she had loved him so much and then he died. And I wondered if it had all been worth it."

"Her love for your dad?"

"In a way, yes."

"Have you looked at your mother lately? She's one of the strongest women I know. Being vulnerable didn't destroy her. And the strength she developed? I suspect life with your dad had put that in some kind of reserve, should she ever need it."

Cass was quiet. She looked at her two friends. "Maybe I'm missing the gene."

"Which gene is that?" Birdie asked.

"The one that makes loving someone a healthy thing. And doesn't turn one of the parties involved into a screwup." She looked at both of them and tried to smile as she began walking around the front of her truck. "In case you were wondering, that would be me—the screwup—not Danny."

In the next minute the truck roared to life and Birdie and Nell stood quietly, watching the taillights disappear down Harbor Road.

$\mathcal{N}$ell fidgeted around the kitchen the next morning, unable to settle in on her day. Images of people she knew—and liked—traveled across her consciousness, back and forth. They were missing something in their conjecturing, overlooking something right before their eyes. And somehow Nell couldn't erase the thought that it had to do with the little house on Ridge Road. It was bursting with secrets, if only they could clear their vision and see them.

When Izzy called to say she had packed up some duplicate wedding gifts that had been sitting in boxes for two years and was going to give them to Jules, Nell welcomed the chance to ride along. Ben suggested they add that small unused television set sitting in the garage.

"Maybe it will help take her mind off things while she's marooned here in Sea Harbor," he said.

A phone call confirmed that Jules would be home—she'd already gotten her morning run in—and she'd love company. She would be home all day, waiting for several repairmen to come by.

An hour later, Izzy and Nell turned onto Ridge Road, a route that was fast becoming almost as familiar as it had been when Izzy lived in the house.

"It looks like we're not her only company," Nell said, pulling up in front of the house.

Mary Pisano waved as she emerged from Karen Hanson's silver Audi.

"We all had the same idea," Karen said, closing the car door and calling back to Nell and Izzy. She took a package out of the backseat. "I am curious to see what she's done with the house."

Mary held up another box. "Bathroom soaps and accessories."

"The best kind of happening. A housewarming party with no planning," Izzy said.

"I have the coffee and donuts," Jules called from the doorway.

Nell was surprised—but pleased—to see Karen Hanson. She had unconsciously pegged her as one who was suspicious of Jules Ainsley, not at all sure of her innocence. She had read her wrong.

"Karen," she said, stopping her at the steps as the others went on in. "I've been wanting to ask you something for days but keep forgetting."

"You're worried about the party. Mary is under control as best I can tell."

"That's good, thank you. But it's not that. It's about something you said to Jeffrey. Or maybe you said it to us and he was just there. It was at the Ocean's Edge."

Karen looked confused. "Was it about one of those new drinks he was concocting? I didn't know Jeffrey all that well."

"No, it was about Jeffrey and your husband."

"Jeffrey and Stan? Oh, I don't think so . . ." She began to walk up the steps.

"It was about their friendship."

Karen stopped and turned back to Nell. "They knew each other a long time ago. Another life."

"You mentioned there were three friends—the Three Musketeers, I think you said. Who was the third?"

Karen's brows drew together, her voice tight. "Yes, there were three of them who hung around together back when they were teenagers—childhood friends." She paused, digging back in her memory. "Stan, Jeffrey, and . . ." She shook her head. "I'm sorry. It escapes me right now. It was such a long time ago."

"That's all right. My memory is like a sieve sometimes. It always surprises me what stays in it and what falls through the holes."

"Are you two coming?" Izzy called from the door.

Nell nodded and dropped the conversation, hurrying up the steps and into the living room. Jules motioned them back to the kitchen, where a pot of coffee waited.

Nell mentioned the television still in the car. "Don't let me forget it when we leave."

Jules gave her a hug. "You're wonderful. All of you. What thoughtful gifts."

"You've done nice things to this place," Karen said. She looked around the kitchen and out the windows to the backyard. "You have an eye for color, Jules."

Izzy agreed. "It changes by the minute. I love it."

"It occupies my time, and that's good," Jules said.

"What are the police saying?" Karen asked.

"Not much. Except they're closer, but that's hearsay, and I don't know if it means they are closer to me or closer to the person who really killed Jeffrey." She stood at the sink, fiddling with the chain around her neck. Nell noticed the gesture seemed to happen when she needed extra support—or when she was uncomfortable with the conversation.

Talk of the murder sobered the group and they all uttered meaningless but reassuring comments. Ben had told Nell that morning that Jerry Thompson said the police were looking into the last few days of Jeffrey's life carefully—meetings he'd missed, arguments at work—not unlike what the knitting group had done the night before.

Nell was relieved. She knew Birdie was right. Follow Jeffrey. He will tell us who did this. And why.

"Karen, how are things on the campaign trail?" Nell asked, attempting to change the conversation.

But the question caused Karen's face to tighten. She took the mug of coffee that Jules handed her. "Stan has canceled a few engagements—and that's not a wise thing to do when you're campaigning. The president of the Rotary Club called Beatrice Scaglia to fill in when Stan canceled." She sat still on the kitchen chair, composed, but clearly upset at Stan's uncharacteristic actions.

"And of course she went?" Izzy said.

Karen nodded. "Of course."

"Well, the debate is coming up," Mary said. "Stan will shine."

"Beatrice scheduled that without asking either of us. She checked with Stan's secretary to be sure he'd be free but never asked him."

"He'll do a great job. Stan is impressive," Nell said.

"Yes, he is. Stan could have been governor if he had put his mind to it. As for the debate, I told him he has to do it. He thought holding a public forum right now wasn't the right thing to do because of Jeffrey Meara's death. But the election is still going to be held, and Sea Harbor still needs a mayor. And Stan is the only person for the job. Sometimes things happen in life that we can't control. We must go on."

Karen stood and forced a smile to her face, then excused herself to use the restroom.

Jules started to get up to show her the way, but Karen was already gone.

"Stan is stressed," Mary said when Karen was out of earshot. "This is such a hard time for him, trying to calm people down, keep his town safe."

Perhaps it was the image of Stan Hanson carrying the weight of Sea Harbor on his shoulders that cleared Nell's memory, but in that moment she remembered the unlikely spot where she had seen Jeffrey Meara shortly before he died.

She and baby Abby.

He was sitting under the shadow of the harbor bridge in an intense conversation with his high school friend Stan Hanson.

Chapter 33

When Karen returned to the kitchen, Jules refreshed her coffee and passed around the plate of donuts.

"I'm getting the days mixed up," Nell said. "What happened when. But I finally remembered where I had seen Jeffrey that week he died. It was like seeing a teacher out of school. Instead of being behind his bar, he was sitting on a bench near the harbor bridge in the middle of the day." She looked at Karen. "Stan was there with him. And the conversation looked serious. Did Stan mention it?" Nell hesitated to say more, feeling a bit like she was revealing a private conversation she had no right to talk about.

Karen answered quickly. "I think maybe you're mistaken, Nell. But if it was Jeffrey and Stan, Stan was probably asking Jeffrey for his support in the campaign. Or maybe he was confirming a speaking engagement at the Edge."

In an out-of-the-way place, and with intense concentration that didn't speak to luncheons or election promises? Nell nodded as Karen talked, but she knew instinctively Karen was the one who was mistaken. Jeffrey and Stan were talking about something personal and important. She was certain of it.

Mary was up and carrying her coffee cup to the sink. "This house looks like you, Jules," she said. "It's how I imagined it would look. You have a fine touch."

Karen agreed, following Mary across the kitchen and signaling with her car keys that she needed to leave. "I'm speaking to a neighborhood women's group on education issues," she said. "They'd much prefer my husband. But I will do in a pinch."

Jules stood on the steps and waved off Mary and Karen while Izzy and Nell gathered their bags.

"We're off, too, Jules," Nell said, following Izzy to the door.

She paused at the bottom step, looking back. It wasn't only her days that were getting mixed up. Her thoughts, too, were piling on top of one another, coming in starts and stops. Pieces of a puzzle falling from the sky and landing topsy-turvy.

"Jules, you mentioned once that Jeffrey thought he had met you before. That he somehow knew you?"

She nodded. "It happened a couple times. He was trying hard to place me, but we had never met before. I'm sure of that."

"But he wasn't the only one in Sea Harbor. Didn't you say there was someone else who had said the same thing?"

"Yes," she said. "It was soon after I arrived here, over at the bed-and-breakfast. And once again, it was someone I know I had never met before. And it hasn't come up again. Weird . . ."

"Who was it?"

When Nell heard the name, it was almost as if she had expected it. It was a piece still searching for its place in the puzzle—but an important place. And an impromptu morning coffee had oddly confirmed it.

Nell's phone pinged as she headed toward Harbor Road. Izzy dug the phone out of her aunt's purse and read the message out loud.

" 'Nell, give me a call.' "

"It's from Jane Brewster," Izzy said. "Should I call her back?"

Nell nodded. Her mind was still mulling over the image of Stan and Jeffrey huddled on the bench at the water's edge. What were they talking about?

"It's not an emergency," Izzy said a minute later, slipping the phone back into Nell's bag. "Ham finished cleaning the years of dust and grime off the Penelope Ainsley paintings. They are lovely, Jane says. She talked to Jules, who told her she couldn't leave the house today because of the repair guys she was waiting for. But she suggested that Jane call you—that you were anxious to see the paintings and maybe you could pick them up for her if you were in the area."

Izzy was up for the detour. Mae had things under control at the shop and she didn't have a class to teach for a couple of hours.

They drove along the narrow road to Canary Cove, alone with their thoughts and the quiet of the September day. It was that special time of year when Sea Harbor residents didn't have to share their town with crowds of strangers and could relish its beauty all by themselves. The lull between summer vacationers and autumn's leaf watchers.

Jane and Ham's gallery was near the end of Canary Cove Road, on the same property they'd purchased nearly thirty years before, when they had fallen in love with this small town on the edge of the sea. Like Willow's Fishtail Gallery next door, the Brewster property had the shop and studio in front, a small garden behind, and a house beyond that, where they'd lived happily, building Canary Cove into an artists' colony, the little sister of the historic Rocky Neck Art Colony, not far away in Gloucester.

Jane waved as they walked in the side door. "Back here," she said, and headed into Ham's workroom.

He looked up from the workbench, his white beard flecked with donut crumbs. "Howdy, ladies. Have a seat." He wiped off his hands on a damp rag and pulled over a stiff portfolio.

"These are very nice paintings," he said, taking one out of the brown container. "I wish there were more. Penelope Ainsley could have made a fine career of her art."

Coming from Ham, the words were more than a polite acknowledgment that someone's relative did a nice job on a painting. Jules's mother had been talented.

Ham handed the first one to Nell. He had placed it in a protective plastic sleeve. "I'd love to frame these for Jules when she's ready. The paper is in remarkable condition, the deckled edge still intact."

Nell took the painting over to the window and sat down with Izzy at her elbow. It was similar to the painting that now hung in Jules's den—a view of the porch and swing, an enormous spray of bright red roses in the corner, and the bright green bush that reflected the light. The porch swing held a wash of color in the pillows, with a small kitten curled up next to one.

A happy painting.

"My guess of its age would match what Jane told me," Ham said. "We're thinking it was done about forty years ago."

"You've done an amazing job with it."

"The artist used good materials. Some of the pigments have become dull over the years, but it doesn't take away its beauty. I'm glad Jules has these. I just hope she gets to keep looking at them."

Izzy looked up from the painting. "She will—I am sure of that," she said.

Nell looked at her niece. She felt it, too. And the feeling grew each day, with each new snippet of conversation, each new insight into the man who was Jeffrey Meara and the people who were in his present—and in his past. Jules Ainsley was not a murderer. And the whole town would know it soon. She looked at what Ham had done with the painting and it matched that same feeling—that they were dusting off years of grime and grit and would soon have a clear idea of who killed a kind bartender.

She handed the painting back to Ham, exchanging it for the second one. This one was more impressionistic than the first, but equally vibrant and filled with light. The elements were hazier, the shapes more amorphous, but it was clear where Penelope had sat or stood to paint it. She had set an easel on the sidewalk in the front of the house. The green shutters were there, the winding pathway between the garage and the house.

She squinted, then looked closer. At first she thought she was looking at an enormous smiley face painted on the garage door.

Izzy leaned over her shoulder for a closer look, then laughed when the image came into better focus.

A laugh . . . followed by Nell's gasp.

It was a car. A British racing green car. A shiny Sprite, smiling at them with its round headlights and oval grille—exactly as it had done just days before.

Ham needed a little more time with the paintings, he said, to be sure they were protected.

Nell agreed to leave them, along with a quick explanation that the car had belonged to Jeffrey, an explanation that conjured up more questions than answers. Nell promised to clarify it all at dinner that night.

On the ride back to Izzy's shop, Nell explained about the car she and Birdie had found a few days before in Jeffrey's garage. At the time it had been little more than a curiosity and slight mystery. Where had Jeffrey gotten a Sprite? And why in heaven's name—as Birdie was prone to say—didn't the man drive it?

Izzy listened, trying to connect the dots as Nell talked. Some were still missing, the dots scattered around in the air. But an image was appearing—emerging slowly, like a knitting motif as row after row of the pattern was carefully knit into the whole.

Izzy climbed out of the car, then leaned back through the window. "Jules told me today that she's beginning to understand what family means. She loved her mother greatly, she said, but there wasn't much affection in their house when she was growing up. Her stepfather was a decent man, but never loving. How sad is that?"

"I wonder if it was difficult for him to raise a child someone else fathered. You'd hope not. Or maybe he sensed the love Penelope had once had for Jules's father—I'm convinced she did love him. Those paintings don't lie." She thought of little Abby, and the copious amounts of love showered on her from all sides, blood relatives or not. It didn't always matter where it came from. As long as it came.

Izzy hurried inside the shop and Nell sat there in her car for a minute, thinking through the events of the morning. And then she thought of Garrett Barros—still a bit of a loose dot, floating around aimlessly.

Garrett . . . Nell started the car, and then an impulse took over, and, hoping Tommy Porter wasn't lurking around the corner, she made a quick U-turn and headed for the Ocean's Edge.

Cass was coming out of the restaurant with Pete and Willow as Nell walked up the steps.

"What's going on?" Nell asked. "Am I missing something?"

"A business meeting," Cass said curtly.

"Pete and I thought Cass needed an intervention," Willow said. She gave Cass a look that defied contradiction.

"It didn't work. She's as stubborn as Ma," Pete said. "Damn that Irish gene."

"They're trying to take the lobster business away from me," Cass said.

"Don't be nuts," Pete said to Cass. Then he turned to Nell. "What we're trying to do is convince Cass that she needs a life besides work.

"I know she has you guys and knitting and all that wine you drink on Thursday nights—you're great friends. But face it—for starters, she's wicked bad at the knitting part. You should see the hats I get at Christmas. And you all have other lives, too. That's what she needs. Balance. Cass needs to broaden her horizons. She needs to have more fun. She needs—"

"Enough, Halloran," Willow said quickly, breaking off his sentence and hoping to avoid embarrassment.

"You don't think Izzy, Birdie, and I are fun?" Nell teased, her affection for Pete and Willow growing by the second. They are crazy in love with each other, she thought, and they're frustrated that Cass is messing up her life with Danny. At least in their opinion anyway. And, Nell had to admit with a twinge of guilt, she shared the sentiment.

Pete looped an arm around Willow's waist, having to lean down slightly to do it. Birdie had once described the small black-haired woman as a waif, and the description wasn't far off. Except when she had first come to Sea Harbor, she was pale and rarely smiled, more of a Dickensian waif. The Willow they knew today, the nearly twenty-six-year-old fiber artist with a thriving gallery and a tall, gangly lobsterman wrapped around her finger, the woman who had a Sea Harbor tan, a blush on her cheeks, and laughed often and loud, was more of an Audrey Hepburn–type waif—charming and irresistible.

"We're off," Pete said. "Oh, and we'll miss dinner on the deck tonight. The Fractured Fish has a gig over at the Dog Bar in Gloucester. I'm hoping that Captain Joey guy will mention us on *Good Morning Gloucester*. Everyone on Cape Ann is reading that blog of his. It'd be great PR for the band. Maybe get us more Gloucester gigs. But anyway, save us some food?"

"Always." Nell laughed as they walked off.

Pete didn't turn around, just raised one fist in the air and bellowed a whoop.

Nell looped an arm through Cass's and asked if she had a minute before she went back to work. Together they walked back into the restaurant and Nell filled her in on the morning's events.

"Crazy," she said, when Nell got around to the story of the Sprite. "So Jeffrey's car has a connection to Jules's house?"

"At least the car visited the house at some point when the Brogans owned it."

"Didn't Maeve also tell you he had found someone to give the car to?"

"Yes. Maybe Jules? But why? And what is his connection to all this? And to Jules's mother? I keep imagining possible scenarios, then tossing them away. But then they come back . . ."

"The timing is right. Jeffrey was probably here in Sea Harbor that summer. And we know he wanted to talk to Jules about something."

"Yes . . ."

"And Jules's mother had a connection to that house," Cass said.

Then she took a deep breath. "Nell, you don't think . . . Jules's father . . . ?"

Nell didn't answer. She wasn't ready to go there. Instead she motioned toward the bar, where Don Wooten stood talking to the bartender. "There's Don. Let's say hello."

Don didn't seem especially happy to see Nell, and she knew it was a direct result of the last conversation she'd had with him at the yacht club. Ben thought she owed him an apology; perhaps he was right. But she had heard Don threaten Jeffrey just days before he died. And she was trying desperately to pull together anything and everything that would lessen Jules Ainsley's burden.

"Nell," he said with a nod. Then, "Hi, Cass."

"Don, we've been friends for a long time—" Nell began.

"I think I reminded you of that just recently."

"Yes, you did. And I'd like to apologize if I came down too hard on you. I know you couldn't murder a flea, Don. I know that. But there are all these loose ends that are floating around, making it hard to get at the truth. I guess I was trying to tie off some of them. Friends?"

Don hesitated for a minute, then shook his head and laughed. "Sure. Rachel would divorce me if we didn't end this thing with a hug. She's says I'm stubborn, I said you were outta line."

"Well, a hug eliminates all of the above."

They complied, Nell adding a kiss to his cheek, just as Rachel came around the corner, lifted an eyebrow, and walked over. "Hanky-panky?"

Cass hooted. "I'm keeping an eye on them, Rachel."

"Good. Thanks, Cass."

"Are you two here for lunch? Dinner?" Don checked his watch. They were caught in between the two. Neither made good sense.

"I had a question about one of the fellows who works here."

"Garrett Barros," Don said.

"Now you're reading my mind?"

"The police have talked to the poor kid three times now."

"He wasn't here the afternoon that Jeffrey was killed," Nell said.

"He lived right next door to where he died. And some of the jobs Jeffrey gave him were not very desirable."

"All true. You've been doing a little bit of sleuthing, my friend," Don said.

"Is that wise, Nell?" It was Rachel, her face pulled into a worry. "This is a murder we're talking about. And you can't get away with asking questions in this town and not have people know about it."

Nell tried to brush her concern off. "You sound like Ben. But Jules Ainsley is getting a bad rap. And maybe Garrett Barros, too. It's difficult to live your life under those kinds of clouds. And they desperately need to get back to living their lives. We all do."

"You're right," Don said. "We're all frustrated. I look at the restaurant every night and worry about it, wanting to be sure the staff gets home safely, then wondering about the people eating here. Is one of them a murderer? It does crazy things to our heads."

"Yes, Don. That's exactly it," Nell said.

Cass looked over and saw Garrett walking into the kitchen. She nudged Nell, who followed her look.

"Would you mind if Cass and I talked to Garrett?" Nell asked Don.

"Will you be nice to him?" Don answered, with a half smile. Then he motioned to a waiter to get Garrett from the kitchen and excused himself to answer a phone call.

Rachel waved a good-bye, but Nell stopped her. "Rachel, a question before you leave. Do you remember any of Jeffrey's other friends from high school? Karen mentioned there were three of them that were tight—"

"Hmmm. I don't remember that. But Karen would know better than I. I remember her keeping an eye on Stan, even back then. She would have known his friends—"

Garrett appeared, ending the conversation, and Rachel moved toward friends waiting for her at a table.

"Hi, Mrs. Endicott," Garrett said. He looked at Cass. "Hi, Cass. We're friends now, right?"

"Gotcha," Cass said.

"I was over at Jules's today," Nell said. "You've done a magnificent job on her backyard. It was very nice of you to help her out."

Garrett's smile grew and he stood a little straighter. "I like doing that. Kinda selfish, too. Now that it's cleared I can use my binoculars to see all the way to the beach. Early mornings are the best time to see the shorebirds. Loons, sea ducks. Sometimes I even see migrating butterflies."

His voice was almost reverential as he described the sight. When Nell looked away, she realized Grace Danvers had come up and was standing next to Cass, listening, too. She was carrying several books.

"Break time, Garrett," she said when he finished. "Are you ready to hit the books?"

Garrett looked at Nell and Cass sheepishly. "School time. She's teaching me to read better."

Their puzzled looks brought an explanation from Grace. "Jeffrey Meara was helping Garrett with his reading. Somehow he got passed along in school without anyone noticing that he couldn't read. After Jeffrey died, Don asked me if I could take over, and we're having a good time. Right, Garrett? I'm not as good as Jeffrey, but close, he says."

Garrett beamed. "She teaches me to read and I teach her about snowy owls and grebes and alcids. Right?"

"I think I get the better deal," the hostess said, motioning toward the side door. It was a sunny day. They'd sit outside today.

Nell and Cass watched the odd couple disappear from sight.

"This must have been why he got the crummy jobs we heard about. It was what he could handle."

"A surprise around every corner," Nell said. "And the question I had for Garrett—how he and Jeffrey got along—was answered without asking it."

Don Wooten was at the front door when they went to leave. "When Jeffrey was on his firing rampage, that guy was the one I wanted to fire first," he said. "Jeffrey adamantly refused. I didn't get it at first. He said the kid needed something to do to feel better about himself. He didn't mind the jobs Jeffrey assigned him. He was grateful. Big Barros doesn't show emotion much, but he was pretty broken up when Jeffrey died. I promised him that his job was safe. That we'd figure it all out."

Nell smiled. "And so you have, my friend," she said.

Chapter 34

"**B**en, did you ever study the *Euthyphro* in college?" Nell handed Ben the cutting board and a bowl of vegetables.

"Graduate school. A business law professor had us read Plato's dialogues to see how well we could mess them up."

"What do you remember about that one?"

"That I had trouble spelling it."

Nell laughed. She poured freshly squeezed lime juice into the food processor. They'd agreed to keep the Friday-night dinner as simple as possible. Grilled coconut lime shrimp and a hearty couscous vegetable salad. The friends coming to dinner were in need of more than carefully prepared delicacies. Friendship and talk would go much further in aiding weary spirits.

"It's actually strange that I remember it at all," Ben said. He pulled out the basket for the shrimp. "But I enjoyed the class and the professor. He wanted to pull out the ethical dilemmas, and then he wanted us to try to construct a justice system that was better than the Athenians'."

"No small task. I imagine you got an A." She added the coconut, rum, honey, and milk to the processor.

"Why are you suddenly interested in Plato?"

"Jeffrey Meara was talking about Plato with Grace Danvers shortly before he died. Sparring with her, she said. They both loved philosophy and spent some of their breaks that way. But that week, right before he died, Jeffrey seemed obsessed with the *Euthyphro*'s theme—exploring the right thing to do in difficult situations. For example, if you thought someone close to you had done something wrong. Should you turn the person in—and upset their life—or let it pass for the sake of the relationship? To keep peace. Not ruin people's lives."

"In the dialogue, Euthyphro turned his own father in, if I remember, because he'd let a slave die."

"Something like that. But it presented an ethical dilemma. Grace seemed to think Jeffrey's interest was more personal than academic."

"That's interesting." Ben took the ice out of the freezer and filled the silver bowl. The furrows in his forehead deepened. "He was going to talk to Jules, but what could he possibly be telling her that would have dire consequences?"

"Maybe that's the question."

The sound of footsteps broke into the conversation and a group came in, all at once, not the ordinary way the Friday-night crowd appeared. Ben disappeared to get the grill and martinis started. Sam deposited Abby with Izzy and he and Danny followed Ben outside to help. Birdie came in with Cass, talking before she reached the kitchen.

Her afternoon with the old gals had been interesting.

"They confirmed that the Brogans were the family who owned the Ridge Road house," she said without preamble. "Stella was right. And yes, it was James, the patriarch, who then sold it. But it's why he sold it that's interesting." She looked around at the expectant faces around the kitchen island.

"There was one child in the family, James the Third. He went to school in Sea Harbor, Amelia Oliver said. She used to teach at the high school and remembered him. His parents were never around—they spent most of their time in Boston. Remember, this was forty years go. They probably had a houseful of servants to take care of things in the main house."

"Things, meaning their son?" Cass asked.

"I suppose. But don't forget that the memories of some of these ladies leave a little bit to be desired. But what Fiona Riley remembers about that summer is that the son was home from college, living in that little house. Apparently he didn't like staying in the mansion over on the Point. And she vaguely remembers that he got in trouble."

"Trouble?" Nell said.

"That's what she remembered. But Amelia argued with Fiona. She said Jimmy Brogan was a wonderful young man."

"What kind of trouble?" Izzy asked.

"Something big, Fiona insisted. But she couldn't remember what. And then he died, she said."

"While so young? How awful," Izzy said.

Birdie nodded. "After the son's death, the family immediately sold everything they owned in Sea Harbor and never returned. They even left furniture behind, Fiona said."

"They were grieving," Nell said.

"Maybe. But Bernice Risso thought it was their pride. They were older, quite aloof. And the whole thing with their son was tarnishing their good name."

"Did any of them remember how he died?"

"It was all hush-hush, Bernice said. But the rumor was that he had killed himself."

"What a sad story," Nell said. But the summer had been a happy one for Penelope Ainsley. What had happened?

She looked out the window at the men on the deck. Danny Brandley was smiling at something Sam said. *Danny*. Their resident expert on finding scoops. Perhaps he would help them fill in the gaps.

When Jane and Ham walked in, the attention turned to art. "Jules wasn't sure if she'd make it over here tonight," Jane said. "But if not, she'll pick the paintings up tomorrow. In the meantime, she said I could show off Ham's excellent restoration skills."

Ham carefully took the paintings from the portfolio and they gathered around the table. There were two paintings, both beautifully restored. Ham pointed out the places where the pigment had lightened, but the attention wasn't on the pigment.

It was on a car. A very distinctive car. British racing green—BRG, as it's known in the field, Ham said.

The rest of the men came in from the deck and passed out the martinis as everyone took a turn examining the paintings closely.

"It's a great little car," Ben said. He turned to Birdie. "You're probably the only one of us who has ever driven one. I took a few spins in the Mark III and IV but never came across one of these, except in magazines."

"Have you lost your mind, Ben Endicott? I never once sat behind the wheel of Sonny's Sprite. It wasn't allowed. That man would have given me the moon if he could have lassoed it—but driving the Mark I? No, that was off-limits. I suspect Jeffrey Meara felt the same."

They looked at the car, then into their memories of the congenial bartender. Somehow the two images didn't mix easily.

The paintings had charged the room with energy. Positive energy. Nell would even go so far as to call it happy energy. And for this brief time, they were putting a murder in their town in the wings and out of their heads. And in its place, a mystery of a different sort was taking center stage. A much more palatable mystery.

Finding Jules's father and giving her back her past.

They gathered eagerly around the story of a young pregnant woman and the child raised without her father.

"The car in the painting wasn't Jeffrey's, not when Penelope painted it," Birdie said. "It was his friend's."

"And that friend may well have lived in the house Jules just bought. The man who owned this car—and perhaps Jules's mother's heart," Nell said.

The third Musketeer.

She knew they were leaping over a chasm without a bridge. The Brogans could have loaned the house to someone. Rented it. But somehow she didn't think so. The chasm was very small, and with a little research perhaps they could step right over it.

Jimmy Brogan. She liked the sound of his name.

The shrimp and couscous were served without a single break in the conversation. They'd been given a beneficent gift: an evening free of murder. An evening filled with hope.

It was only when Nell crawled into bed and turned out her light that the darker thoughts came back, the ones she had pushed as far out of her mind as was possible.

What was the connection between Jules's father and Jeffrey Meara's murder?

She lay on her side and curved her body into Ben's, the pillow cushioning her head and his body supporting and warming her, his arm looped around her. She pressed into his chest until she could feel the beat of his heart on her back, and she willed the thoughts away.

But they were stubborn thoughts, ones that lingered long into the late night.

Chapter 35

Birdie called Maeve from the table at Coffee's. It was warm enough to be outside, cool enough to be wearing soft wool sweaters.

"I have the whole day off," Izzy said to Birdie when she was off the phone. Abby sat on her lap, her large blue eyes following the coffee cups and bright colors moving across the patio.

Nell brought over a tray of coffee mugs and passed them around the table.

"Maeve is out this morning but will be back this afternoon," Birdie said, putting her cell phone back in her bag. "We can go over then. I didn't tell her that we wanted to prowl around in her garage rafters looking for the box she saw Jeffrey holding that day. Some things are better said in person."

They had decided not to tell Jules, either. There were still too many holes in their theories, and getting her hopes up that they might have found her father seemed to serve no purpose. Especially when the details surrounding their suspicions were hazy—and perhaps dark.

The evening before, before they had left the deck, Danny had suggested a course of action. Look up the obituary. Find some concrete dates. Then newspaper clippings. They might find some of it online, he said. But the library would be useful.

"Decide exactly what you're looking for," he'd said. And then he climbed into his car and drove off alone.

"The last thing Danny said should be first on our agenda. What are we looking for?" Birdie said.

She brought out her iPad and began to type.

Information about Jimmy Brogan, she wrote, then looked up. "We're assuming, of course, that Amelia's memory is correct and he was staying in the small house his parents owned."

"And that he had a Sprite."

"The timing is too exact for it not to be the case," Izzy said. "I know we are on the right track. I never imagined when I lived in that house what secrets it held."

"Maybe that's a good thing," Birdie said. "Sometimes it's difficult to sleep with too many secrets weighing you down."

Izzy agreed. The house had held them close all those years, but now was releasing them one by one.

"Hopefully we'll uncover more secrets at Maeve's—maybe something in the car that will confirm things or tell us more about Jimmy Brogan," Nell said. "And maybe . . ." Nell took a drink of her coffee. "So, we're set, then?"

"Except for that last 'maybe,'" Izzy said. "What were you going to say, Aunt Nell?"

Nell shook her head, as if to brush it away and move on. But that would be difficult to pull off with Izzy, Birdie, and Cass. So she finished her thought. "I know that this is all about helping Jules find out who her father was. But it's more than that."

Birdie nodded, and Cass's and Izzy's expressions showed no surprise. The paths had been merging for days, maybe from the beginning, although they wouldn't have said so then.

As Nell often said, *There are no coincidences.* And clearing their newfound friend of an evil act might well bring great distress to other people in their town. She thought back to Jeffrey's—and Plato's—dilemma.

Birdie stood up and brushed the crumbs from her lap. "If we look in the right places—and we certainly will—we'll find more than we're looking for. We've always said Jeffrey would lead us to his killer. He simply forgot to mention that we'd have to go through the garage to get to him."

They dropped Abby at home with a sitter and headed to the library. The computer room was nearly empty when they arrived and they commanded two machines—Izzy and Nell on one, Cass and Birdie on the other, all looking up obituaries.

"We should check the *Globe* as well as the Sea Harbor paper. And who knows where else the Brogans may have lived," Birdie said.

It took Cass two minutes to come up with the senior Brogans' obituaries. "It looks like they died a dozen or so years after that summer—and within months of each other. They say that often happens with older couples."

Birdie scrolled through a long body of text. "He was on many Boston company boards, owned some real estate, a house in Florida where they retired . . ." She looked closer. "Well, that's interesting."

Cass leaned over. "What?"

"They moved to Florida the year they sold the cottage up here—and their other Cape Ann properties. They sold the Boston residence, too. It looks like they sold everything and moved on."

Because of grief?

"Does the obituary mention family members?" Nell asked.

"It says they had one son who preceded them in death. 'Name withheld for privacy reasons,'" Cass said.

"Withholding children's names in obituaries used to be very common," Birdie said. "Especially in wealthy families."

"But it seems a little strange when the person preceded them in death," Nell said. "I wonder if they were ashamed of their son."

"Maybe they had reason to be," Cass said.

That quieted them, except for the clicking of the computer keys, and they realized how much they wanted this story to have a happy ending.

"Here is the James III obituary from the Sea Harbor paper, along with a small photograph that looks like a high school graduation photo," Izzy said, pulling up a computer screen. She read out loud: "James Arthur Brogan III. Died November 22. James, called Jimmy, was the son of James Brogan, Jr., and Florence Brogan of Boston, Massachusetts, Palm Beach, Florida, and Sea Harbor. He was an honor student and studied at Yale University."

They waited.

Izzy looked up. "That's it. That's all there is."

Nell reached over and scrolled down. Nothing.

Cass shook her head. "I just pulled one up from the *Boston Globe*. It's identical."

"There's something terribly sad about all this," Nell said. "Even those who die young leave more of a legacy than that."

"The dates line up, though," Izzy said. "Stella said the house sold that next January."

"And it looks like that's when the parents got out of Dodge," Cass said.

"The death of a child is a terrible thing, but this makes me think there's more to the story."

And there was, which the next hour of poring over articles, using Jimmy Brogan's name as the key search word, proved. But none of them said very much. Cass clicked on the printer and they pulled out the pages.

There was one article that held their attention, one written at the end of that August—that magical time when wild parties and anticipation precede college kids' return to school—that told of an accident, a hit-and-run in the wooded area just outside Sea Harbor.

George C. Claiborne, 87, of 22 Seacliff Road, was walking his dog around 1:30 a.m. in a wooded area of Sea Harbor when he was hit by a car. He was killed instantly. Police say the driver, who was speeding around a curve, lost control of the car and left the scene. The driver has not been found. Police are questioning people in the area.

But it was the next article, posted a few days later, that brought their searching to a halt.

Police have found the owner of the car that killed George Claiborne last Friday night. James Brogan of Ridge Road has been arrested.

And two months later, a short, succinct notice was printed on page four of the Sea Harbor newspaper.

James Brogan, 20, formerly of Sea Harbor, was found hanging in a jail cell. His body was cremated.

"Now I understand why you don't remember this, Birdie," Izzy said, sitting back in her chair. "There is barely any mention of it. How can that be?"

"A story like this would have legs," Cass said.

"Mary Pisano's grandfather, old Enzo Pisano, owned all the newspapers around here at the time. I wonder if Mary remembers hearing any stories about this and why there wasn't more coverage," Birdie said. "Enzo was a character, and, well, in a word, he could be bought."

Cass laughed and several library patrons shushed her with frowns.

"I found one article that was chatty," Izzy said, "but it was printed in a free newspaper, one that had a short life, apparently. So the legitimacy of it might be suspect."

The article talked about a party at Jimmy's house the night of the hit-and-run—an end-of-the-season wild college student bash. According to people interviewed, everyone drank way too much, and by party's end the man who lived in the house, Jimmy Brogan, along with several friends, had passed out on the floor. Jimmy couldn't have been driving the car, according to his friends. He rarely drank, but was celebrating something special that had happened in his life, and he ended up dead drunk.

But the facts said otherwise. The police found the car keys beside him, half out of his pocket. The car belonged to him. And marks on the car proved it to be the vehicle that had killed the old man. End of story.

And the end of the free newspaper.

"There isn't a single mention of Penelope," Cass said. "In fact, there are few names anywhere."

"Jeffrey would have been at that party," Birdie said.

"And Stan Hanson," Nell said.

The Three Musketeers.

"None of these articles say that Jimmy was proven to be the driver of the car. Just that they couldn't prove he wasn't," Nell said. "I wonder if Jeffrey knew more. Maybe somehow he had proof that Jimmy couldn't have been the driver."

"And he would have wanted Jimmy's daughter to know—and maybe other things about her father," Birdie said. They gathered up their things and walked out into the sunny day, their minds reeling. In the distance, the sounds of gulls and horns and people moving through a lovely day masked the sinking feeling that a long-ago party had somehow laid the way to a murder forty years later.

They walked into Harry's deli, looking for a booth out of main-stream traffic. The familiar aroma of garlic and wine, butter and oregano filled the warm air.

"I gain three pounds walking through here," Izzy said. "But it's worth every ounce."

They settled into a booth and picked up the menu, which rarely changed, knowing what they would order before Patti, Harry's niece, approached. Until Mary Pisano spotted them from across the room and suggested the meat loaf. "It's never been better," she said, scurrying over to their table.

"Mary, you're exactly the person we need to talk to," Birdie said.

She scooted over on the padded bench, nudging Izzy closer to the window. "Sit, dear. You've eaten, I presume?"

Mary had, and had all but licked her plate, she said, detailing the ingredients Harry had blended into the meat loaf—fresh basil and oregano, wine and his special tomato sauce. "And his homemade sausage can't be beat. Magnificent," she said, and told Patti to bring four specials for her friends.

When the waitress had left, she said, "You're wanting more information about the anniversary party. I've been negligent."

"Reports are definitely not necessary," Nell assured her. Today they needed a bit of Sea Harbor history, and if there was anyone who could give it to them, it was she.

Mary listened carefully, her reporter antennae on high alert.

It was true that her grandfather, Papa Enzo, would have been the man in charge of the Pisano-owned papers back then. He had a dozen under his thumb, but because Ravenswood by the Sea was his estate and where he spent most of his time, he paid special attention to the locals and the Sea Harbor paper. From the stories Mary had heard, he had his fingers, every single one of them, in just about everything in town.

Birdie remembered Enzo in his prime. "Someone should have made a movie about his life. Except he turned into such a sweet teddy bear when he retired that no one would have believed it."

"He wasn't exactly the Godfather," Mary said. "But he would have liked to have been. His own version, anyway."

Mary agreed that it was odd to downplay a story like the hit-and-run. It had all the ingredients Enzo loved: a wealthy family, Ivy League kids, Boston connections. And a suicide on top of it? He would have been in heaven, she said.

She took out a small pad of paper and a pen, took some notes, and promised to get in touch with one of her relatives who still had his hands in the inheritance pie. "Uncle Petey loves talking about the old days. I'd bet my bottom dollar he'll know exactly what went down with this."

. . .

Mary had been right about the meat loaf. Forty-five minutes later, they pushed themselves out of the booth, collected their doggie bags, and headed to Maeve Meara's on full stomachs.

Maeve met them at the door and was thrilled that the group had grown. She ushered them inside, where coffee and tea were waiting in the living room, along with a plate of petits fours.

When they were settled in easy chairs, with coffee poured and cream passed around, Maeve got down to business. "I understand you're interested in the car. Now what can I do to help?"

They had decided on the way over that there was no reason to keep the story of Jimmy Brogan from Maeve. Jeffrey was involved, after all, and maybe hearing it would trigger her memory.

Only afterward would they suggest they take her spotless garage apart.

Maeve listened carefully, frowning at some places, nodding at others.

"I don't remember the accident, but I wasn't living here then. My mother did have the rather annoying habit of cutting things out of the Sea Harbor newspaper that she thought I'd be interested in—people getting married, winning awards, taking trips to Europe or having babies, that sort of thing. They always came with a secret agenda, hidden messages, like, 'Wouldn't you like to have a wedding, Maeve?'"

"My mother did the same thing." Nell laughed.

Maeve offered her another petit four. "Such a sad story. Both the man being killed, but especially Jimmy going to jail. Everyone knew the Brogan name—they had that huge mansion over on the Point—and we always wondered how three people could live in that gigantic house and still keep in touch with each other. But then you'd see Jimmy around and he was just this nice kid who didn't see himself as anything special."

"So you knew Jimmy?"

"Not really. He was like Jeffrey—enough years younger than me to be unimportant. But his family was known here, so I remember the name—and some of the rumors. I remember people liking their son, even though they didn't expect to. With all that wealth I suppose people thought he'd be a spoiled little kid. I can't imagine his life ending so terribly." She looked across the room, toward the back door. "And I can't imagine that I've had Jimmy Brogan's car in my garage all these years. My Jeffrey is continuing to surprise me." That thought amused Maeve and her eyes brightened.

Birdie leaned forward, carefully balancing her coffee cup in her palm. "Maeve, we think maybe Jeffrey was going to talk to Jules about her father the day he was killed." They all knew they were making assumptions about Jimmy fathering Jules. But it fit such a big hole in their puzzle that none of them doubted it. Maeve Meara didn't, either.

"Do you think he was going to tell her that her father committed suicide?"

"Maybe more than that," Nell said. "I think he was going to tell her what you just told us. That Jimmy Brogan was a very nice person who probably loved Penelope very much. And that he would never have driven the second love of his life—that car in your garage—while drinking. And that he couldn't possibly have been the person who killed that old man. He might have told her that she had a wonderful father."

Maeve was quiet for so long that they wondered whether she had stopped listening or fallen asleep. Her eyes were on her teacup, her small fingers gripping it tightly. Finally she lifted her head, her eyes moist.

"Did you know Jeffrey never drank a drop of alcohol in this house? He told me alcohol had killed one best friend and killed a friendship with another man. Imagine that—a bartender who didn't drink."

Nell smiled. Ben had told her once that Jeffrey didn't drink. A little taste now and then to be sure his concoctions at the bar were palatable. But not much more. Customers sometimes teased him about it, but he'd just laugh and say, "Each to his own."

"The day Jeffrey died we had breakfast together," Maeve continued, wiping away the moisture in her eyes with a small cloth napkin. "I made his favorite French toast and café au lait. It was lovely. And he was lovely, too. The way I will always remember him. The tension that had been building that week was disappearing. It was going to be a good day, he told me. He was going to right some wrongs."

She put down her cup and stood up, looking at the four women eating her petits fours. "Now tell me, ladies," she said, "what can we do to make Jeffrey's good day happen?"

Maeve's energy and awareness surprised them all. Maeve Meara was proving to be a wise woman, one who knew there was a time for everything, a time to be silent, and a time to speak—just as her husband had.

They stood in the garage, the Sprite in front of them, its shine lighting up the space. Maeve pointed to a ladder that pulled down from the ceiling. "That will take you up to the rafters, where Jeffrey kept his treasures."

Cass was elected to do the climbing, and in minutes she was handing down several boxes to waiting hands.

Maeve ignored the dust that fell with them and suggested they line them up on the floor and dig in.

"That's it," Cass said, climbing back down. "There's not much else up here, just some old skis and a kayak that looks like it has a hole in it."

"Jeffrey had trouble getting rid of some things. He was always going to fix that kayak and take me out for a moonlight ride. Imagine that," Maeve said, smiling.

The boxes proved to be filled with more things of little consequence—bike helmets, more books, old winter jackets, hiking boots that had long before outlived their usefulness.

Izzy sat cross-legged on the floor and shook her head. "I don't think there's anything here."

One by one they replaced the covers on the boxes. Maeve suggested they put them back up on the rafters for now. She'd deal with them another day. "The odd thing," she said, "is that none of these boxes was the one Jeffrey held in his lap the day I found him sitting in the car. It was small, not much bigger than a shoe box."

Nell stood beside the Sprite, her hands on her hips, staring at it, as if begging it to talk to them. "Maybe in the trunk of the car?" she said.

Izzy's eyes lit up. "My smart Aunt Nell." She walked behind the car and smoothed her hand over it, feeling for a latch. "There isn't a trunk," she said, and shook her head in disappointment.

Birdie walked over and looked at the back of the car. She frowned, repeated Izzy's movements, then suddenly threw both hands up in the air. "So silly of me," she said, startling the others.

She walked around to the door and reached inside to open it, then motioned to the others to watch. "Sonny loved this." She pushed the seat backs forward and gestured to a dark open space behind the seats and under the body of the car. "Voilà. The trunk. It's right here, right in front of our eyes. This is the only way to get to it."

And Birdie was right. There it was, complete with the spare wheel in pristine condition—and a small brown box. Just a bit bigger than a shoe box.

Birdie leaned over and carefully lifted it out.

The box was light. But when they took it inside and opened it at the dining room table, the contents seemed profound.

First they removed old photographs covered with dust. They blew it off, then smoothed them out on the table.

The largest photo was of the Sprite with Jimmy Brogan at the wheel. And sitting next to him was a beautiful woman with dark brown hair floating around her shoulders and an enormous smile filling her face. A familiar smile.

"It's hard to see," Maeve said. She opened a drawer in the sideboard and took out a magnifying glass. "My constant companion these days," she said, handing it to Nell.

Under the lens, the figures took on new life. The green Sprite was faded, but the people in it were alive and exuberant. Had they not known better, they would have sworn it was Jules Ainsley sitting in the beautiful car.

The next photo was a close-up of the woman alone, with a blue sky in the background. The familiar smile was there. And something else. Nell held the photo up and looked closely, holding the lens over a spot just below the woman's neck.

A gold chain and a charm. And on it, a small seashell, brighter than it was now, not yet worn down by fingers caressing it.

The letter to Jeffrey had been folded and unfolded so often the creases had been taped together. It was dated the day before Jimmy Brogan died.

In it he thanked Jeffrey for never missing a week of visiting him in jail. For giving him the news, as best he could. For sharing his joy when he and Penny discovered they were going to be parents. For sharing his anguish when the joyful celebration turned into the worst night of his life. The night of the hit-and-run. For comforting him when he learned from the Johnsons' lawyer that his Penny was gone, swept away by parents who convinced their daughter that raising a child whose father was a criminal was a terrible thing to do for that daughter. Jimmy would never see Penny again, the lawyer promised him.

And in the same letter Jimmy asked Jeffrey to take his car. To keep it for him. The keys were on the hook in the house where they were always kept, the registration papers in the glove compartment, along with a couple of other things Jeffrey should hang on to. A small box. Some photos.

Keep it for me, Jeffo, he wrote.

The letter was a testimony to friendship.

A testimony to his love for Penny and their unborn child.

A testimony to his sadness over knowing he'd never see Penny again—nor the baby she carried.

A testimony to his innocence.

And then he added one favor. He charged his best friend with someday letting his child know how much he loved him or her. *Tell my child that I am not that man in jail. Tell her I was a good man who loved deeply and wanted nothing more than to be her father.*

And an innocent man. *You'll fine the proof, Jeffo,* he wrote. *Somewhere in that car, you'll find the proof.*

And he had. The day after Jimmy took his life.

Too late to matter. It would have simply brought up a horrible accident, and ruined even more people's lives. But Jeffrey had kept everything safe in an old shoe box—the single earring, the coin purse small enough to be hidden in the crease of the car seat—and had hidden it away in the trunk of the car Jimmy Brogan loved. Along with a small velvet box holding the diamond ring that was to go on Penny Johnson's finger.

Safe for all the years, even from someone tearing Jeffrey's den apart all those years later.

Chapter 36

It was a cell phone call from Ben that turned their day in another direction completely.

"Did you forget?" he asked Nell.

The political debate that Beatrice Scaglia had plotted and planned and that they had all promised to attend was to begin in a few hours.

Nell moved into the other room to talk and filled Ben in, as best she could, on the events of their day. The articles that had matched their suspicions, the things they'd found in the car.

He suggested they meet at home before the event. He'd be there soon. Also, Mary Pisano had left a message earlier that she was dropping off the information Nell had asked her for.

"A slight detour in our plans," she said to the others when she hung up. There was enough time to shower and change and collect themselves before the evening event. Time to decompress . . . and think, refreshed.

"Perhaps it's fortuitous. We need to move cautiously. 'Knowing' is one thing, but being able to prove it definitively is another." They needed Mary's information to confirm what they were beginning to accept. But none of their discoveries was bringing joy, only a hopeful relief that justice would be done and an end put to innocent people's suffering under the cloud of suspicion.

Everyone would be at the debate. Beatrice Scaglia had seen to that. Yes, it was fate.

Cass offered to come back and give Maeve a ride to the event, but she said she was tired. And politics tired her even more. Besides, it seemed to be a day of weeding things out, and she had a garden in back that needed some attention.

The drive back into town was quiet, although now and then a question would be thrown out and they'd think through the night that Jeffrey died. And the night Jimmy Brogan's car was involved in a hit-and-run. A wild party.

One of the articles had indicated it wasn't a stag party, but they already knew that to be the case. Women were there. But had Penny been one of them?

No. They were sure she wouldn't have been.

Jules had portrayed her mother to be a careful, well-ordered woman, even when she was very young and pregnant. She would have been back in her room at the resort where she worked, allowing her Jimmy to celebrate with his friends that one time. She would probably have been sound asleep while across town her future was being torn apart.

They found only one newspaper article in the box Jimmy had given to Jeffrey—something Jeffrey had probably torn out of the paper and dropped in the box himself. It was a letter to the editor that had somehow slipped by the newspaper censors and been published in its entirety. Its headline read:

TEN REASONS WHY JIMMY BROGAN IS INNOCENT

Several items in the article addressed his character, scholarly awards, and class leadership honors. But others were facts, two about his car keys:

- Car keys were always kept on the brass hook in the kitchen, never in his pocket.
- Jimmy was right-handed; the keys were found in his left pocket.

- Jimmy fell asleep against the wall in the den, with friends lined up between him and the door—and that's where he was in the morning when he woke up. He couldn't have left the room in a drunken state without tripping over people.
- Jimmy drove his car with reverence, never carelessly, always cautiously.

The letter wasn't signed.

All good, sound facts. And none that the police would particularly care about. Plenty of good people did bad things.

Ben wasn't home when Nell got there. She put Jeffrey's box and the articles they'd printed out on the kitchen island and went upstairs. She was secretly grateful to be alone, to have time for a quiet shower. A chance to clear her head before revisiting it all over again. The week had been a roller-coaster ride, and today, especially, had allowed little time to process feelings. It hadn't allowed the time to imagine real people in front of the runaway train.

The fact that she knew those people filled her with an enormous sadness. She turned her face to the shower, its hot spray washing over her.

When Ben's car pulled up, she was almost ready. And then she heard another car. They weren't expecting anyone. They had all arranged to meet at the community center.

She dressed quickly, slacks and a blouse, a dab of blush.

She recognized the voice before she reached the bottom step and walked into the kitchen. Ben and Chief Jerry Thompson were standing near the island, examining the contents of Jeffrey's box, now lined up in a row. Jewelry, a small monogrammed change purse. A simple, elegant engagement ring in a velvet box. Old items that had spent nearly forty years undisturbed in the back of a well-cared-for Austin-Healey Sprite.

They greeted her with somber expressions. Ben held up a manila envelope tied with a string. "Uncle Petey came through. Mary dropped this off and not ten minutes later I got a call from Jerry."

"Petey Pisano is a character," Jerry said. "I've known him for years, ever since I came on the force." He shook his head. "Pete wants to be just like old man Enzo, though he hasn't quite made it. That being said, he's a font of information, and in a magnanimous gesture he sent me copies of everything he sent you. He just wants me to know he's always willing to help the 'coppers,' as he put it. I wouldn't be surprised if he sent it to a couple of others, too."

"This makes things more urgent," Ben said.

Jerry agreed, then excused himself to call Tommy Porter.

Ben opened the envelope and pulled out the papers Petey Pisano had provided. "As Mary so aptly put it, 'Uncle Petey got into the story with lots of gory details. All now documented.' Mary said he made it clear he's only willing to part with this information because lots of these people are dead."

"Hopefully not by his hand," Nell said, putting on her glasses and looking at the papers. Some of the people may be dead, she thought, but they weren't all dead. And this would change their lives forever, just like an inept driver in a careless hit-and-run had done all those years before.

Ben stood beside her, reading along with her. "You were right. The Pisanos made some money by keeping that story out of the public eye. Apparently, it wasn't that uncommon. Money spoke."

Then he ran one blunt fingertip beneath the name of the signature on the checks.

Nell took a deep breath as all their suspicions fell into place with a painful clang that must have been heard all the way down on Harbor Road . . . and as far away as the little house at 27 Ridge Road. And it wasn't James Brogan III, nor his wealthy family, who had kept some of the facts quiet.

The community center parking lot was nearly full when they arrived for the debate. Beatrice Scaglia, true to her word, had brought out a crowd. She'd timed it carefully so it wouldn't interrupt people's lives too severely. Dinner and evening plans could still be intact.

Nell walked in, her eyes peeled for Birdie, Izzy, and Cass. They'd agreed to meet in the lobby of the center, which was now teeming with people.

"They're over there," Ben said, pointing to a corner of the lobby. "I'll find Sam and Danny."

Mary Pisano reached the small group of women at the same time as Nell did and immediately began talking, trying to be heard over the noise of the crowd.

"You were right, ladies." Her voice was animated and she pulled them close in a huddle, keeping her words private. "The hit-and-run story was pulled and censored from the paper."

She repeated to the others the story that was already ingrained in Nell's head.

Without knowing names or details that would add tragic weight to her information, Mary was free to enjoy the excitement of it—and the flush of success. "I feel like a young reporter again," she said. Then tilted her head to the side and chuckled. "Mary Elizabeth Margaret Pisano Ambrose at your service."

"Thank you, Mary," Birdie began, but Mary was already off, having spotted Rachel and Don Wooten standing with a group of longtime Sea Harbor residents near the door.

Nell watched her walk toward the group of friends, people they'd all known forever.

Friends. The room was filled with them.

Mary was unaware that she had helped them in a profound way in discovering who murdered Jeffrey Meara. It wasn't proof . . . but the next best thing. Helping connect those final dots. She made a mental note to call Mary the next day and make sure she understood that they couldn't tell her more at the time. But knowing Mary Pisano, she wouldn't feel taken advantage of. Not if she was helping remove a murderer from the streets of the town she loved—even if the murderer was someone she knew.

As Mary disappeared from sight, Stan Hanson came into view, walking through the front doors of the building. He moved slowly through the crowd, shaking some hands, greeting people, speaking softly. Next to him, Karen stood straight and composed, one hand on Stan's tailored suit sleeve, directing him toward the community room. She wore a tailored gray dress and pearls, diamond stud earrings that caught the light, and her hair smooth and curled under at the ends. Nell thought of yearbook pictures from another era, where all the girls looked alike—identical smiles, the same sweater, the shoulder-length pageboy cuts. Conservative jewelry. Easier times.

She didn't realize she was still looking at the couple until Stan's eyes met hers and held her there. Startled, Nell met his gaze. It seemed to last for minutes, although it was probably just a few seconds. She couldn't read his look but was sure she read sadness in it.

Finally Stan released her, looked away, and continued on into the crowded debate room.

Nell couldn't spot Ben in the crowd, and suspected he, Danny, and Sam had gone on in. She saw Tommy Porter, in uniform tonight, standing in the back of the room.

"A sold-out crowd," she whispered.

Tommy's smile was halfhearted, one that told Nell he had talked to the chief. She patted him on the sleeve and followed Birdie to a cleared space near the door.

"I would rather stand than be squished," she said, and the others agreed, lining up next to her. A breeze coming in from the lobby offered some relief in the overcrowded room.

Once they were settled, their backs to the wall, Birdie whispered to Nell. "There's something not quite right about all this."

Nell had sensed it, too. The setup was normal—two podiums on the stage, a small table for the moderator. Chairs neatly arranged. Stan in his handsome blue suit, Beatrice looking stylish in a pink silk jacket dress, slightly nervous, but confident and smiling, talking at the side of the stage. Waiting to be introduced.

But there was a feeling, visceral and disturbing, traveling through the room. Birdie shivered.

The green stillness before a tornado swoops down and destroys.

It was as if the entire town had been privy to their day, watching them on some giant television screen as they had prodded and pulled apart and pieced together lives . . . and deaths. As if they, too, were aware that something ominous was hanging over the wood-beamed room in their beautiful community center. As if they were aware . . . that a murderer sat in their midst.

But of course that was foolish. Nell pressed one hand against her heart, calming the painful feelings.

The shrill buzz of the microphone being tested hushed the crowd.

Lily Virgilio, Izzy's obstetrician and director of the community center's free health clinic, was the moderator. A wise choice, Nell thought.

Lily stepped up to the microphone and smiled warmly at the crowd. She thanked them for coming and explained the event's format: a brief statement by each candidate, followed by questions that had been gathered from e-mails and a library collection box. Lily would be the timekeeper, and if there was time, there'd be questions from the audience at the end.

First, the moderator introduced Beatrice, who stepped up to the microphone and launched into an impressive and brief presentation, just as Lily had requested, of her hopes for the town. She ended with sincere compliments to Stan Hanson for the wonderful things he'd done for the city over the past years. "And now," she said with a beguiling smile, "it's my turn."

The crowd laughed and clapped and Beatrice took it all in. Then she sat back down, folded her hands on her lap, and waited for Stan to take his turn.

The room grew quiet as the respected mayor stood before them. For a long moment, Stan didn't speak. He looked out over the audience as if seeing some of them for the very first time. His head turned, looking from one side of the room to the other.

Karen Hanson sat on the far side of the stage, where a few chairs had been set up for family members. She edged forward in her seat, her eyes glued to her husband, her body tight.

Nell watched her, sensing her concern. She looked for Ben and spotted him at the end of an aisle halfway down. He was watching Karen, too.

Bodies shifted on wooden chairs.

On the stage, Lily Virgilio started to stand up to check the microphone and make sure Stan had water. But before she could take a step, Stan began to speak.

After a gracious thank you to friends and supporters, he took a drink of water, then removed the microphone from its stand and walked informally to the edge of the stage. Again, he stood still for a minute and looked out at the crowd. And then he began.

"This is an unusual night for me, folks. I know you came out expecting a rousing debate between my worthy opponent and me—" He looked over at Beatrice and smiled, and then he began clapping for her until the crowd, unsure of his gesture, joined in. When the applause died down, he looked back at the sea of faces and the people who had put him back in office term after term.

"Well, you're not going to get that rousing debate." His eyes turned to his wife briefly, then back to the crowd.

Nell looked over at Karen. The color had drained from her face but her eyes remained focused on her husband. Even from where she stood, Nell could feel the intensity in her look, powerful and commanding. Without averting her gaze, she stood and moved to the far wall of the stage, into the shadows near the fire exit, and away from the glare of the crowd.

"I made some decisions this week," Stan went on. "Tough ones. And I wanted to figure out a way to tell you all personally—and then Beatrice Scaglia made that possible by arranging this great gathering." He nodded to Beatrice, thanking her.

"The time has come for me to let someone else have a turn, as Beatrice here so aptly put it. I've cared about this town as well as I'm able, and I hope we've done a few good things. I'll always be grateful to you for your acceptance and support. And I hope you will be as fair to Beatrice Scaglia as you've been to me. She will be a terrific and worthy mayor—far more worthy than I.

"You've been wonderful to me. And to my wife, Karen, too. I hope . . ." His voice faltered slightly, then grew strong again. "I hope you will continue that support. I thank you for your humanness, your fairness, and your understanding."

He paused for so long that a few people clapped, not sure of what he was saying, but with the thought that he was finished. But then he looked up again and went on.

"I ask for your forgiveness for errors in judgment I've made. I've loved my job. I've loved working for all of you. I've loved . . ." His voice faltered, but this time the crowd didn't fidget. They sat quietly and waited. Stan looked down at his hands, then back at the crowd. "The truth is that sometimes loving can present dilemmas without clear answers."

"He isn't talking about his love for his job," Birdie said softly.

Nell nodded. Stan's dilemmas were born of a different source.

Stan walked back and replaced the microphone in the stand. And then he raised one hand in a slight wave. "And now, good people, it's time to say good-bye."

He smiled then, and a look of profound relief settled over him. He seemed to stand taller, as if one burden was being lifted from his shoulders before he took on another. He began to walk off the stage.

At first the crowd sat in silence, unsure of what they had just heard.

And then they began to clap, politely at first, and then with more enthusiasm as a surprised Beatrice Scaglia stood and walked quickly over to Stan, grasping his hand in her own and pulling him back to the center of the stage. She lifted their entwined hands dramatically into the air to rousing applause. And then the crowd effect took over and the noise grew louder as people stood up and cheered. Some because their neighbors were doing it, others because they liked Stan

Hanson, even though they didn't understand much of what he had just said, and still others because it was a beautiful night and they were happy to be with friends.

In the back of the crowded room, Nell saw Ben trying to make his way toward the stage, moving against the tide of people and not getting very far.

Nell stood as tall as she could and scanned the stage.

"She's gone," she said loudly, motioning to Izzy, Cass, and Birdie to follow her.

"Karen's gone."

$\mathcal{W}$hen they thought back on it later, they weren't sure what their intentions were, where they were going, or what they intended to do when they got there.

But instinct trumped reason and in seconds they were following Cass down the front steps of the community center and across the grounds to where she always parked—right at the edge of the lot, for an easy exit.

Cass drove fast, her four-by-four truck spewing gravel as they raced out of the parking lot and onto the winding narrow road leading into the town.

In the distance, they spotted the bright silver Audi speeding erratically into the night.

"To where?" Izzy asked. "Where is she going?"

But the question was never answered.

In the next stretch of road, they watched helplessly as the driver sped around a tree-lined curve, lost control, and careened into the thick, tangled shrubbery that edged the woods, crashing into a pole. The sound of metal against metal echoed in the night. Nell pulled out her phone and dialed 911.

Izzy was the first one out of the truck, with Cass a footstep behind. They pulled open the driver's door.

Without the protection of a seat belt, Karen's body had pummeled forward, cracking the windshield. She was hunched over the wheel, her face pale. A river of blood ran from her scalp down her face.

"Karen, you've been in an accident. We've called for help," Izzy said.

She forced open her eyes and pressed her hand to her head, then stared at her bloody palm.

"I'm all right."

Nell took a tissue from her purse and pressed it to Karen's forehead.

It was that gentle touch, they decided later, that triggered Karen's uncharacteristic move.

With her hands still on the wheel, she buried her head in the shadow of her arms, a trail of tears running freely down her cheeks.

They waited quietly, but just as quickly as the tears started, they stopped. Karen pushed herself back, her face pale against the dark leather seat. "Why . . . are you doing this? Why are you ruining our lives?"

Nell looked at Birdie over the top of Karen's head. She was clearly injured badly. Did she know what she was saying?

"It's her. Jules Ainsley, isn't it? She started all of this." She stared at the blood, which was now running onto her suit. "No one should prod around in the past. It should have stayed buried. Digging it up helped no one."

"Except a daughter looking for her father," Birdie said. "A daughter wanting to know what kind of a man Jimmy Brogan was."

Karen seemed not to hear.

Nell filled in the silence, waiting anxiously for the sound of sirens. "We know about the hit-and-run, Karen. We know you were driving, and your parents paid to keep it out of the press so it would go away."

"How . . . how did you . . . ?"

"You were familiar with Jules's house. You even found the hidden bathroom without direction. You knew there was a potting shed. You told us yourself about the Three Musketeers—and then later, after Jeffrey was killed, you suddenly, conveniently, couldn't remember Jimmy's name. Jimmy, one of your husband's best friends."

"It was an accident, you know, all of it. Everything," she said. "I knew the old man was dead that night as soon as I hit him. He . . . he was dead. There was no reason to stay. Who would have been helped by that? My parents agreed—there was no reason for people to know who killed him. The . . . the deed was done. So they took care of it. Stan and I were talking marriage. Our life was just beginning."

Her voice was steady now, but her eyes looked glazed, and Nell wondered whether the blow to her head was causing the words to flow so freely. She put up a hand to quiet her, but Karen refused. "You need to know that it was all a mistake," she said.

"It was easy for my father to have one of his workers take the car back—all the partiers were gone or passed out on Jimmy's floor. I told him where to put the keys, but he wasn't very smart and put them in Jimmy's pocket. A mistake, but not a serious one. Only a few of us knew that the keys were always kept on the kitchen hook. It was taken care of. No one was hurt."

"Karen, a young man committed suicide because of that cover-up."

"Jimmy was prone to depression. It was a foolish thing to do. He probably would have gotten off after a few years. Love does stupid things to some people. He needed . . . control."

"Did Stan know about your involvement?" Izzy asked.

She rested her head back, wincing, and again Nell tried to keep her quiet, but she pushed her hand away. "No. Not until all these years later when Jeffrey Meara decided to take people's lives into his own hands." Her voice was becoming more sluggish now, but muffled bitterness still coated the words. "He recognized that woman. She looks just like Penny, and she always wears that charm Jimmy gave her. It brought it all back to Jeffrey—all those memories, Jimmy's suicide.

"He told Stan that he was going to tell Jules everything he knew—honor among friends, he said. They owed Jimmy's daughter, he said. And then he told Stan about the things he'd found in the car. My purse, the earring."

"But the hit-and-run might not have even interested the police, not all these years later. It might not have hurt you, Karen . . ."

"Hurt me?" The words came out slowly, painfully. "Who knows what Jules would have done with the information. Sued us? Dragged our good name through the mud? Ruined Stan's career? We don't know her, Nell. She's not one of us."

Her eyes closed briefly, then opened again. "I begged Stan to stop Jeffrey, to convince him to leave it all alone. Jules Ainsley could lead a fine, long life without knowing who her father was.

"But Stan said no. We needed to let it go. We'd deal with whatever happened. So . . . it was up to me. To talk Jeffrey out of it."

Her words were so soft they had to lean in to hear.

"Karen, I think you should stay quiet." Birdie reached over and felt her pulse.

Nell looked up as the sounds of sirens blended with the night sounds.

Karen seemed not to notice. Her head moved slightly on the headrest and her voice grew stronger, buoyed somehow by a need to keep talking.

"Stan told me when Jeffrey was going to meet Jules. I left a message at the Edge telling him the meeting was earlier. And I met him there. He was wandering around . . . reliving the old days. 'No,' I said. 'Don't relive those days. Don't . . .'

"We moved into the shed to talk, for privacy, I said. Just old friends. He should think of us, Stan and me. Our life. But no. He'd made some promise. It was about a promise. A promise. I tried and tried—"

Nell took over, trying to stop Karen from using up oxygen. "So you were angry, of course. You grabbed the glove, the knife—"

"To scare him . . ." Her voice slowed. She tried again. "Scare him . . . Stan loves me . . ."

"Yes, he does," Birdie said, her voice soothing.

"Stan . . . loves me. But tonight I knew . . . tonight I knew . . . he was going to the police. That's what he was saying up there. He couldn't live anymore with . . . all those secrets. He couldn't live . . . He . . ."

She closed her eyes and didn't notice the police cars, the ambulance that had rounded the bend of the narrow road, their spinning lights filling the night air, and the uniformed men running toward the small silver Audi.

She only noticed Stan, holding her gently as the ambulance took her away.

Chapter 38

"**I**t was a tragedy back then. And it still is. Nobody won in any of this." Ben leaned back against the counter and rubbed his temples. "And two people died."

They were gathered in Ben and Nell's kitchen, the weight of the day pressing down on them.

Although the paramedics hadn't said much, it was clear Karen's condition was deteriorating. Possible swelling in the brain from the trauma, Chief Thompson said. It didn't look good.

Sam and Izzy had picked Abby up from the sitter's before circling by Jules's house. Who knew how long it would take for some reporter to catch wind of what had happened and show up on Jules's doorstep? She needed to know what was going on. And she needed to be with friends.

Rebecca's car was in the drive when Sam went in, inviting them both to a magnificent pizza dinner at the Endicotts'. They accepted instantly.

Danny picked up the pizzas and Nell pulled out an assortment of wines and beer.

Jeffrey's box was gone, now safely in Chief Thompson's hands. The diamond stud earring that Jeffrey had found squeezed down in the seat of the Sprite went with it, along with a tiny leather coin purse with a folded note scrunched inside that Karen had written in her distinctive left-handed script, reminding her to pick up her laundry the next day. The day after an old man died from a hit-and-run—a forty-year-old note, yellow now with age.

"Reminders before messaging and iPhone calendars existed," Izzy had said, with a sad smile. The monogram on the purse was a scrolled KES. Karen Elizabeth Siegel.

"The police will have to work out what Stan knew. Didn't know," Sam said. He filled the wineglasses lining the island.

"I don't think he knew for sure that Karen killed Jeffrey," Ben said. "But he must have suspected it. Few people knew Jeffrey was going to meet with Jules, but Stan did. And he had told Karen about it."

But he loved his wife, Nell thought. Just like Karen said. He'd want to protect her.

"He faced the same dilemma that Jeffrey Meara faced," Birdie said. "Should Stan fill the police in on the past, on possible motives that his wife might have? Would that bring Jeffrey back? Or should he protect Karen, protect their life together?"

They were quiet then, each sorting through the dilemma and their own feelings, their own lives and loves.

Karen was an enigma, everyone agreed. A woman as steely as she was gracious.

"She grew up in a bubble," Birdie said. "Her parents controlled any obstacle in her life as diligently as they did their business. Even when it meant covering up a hit-and-run that might tarnish their family name."

Nell looked over at Abby resting in Sam's arms, a pacifier bobbing between her small lips, and read their thoughts. Izzy leaned in to Sam's side, one finger touching a curl on the baby's head. Thinking of their own parenting ways. The stumbles their daughter would make, the challenge to let her make them, let her solve them. And she knew as certainly as anything in her life that Abby—and her parents—would handle it all just fine.

Danny took over the kitchen, dishing up the pizza, and Nell

began tossing a salad with anything she could find in the refrigerator—arugula, scallions, pine nuts, cheese. They filled their plates and sat around the fireplace, warmed by the comfort of each other's company.

Ben looked over at Jules, concerned with all the news she had just begun to process. "How are you doing?"

Jules had shed some tears. "Jimmy Brogan," she said, tasting her father's name on her lips. "I was sure I had some Irish in me. See this red?" She lifted up a strand of hair.

Rebecca handed her a tissue. "It's terribly sad, it's tragic, it's awful—but there's plenty of good in all this. You guys—" She looked around at Nell, Izzy, Birdie, and Cass. "You four have given Jules a wonderful thing: a love story. Her parents truly loved each other." She gave Jules a hug. "And that's a good thing."

They all agreed it was definitely a love story. And a good thing.

Ben reached in his pocket and pulled out a small box. He handed it to Jules. "The police didn't need this. And it rightfully belongs to you, Jules. It was intended for your mother."

Jules opened the box and took out the ring so carefully chosen for the love of Jimmy Brogan's life.

"A love story," she murmured. She slipped the ring on her finger and looked at Nell. "What happened to Jimmy's . . . to my father's parents? Did they know about me, about my mother?"

"I don't think so, dear. Jimmy wasn't close to them. They thought he had dragged their good name through the mud and they couldn't forgive him for that."

"Even if he was innocent?" Rebecca asked, her voice filled with fight.

"From what people remember and what we've been able to uncover in news clippings, they moved away—"

"And never looked back," Cass added. Her voice expressed her opinion of the elder Brogans.

"Jeffrey Meara was a good man, Jules. He was your father's best friend. You two would have liked each other," Birdie said. "And I suspect you'll find a new friend in his lovely wife, Maeve."

"And there's someone else," Ben said. "It may take Stan Hanson a while to piece his life back together, but he loved your father, too. And I suspect he will want to share many memories with you in time."

Jules sat still, soaking in every word as she pieced together her past.

"Jeffrey Meara was going to tell you exactly what you came here to find out," Nell said. "He was going to tell you that your father was a wonderful man, that he hadn't committed any crime, that he was a great friend, and, most of all, how much in love he and your mother were—and how excited they were to be bringing you into the world."

She remembered Jeffrey's discussion with Grace Danvers and the ethical dilemma he struggled with. He had resolved the dilemma one way as a young man, but forty years later his decision was completely the opposite.

Jules Ainsley had come to Sea Harbor.

It was the daughter who made the difference.

Chapter 39

$\mathcal{I}$t was Jules Ainsley's idea, and one that Ben Endicott declared brilliant. A stroke of genius, he said.

That's how it happened that Nell and Ben, on the anniversary of their forty years of marriage, drove a British racing green Sprite through the gates of Ravenswood by the Sea on a gorgeous autumn day.

And that's how it happened that friends and family, storekeepers and councilmembers, waitresses and bartenders, children and dogs lined the long, winding driveway of the bed-and-breakfast and cheered wildly at their entrance.

Birdie had outfitted Ben in a herringbone driving hat that she'd purchased for Sonny on a trip to England. Sonny would have been thrilled, she said.

And Nell—looking like Isadora Duncan and hoping to avoid the dancer's fate—looped a long, flowing scarf and a waist-length string of pearls around her neck.

Izzy had picked out her aunt's dress, shimmery silk in a deep liquid blue that matched Nell's eyes.

Angled over the back of the soft leather seats, catching the fading afternoon sunlight, was a ruby red afghan, the hearts and cables and twisted panels a tribute to forty years of a life well lived and a promise of the years to come.

Birdie, Izzy, and Cass had given it to Ben and Nell that morning when they were barely awake. The threesome stood on the bottom step and called them down from their bedroom. Mimosas and sweet crepes from the bakery were waiting. And dear friends.

And an anniversary afghan knit with love.

It was all quite perfect.

The day, the event, and the gathering of family and friends.

A true celebration.

Nell and Ben spoke little on the drive over, cherishing the only time they'd be alone together that day. Nell leaned her head back against the leather seat, her eyes on the man who had entered her life the first day of a Harvard logic class—and had never left. Ben insisted, however, that he had fallen in love with her before that fortuitous class schedule. It was a beautiful fall day and she was alone, he remembered. She was walking across the quad, her hair tangled by the wind and her high cheekbones blushed by the sun. And smiling. At what? he wondered. The day? The sky? *Wicked amazing* was how he remembered the day and the woman.

Forty years ago today . . .

They were married on the Kansas ranch that Nell's family owned. It was a unique and splendid affair, with the Boston Brahmins landing their planes on a strip in the middle of a field smoothed clean by Nell's dad and ranch hands. Guests donned cowboy hats and rode horses and licked their plates clean of barbecue and beans. Nell loved Ben's desire to embrace her roots.

She watched the curve of his lips now, reading his eyes as his mind went back over those forty magnificent years—years filled with learning about each other, with suffering through the heartache of failed pregnancies, years of opening their arms to friends and family and to dear Izzy, as close as a daughter could be. A marriage that grew with understanding, with togetherness, with separateness. Years nurturing a dynamic love as strong as the Cape Ann granite that fortified their town.

Their eyes met now, smiled, and held for a moment as their memories merged.

Then Ben slowed the car and pulled up in front of the bed-and-breakfast, turning the engine off.

"One dream to cross off my bucket list," he declared as he helped Nell out of the car. He bowed slightly to the crowd, then looked up at the sky and tipped his British driving hat to the heavens. "With special thanks to Jimmy Brogan and Jeffrey Meara," he said in a booming voice that even those standing on the B and B's porch could hear. "I know you're up there keeping an eye on us."

Maeve stood next to Mary Pisano, beaming. Her Jeffrey was watching; she knew he was. As she told Ben later, "There was no way on earth he'd let that car be driven by anyone without being there to guide it to safety. He had promised Jimmy as much."

"Everyone in back," Mary called, fluttering her hands in the air. Don Wooten stood beside her, taller by a foot and a half, and helped direct traffic.

As if choreographed, the mass of people moved around the wide, sweeping porch, along the pathway that led around the carriage house, and out to the carefully kept lawns behind the inn. Narrow paths wound like pieces of yarn past flower beds and stone benches, all the way to the backwoods.

Ben waved at Jules and thanked her with a courtly bow and tip of his cap. She blew him back a kiss, then melted into the crowd to join the celebration. Happier than she'd ever been.

Mary had wound dozens of trees in the back with tiny Christmas lights and then laced the lights through the gazebo.

It was as she had promised: simple and casual, but perfect in every way.

Ben had invited Stan Hanson to come, but the former mayor said the time wasn't right and Ben concurred. No matter what she had done, Stan loved his wife. She had devoted her life to him, and although it might not have always been a healthy love, it was a deep love.

Karen had lived only a day, the swelling caused by the accident inoperable. She awoke once, told Stan she loved him, and then she was gone. Stan's grief was profound.

Although Chief Thompson and the lawyer Ben had recommended had worked out a deal that wouldn't involve criminal action, Stan's reticence to go to the police with his suspicions about Karen, about their past, was a decision that would follow him.

But Stan would survive this, and no one doubted that he would make up for what he had done in a manner that would benefit Sea Harbor and make him whole again.

Nell found Ben again, and they stood together on the edge of the crowd. Danny came up, bringing hugs and a smile. She had checked on him the previous day, making sure he was coming. He had missed Friday dinner the week before and it concerned her.

"I don't miss Ben's martinis and grilled fish lightly," he'd assured her, explaining his absence involved a book signing—nothing more or less. "You're not rid of me, not by a long shot."

She hugged him now, and he read her thoughts. "Don't worry, Nell. Things will work out, however that's meant to be."

They watched him walk off, waving to friends, smiling.

"The way I see it, Nellie," Ben said, "he and Cass are apart, but within reach. They'll do what's best for them. Give them time."

Nell was trying to do exactly that. As was Birdie. And Izzy.

She looked around for Izzy and spotted her standing with Sam near the gazebo, watching Abby roll on the grass at their feet. Behind them, the Fractured Fish were tuning instruments, ready to make music.

Pete strummed and Merry trilled her fingers up and down the keyboard. Andy Risso sat behind them, his blond ponytail moving to the practiced beat of his drums.

All across the lawn, waiters carried trays of cocktails and Tyler Gibson's special anniversary drink, a ruby red concoction that he promised they'd remember forever. Jeffrey had taught him how to make it.

Food stations were scattered beneath the trees—lobster rolls and calamari, Harry's salads and mounds of fruit in Jane Brewster's beautiful handmade bowls.

Nell found Mary Pisano walking along the back porch checking the drinks, the food, the music, the guests. Nell came up behind her and wrapped her in a hug. "It's absolutely perfect, my dear friend."

Mary turned around and hugged her back. "Yes, it is, isn't it? It's a perfect celebration. And we have much to celebrate. Amazing friends, good food. It's not all about you, you know. So let's get the toast over with, shall we? And then get on with the party and dance the night away."

Izzy was already at the microphone, gathering the crowd and promising to be brief.

Ben walked up to the gazebo and picked Abby up off the blanket, swinging her into the air until her giggles became contagious and a wave of laughter vibrated through the crowd.

Nell hooked her arm into Ben's, and before Izzy could have her say, they took the microphone away. Nell kissed her niece on the cheek and whispered, "You're next, my Izzy."

Then Ben thanked their friends for being in their lives.

"You are the threads that add richness and support and joy to our lives together," Nell added. And then her voice gave way and she took the handkerchief Mary had ready.

Ben kissed his wife full on the lips with a passion that had only grown richer over the forty years. The crowd cheered. And that was it. Simple and sincere.

Izzy was next, with Sam standing next to her.

"No toast," Izzy said. "Just love. Lots of it . . . forever and ever. And a gift that you loaned to Sam and me for our own wedding. Here it is, back at you . . ."

She turned to Pete, who turned to Merry and Andy.

Izzy and Sam stepped away, their arms looped around each other, their eyes on Ben and Nell. Pete strummed the first chords as Mary brought the keyboard to life and Andy joined in with the drums. Then Pete and Merry took to the microphones and began, their voices filling the air.

Our love is here to stay . . .

The song Ben and Nell had danced to on a ranch in western Kansas forty years before . . .

Not for a year, but forever and a day.

The same song Izzy and Sam had danced to in Sea Harbor, Massachusetts, just a short memory ago.

Together we're going a long, long way.

Our love is here to stay.

And they danced the night away.

Nell and Ben Endicott's Anniversary Afghan

Designed for *Murder in Merino* by Cindy Craig

Cindy Craig—a gifted designer, teacher, author of *The Kids' Knitting Notebook*, and guru of all things knitting—is the manager of the Studio Knitting & Needlepoint store in Kansas City, Missouri. Cindy designed this shawl for Nell and Ben's anniversary, working into the pattern symbolism of their forty years together.

The ruby red color symbolizes forty years of marriage. The main section of the blanket—a heart cable—represents marriage as the center of a family's life. The zigzag cable reminds us of those times in life when a couple travels through curves and turns and unexpected happenings. The two lacy heart panels are symbols of the openness and flexibility partners maintain to ensure a long and honest relationship, and the diamond cable border symbolizes a couple's relationship to the world in which they live and love.

For more information about the Studio and Cindy's creations, please visit their Web site: www.thestudiokc.com

The Pattern

This blanket is knit in strips and sewn together. It simplifies knitting a large afghan and also lends itself to a group project. The panels vary in textures and skills required, to keep it interesting. You can customize the finished size of the blanket by adding or reducing the number of panels.

Finished Size: 48 inches wide by 60 inches tall

Gauge: 4 sts per inch and 6 rows per inch in stockinette stitch

Yarn: 20 skeins Trendsetter Yarns Merino 8, 100 percent merino wool—50 grams/skein. Motto 10 ply, 100 yards/skein

Needle: U.S. No. 9/5.5 millimeter, or needle needed to obtain gauge; a cable needle (cn)

Crochet Hook: If desired to attach panels

ABBREVIATIONS

cn	cable needle
CO	cast on
k	knit
k2tog	knit 2 stitches together
p	purl
rep	repeat
RS	right side
ssk	slip, slip, knit
st(s)	stitch(es)
WS	wrong side
yo	yarn over

2/1 RPC	Slip next st onto cn and hold in back; k2; p1 from cn
2/1 LPC	Slip next st onto cn and hold in front; k2; p1 from cn
2/2 RC	Slip 2 sts onto cn and hold in back; k2; k2 from cn
2/2 LC	Slip 2 sts onto cn and hold in front; k2; k2 from cn
2/2 RPC	Slip 2 sts onto cn and hold in back; k2, p2 from cn
2/2 LPC	Slip 2 sts onto cn and hold in back; k2, p2 from cn

Seed Stitch Over Even Number of STS
Row 1: *K1, P1; rep from * to the end

Row 2: *P1, K1; rep from * to the end
Repeat these 2 rows

Seed Stitch Over Odd Number of STS

Row 1: K1, *P1, K1; rep from * to the end
Row 2: P1, *K1, P1; rep from * to the end

HEART CABLE PANEL (MAKE 1 10" PANEL)

CO 56 sts
Work seed stitch for 8 rows
Work heart cable pattern stitch until piece measures 59 inches from
    cast-on edge
Work seed stitch for 8 rows

HEART CABLE PATTERN STITCH

Row 1: (RS) (k1, p1) twice, 2/1 RPC, p3, k4, p3, 2/1 LPC, 2/2 LPC, 2/2
    RC, 2/2 LC, 2/2 RPC, 2/1 RPC, p3, k4, p3, 2/1 LPC, (p1, k1)
    twice
Row 2: (WS) (p1, k1) twice, p2, k4, p4, k4, p2, k2, p12, k2, p2, k4, p4, k4,
    p2, (k1, p1) twice
Row 3: (k1, p1) twice, k2, p4, 2/2 RC, p4, k2, p2, 2/2 RCP, k4, 2/2 LPC,
    p2, k2, p4, 2/2 RC, p4, k2, (p1, k1) twice
Row 4: (p1, k1) twice, p2, k4, p4, k4, (p2, k2) twice, p4, (k2, p2) twice,
    k4, p4, k4, p2, (p1, k1) twice
Row 5: (k1, p1) twice, 2/2 LPC, 2/2 RC, 2/2 LC, 2/2 RPC, p1, 2/1 RPC,
    p2, 2/2 RC, p2, 2/1 LPC, p1, 2/2 LPC, 2/2 RC, 2/2 LC, 2/2 RPC,
    (k1, p1) twice
Row 6: (p1, k1) twice, k2, p12, k3, p2, k3, p4, k3, p2, k3, p12, k2, (p1, k1)
    twice
Row 7: (k1, p1) twice, p2, 2/2 RPC, k4, 2/2 LPC, p2, 2/1 RPC, p3, k4,
    p3, 2/1 LPC, p2, 2/2 RPC, k4, 2/2 LPC, p2, (p1, k1) twice
Row 8: (p1, k1) twice, k2, p2, k2, p4, k2, p2, k2, p2, k4, p4, k4, p2, k2,
    p2, k2, p4, k2, p2, k2, (k1 p1) twice

Row 9: (k1, p1) twice, p1, 2/1 RCP, p2, 2/2 RCP, p2, 2/1 LCP, p/1, k2, p4, 2/2 RCP, p4, k2, p1, 2/1 RCP, p2, 2/2 RC, p2, 2/1 LCP, p1 (k1, p1) twice

Row 10: (p1, k1) twice, k1, p2, k3, p4, k3, p2, k1, p2, k4, p4, k4, p2, k1, p2, k3, p4, k3, p2, k1, (p1, k1) twice

DIAMOND TWIST CABLE PANEL (MAKE 2 3" PANELS)

CO 32 sts

Work seed stitch for 8 rows

Work diamond twist cable pattern stitch until piece measures 59 inches from cast-on edge

Work seed stitch for 8 rows

Bind off all sts

DIAMOND TWIST CABLE PATTERN STITCH

Row 1: k1, p1, k1, p11, 2/2 RC, p10, k1, p1, k1, p1

Row 2: p1, k1, p1, k11, p4, k10, p1, k1, p1, k1

Row 3: k1, p1, k1, p10, 2/1 RC, 2/1 LC, p9, k1, p1, k1, p1

Row 4: p1, k1, p1, k10, p6, k9, p1, k1, p1, k1

Row 5: k1, p1, k1, p9, 2/1 RC, k2, 2/1 LC, p8, k1, p1, k1, p1

Row 6: p1, k1, p1, k9, p8, k8, p1, k1, p1, k1

Row 7: k1, p1, k1, p8, 2/1 RPC, 2/2 RC, 2/1 LPC, p7, k1, p1, k1, p1

Row 8: p1, k1, p1, k6, p1, k1, p2, k1, p4, k1, p2, k7, p1, k1, p1, k1

Row 9: k1, p1, k1, p7, 2/1 RPC, p1, k4, p1, 2/1 LPC, p6, k1, p1, k1, p1

Row 10: p1, k1, p1, k7, p2, k2, p4, k2, p2, k6, p1, k1, p1, k1

Row 11: k1, p1, k1, p6, 2/1 RPC, p2, 2/2 RC, p2, 2/1 LPC, p5, k1, p1, k1, p1

Row 12: p1, k1, p1, k6, p2, k3, p4, k3, p2, k5, p1, k1, p1, k1

Row 13: k1, p1, k1, p5, 2/1 RPC, p3, k4, p3, 2/1 LPC, p4, k1, p1, k1, p1

Row 14: p1, k1, p1, k5, p2, k4, p4, k4, p2, k4, p1, k1, p1, k1

Row 15: k1, p1, k1, p4, 2/1 RPC, p4, 2/2 RC, p4, 2/1 LPC, p3, k1, p1, k1, p1

Row 16: p1, k1, p1, k4, p2, k5, p4, k5, p2, k3, p1, k1, p1, k1

Row 17: k1, p1, k1, p3, 2/1 RPC, p5, k4, p5, 2/1 LPC, p2, k1, p1, k1, p1

Row 18: p1, k1, p1, k3, p3, k5, p4, k5, p3, k2, p1, k1, p1, k1

Row 19: k1, p1, k1, p3, 2/1 RPC, k2, p5, 2/2 RC, p5, k2, 2/1 LPC, p2, k1, p1, k1, p1

Row 20: p1, k1, p1, k3, p3, k5, p4, k5, p3, k2, p1, k1, p1, k1

Row 21: k1, p1, k1, p3, 2/1 LPC, p5, k4, p5, 2/1 RPC, p2, k1, p1, k1, p1

Row 22: p1, k1, p1, k3, p3, k5, p4, k5, p2, k3, p1, k1, p1, k1

Row 23: k1, p1, k1, p4, 2/1 LPC, p4, 2/2 RC, p4, 2/1 RPC, p3, k1, p1, k1, p1

Row 24: p1, k1, p1, k5, p2, k4, p4, k4, p2, k4, p1, k1, p1, k1

Row 25: k1, p1, k1, p5, 2/1 LPC, p3, k4, p3, 2/1 RPC, p4, k1, p1, k1, p1

Row 26: p1, k1, p1, k6, p2, k3, p4, k3, p2, k5, p1, k1, p1, k1

Row 27: k1, p1, k1, p6, 2/1 LPC, p2, 2/2 RC, p2, 2/1 RPC, p5, k1, p1, k1, p1

Row 28: p1, k1, p1, k7, p2, k2, p4, k2, p2, k6, p1, k1, p1, k1

Row 29: k1, p1, k1, p7, 2/1 LPC, p1, k4, p1, 2/1 RPC, p6, k1, p1, k1, p1

Row 30: p1, k1, p1, k8, p2, k1, p4, k1, p2, k7, p1, k1, p1, k1

Row 31: k1, p1, k1, p8, 2/1 LPC, 2/2 RC, 2/1 RPC, p7, k1, p1, k1, p1

Row 32: p1, k1, p1, k9, p8, k8, p1, k1, p1, k1

Row 33: k1, p1, k1, p9, 2/1 LC, k2, 2/1 RC, p8, k1, p1, k1, p1

Row 34: p1, k1, p1, k10, p6, k9, p1, k1, p1, k1

Row 35: k1, p1, k1, p10, 2/1 LC, 2/1 RC, p9, k1, p1, k1, p1

Row 36: p1, k1, p1, k10, p6, k9, p1, k1, p1, k1

ZIGZAG CABLE PANEL (MAKE 4 3" PANELS)

CO 27 sts

Work seed stitch for 8 rows

Work zigzag cable pattern stitch until piece measures 59 inches from cast-on edge

Work seed stitch for 8 rows

Bind off all sts

ZIGZAG CABLE PATTERN STITCH

Row 1: k1, p1, k1, p1, p8, 2/1 RPC, p2, 2/1 RPC, p5, k1, p1, k1

Row 2: (k1, p1) twice, k5, p2, k3, p2, k7, p1, k1, p1, k1

Row 3: k1, p1, k1, p7, 2/1 RPC, p2, 2/1 RPC, p6, k1, p1, k1

Row 4: (k1, p1) twice, k6, p2, k3, p2, k6, p1, k1, p1, k1

Row 5: (k1, p1, k1) twice, p6, 2/1 RPC, p2, 2/1 RPC, p7, k1, p1, k1

Row 6: (k1, p1) twice, k7, p2, k3, p2, k5, p1, k1, p1, k1

Row 7: k1, p1, k1, p5, 2/1 RPC, p2, 2/1 RPC, p8, k1, p1, k1

Row 8: (k1, p1) twice, k8, p2, k3, p2, k4, p1, k1, p1, k1

Row 9: k1, p1, k1, p4, 2/1 RPC, p2, 2/1 RPC, p9, k1, p1, k1

Row 10: (k1, p1) twice, k9, p2, k3, p2, k3, p1, k1, p1, k1

Row 11: k1, p1, k1, p3, 2/1 RPC, p2, 2/1 RPC, p10, k1, p1, k1

Row 12: (k1, p1) twice, k9, p3, k2, p3, k2, p1, k1, p1, k1

Row 13: k1, p1, k1, p3, k3, p2, k3, p10, k1, p1, k1

Row 14: (k1, p1) twice, k9, p2, k2, p3, k4, p1, k1, p1

Row 15: (p1, k1) twice, p2, 2/1 RPC, p2, 2/1 RPC, p10, k1, p1, k1

Row 16: (k1, p1) twice, k9, p3, k2, p3, k3, p1, k1, p1

Row 17: (p1, k1) twice, p2, k3, p2, k3, p10, k1, p1, k1

Row 18: (k1, p1) twice, k9, p3, k2, p3, k3, p1, k1, p1

Row 19: (p1, k1) twice, p2, 2/1 LPC, p2, 2/1 LPC, p10, k1, p1, k1

Row 20: (k1, p1) twice, k9, p2, k3, p2, k4, p1, k1, p1

Row 21: (p1, k1) twice, p3, 2/1 LPC, p2, 2/1 LPC, p9, k1, p1, k1

Row 22: (k1, p1) twice, k8, p2, k3, p2, k5, p1, k1, p1

Row 23: (k1, p1) twice, p4, 2/1 LPC, p2, 2/1 LPC, p8, k1, p1, k1

Row 24: (k1, p1) twice, k7, p2, k3, p2, k6, p1, k1, p1

Row 25: (p1, k1) twice, p5, 2/1 LPC, p2, 2/1 LPC, p7, k1, p1, k1

Row 26: (k1, p1) twice, k6, p2, k3, p2, k7, p1, k1, p1

Row 27: (p1, k1) twice, p6, 2/1 LPC, p2, 2/1 LPC, p6, k1, p1, k1

Row 28: (k1, p1) twice, k5, p2, k3, p2, k8, p1, k1, p1

Row 29: (p1, k1) twice, p7, 2/1 LPC, p2, 2/1 LPC, p5, k1, p1, k1

Row 30: (k1, p1) twice, k4, p2, k3, p2, k9, p1, k1, p1

Row 31: (p1, k1) twice, p8, 2/1 LPC, p2, 2/1 LPC, p4, k1, p1, k1

Row 32: (k1, p1) twice, (k3, p2) twice, k10, p1, k1, p1

Row 33: (p1, k1) twice, p9, 2/1 LPC, p2, 2/1 LPC, p3, k1, p1, k1

Row 34: (k1, p1) twice, k2, p2, k3, p2, k11, p1, k1, p1

HEART LACE PANEL (MAKE 2 6" PANELS)

CO 29 sts

Work seed stitch for 8 rows

Work heart lace pattern stitch until piece measures 59 inches from
   cast-on edge
Work seed stitch for 8 rows
Bind off all sts

HEART LACE PATTERN STITCH

Row 1: (RS) (k1, p1) twice, k21, (p1, k1), twice
Row 2: (WS) k1, p1, k1, p23, k1, p1, k1
Row 3: (k1, p1), twice, k10, yo, ssk, k9, (p1, k1), twice
Row 4: k1, p1, k1, p23, k1, p1, k1
Row 5: (k1, p1), twice, k8, k2tog, yo, k1, yo, ssk, k8, (p1, k1), twice
Row 6: k1, p1, k1, p23, k1, p1, k1
Row 7: (k1, p1), twice, k7, k2tog, yo, k3, yo, ssk, k7, (p1, k1), twice
Row 8: k1, p1, k1, p23, k1, p1, k1
Row 9: (k1, p1), twice, k6, k2tog, yo, k5, yo, ssk, k6, (p1, k1), twice
Row 10: k1, p1, k1, p23, k1, p1, k1
Row 11: (k1, p1), twice, k5, k2tog, yo, k7, yo, ssk, k5, (p1, k1), twice
Row 12: k1, p1, k1, p23, k1, p1, k1
Row 13: (k1, p1), twice, k4, k2tog, yo, k4, yo, ssk, k3, yo, ssk, k4, (p1,
   k1), twice
Row 14: k1, p1, k1, p23, k1, p1, k1
Row 15: (k1, p1), twice, k5, yo, ssk, k1, k2tog, yo, k1, yo, ssk, k1, k2tog,
   yo, k5, (p1, k1), twice
Row 16: k1, p1, k1, p23, k1, p1, k1
Row 17: (k1, p1), twice, k21, (p1, k1), twice
Row 18: k1, p1, k1, p23, k1, p1, k1

FINISHING

Block panels and make sure they are all the same length.
Using yarn and a knitting needle (or crochet hook), sew or crochet the
nine panels together in the following order:

1. Diamond Twist Cable Panel
2. Zigzag Cable Panel

3. Heart Lace Panel

4. Zigzag Cable Panel

5. Heart Cable Panel (center panel)

6. Zigzag Cable Panel

7. Heart Lace Panel

8. Zigzag Cable Panel

9. Diamond Twist Cable Panel

Weave in all ends and enjoy.

For additional tips and a diagram of the anniversary afghan pattern, go to www.sallygoldenbaum.com.

Seafood Salad

(The seaside knitters often order this at the Ocean's Edge.)

Serves 6

Salad Ingredients

12 cups loosely packed arugula leaves (or 6 cups arugula,
    6 cups spinach)

¾ cup diced celery

1½ cups cherry tomatoes cut in half

1½ pounds large shrimp, shelled and deveined (about 25–30)

1 pound sea scallops (approximately a dozen); these can be cut
    in half if desired

2 cups croutons

freshly ground salt and pepper

3–4 T olive oil

2 T unsalted butter

For the dressing

2 cups loosely packed torn basil leaves

5 T chopped parsley

3 T olive oil

1½ T lemon juice

zest of one lemon

2 T white wine vinegar

1 t minced garlic

2 t stone-ground Dijon mustard

1 shallot, thinly sliced

freshly ground salt and pepper

Preparation

Dressing

Heat the olive oil over medium heat; add lemon zest and shallot; cook, stirring, for 1–2 minutes. Remove from heat and whisk in remaining ingredients. Adjust seasonings to taste and set aside.

Seafood

Heat 2 T olive oil and 1 T butter in large skillet over high heat.

Dry scallops thoroughly and sprinkle with salt and pepper.

When oil is hot, gently add scallops, making sure they don't touch one another. Sear the scallops on each side for approximately 1½ minutes. They should have a golden crust on each side and be opaque in the center. Remove from pan and put in a bowl.

Reduce heat to medium high and add 1 T butter and 1–2 T olive oil to pan. Sprinkle shrimp with salt and pepper and add to pan. Turn several times until shrimp turn pink and are opaque in the center, about 3–4 minutes. Don't overcook.

Assembly

Combine greens, herbs, celery, and tomatoes in a large bowl. Add scallops and shrimp. Toss lightly.

Drizzle with warm dressing and toss to coat. Add salt and pepper if needed and sprinkle croutons on top.

Serve with a smile.

Read on for an excerpt from
the next Seaside Knitters Mystery,

A Finely Knit Murder

Available in hardcover from Obsidian

The glass in the headmistress's door rattled, but it was the chilling echo of footsteps on the polished floors that rattled Dr. Elizabeth Hartley's soul. She stood still at the office door and stared through the reception area and into the round entry hall.

Captain Elijah Westerland, the subject of the school hall's gigantic painting, looked in at her, his bushy eyebrows pulled together, his eyes black and small and piercing. Judging eyes.

What had she done now? This woman who held his beloved home in her hands?

But that was foolish. It was a painting, after all, and the captain had been dead for nearly a hundred years. Moreover, his home was no longer a home, but a wonderful school.

She took a deep breath and tried to shake off the unease. Elizabeth hadn't anticipated the volcanic anger or the teacher's abrupt departure. Maybe the captain hadn't, either. But neither of them should have been surprised. Of course he'd be upset. People didn't like it when you messed with their livelihoods—and Josh Babson was soon to be out of a teaching job in a town with few openings.

But the decision had been taken out of her hands. Josh's recent absences were known to the board, his faint excuses not very credible. And although he had a charming manner, he could be prickly.

Elizabeth had attributed it to his artistry. Weren't artists supposed to be temperamental? The few paintings she had seen of his were lovely, and his students liked him. If only he had toed the line a little more precisely.

She'd tried to reason with him as best she could, hoping to help him see that missing work and confronting board members didn't go over well at Sea Harbor Community Day School. She needed the art teacher to be there when the bell rang, when eager students filed into his classroom. And he was getting better, paying closer attention to the artist's clock that sometimes kept him painting at home after the magnificent girls' school on the hill opened its doors, preparing for a new day.

Josh was getting better . . . but once a few of her board members got involved, it was too late. It wasn't within the purview of her position to rehabilitate the teachers or staff, one had pointed out to her.

Controlling his exit, however, was her job.

And that had gone badly.

On the other side of the administrative suite, the door to a smaller office opened and the assistant headmistress stepped into the reception area. Mandy White stood tall and composed. She glanced at Teresa Pisano, who was shuffling papers behind the reception counter, trying to look busy. "What's going on?"

The school secretary lifted her bleached-blond head and shrugged one shoulder. It was an off-putting mannerism, one Teresa had recently developed.

Mandy looked back at the headmistress, still standing in the doorway. "Do you need help, Elizabeth?" she asked.

Elizabeth met Mandy's look and offered a half smile and a slight shake of her head.

I'm fine, the gesture said. Everything was under control.

Before Mandy could pursue the issue, Elizabeth closed her office door and moved back into the safe shadows of the room.

The elegant office seemed tarnished by the anger and harsh words that had filled it moments before. In spite of the faded drapes and worn Oriental carpet, the room seemed to demand quiet and respect, intelligent conversation. Not the hand waving that had scattered the paperwork she had carefully put together to document her decision.

Elizabeth looked down at her computer and checked the next appointment. Ten minutes to collect herself.

And it was just the beginning of the week. If she had had her way, she would have waited until Friday to talk to Josh. Then he would have had the weekend to come to grips with being fired, and he could have come back on Monday to finish up the remaining week in the quarter. Then depart from his students gracefully. She had suggested he tell the students he was moving on to other opportunities. He was talented, she said to him. He shouldn't forget that. There was a life beyond teaching. And she would help him in any way she could.

Sea Harbor was a small town; she owed him some support.

But her plan to wait until Friday was thwarted by the planned Tuesday board meeting, and Elizabeth was asked to tie up this loose end so she could report on it at the monthly meeting the next evening.

Tie up this loose end . . .

Was that what she had done?

Or had she created another loose end, a life left frayed and dangling?

Elizabeth set her glasses on the desk, rubbed her temples, and walked over to the lead glass windows fronting the school. The view beyond the windows was a tonic. She would have given up the ornate desk and elegant bookshelves in a heartbeat. But the view? That she would never give up.

From the day she had arrived in Sea Harbor, the magnificent seaside had soothed her, helped her acclimate to the new headmistress position, helped her through rough days of budget negotiations, decisions to reduce staff and adjust protocols, and dealing with student problems and board disagreements.

She pushed away the sliver of fear that had come with the slamming of the door. The parents and board didn't think of her as fearful. *Audacious. Brave. Intrepid.* Those were the words some of them used—although she sometimes had to stop herself from saying, "No—that's not me. Not really." Fear wasn't a stranger to Dr. Elizabeth Hartley, and it often surrounded the tough decisions she had to make. She was good at this job. Very good.

Her heartbeat slowed as she pushed the heavy windows open and welcomed in the salty breeze. It lifted strands of brown hair from her forehead, cooling her flushed skin.

Just a short distance below the windows, tiers of stone terraces gradually gave way to a wide lawn that rolled down to the sea, its expanse broken only by the granite boulders that seemed to have been tossed haphazardly about the property by some giant prehistoric claw. Beyond the lawn was a narrow road, nearly empty at this time of day save for a jogger or two and an old man walking his dog. And across from it was the old boathouse wedged in among the giant boulders, once filled with the Westerlands' oceangoing sailing vessels, canoes, and motorboats. Another thing on her to-do list. Tear it down? Fix it up? Turn it into a little theater or art studio as students and teachers had suggested?

The thought pushed Josh Babson back into her head. Although the run-down boathouse was used mostly to store odds and ends, there were reports that some—Josh Babson and others—had sometimes used it as a personal hideout to rendezvous with a beer or a woman or a joint.

Or so the rumors went.

But even the boathouse was a part of the view she loved, its history and gray weathered sides merging into the color of the sea.

The view continued on forever, across the boulders, over white-capped waves—until finally it touched the sky and melted into one single masterpiece.

Peace. She had found it here.

And she would protect it with her life.

Just a floor below, mixing in with the familiar odors of a science lab and cleaning supplies, the lilting voice of a recently enrolled student filled the wide hallway.

"Angelo, my Angelo—"

The singsong words hung in the dusty air like a hummingbird, fluttering lightly.

Angelo Garozzo looked up from his desk as the long-legged girl with the infectious voice filled the doorframe of his office.

"What was your mom thinking to give you that name?" Gabrielle Marietti asked, a frown teasing the man behind the desk. "Angel? I mean, seriously?"

"Humph." Angelo sneezed. His rimless glasses slipped down to the ball that formed the end of his nose.

Gabby leaned her head to one side, an uncontrolled mass of thick hair falling across her cheek. "But maybe it fits. You're sort of an angel to me. My nonna thinks so, anyway. Even though you're wicked cranky sometimes. I probably should have been more discriminating when I put in my order for a guardian angel."

Angelo laughed at that, his head pressing back into his high-backed chair. Then he leaned forward and glared at his visitor. "Don't you know New Yorkers don't get to use the word *wicked*? You trying to fit in here or somethin'?"

Gabby loved Angelo's accent, the absence of *r*'s. Sometimes she tried to think of questions for Angelo that would require only *r* word answers. "I went to a Sox game with Sam and Ben last weekend," she said, walking into the small room. A slice of sunshine fell from the high casement windows onto her blue-black hair. "So that counts for something, right?"

She brushed a layer of dust from a folding chair and sat down. The small room was crowded with manuals and tools, shoved onto shelves that lined one wall. A single filing cabinet stood beside Angelo's metal desk, a small table holding a coffeepot and lunch box against another wall. The only other furniture were Angelo's high-backed office chair, a heavy table with a printer on it, and a few folding chairs.

But the bright posters lining one gray wall made the office wonderful in Gabby's mind. Broadway shows performed at the local high school, Sea Harbor Community Day School productions, shows performed in a small theater over in Gloucester. Angelo himself had sung a tune or two in his day, he confessed to Gabby one time.

But no matter, he loved them all, and donated generously to keep their doors open.

And Gabby loved that he loved them.

"Whattaya doin' down here, anyway?" Angelo growled. "Shouldn't you be in class somewhere, learning how to behave like a lady?" He waved one fist in the air as he talked, his bushy eyebrows tugging together until they almost touched—a white caterpillar shadowing piercing eyes.

Gabby grinned and flapped a folder in the air. "I'm Miss Patterson's errand girl. I was about to fall asleep in her history class and she took pity on me."

Angelo tsked and shook his head. "You watchit, Marietti. Your nonna holds me responsible for you, God knows why. You get yourself booted out of here and it's all on poor Angelo."

His words were soft, his gruff expression fading into a lopsided smile. He picked up an envelope from the corner of his desk, half rose, and shoved it toward her. "Might as well give you an excuse for coming down here. This gets put directly into Dr. Hartley's hands. And don't lose it, you hear me talkin' to you?"

Gabrielle shoved it under her arm. "Do you doubt me for a second? Of course I'll do your bidding, fair Angelo. Your wish is my command." She stood and bowed elaborately, her arms stretching out and knocking a stack of papers off his desk.

"Outta here, pest." Angelo shooed her off with a wave of his hand.

Truth be told, he loved Gabby Marietti's detours to his office. He loved her sass and her smile. She'd come late to Sea Harbor Community Day School, missing the first few weeks of the quarter after moving up from New York. But no one would have known she was a newbie. In the brief time she'd been there, Gabby had made a place for herself, brought sunshine into the cavernous mansion that housed the old school. Or at least into the office of the chief maintenance engineer, as the black-and-white sign on his door so presumptuously declared. Sunshine was good.

Gabby scooped up the papers and set them back on his desk. She wrinkled her nose at him, the freckles dancing on her fine-boned face. And then as quickly as she'd come, she spun around, arms and legs flying, and disappeared from Angelo's view as she raced down the hall toward the staircase.

The urgent sound of boots on the hardwood stopped Gabby in her tracks just before she reached the bottom step.

"No running in the halls," she imagined the person saying to her. "Decorum, my dear."

But the sound on the steps was loud in the quiet hall, ominous, certainly not an administrator checking lockers or taking someone on a tour—and Gabby instinctively stepped back into the shadow near a utility closet.

The familiar figure that came barreling down the steps was mumbling fiercely, the sound pushing Gabby deeper into the shadows. She wanted to be invisible.

Mostly she didn't want to embarrass Mr. Babson, the slender teacher who was teaching her to paint en plein air and never once considered her ramshackle watercolor of the old boathouse something that belonged in MOBA. Surely it would embarrass him to know a student was privy to the string of obscenities that filled the dusty basement air. Some of the words were ones Gabby had never heard before, even when she hung out at the fishermen's dock, helping Cass and Pete Halloran repair lobster traps. These were unfamiliar, and seemed out of place coming from the mouth of the teacher.

Gabby backed up until she could feel the ridge of the firebox between her shoulder blades, dust motes filling the air in front of her. A sneeze was threatening to break her silence. She pressed one hand over her mouth, the other clutching the papers she was supposed to be delivering. One second before the tickle became utterly painful, Mr. Babson disappeared into the downstairs teachers' lounge, his strangely animated voice trailing after him. Words like *hussy* and *revenge* were mixed in with the curses, until the door finally banged shut behind him, filling the hall with silence.

Gabby released a sigh of relief, pitying the final hour's art class, who would have to face the angry teacher. It wouldn't be pretty.

With a sudden desire to return as quickly as possible to the safety of her class and the trials of colonization, she raced up the steps to drop off the envelopes, pausing more briefly than she usually did in the lobby.

She always skidded to a stop here—even if she only had a minute—planting her feet on the striped hardwood surface and tilting her head back. The portrait demanded it. There was something about the austere expression on the man's face that froze Gabby in her tracks. He'd had something like nine sons, her nonna had said. And they all lived in this house. She gave him her brightest smile. She'd crack that facade. Someday he'd smile back, she told herself.

Sure he would.

And then she rushed into the office suite, startling the secretary to attention.

"Gabrielle, where is the fire?" Teresa leaned over the tall counter and peered at the student, her long face somber.

"Delivering papers to Dr. Hartley."

"I'll take them," Teresa said, reaching out her hand.

Gabby stared at her arm. It was thin, with knobs at her wrist. The kids talked about the secretary sometimes, but Gabby worried about her. She was so skinny, and had recently done something terrible to her light brown hair. It was a dull blond color and seemed to move in odd directions. Maybe it was just a wig, Gabby thought, somehow relieved at the idea.

"It's okay, I told Angelo I'd deliver them—"

"And so you have. To me. You're two seconds too late to see Dr. Hartley. An important board member beat you to it." Teresa reached across the counter and took the papers from Gabby's hand. "Now, off with you, back to class, missy," she said, and motioned toward the door.

Gabby turned back just once. Just long enough to see the back of a woman with platinum hair, standing perfectly still on the other side of the headmistress's glass door.

Teresa had turned and was looking at her, too, in an admiring way as if she wished her bleached blond hair didn't frizzle around her face, but floated back smooth and perfect, every hair in place.

For a second Gabby thought the woman beyond the door was a mannequin, but just then Teresa Pisano turned back in her direction, and her glare prevented Gabby from finding out. She hurried down the hallway to learn more about the founding fathers.

Photo by John McElhenny

Sally Goldenbaum is a sometime philosophy teacher, a knitter, an editor, and the author of more than thirty novels. Sally became more serious about knitting with the birth of her first grandchild and the creation of the Seaside Knitters mystery series. Her fictional knitting friends are teaching her the intricacies of women's friendships, the mysteries of small-town living, and the very best way to pick up dropped stitches on a lacy knit shawl.

CONNECT ONLINE

sallygoldenbaum.com
facebook.com/authorsallygoldenbaum
twitter.com/sallygoldenbaum